PRINCESS OF WISDOM
A BRAVE YOUNG WOMAN
ON A
REMARKABLE JOURNEY

A Novel
by
Mayra Sonam Paldon

Mayra Sonam Paldon

"The basis for realizing enlightenment is a human body.

Male or female, there is no great difference.

But if she develops the mind bent on enlightenment

the woman's body is better."

-Padmasambhava 8th Century A. D.

Mayra Sonam Paldon

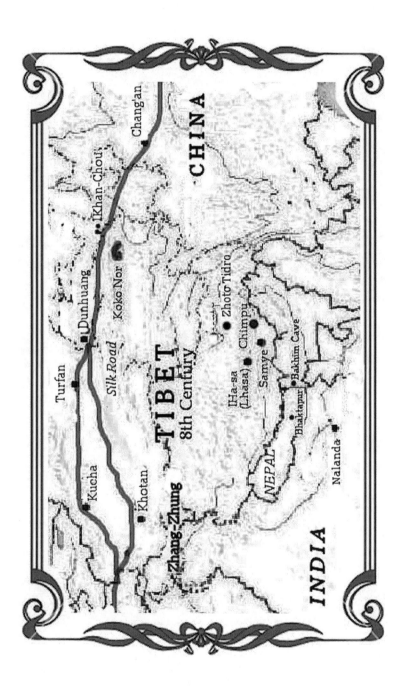

Mayra Sonam Paldon

PART ONE

Mayra Sonam Paldon

1

TIBET 770 A.D.

The thundering of hooves broke the cold silence of the morning as the sun's rays cut over the mountain pass, filling the valley with light. The riderless black mare bolted from her peaceful grazing as the ten horseman bore down upon her.

"It is the Princess's horse!" the young warrior shouted.

"Catch the mare!" exclaimed General Senge.

General Senge and his nine warriors, a search party for King Pelgyi of Karchen, galloped after the black mare named Lungta. Each man's recurve bow, arrows and their sheathed swords, held firmly at the waist, slapped wildly as the warriors sped their horses to catch up to the fleeing mare. Three of the warriors caught up to the mare, two along either side of her. The third, Dorje, whipped his horse wildly to gain the ground in front of Lungta's quickened hooves.

Lungta shied away from warrior Kipu's grasping hand as he leaned sideways, reaching for the rein hanging slack on her neck. Kipu caught himself from falling as the mare instantly widened the gap, his fox-fur hat spinning in the air before it landed on the ground, abandoned. Lungta sped up, cutting in front of the warrior, Chudak, to her right. His gelding shied away, avoiding a collision with the mare.

This last surge of power freed Lungta from the men. They

watched in frustration as the mare galloped full out, leaving them behind. Chudak cursed as he pulled and kicked his horse back to the chase. Kipu laughed and whooped, balancing himself back in the saddle as his horse bolted after the mare. Dorje, who had gone out ahead, was able to cut in front of Lungta. Seeing the warrior suddenly coming at her, Lungta shied sideways to avoid Dorje. Keeping his horse at her left, he forced her to run in a circle, slowing her flight. Chudak and Kipu caught up quickly, falling in at her side, preventing escape. As the men gradually herded Lungta into a smaller and smaller circle, Chudak urged his mount alongside the mare, grabbing at the flopping reins. At last he felt the leather in his fist. Feeling the tug of his hold on her reins, Lungta bucked and pulled, shaking her head, trying to free herself. Chudak cursed and demanded her to yield. Kipu and Dorje closed around, all four horses now slowed to a trot, then to a walk. Lungta finally relaxed, submitting to the herd, as the warriors led her to General Senge who watched the chase from a small rise.

General Senge nodded approvingly at the skill of his men, as they approached him.

Coming to a halt before the General, Chudak gasped in alarm, "Sir, the Princess's horse alone in this valley? Where can she be?"

Handing Lungta's reins to Kipu, Chudak dismounted his horse. His sword and recurve bow and arrows in their quiver hanging from his belt tapped his legs as he strode to Lungta's side.

General Senge and the other men sat on their horses, gazing at the high peaks surrounding the valley.

"Where can she be?" Senge mused aloud. His lacquered-leather breastplate glistened in the low morning sunlight.

Standing next to the black mare, Chudak ran his hands gently down her legs, feeling for any swelling. Then, he stroked her neck, reassuring her. Her black coat was hot and wet with sweat. "She is a fine horse, is she not, General?" Chudak asked, relieved she was not injured in the chase.

"Yes, bred of the finest in the King's herd," Senge murmured absently, as he scanned the mountainsides for any sign of a path or a climbing figure.

Chudak's hand glided over the fine silver-work of the pommel, intrigued by the patterns and scrolls, then rested for a moment on the padded seat of bright red carpet. The soft seat was cold under his hand. He reached for the flap of the saddlebag, behind the high-backed cantle rimmed with silver. Chudak lifted the red-felt cover flap, the gold-thread garudas embroidered upon it twinkled in protest as he felt inside the bag. Realizing the bag was empty, he passed around the back of Lungta, his hand sliding along her rump to look into the other bag.

"These bags are empty, General," Chudak said, feeling once more into the bags as though he could possibly have been mistaken.

"So, she has taken food and water with her," Dorje said. "She escaped in great haste, yet certainly there was food and water in those bags."

"You, Kipu, take two men with you and ride as swiftly as your horses can carry you back to the palace. Tell the King we have found Lungta, fully saddled and with her saddlebags empty, yet the Princess is nowhere in sight. Assure him I will continue the search. We will keep the mare with us," the General ordered. "Be careful, be vigilant of attack as you travel."

"Yes, General," Kipu replied. With a glance indicating the selection of two of the warriors, the three spun their mounts and charged away, Kipu taking the route toward retrieval of his hat.

"Why is Lungta alone here? Why has the Princess taken afoot?" Chudak asked as he looked up and around at the mountains. "There is no place up there for her to go."

Chudak swallowed hard, his throat clamped tightly as his concern for the safety of the young Princess grew. With pressed lips he held back his rage as he walked to his horse. Cinching the coarse silk belt around his woolen robe, he arranged the sword that hung from it. Placing his felt boot into the iron stirrup with silver inlay, he swung gracefully up onto his horse. Looking around at the size of this valley, he wondered aloud, "Why would she have gone without her beloved horse?"

Senge shifted his attention to Chudak, noticing the hard look on the young warrior's face. Senge was aware that Chudak, like many of the subjects of King Pelgyi, loved the Princess and were angry at the causes of her running away.

"She cannot have gotten far without her horse. Spread out and look for tracks," General Senge ordered his men. "We must find a sign."

Rocks rolled down the steep cliffside as her hands and feet grasped for each hold. The cliff was not so steep as vertical but was nevertheless difficult. The young girl struggled up the trail, her felted wool boots slipping on the loose rocks. Her cotton robe was dirty and torn, her leggings tucked into her boots did not protect her when she often slipped and fell to her knees. Her shoulder ached as the leather strap of the heavy bag she carried cut into her flesh under the thin cotton.

At last she reached the cave and stumbled inside. Exhausted, she pulled the bag over her head, letting it drop to the floor. She could see there had been others that had occupied this cave over the centuries: Hermits, Bon practitioners and Buddhist adepts; obvious by their leavings, an old butter lamp, rocks positioned for sitting and cooking.

She noticed a bundle along the rock wall. Walking over to it, she lifted it to see it was an old sheepskin coat, left here in some distant past, yet still serviceable for warmth. She was glad for this gift as her cotton robe would be of little warmth in the night. She had been able to bring only a few dried apricots, walnuts and water with her. No one had been here for a very long time. Of that she was certain, this cave was secret.

"No one will find me here," she spoke aloud in an attempt to encourage herself.

Then, the Princess Tsogyal of Karchen, once a Royal dressed in the finest of silks and jewels, legend to be the most beautiful young woman of the land, the reincarnation of a Goddess, sank to the cold dirt floor of the cave, buried her head in her hands and wept.

2

ONE SPRING EARLIER
IN THE SMALL KINGDOM OF KARCHEN
TIBET

"Princess, please! Wait! Not so fast! Let me catch up!" shouted Chudak, gasping for breath.

The young Princess's raven-black braid whipped her back as she crouched over the neck of her speeding mare, Lungta. Twisting in the saddle to look back, she laughed, seeing the frustration on Chudak's face and hearing his pleading shouts as she left him farther behind.

"Ha, ha!" she encouraged her mare. "Faster, my beauty!"

Lungta surged even faster, her hooves as lightening over the rocky valley floor, the sheen of sweat glistened on her black coat. Ahead, the rushing waters of the Yarlung River that ran the length of the valley, appeared before them. Princess Tsogyal positioned her body to aid her mare's balance as she prepared for the leap over this narrow yet deep section of water. They had practiced the jump over this section of river many times. Slowing just a bit to collect herself onto her powerful hindquarters, Lungta pushed off, soaring over the rushing water below, her hooves landing just on the edge of the other shore.

Chudak raced up behind Tsogyal, yet his gelding, Goba, fearing the crossing, balked. The gelding's sweaty golden-red coat shimmered in the sunlight as he shied sharply sideways. Though a fine horseman, the sudden change of direction almost unseated Chudak. Circling Goba, Chudak cursed as he watched his charge rapidly disappearing over the rise.

Then he laughed and said, "Oh, Princess, you are as wild as you are beautiful." Patting his horse's neck to reassure him, Chudak encouraged, "Come Goba, we will find a place where you can cross. How can I expect you to jump like that fine horse of the Princess?"

Wishing his horse, whose name meant Eagle, could fly like Lungta, Chudak trotted Goba upstream to find a shallow crossing. Goba, now distressed at being separated from his herd-mate, crossed the shallow yet rushing water with confidence and they continued at the gallop to catch up to the Princess.

Tsogyal slowed her mare and fell over her neck, hugging her tightly. "Oh, Lungta, you are as your name, a splendid horse! Now, let me give you a much deserved rest and drink."

They trotted upstream to a place where the water was calm. Tsogyal dismounted and let go of the reins. Lungta walked to the riverside, lowered her head and sipped the fresh cold water.

As Tsogyal sat on one of the many rocks that studded the shore, she tightened the loosened belt at the waist of her soft dark blue woolen robe. The gold silk trim sparkled in the sunlight. Placing her felt wool booted feet onto a rock to avoid the boggy ground, she took in a deep breath of the cold clean air, mingled with the scents of the tufts of green grass and damp earth. Looking up at the snowcapped mountains that surrounded the valley, she felt safe, enclosed by their mass rising dramatically from the valley floor. She wondered if there really was a protective God in those mountains and if it was true, what did he look like?

Pushing all thoughts aside, she threw her head back and gazed at the clear blue sky enjoying the warmth of the sun on her face. "Ah, such a beautiful sky," she murmured, letting herself melt into the sounds of trickling water and the chirps and whistles of the many birds flying about.

Hoofbeats brought her attention back as Chudak appeared.

"There you are!" he said, exasperated.

Tsogyal could not hold in a laugh. "You must practice that jump, Chudak, if you are going to be as great a horseman as I and if you wish your Eagle to fly ."

Chudak shook his head as he dismounted. "You have the finest mare of the realm, Noble Daughter. How can my gelding compete with her abilities?" Chudak said, defending himself.

Leading Goba to the river's edge, Chudak released his reins, allowed him to drink. Lungta nickered as Goba came close to her. The two horses touched noses; blowing, they exchanged their breath.

"Princess, you should not run away from me. Your father fears for your safety. He would be very angry with me if anything should happen to you," Chudak scolded. Then, softening his tone, he implored, "It would be a great shame for me if you were to come to harm. It is my task to protect you."

"Come, Chudak, sit and rest. All is well," Tsogyal said, as she gestured to a large rock a short distance away from her.

Chudak pulled his fox-fur hat off and lifted the tip of his sword, Wolf Tooth, at his side, to clear the soggy ground as he seated himself on the small boulder. Untying the loosened thong at the back of his neck, he gathered the locks of hair that had escaped in the chase, then tied his long black hair back again. His wispy mustache and chin-hairs bristled around the frown of concentration on his face.

Rising from the boulder she sat upon, Tsogyal walked over to her mare. She opened one of the red felt saddlebags tied behind the saddle and dug inside. Lungta, grazing on tufts of grass growing between the rocks, lifted her head, bending it around to see what her mistress was retrieving. Tsogyal pulled out a cloth bundle and opened it to reveal several sweet dried apricots. Seeing these, the mare spun her body full around and nipped at the bundle.

Pulling it from Lungta's reach as she gently pushed the mare's muzzle aside, Tsogyal instructed, "Wait." Then, slowly taking one of the apricots from the bundle, Tsogyal held it out for her mare, saying, "This one is for you, my dear friend."

Lungta reached out and gently nibbled the fruit from her

mistress's small delicate hand. Noticing the treats being handed to Lungta, Goba came over to receive one. Then Tsogyal walked over to Chudak and held out a sweet apricot for him.

"And this one is for you, my protector," she giggled.

Delighted to be offered the fruit, Chudak opened his large course hand, allowing her to drop the small shriveled delicacy into it. Though he was anxious to bite into the fruit and taste its sweetness, he disciplined himself to wait until the young Princess seated herself on a rock.

Chudak, a man of twenty springs and married with a son of his own, was a bit dismayed by this girl. At only twelve springs of age, her beauty was striking. Her facial features were considered by all to be most exotic. Her almond-shaped black eyes with long black eyelashes were large and kind, her clear flawless skin was soft light brown, her long hair was silky and black as a raven's wing. Though she held a high station, she did not wear as much coral and turquoise jewelry as was customary for a Noble. She moved with the grace and poise of a grown woman, yet she was playful like a girl. She was strong and willful, those kind eyes turning to fire when she had decided on a course she would take, constantly challenging herself. To ride faster, jump farther, to climb the mountainside, she was always wanting to do something she had never done. These thoughts swirled around in Chudak's mind as he bit into the sweet dryness of the apricot. Looking at her small form sitting serenely on the boulder, gazing at the water placidly swirling by before them, he considered that her birth was now a legend, claiming her as being a reincarnation of a great Goddess. It was said that her mother bore no pain during her birth and that there were unusual natural occurrences. When she was born, the earth shook and a spring of fresh water spontaneously burst from the ground, turning a small pond next to her house larger, into a lake. Thus, her parents named her Yeshe Tsogyal, Ocean of Wisdom. Many now call that lake, Lha-tso, the Divine Lake.

Well, the great mountain God, Sheldrak, shakes the mountains here every ten or so seasons, grandfather has told me. So maybe that is not such a strange occurrence, Chudak thought. *And when he caused the ground to shake, the splitting of rocks would have awakened the water Nagas. That would certainly have caused the flow of water up from below to make the pond, which was already there, much larger in size. That is not so unusual,* he mused, as he chewed slowly on a small bite, wanting to make the fruit last as long as possible.

Yet, this Princess was unusual herself, as compared to any of the girls or women he had ever known. She had an air of something he could not describe to himself. Though she was renowned already, the daughter of a powerful King and desired by many important suitors, she was kind and gentle to everyone.

Though the girls and women in Karchen are all strong, he considered, *yet there is something about this Princess that is different.*

"My father is only worried for my safety so his Princess daughter will marry the Emperor or one of the Kings," Tsogyal said, breaking the silence between them.

Startled out of his reverie, Chudak swallowed his last bit of apricot, confused by her statement. Then, realizing she was continuing their conversation of many moments past, he said, "You are a Princess, all Royals must be protected."

Ignoring his statement, Tsogyal continued, "He will be surprised when I refuse all suitors."

Surprised by this admission, Chudak asked, "Noble Daughter, why will you refuse? Is it not a great thing to be married to the Emperor or a King? Is that not a dream of every woman to live in splendor?"

Looking intently at him, Tsogyal inquired, "Chudak, you are aware that my father embraces the teachings of Lord Buddha?"

Feeling uncomfortable about the subject, Chudak shifted his position on the rock, as he answered, "Yes, Princess, I know this."

"What do you think of these new teachings?" Tsogyal inquired.

Placing his hands on his muscular thighs, he straightened his back, his felt-booted foot tapped the ground absently as he thought for a moment, considering how to answer. Letting out his breath, he decided to just tell the truth of his thoughts about this subject. "What of our Gods, will they protect this land if we turn from them? It is known by many that these teachings, coming from the lands of India, anger the Kings of the other clans as well as the Bonpo priests. Noble Daughter, your family has been Bonpo since your grandfather's time, my grandfather has explained this to me." Shaking his head slowly, he continued, "For generations Tibet has followed the way of Bon. I do not see the need for these ideas of the one called Buddha. Yet, if your father wants to receive these teachings, even if doing so angers the Gods, he may do so, he is the King of Karchen."

"Yes, he is the King," she said, rising up from the rock she sat upon. Walking toward the water's edge, her anger growing, she continued, "My father has made it clear to all that he embraces the dharma of the great awakened one, Sakyamuni." Stamping her foot on the ground as she raised her voice, she declared, "As do I."

Exasperated, Tsogyal deftly stepped from one large rock to the next, pacing over the river rocks. With her hands held out in supplication, she explained, "My father is blind to my need for freedom, to my intention to find a teacher and practice the yoga of the Buddha's teachings."

Turning to Chudak in frustration, she exclaimed, "I can not do so if I am married!"

Chudak looked at her in astonishment. "A Princess who does not marry? Your father will never allow it," he declared. "You must make alliances with one of the other Kingdoms. Or, if you become one of the Emperor's wives, your father will be very powerful indeed."

With a huff, Tsogyal picked up the empty bundle and stomped over to Lungta, who was nibbling on grass where there were not so many rocks on the shoreline. Stuffing the bundle hard into the saddlebag, she glared at Chudak, frustration twisting her beautiful face, as she tried to think of how to answer this. Then a smile crept along the hardened edges of her expression, softening it into mirth. With one swift movement, she grasped Lungta's reins, placed her foot into the stirrup and swung her leg over the carpeted saddle, spinning Lungta around. Her mare needed no kick as she knew what her mistress wanted. The powerful horse leapt up the small embankment onto the valley plain.

As they galloped away, Tsogyal shouted, her faced raised

skyward in jubilation, "I will be free! No one will bind me!"

Surprised and alarmed, Chudak jumped to his feet and ran to Goba, grasping the reins as the gelding bolted past him attempting to follow the mare. Cursing, Chudak struggled to mount as Goba spun in circles trying to run after Lungta. Finally on Goba's back, seconds seeming as many minutes lost, Goba burst into a gallop, leaping up the embankment after Lungta and the Princess.

3

General Senge sat astride his silver-gray horse, Ketu, atop the hill overlooking the practice field. Ketu stood perfectly still, the faint stripes from distant ancestors visible along the backs of his charcoal-colored legs that stood rooted to the earth. General Senge nodded to the flagmen to signal the charge.

Seeing the signal of the waving flags, the line of three hundred mounted warriors let loose their horses, thundering in a line abreast. Then, the line coalesced into an arrow shape. Like a flock of birds flying along the ground, communication magically passed between them. Their shape changed again as they flared out, perfectly spaced, allowing each horseman to pass between the targets spread across the field. The first wave of warriors thrust their spears into the first target, then drew their bows from the bow quiver at their side. Hundreds of arrows found their marks on the next targets on the field. Five more targets presented themselves, challenging the warriors at the gallop. Every shot hit home. At last each man drew his sword and sliced through the blocks of wood set up for them at the end of the run.

Senge's long mustache curled around his stern mouth. Standing in his stirrups, he studied his men as they executed the pattern of attack he created. His troops were an extension of himself on the practice field.

Then he nodded. "Very good, perfect," he exclaimed, watching his men perform in exact formation, each warrior finding their target and with cold precision, executing perfect killing blows. Letting out a breath of satisfaction, Senge smiled as he sat back in his saddle. Resting his hand on his sword, Dragon's Claw, his calloused strong fingers curled around the exquisitely-crafted hilt of the sword, feeling the cool form of the protector God's face molded in bronze with gold inlay.

This sword was had been given to him by his father, General Namzhung, presented to Senge when Namzhung retired as the general of this very army of King Pelgyi that Senge now led. This sword had the blood of many a Chinese on its blade, by both his father's hand and his own.

General Senge felt the urge to draw his sword, to admire once again its beautiful blade, wide at the hilt, tapering to a sharp point, with an inscribed dragon twisting along the blade. He longed to feel the heft of its perfect balance in his hand.

"Dragon's Claw, you will have prey soon," he whispered.

As his men reformed to begin the practice again, Senge's mind wandered to the great battle of Talas. Images filled his mind of the massing of troops as he, then a young man of eighteen springs, rode alongside his father. His breast felt full as the memory of himself galloping next to his father with their bows drawn, releasing arrow after arrow into the ranks of the Chinese forces. The distant memory of the screams and smell of blood and dying men flooded his mind. He contemplated the brilliant plan and execution of that battle. Arabs and Tibetans had charged the Chinese front. The Turkish forces, thought by the Chinese to be an ally, rode at the flank of the Chinese army. Yet, instead of providing a strong rearguard, they attacked the Chinese at their flank, surprising the Chinese with their treachery and sealing the fate of the battle. This great battle defeated once and for all the Tang Chinese influence and power in the Talas valley. Thus control of that part of the ancient trade route fell to the Emperor of Tibet. Arabia and the Turkish lands, now allies of the powerful Empire of Tibet, realized great profits in trade along the route. Now, a man of thirty-four and with much experience, having been taught strategy well by his father,

Senge won many a battle and made his King Pelgyi very rich and powerful.

The forms of two riders in the distance at the gallop, approaching the practice area, broke Senge out of his reverie.

Pointing, Senge bellowed, "Who are those riders?!"

A warrior at the edge of the field called out, "It is the Princess and Chudak, General."

"May the Gods hold my temper," Senge growled. "Signal to hold the charge," he called to the flagmen.

The flagmen waved their flags furiously. The order was passed from man to man like a wave across the field. A hush fell over the army, all eyes were on the charging pair as they passed the practice field at its edge, heading in the direction of the Palace. As Tsogyal and Lungta galloped passed the men, Tsogyal stood in her stirrups and waved. Delighted with her skill on her beautiful horse and her gesture toward them, three hundred warriors raised their bows and cheered, "Hurrah," the sound like rumbling thunder. Then a roar of laughter rose from the gathered army as Chudak appeared, his horse Goba trying to catch up to the Princess, who now was far ahead.

"General?" Temba said, looking up at Senge.

"Yes, Lieutenant, what is it?" Senge clipped, looking down at the warrior.

"General, a messenger is here with a message that the Oracle Shatri is ready to confer with you on propitious dates to begin the march."

"Very well, Lieutenant, oversee the exercises while I am occupied with the oracle," Senge ordered.

Urging Ketu to the trot, Senge headed for the Bonpo Oracle's hut in the nearby hills. Taking a detour along the edge of the practice field, Senge kicked Ketu into the gallop. Sliding Dragon's Claw from its scabbard, he drew back his arm, the practice post coming closer and closer. At the perfect moment he swung Dragon's Claw, thrilling at the feeling of impact as the sword sliced easily through the block. The severed end twisted in the air, then thumped onto the ground.

Shatri sat upon his cushion in quiet meditation. His once empty mind was now filled with images of slashing swords, cutting of flesh, severing of heads, screams of pain and terror. A shiver ran through his body. Mindful, he allowed the images to dissolve away on their own, aware not to grasp these images as an effort to dispel them, instead he paid them no attention. Silence and emptiness returned to him.

The sound of crunching footsteps drew him out of the silence. Loud words boomed into his abode, bringing his attention completely back into the room.

"Oracle Shatri, I have arrived," Senge's commanding voice filled the space.

"Enter, General," Shatri's answered, in a soft tone.

Senge pushed the wooden door open and ducked his head as he stepped into the hut.

"You have divined a day for our departure?" Senge asked, as Shatri looked up at him.

Senge looked down at Shatri. Though seated he knew the oracle was a head smaller in stature than he. He noticed his white beard had grown to the middle of his chest now, causing him to realize it had been a long time since he had seen the man. His light brown eyes, deep under heavy brows, were calm yet piercing. His skin was like brown leather. Long grey hair hung loose down his back, reaching the cushion he sat upon. A single long braid hung along the left side of his temple, over his shoulder and down the front of his willowy chest. Turquoise and amber beads woven into the braid twinkled in the flickering light of the butter lamps placed around the small abode.

"Please sit, General," Shatri said, gesturing to a cushion across from him. "Your presence is required if the divination is to be accurate."

Senge crossed to the cushion. Untying the belt that Dragon's Claw was attached to, he leaned the sword against the wall, the belt dangled from the ring of the scabbard. He loosened slightly the second silk belt he wore around his zhuba, his thick woolen robe. The dark blue of his robe was dusted gray with the dirt of being on the practice field day after day. Seating himself on the thick cushion, he pulled each felt-booted foot into place under him, crossing his muscular legs. Pulling off his fur hat, he ran his fingers through his short hair, it reaching barely to his shoulders. He kept his hair shorter than most men, thus removing the opportunity a long braid gave an opponent in battle to grab hold of. The image of his wife, Michewa, cutting his hair with the sharp blade of a knife just last night flashed through his mind, her dark eyes looking down at him, stoically holding back her tears that he was leaving soon for battle. Shifting on the cushion, he rid himself of the images that caused a tightness in his chest.

Shatri took in the energy and form of the General. The dark long mustache curled around the firm mouth, and the short thick black hair that looked to Shatri more like the mane of a lion than the hair of a man. Shatri could feel the tension in Senge's body and mind. Senge's eyes were stern and dark, his shoulders tight, his fingers fidgeted on his knees.

General Senge stared down at the carpet that was placed between them. It measured eleven hands in length and six hands in width. The weave displayed symbols of two snow lions. Laying on the left side of the carpet were two silk bags. One was small and black, just fitting into the palm of Oracle Shatri's hand. The other was larger, green with gold threads woven in designs of clouds. Next to these two silk bags lay a square wooden board, the length and width of the priest's forearm. Carved into the wood was a lattice design of nine squares. On top of this board was a stick of charcoal for writing.

Shatri took in a breath and, as he let it out, he sank into relaxation. This was an example to the General to calm himself. Senge's strength of body and intensity of spirit unsettled the Bon sorcerer.

"General, it will be beneficial if you would calm your mind and relax your body," Shatri instructed.

Senge glared at Shatri, ignoring his admonition. "Oracle, as well as the propitious date for our leaving, I request you divine the future of our enterprise. I wish to know if there may be obstacles to my success in this battle. We are marching northeast to the Kan-chou oasis on the trade route. The Emperor's garrison there is having trouble with one of those frontier general dogs who seeks to make a name for himself in the Tang imperial court. He seeks to gain favor by taking the oasis from our control."

Shifting on his cushion, Senge continued, "A messenger has recently arrived, bringing news that this general's force has killed most of our garrison troops and now has taken control. It would be a small matter to take back our garrison there, but the bandit in lacquered armor has gathered 3000 men and many are trained solders. Our great Emperor Trisong has requested that our King Pelgyi, along with all the other Kings of Tibet, commit troops to add support to his army in a battle. Emperor Trisong wants to make sure these interlopers are killed to the man. This will send a message to all: Chinese, Arabs and even to our allies the Turks, that Tibet controls Kan-chou and will soon rule all of the trade route."

Thumping his fist on his thigh, Senge growled, "Tibet is the most powerful empire in the world. This message will be given to all who think they can challenge us. The Emperor's armies are ever expanding the empire, he does not wish to waste men and resources on these little dogs who nip at our heels."

Leaning forward with gritted teeth, Senge declared, "We will trounce them. We will slaughter them to the man. I need to know of any obstacles so I can avoid them or overcome them."

Shatri leaned back, the force of the General's intention caused fear to scurry up his back. Gaining his composure, Shatri asked, "Do you have a trade item for me from this garrison, General, as I requested?"

"Yes, here," Senge said, as he drew a translucent green form from the pocket made by the front fold of his zhuba and held it out to Shatri. Shatri reached for the cool stone, taking it from Senge's hand. He was impressed with the weight of it as it fell into his grasp. Turning the statue in his hands, he admired the exquisite lines and cuts that formed a dragon in twisted elegance.

"Very good," Shatri whispered.

Senge shifted on his cushion, impatient with the slow

movements of the oracle.

"Is that enough payment for your services?" Senge said in a low growl, not even trying to hide the contempt he felt for this little man. He needed the oracle's divination, yet the idea of having to seek counsel from this small weak man irritated him. It was strength and skill with weapons that won his admiration, not throwing little sticks to decipher some meaning in their tangled display or counting pebbles on a board to find outcomes. Even worse, he was suspicious of those claiming to travel into other worlds, cavorting with shadowy figures. Behind his contempt and fierce exterior, the General hid the truth; that he feared these sorcerers and magicians. For if their magic became strong and was turned against him or the realm, he knew no strategy for fighting against their spells.

"I did not request an item from the trade route for myself, General, though I need to eat as you do," Shatri said, shielding his psyche from the General's negative energy that washed over him. He did not care about the General's obvious dislike of him and his trade. He was the oracle of King Pelgyi, so must give divination requested by the King's officials.

"I requested an item to aid in the divination. This carved jade carries the energy of your destination," Shatri explained as he turned and placed the jade dragon on a small table behind him. "Please settle yourself and quiet your mind, General, we will begin now."

Shatri picked up the two small bags made of silk lying on the carpet. He opened the larger of the silk bags and poured forty-two crystal pebbles onto the carpet. He gently patted this pile of pebbles flat. Then the oracle picked up the small black silk bag and opened it, three black smooth stones dropped into the palm of his hand. Shatri placed the three black stones to the right of the crystal pebbles, he rolled the black stones to the left three times before the group of crystal pebbles. Then he picked up the black stones and slowly passed them in his clenched fist over the crystal pile. This done, he took the black stones and hid them under his cushion seat.

"All negativity is now eliminated from the crystals," Shatri explained to the General.

Then Shatri whispered the secret words three times while invoking the questions in his mind, *How will General Senge and his fine warriors succeed in their duty to the King and to the Emperor? And in how many days shall they begin the march for their success?*

He divided the forty-two crystal pebbles into three heaps with the side of his hand. From the first heap he took four pebbles and moved them away, then four more and moved them away and four more, moving them away. He was now left with two pebbles. He picked up the board and wrote the number two with the charcoal stick in the first square. Then Shatri moved four pebbles from the next pile, four again and again until he was left with three pebbles. With the third pile, moving pebbles away in fours, he was left with one remaining. He wrote the numbers on the board. Gathering the pebbles together again, he repeated the procedure, writing the numbers in their places on the board. Now for the final time he counted the pebbles. The nine lattice squares were now full with the numbers given by the crystal pebble counts. Shatri pondered the numbers written on the board. Senge leaned over his crossed legs in deep concentration watching the divination of the pebbles.

"Well, what do you see?" Senge asked, impatiently.

"Silence," Shatri quietly commanded.

Senge sat back on his cushion with a deep sigh. Allowing himself to relax, he took in the sweet earthy scent of incense smoke curling from a bowl on the small altar at one side of the room. He became absorbed in the chirps and whistles of a songbird outside. His thoughts wandered to his earlier irritation at the Princess Tsogyal for having interrupted his army's practice. *She is so willful, disturbing my practice field,* he thought, irritated. *But, by the Gods she is a great rider, no one can deny it. And that fine mare of her's, bred from the finest stock in Ferghana.* Stroking his mustache absently, he mused, *She is brave, what a great warrior she would have made if she had been born a son of the King instead of his third daughter. If born a boy....*

"It will be most auspicious if you leave on the fifth day from this day," Shatri said, breaking Senge's wandering thoughts, bringing him back into the hut.

"Five days?" Senge inquired more to himself than to the oracle, wondering if it was enough time to make all ready. Taking a quick mental inventory, he knew that was plenty of time.

"Five days, yes, very good. Is there more you see?" he inquired.

"I see a lion devouring a ram. Your warriors are well trained and strong. The frontier soldiers will be no match for your army, General Senge."

"Very good," Senge said, placing his hat on his head as he rose to his feet. Lifting Dragon's Claw, he pulled the belt tight around his waist as he strode to the door. At the door, his hand ready to pull it open, he turned and said, "I will be arriving at the palace to inform the King at sunset. Will you be there to confirm the date of our departure?"

"Yes, General," Shatri said, still musing over the board of divination.

Raising his finger, Shatri said, "One more thing, General."

Senge froze. "What, more?"

"General, the young Princess is not a mere girl. Respect the Princess and protect her," he warned.

Senge, irritated and confused by this mention of the Princess, retorted, "I do respect the family of the King."

Shatri looked up at the General. In a firm yet soft voice, he repeated, "Respect the Princess Tsogyal and protect her, General."

Senge glared down at the wizened man, then turned and pulled the door open. Stepping out into the bright sun, he was blinded for a moment. Closing his eyes, he raised his hand to shield them as he pulled the door shut behind him. Squinting, he adjusted to the brightness as he hurried down the path to Ketu, who waited patiently, his reins tied around a large rock. Mounting, Senge turned Ketu and trotted down the winding path. The words, five days, the lion devours the ram, respect her, protect her, repeated like a mantra, around and around in Senge's mind, like beads on a mala.

4

Queen Getso of Karchen placed the bundle of sage onto the red glowing coals in the terra cotta receptacle. The smoke of the smoldering sage rose up through the five-foot-high chimney of the burner. The gray cloud of sweet pungent smoke wafted into the blue sky. Folding her hands, she felt the chill of the late morning cold in her fingers pressed together in prayer. A shiver ran through her as she recited the mantra taught to her by the Buddhist teacher she retained in the palace for herself and her daughters. Glancing up, she noticed the movement of a guard disappearing into the doorway. She bristled, realizing he had been watching her. She struggled to release the irritation from her mind, yet the harder she tried, the stronger the thoughts seized her. Then she remembered to relax and allow the thoughts, not paying attention to them. A smile replaced her frown when peace came back to her.

"Om, Ah, Hum," she recited over and over again in a whisper.

"There you are, my beautiful Queen." The words broke her concentration. Raising her head, she watched as her husband approached. His knee-length padded silk robe glistened lapis lazuli blue. The gold-embroidered dragons twisted in their celestial dance as he strode to her in the morning light.

"When I could not find you, I knew you must be hidden here,

on the roof of the palace," King Pelgyi said.

"I find peace here and give offerings to the Buddha and the Three Jewels," Getso replied. Then, taking a moment of silence, her lips silently moving, she quickly finished her prayer.

Getso turned from her offerings to the strong lean form of her husband, the King. She glanced beyond him to see the guard standing at attention at the doorway, watching them. Taking his strong hand in hers, she turned toward the view off the terrace toward the mountains.

With a whisper, Getso implored, "Husband, is there nothing you can do to keep the Bon guards from following me everywhere I go and standing everywhere I am?"

Perplexed, Pelgyi said, "It is their place to protect the Royal Family."

Then, noticing the guard watching them, Pelgyi waved his hand at the man in dismissal. The guard shrank off the terrace into the darkness beyond the doorway.

Placing his hands on his wife's shoulders, he gazed into her dark almond-shaped eyes. He marveled that he never tired of her, that her beauty never faded. Every day of the twenty-three springs they had been married he delighted at the sight of her, at her touch. They were married when he was just a boy of fifteen seasons. Yet, soon after his marriage to Getso, his father had died, making Pelgyi the King of Karchen.

Concern in his voice, he asked, "Have they been rude in any way, wife?"

Shaking her head slightly, Getso said, "It is that they are everywhere, I can find no peace from their prying eyes. Do I need so much protection in the palace?"

"Yes, you do," Pelgyi assured. "Yet, I am sure these guards are more spies of the Bon Ministers than protectors," he concluded.

Getso gently removed Pelgyi's strong, yet soft, hands from her shoulders. She kissed his right hand, then turned and walked to the edge of the rooftop terrace and leaned against the short wall there. Her thick woolen robe shielded her from the strong breeze that eddied up the palace walls then onto the open terrace of the rooftop. The gold silk trim of her robe sparkled in the sunlight as she gazed out over the valley and surrounding mountains. Relaxing, she let herself be absorbed for a moment in the clarity of the intensely blue sky, the tension she had felt moments earlier melted away.

"Husband, can you not find personal guards that are devoted to the Buddha dharma and not the Bonpo?" Gesto asked. Taking in a breath of the cold air and letting it out, she added, "I am concerned that the Bonpo ministers are trying to find ways to remove the Buddhist influence from our court. That is why they spy on us."

Pelgyi walked over to Getso. Standing behind her, he gently stroked her long black braid. Getso leaned into his strength as she went on, "Husband, I worry at their power, I fear them. Even your great General Senge is a Bonpo and not Buddhist."

Placing his arms around her, Pelgyi assured, "Do not be concerned about Senge, he is loyal to me as his father was loyal to my father."

Getso tensed slightly. "Yes, but your father was a Bonpo practitioner, as was your grandfather, who created the largest Bonpo coven around him. Does Senge embrace the Buddha dharma? I see no evidence of his conversion."

Pelgyi laughed. "Senge embraces his sword, his bow and the girth of his horse at the full gallop! That is what Senge embraces. You need not have concerns about Senge. The General is a warrior, he cares only for victory in war and being free as the leader of my great army. He will never betray us, he will protect us and our interests, I can assure you of this, my dear."

Softly swaying in loving embrace, they gazed out to the expanse that lay before them. Wafts of the sweet pungent smoke from the sage offering blew over them on a swirling breeze. Clouds, as big as the mountains themselves, were forming around the peaks in the distance.

"Do you think your army has arrived at the trade garrison by now? Could they be in battle at this very moment?" Getso wondered.

Pelgyi looked inward, thinking, as he answered, "They began the march two moon cycles ago, the journey is many leagues. It is hard to say." Tightening his lean strong arms around her, he assured, "It is of no importance now, as they will not return for many moons. I have no doubt they will return in victory and with much treasure for our coffers."

Then Pelgyi whispered into his wife's ear, "I will arrange new guards for you, those that embrace the Buddha dharma. You are safe, my love."

"Thank you, husband," Queen Getso sighed, her body relaxing into his embrace.

"Was there a reason you were looking for me?" she inquired.

King Pelgyi stiffened. Releasing his embrace, he moved beside her to the terrace edge and turned his back to the view to face Getso.

"It is about our daughter, Tsogyal," he sighed. "There are many who ask for her hand in marriage to form an alliance with our family. Too many. They arrive every week asking for her. Our two other daughters are beautiful, older and accomplished as well, yet the suitors only want Tsogyal."

Getso made a wry face. "She has become a legend, a great prize."

"Yes, she was born with auspicious signs," Pelgyi continued. "If I give her in marriage to one clan, the other clans will feel slighted. Those slights will lead to animosity and possibly to war. I have therefore decided it would be best to refuse her to all. I will let it be known she is only available for the Emperor, if he would desire her."

"Husband," Getso began, not knowing if she should say anything, yet deciding it would be best to do so. "Tsogyal has taken to the Buddha dharma quite enthusiastically. She has told me she does not wish to marry. Her desire is to become a great adept as in the Nepali legends."

Pelgyi's face became hot. Glaring at Getso, he said, "She will do as she is told! She has become too willful. If the Emperor wants her as one of his wives, then by the Gods she will become his wife!" Pelgyi's voice rose as his irritation grew. "She is living in a fantasy." Clenching his fists at his sides, he strode across the terrace, then spun around to face Getso, "Does she not know the way life is? You must teach her what is required of her!"

Getso, alarmed by the sudden anger of her husband, went to

him and took his hands in hers. "Husband, please, calm yourself. I will make sure she understands her life and her place."

Pelgyi took a deep breath and let it out. "Very good, please do so. I must go now, the ministers are meeting," he said. Unable to cool his anger, he turned and quickly strode away.

Getso sighed as she watched him disappear into the darkness of the doorway. She could see the faint silhouette of the guard hidden in the shadows beyond. Resigned, she turned and walked over to the smoldering sage. Folding her hands she prayed, "I take refuge in the Buddha, please keep us safe."

5

"Yes, that is correct, hold the brush thus and draw the stroke. Relax your grip. Yes, that is correct, very good, Princess," Tutor Thargye-la encouraged Princess Dechen, King Pelgyi's first-born child.

Dechen held the carved sandalwood handle of the delicate paint brush lightly as she completed the brush stroke. Dipping the fine sable hair tip of the brush into a small silver cup of liquid gold, she took in a slow breath and let it out softly as she applied another gold line to the edge of the colored area.

When she had begun this painting, she had cautiously painted over the lightly pre-drawn lines made by her tutor. Her confidence had grown from those first timid strokes weeks before. Exhilaration filled her now as she deftly applied the gold in fine exact lines, thus completing her first thangka.

Thargye-la, a master thangka painter, had been invited from his homeland in Nepal by Queen Getso. Now he looked on, appreciating his student's concentration on her work, as Dechen's paint brush slid effortlessly over the surface prepared by the master himself.

The preparation of the blank thangka for painting was a long process. Master Thargye-la began by stretching cotton muslin, imported from India, between a frame he made of sticks lashed together at the corners. Then he painted this stretched cotton with a layer of gesso.

Using the smooth stones he had gathered at the river's edge, he rubbed the surface until it was smooth. After this, a layer of hide glue, made from yak-skin, was applied to both sides of the surface. While this was wet, Thargye-la tightened the strings attached to the cotton and stick frame, evenly pulling the canvas tight. As it dried, the canvas shrunk, making the surface taut and smooth. The canvas completed, Thargye-la drew onto the white surface with a willow stick of charcoal specially made for the fine light drawing. Painstakingly, he drew the sacred image to the exact measurements and proportions for that particular deity. His students learned by painting over the master's drawings.

Deep in concentration, the Princess guided the shimmering gold as it flowed from the sable hairs. Finishing her stroke, Dechen leaned back to inspect her work. Delighted at the result, she smiled and looked at her tutor seated on the cushion next to her.

"Oh, how beautiful!" A voice came from behind them as small hands grasped Dechen's shoulders. Then the head of her little sister, Tsogyal, appeared, leaning over her right shoulder.

"Oh, sister, it is exquisite. I have never seen painting like this," Tsogyal marveled, her eyes wide, taking in the rich green made of powdered malachite, the intense blue made from azurite. "What is this you are painting on now, sister? Is this real gold? I have never seen painting like this," Tsogyal said, as she came around Dechen and plopped onto the cushion beside her sister.

Leaning forward, inspecting the painting, Tsogyal enthused, "Sister, you are very good."

Glowing at the praise, Dechen explained, "This painting style is new. Master Thargye-la is one of the few who know of it and can teach it."

Tsogyal gazed at the image of a Goddess standing on a lotus. The graceful figure gestured to a text, a stack of parchment paper pressed between two boards and wrapped in gold brocade, floating in the sky on a swirl of silk extending from her hand to the left of her. In her right hand she held a lute. The colors were so bright, so rich, they sparkled. Tsogyal was drawn into the Goddess's eyes. They looked back at her with love and compassion. Enchanted, Tsogyal turned to look at her sister sitting beside her. Dechen appeared radiant, her silk robe flowed around her like glistening clouds, she herself was a Goddess. Looking at Thargye-la, who was sipping from a cup of tea, Tsogyal was amazed that the tea was shimmering like silver nectar. Tharge-la's robes sparkled. Seated there with a look of benevolence, he appeared as a celestial God. Tsogyal could see into him, his great talent, his many previous lives as an artisan. Looking around her, the room itself seemed to sparkle like a pure space. Every object she laid her eyes on was clean and bright, shimmering silver and gold. Turning her attention back at the figure in the painting, Tsogyal felt the Goddess within the frame calling to her. Pulled by her call, Tsogyal reached out to touch the figure in the painting. A sudden grasp on her wrist stopped her.

"Little sister, do not touch it, the paint is still wet, you will ruin it!" Dechen warned, staying her hand with a grasp on her wrist.

Tsogyal drew her hand back, realizing her error, as Dechen released her hold. Looking away from the painting to break its spell, the shimmering of the room faded away. Dechen's face and silks were no longer radiant. Thargye-la's tea was milky brown. Dechen and Thargye-la were looking at her in dismay, wondering what was the matter with her.

Shifting on the cushion, composing herself, Tsogyal asked, "Who is this Goddess in the painting?"

"This is Sarasvati, Princess," Thargye-la answered. "She is the Goddess of learning and music. She is knowledge of ultimate truth."

A shrill voice boomed from the neighboring room, "Tsogyal, we are waiting!"

"Yes, I am coming," Tsogyal called out.

Pressing her cheek against Dechen's, Tsogyal said, "Keep painting, sister, for ever and ever. You are so good."

In one graceful movement she rose and ran on light feet through the doorway into the adjacent room.

"Why are you late, little sister?" Nyima, second born princess of Pelgyi, scolded as Tsogyal entered the room. "You have kept us waiting."

"I am sorry, sister and Master Jangbu," Tsogyal said with a quick bow. "The rising of the sun was so beautiful. I went out riding Lungta and lost attention to lateness of the morning," she explained, as she alighted upon the cushion next to her sister and in front of the writing master. "Oh, you should have seen the sunrise, the sky was rose and..."

"Princess Tsogyal," writing master, Jangbu, interrupted. "It is time now for your lesson, you have caused us too much delay, we must begin now."

Startled out of her reverie, Tsogyal bowed her head. "Yes Master, I am sorry, please begin."

Before her on a low table, was a tablet of smooth wood with charcoal sticks atop it for writing. Tsogyal took a stick into her fine hand and looked up to Master Jangbu.

It was Queen Getso's wish that her daughters be educated in painting, writing, music and the dharma. She also had them learn a basic history of Tibet, China, Nepal and India. In addition to this, they studied the fundamentals of astrology and medicine. And even though they were served by servants, and would marry a man who in turn would have servants, she encouraged them to learn how food was prepared.

Getso also wanted her daughters to understand the world of men and politics, and she even had plans to have them learn fundamental military strategy. This she knew would be scorned by her husband, the King. Nevertheless, she had every intention of it being so, sometime in their future. She wanted her daughters to understand as much of the world and its complexities as possible. This was not only for their safety but also that their knowledge of such things would make them assets to their future husbands. Because Queen Getso knew that a woman's beauty will satisfy a man only for a short while. However, a strong and knowledgeable woman can help a husband succeed and see danger close to him when he is blind. These assets will make her valuable to him.

6

"Mmm, I am so hungry," Tsogyal said as she sat with her mother and sisters at a large low table as servants filed in, carrying bowl after bowl of fine food and pots of tea. Tsogyal was starving after her busy morning riding Lungta and in deep concentration on her writing lesson with Master Jangbu. She looked on hungrily as her mother then elder sisters were served the midday meal. Finally, a bowl of stew, goat meat with potatoes and spices, was set before her, the thick aroma of the delicate spices enveloping her. Next to this, the servant placed a plate of momos, dumplings filled with spiced mutton. And finally, a bowl of yogurt; a real treat for them all. Her special silver cup was filled with hot butter tea.

Rocking on her cushion, holding herself back from grabbing at her food, Tsogyal's stomach rumbled as she waited for her mother to begin.

Getso looked at her youngest daughter. "Tsogyal, can you not hold yourself still?"

Ceasing her rocking at this reproach, Tsogyal answered sheepishly, "Yes, mother, I am sorry."

Getso sipped at the spicy stew. "Mmm, very good," she said to the servant. "Tell our new cook I am well pleased."

The servants bowed and left the dinning room.

Looking at her daughters, she explained, "We have a new cook from India. He has brought many new spices to add to the preparation of our meals."

With a nod to her daughter, Queen Getso said, "You may begin now, Tsogyal."

Dechen and Nyima giggled at their little sister as they began to eat. Tsogyal grabbed a dumpling and bit into the sticky dough, the juicy meat savory with spices filled her with pleasure. "Oh, my, this is delicious," she exclaimed, the words muffled by her full mouth.

Murmurs of appreciation and sounds of chewing fell like a soft blanket over the room. Queen Getso took a sip of tea, then placing the cup on the table, she said, "Today we have a great teacher from the Emperor's palace visiting. He is the Abbot Santaraksita, of the great monastery the Emperor is building at Samye. The Abbot is traveling to Nepal. Your father has invited him to stay with us for a few days to teach us the dharma of Lord Buddha. He has accepted our invitation."

Wiping a dribble of spicy juice making its way down her chin with the small cloth of muslin she kept in the fold of her robe, Tsogyal looked up, swallowing hard.

"Oh, how wonderful, will he tell us stories of the great adepts? I hope so, I am going to be a great adept and meditate and become enlightened," Tsogyal exclaimed, as she picked up the bowl of delicious yogurt. Sipping the yogurt, she licked her lips, then replaced the bowl on the table. Happily, she bounced on her cushion as she continued, her arms raised up like a bird's wings, "I will rise up into the sky and look down on the land. I will fly, like the great Taoist masters."

Getso looked to her eldest daughter Dechen, who was gazing at Tsogyal, slowly shaking her head. Then mother and eldest exchanged a look of incredulity.

Seeing the silent exchange between her mother and sister, Nyima scolded, "Little sister, you are living in a dream. You will be married and run a household, as all of us will."

Tsogyal frowned at Nyima, lowering her arms. "I have no desire to be married to anyone. I wish to be a yogini," she declared, reaching for a dumpling.

In her gentle tone, Dechen said, "Little sister, you must do as is custom. Besides, there are no great women yogis or adepts; that is for men. Women are meant to be good wives and bear children."

Tsogyal's face flushed as her throat clenched. She chewed quickly and swallowed, resisting the urge to jump up in a rant and storm out of the room. Taking control of her emotions, she grasped her knees and willed herself to sit still. Looking over the delicious food remaining on the table before her, she decided better to stay and enjoy than to waste it all by leaving in a rage.

With a quaver in her voice, she replied softly, "You will see, sister."

Abbot Santaraksita sat upon a pile of large cushions, made of splendid brocade of woven designs in red, gold, green and blue, as he explained, "Your bodies and minds are the result of many rebirths; of the accumulation of the karma created from each of those lives. You should use this precious existence as a human to gain enlightenment, instead of wasting time in pursuit of desires and pleasures." Raising his long index finger, the scholar continued, "Life is samsara. For even good food will turn to poison, if you eat too much. Youth turns to old age, health turns to sickness, fortune turns to poverty and on and on. Today, life may be good, but all things pass. Life shows us that good can turn to bad in a moment's time."

"Can anyone gain enlightenment?" Dechen asked.

Santaraksita looked down upon the beautiful young woman, sitting with the Royal Family below and before him on cushions. King Pelgyi sat in the middle, Queen Getso sat to his right, Princess Dechen to his left. Princess Niyma sat next to Dechen and Tsogyal sat next to her mother Getso.

Santaraksita smiled as he answered, resting his hands in his lap, "Yes, man or woman, it makes no difference. What is most important is finding a qualified master to teach you and guide you along the path of the Buddha dharma. For most, it takes many lives to attain enlightenment. Why is this so? Because, we are the sum total of positive and negative karma. When we practice the dharma we are set on the path of gathering positive karma and wisdom from each of our lives. This accumulates, making each life more positive and spiritual until we become able to realize our Buddha nature and be free forever from samsara existence. Then we will live forever in Nirvana."

Raising his hand palm up he gestured toward the seated family before him as he instructed, "So, you see, it is of great importance that you use this life to practice the dharma. If you do, you will, either in this life, if you are ready, or in one of your future lives, because you have been practicing the dharma, gain enlightenment."

Slowly shaking his head with a frown, he continued, "Those people that only chase desires and pleasures, that never understand their passions, create more and more negative karma. They will perhaps take eons to gain enlightenment. Because of their negative karma they are not attracted to the dharma. Eventually these people, whom create heavy negative karma will find themselves reborn as an animal. Or, perhaps, when they die they will wake up in the Hungry Ghost Realm or in a Hell Realm. They will exist there for a very long time. Eventually, they will be reborn again as a human. Being reborn as a human they have the chance to find the path of the dharma toward gaining enlightenment."

Sitting back, Santaraksita looked over the Royal Family, his face serene. "Do you have any further questions?" he asked.

"Master?" Tsogyal spoke. "The mornings, when I ride my wonderful horse, are so beautiful. I love my horse and good food, my mother and father and my sisters. Is this attachment? Is this desire, to long to see and relish the beauty of a sunrise or a sunset, the feel of my fine horse at the gallop, my love for my family. Is this the desire and attachment to which you speak?"

Santaraksita looked down at the girl, whose features he had not really taken in. She was exquisitely beautiful. Her question surprised him as to her intelligence.

"My dear Princess, your question is very good. It is not that you do not appreciate the world's beauty and those you love. It is that you realize the reality of the impermanence of all things. This realization will guide you not to let grasping and desire rule your actions. To grasp at anything of this life is like grasping at sand. You will only experience it slipping through your fingers. You cannot hold onto anything. You can and should, however, appreciate everything. This realization of impermanence heightens one's appreciation of life; because every moment is new and fleeting, becoming yet a new moment."

His gaze turning to look out the large open window in the room, he continued, "The beautiful sunset fades to night, the taste of good food ends rapidly in your mouth and turns to excrement in the end. Your fine horse will one day go lame and be too old to carry you. And your dear family, as yourself, will grow old and die." Looking into the young girl's eyes, he said, "This is reality. This understanding is also the water that nourishes the seeds of compassion. The deep comprehension that all is impermanent."

The trill of a song bird outside rippled across the silence that fell in the room as the Royal Family considered the Abbot's words and their meaning.

"Now, we shall read the scriptures," Santaraksita said, gesturing to the low table before him. On it was a tablet of papers held together with two rectangular boards, one on the bottom and one on top, wrapped in silk and bound with string.

"Very good," Pelgyi interrupted. "Wife, please read with our daughters while I speak privately with the Abbot. We do not need to take his time this way. He will return tomorrow to answer any questions you have from your reading."

Pelgyi stood up and gestured to the door. The Abbot slid from the high cushions to his feet. Then he stepped into his leather sandals and followed quickly behind the King out of the room. Silently they walked down a long hallway, then went up stairs and through another hallway, to a room with three large windows. The day was warm so the wooden shutters lay open. The afternoon sunlight flooded in, along with the distant sound of a falcon's screech. Santaraksita looked out the window to see the large bird circling above the palace. With a look of amazement, he took in at the magnificent view of the valley and mountains. The walls of the room were covered with tapestries. Santaraksita felt the thick fine carpets under his sandaled feet. He placed his hand on one of the ancient carved wooden pillars that supported the timbers of the ceiling.

Pelgyi gestured to a cushion. Santaraksita made himself comfortable as the King sat across from him. Santaraksita, of the Brahmin caste and the son of the King of Zahor, felt comfortable in the presence of Pelgyi as he did also in the presence of the Emperor. Powerful men were familiar to him. He was their equal in royal heritage. A servant entered the room with a tray of tea and placed a steaming cup before each man. Then the man stood waiting for instruction.

"Leave us," Pelgyi ordered.

The servant bowed and silently left the room. Pelgyi considered the Abbot sitting on the cushion before him. His clean-shaven face bore serene chiseled features. His saffron-dyed woolen robes were plain yet clean. He tied his belt with a precise knot, ornate in its simplicity. Santaraksita was known for his great intelligence as a renowned scholar of the Buddha dharma. As well, he had drawn the architectural plans for Samye and now oversaw their execution. Abbot of Samye and of Nalanda University, he was a very busy man. The serious bright eyes of the Abbot waited patiently for his host to begin. The scent of honey-sweetened China black tea wafted up from the steaming cups.

"I am very curious what the news is from court," Pelgyi began, "however, first I have a question regarding the dharma."

Sanatraksita bowed his head, "As you wish, Sire. I do have news from court. And I will be happy to answer any question of the dharma I am able to."

Agitated, Pelgyi stood up and walked to the window, deep concern in his expression.

Gazing out, his back to Santaraksita, Pelgyi asked "What of the Gods?"

"The Gods?" Santaraksita inquired, leaning forward on his cushion with a quizzical look.

Pelgyi gestured to the expanse revealed by the window. "Yes, the

Gods, what of the Gods?" Pelgyi repeated, irritation in his voice. Turning to look at Santaraksita, he explained, "The people revere and fear the wrath of the Gods. Our people have been revering the ancient Gods of Bon for generations. How will the Buddha dharma appease the Gods in the eyes of the people? Why will the people want to follow the teachings of the Buddha, when they see no power in the Buddha and they only know the power of their Gods?"

Santaraksita sighed and sat back on his cushion. "King Pelgyi, this is, of course, a very astute question. The answer is that the fruit of enlightenment takes one beyond the Gods' Realm."

Pelgyi stared at Santaraksita with interest. "Beyond the Realm of the Gods?" he inquired.

Santaraksita continued, "The realms of the Gods and demigods will be transcended at the fruition of the path to enlightenment."

Pelgyi walked over to the low table and picked up the cup of tea. Absently, he sipped the warm sweet fragrant tea as he considered. "Transcend the Gods?" he asked "Explain this Realm of the Gods."

Santaraksita placed his own cup of tea back on the table as he swallowed. "First, you must understand that there are six realms of existence and that all realms are samsara. There is the Hell Realm, this is where those who are cruel and evil arrive after their death. This realm is filled with pain and suffering. The Hungry Ghost Realm, this is where those who are greedy and miserly end up. This realm is filled with hunger and thirst. There is the Animal Realm, this is where those who remain willfully ignorant with no striving for knowledge, who only chase their desires, having no regard for others, are reborn. The Human Realm, where one has the best conditions for following the dharma and for gaining enlightenment. There is the Demigod's Realm, where those of the God's Realm fall when they become jealous of other Gods. And there is the God's Realm, where those that are good and kind, who almost gain enlightenment and have great compassion, exist. These beings are immaterial spirits of light existing in a realm of beauty and pleasure for a very long time. They are on the edge of enlightenment yet they are caught in subtle grasping. Their curse is there is nowhere to go but down when their karma is exhausted. After living such a long and wonderful life, it is extremely painful to lose it all and fall into lower realms of existence. It is possible to achieve enlightenment in the God's Realm, yet the step to enlightenment is very subtle, therefore difficult."

Santaraksita looked at Pelgyi now seated on the cushion across from him in rapt attention.

"To realize one's Buddha nature, to become fully enlightened, one transcends all the realms of existence and exists forever free, in Nirvana," Santaraksita concluded.

"I see," Pelgyi murmured as he stroked his mustache. Rising, he strode to the window and gazed out, considering. Then he asked, with a wave of his arm gesturing to the mountains beyond, "But what of these Gods, the ones that exist in the lakes and rivers and the mountains. How do we live with them, now that we are devoted to the Buddha, and not incur their wrath?"

Rising from his seated position, the Abbot answered, "The Emperor has invited a powerful Tantric master from Oddiyana, to subjugate the forces of demons and demigods that may try to hinder the practice and spread of the Buddha's teachings in Tibet. These forces are causing much trouble in the building of our great monastery at Samye."

"Who is this master?" Pelgyi asked, while looking out at the clouds gathering around mountain peaks in the distance.

"His name is Padmasambhava," Santaraksita answered.

"Padmasambhava?" Pelgyi repeated as he turned to look at Santaraksita. "I have never heard of him."

With a slight bow of his head, Santaraksita assured, "Master Padma is very powerful in the arts of subjugation of demonic forces."

Clasping his hands behind his back, Pelgyi turned once again to gaze at the expanse cascading down and away from the window. "I shall look forward to hearing more of this Master Padma, in future. Now then, tell me the news from the Emperor's court," he asked.

Santaraksita walked to the window and stood beside the King, looking out as he began. "A fortnight ago the Emperor called upon the Oracle. The Oracle warned of great calamity befalling the Emperor himself and all of Tibet."

King Pelgyi look up at the Abbot, the man a head taller than himself, in surprise and concern. Santaraksita waved his hand in dismissal. "All is well, my King, you need have no concern as the matter is resolved. The Oracle had stated that a sacrifice must be made to avert the calamity. Minister Ma-zhang and Minister Lugong were named by the Oracle to give their lives and forever live in the tombs as living dead."

In astonishment, King Pelgyi gasped, "Ma-zhang is the most powerful Bon minister in the Emperor's court. Who is this Lugong, I have no knowledge of the man?"

"Lugong is powerful as well," Santaraksita explained. "Unfortunately he has escaped. But Ma-zhang died in the tombs."

In a somber tone, Santaraksita continued, looking sideways at Pelgyi, "It was very good of him to offer his life to avert such a calamity."

The light of realization washed over Pelgyi's face as he said wryly, "Yes, I see. And the Oracle has more coin in his chest after such a decree."

Santaraksita chuckled, then in a solemn tone, he explained, "Well, my King, the dharma must survive and to do so obstacles must be removed."

Silence fell between them. The scent of snow from distant mountains was strong on the soft breeze blowing through the open window. "Very well, Abbot," Pelgyi said, signaling their conversation was completed. "I wish you a good journey to Nepal. Will you leave upon the morrow?"

"Yes, it was my plan," Santaraksita said. "May I have an audience with the Queen and the Princesses to answer any questions they may have before I leave?"

"Yes, of course," Pelgyi answered absently, deep in thought. "Have a pleasant evening, Abbot."

Santaraksita turned from the window and walked across the room. Then he turned back to Pelgyi, saying, "King Pelgyi, you are correct." The King turned to look at him, as the Abbot went on. "The people need a replacement for the Gods of their Bon tradition. We shall give them Avalokishvara, the principle of compassion. Manjushri with his warrior's sword, the principle of wisdom. Tara the Mother of all the

Buddhas who answers all who call upon her. And we will give them many more." With a bow to the King, Sataraksita turned to leave.

"Abbot?" Pelgyi called out.

Santaraksita stopped at the doorway, turning around to face King Pelgyi.

"Abbot, what is enlightenment?" Pelgyi asked.

Santaraksita looked at the King for a long moment. Then he replied, "It is the full expression of a human being; free from delusion, free from hope, free from fear."

Pelgyi stroked his mustache, considering. "And one becomes free?" he asked.

"By learning and practicing the yoga Tantras, my King," the Abbot answered, then he turned and was gone.

7

Senge felt the man's rapid pulse under his fingers as he clasped the soldier's chin, pulling it up hard, exposing his neck. With his back against Senge's knees, the warrior thrashed and struggled against Senge's relentless iron grip. Hot blood gushed as Dragon's Claw sliced through the man's neck, the sharp blade cutting deeply through flesh and arteries, almost severing head from body. Suddenly a form was rushing at him, seen from the periphery of his vision. Letting the body drop, Senge spun and sliced, making contact under the charging solder's arm. The man screamed, stumbled and fell, his helmet falling off when he hit the ground. Senge lunged to the man's side and hammered the heavy pommel of Dragon's Claw down in a crushing blow to the head. Brain oozed from the cracked skull as Senge stepped over the corpse, his feet slipping on the bloody ground as he looked around him for more of the enemy to kill.

Swirling around General Senge, the battle raged with men hacking and punching, slicing and crushing. Senge was elated, a whirlwind of raw energy and precision. His body spun and sliced, stabbed and finished off every man who came at him. He was beyond thinking, his body and reflexes were his intelligence. His mind could only catch up later and would not remember the details of most, but would remember the details of some things, and these would remain with him forever.

Senge was off his horse Ketu, fighting on the ground. For when he had charged into the Frontier General's Chinese forces, a solder had tripped Ketu, sending Senge crashing down, hitting the ground hard, embraced by the weight of his Persian armor. Rolling to his knees, getting his feet under him, he rose up still holding Dragon's Claw firmly in his grasp. The General spun at a soldier near him and sliced the man's head off in a single stroke. Then he spun again, sliced and stabbed, in the roar of screaming, groaning and cursing, as men fought all around him in the dance of battle.

A Chinese warrior rushed at Senge with a spear. Senge leapt to the side and as the warrior passed him, he swung Dragon's Claw, hitting the warrior hard on the back. The man's chain-mail kept the hard blow from cutting him, yet the force of it caused him to stumble and fall. The warrior lay face down in the bloody muck as Senge turned his sword and drove Dragon's Claw's point into the man's back at the base of his neck, slicing between the vertebra, killing the warrior instantly. Pulling his sword out of the bleeding corpse, Senge spun around, sword held ready, anticipating more Chinese warriors. Yet he only saw his men and the other Tibetan forces around him.

"General Senge!" a man called. "Look!"

Senge looked to where the man was pointing. There on the hillside beyond, the Frontier General with his remaining Chinese forces galloped away from the battlefield. Senge watched as they disappeared over the rise and were gone.

"It is over, we have won!" the men cheered.

"Cowards, pigs, thieves!" Senge cursed toward the empty hill top as he swung his sword. "Come back and fight!"

It was over. After three moons of trudging and pulling horses and supplies over snow-covered passes, traveling through valleys and forests. Freezing nights sleeping on the ground or in felt tents. At last they had reached the Great Blue Lake outside Kan-chou. There the Tibetan army camped for five days as General Klu-pal, the commanding general for the Emperor Trisong Detsen, the Emperor's son Mune and the other generals leading armies of warriors sent by several Kings of

Tibet, planned their assault on the Frontier General's Chinese forces inside Kan-chou.

They made their attack at dawn. The battle raged on all day. The sun was low in the sky now as the Chinese Frontier General, representing the interest of the Tang Dynasty, and what was remaining of his army, who tried in vain to hold Kan-chou after seizing it from the Tibetan Emperor's garrison, ran for their lives. Senge watched as the Tibetan calvary charged up the hillside after the fleeing Chinese, close on their heels.

Senge looked around. "Where is Ketu?" he murmured.

His gaze searched the forms on the field as he walked, stepping over corpses. Noticing a Chinese warrior laying wounded in the bloody mud, Senge quickened his death. He cast his gaze out, searching among the many riderless horses that were standing on the field, for the familiar form and color of Ketu. Many horses lay wounded or dead. He came upon a horse laying in a pool of blood still alive and suffering. Senge thrust Dragon's Claw to sever his carotid artery. Turning from the dead horse he noticed his own saddle laying sideways. His mind froze, not comprehending the sight. Realization dawned. Senge ran to Ketu. Falling to his knees at his horse's side, he saw at once what had caused him to fall. Ketu had not been tripped, his front legs had been sword-cut and bleeding from the time of his fall.

Senge calculated, *How long?* All hope was dashed as he realized it had been too long, the horse had lost too much blood. Ketu's eyes were open. They shifted to look at Senge. Ketu issued a soft rumble of recognition as Senge stroked the stallion's neck.

"Oh, my great warrior brother." Tears welled in Senge's eyes. "You have been true and great," Senge said. "You will be reborn with riches and in a happy life, I will see to it. I will pay the priests of the Bon to perform the rites for your passage into your next life."

Senge drew Dragon's Claw and drove the blade into Ketu's heart to end the stallion's pain and suffering. Withdrawing the bloody blade, Senge felt as though the blade still remained in his own heart, the pain of Ketu's loss searing in his chest. He stroked the charcoal-colored neck, feeling the silky coat under his fingers. As he knelt by Ketu's warm body, images flooded his mind of all his seasons with this fine horse.

Though Senge had many horses, Ketu always had stood out. He remembered the first day he noticed the two-springs old Ketu in his herd, wild and proud. The memories of the weeks of training to ride him played across his mind. The stallion had fought Senge to remain alpha of their herd of two. Senge, never relenting in his mastery, finally won the horse's allegiance. Senge then spent many more moons to train him for battle. He was pleased with how quickly Ketu learned and responded to every cue. Man and horse had become as one. Images of the springs of battles this fine horse had carried him through passed across his mind's eye. Now, Ketu lay in the blood-soaked earth; he was gone. Senge's body convulsed as tears flooded down his face.

"We come from the land of the Gods.
We come from the seven stages of the blue heavens.
We are the sons of the Gods,
the protectors of our people.
Of all the kingdoms of men in this earthly realm,
there have never been warriors equal to ours.
We are the warriors of Tibet!
We crush all in our path.
We are the invincible soldiers of Tibet!"

Tibet's warriors all sang in a roar, their silver and horn cups raised. The generals and soldiers celebrated their victory in one of Kan-chou's great halls. This hall was owned by Akeem, a Saracen whose family had been traders in Kan-chou for generations. Servants carried platters of seared meat and jugs of chang beer supplied by the merchants of Kan-chou to the tables set up for the Tibetan army. The aroma of spiced meats, chang beer, clashed with the stench of sweat and bloodied sheepskin robes worn by the warriors in the hall.

"Congratulations on your victory, General. We all are pleased to have our Tibetan brothers once again as lords of this great oasis," Akeem said with a slight bow of his head to General Klu-pal who was seated next to him.

"We shall expect the Emperor's taxes be ready when we leave," Klu-pal said gruffly, as he reached for the platter of goat meat.

"How long do you plan to stay in Kan-chou, General?" Akeem queried,

Tearing a mouthful of meat from the leg he held in his hand, Klu-pal considered the question as he chewed. Swallowing, he answered, "We all need rest. We will remain until the men are well rested. Then we march east to the capital at Chang-an," Tearing another mouthful of the juicy meat from the bone, he lifted his silver cup of chang and took a gulp of the rich beer. Wiping his mouth with his sleeve, he continued, "We will show these cowards who the masters of this land are."

Noticing Akeem had not taken a bite of the food that lay heaped on the platter before him, Klu-pal waved his hand. "Eat, man! All food and drink for us and our men may be deducted from the taxes owed," he assured.

"Very well, General," Akeem said with a bow of his head as he reached for a morsel of sliced meat, relieved that the Tibetans had come and conquered the occupying Tang forces, before the Tang had received the taxes that they had demanded from Akeem and all the merchants of Kan-chou.

"Chang-an, the capital," Akeem said, as he lifted his cup of chang and took a sip. "Very impressive, General. There are many soldiers guarding the capital, are there not?" he queried.

Klu-pal laughed, waving the goat-leg in dismissal. "They will be no match for our warriors, we will capture Chang-an."

Akeem nodded, clearly impressed. "Our Tibetan brothers are powerful indeed."

Klu-pal tossed the leg bone onto the platter. Leaning back, taking a long deep breath then letting it out, he placed his hands on his full belly as he continued, "I will be appointing a larger number of men to garrison here than before."

"That is understandable, General," Akeem said as he bowed his head slightly. "In case of another attack by the Frontier General?"

Klu-pal smiled. "We expect no more trouble from that Frontier Coward, " Klu-pal said, "We have captured the fleeing General and all with him. He and the prisoners shall all lose their heads on the morrow, when their work clearing the field of the corpses of their brethren and horses is completed."

Akeem held in his surprise. "I see, General."

A high-ranking soldier marched into the hall to the long table where the generals were sitting. Addressing General Klu-pal, he bowed, announcing, "We have the valuables taken from the field."

"Very good!" Klu-pal said. "Bring all in now. Leave the horses, we will inspect them on the morrow in the light of day."

A line of warriors came in, each carrying an armload of bounty. On the floor before the General's banquet table they placed chain-mail, swords, spears, shields, beautiful recurve bows made of horn and sinew, arrows, exquisite armor of lacquered boiled leather with intricate designs, horse bridles decorated with gold and silver medallions, saddles with inlayed gold and silver on the cantles and pommels and horse armor; all had been stripped from the dead on the battlefield. Then more warriors came in, piling sacks of gold and silver, taken from the tents and houses the Chinese forces had occupied during their occupation of Kan-chou.

Everyone nodded approvingly at the wealth the Emperor's general, Klu-pal, would divide between all of the generals. Each general in turn would divide their share between their men for their service to their King or lord. All could see from the mountain of goods that they all would go home with a tidy sum.

General Klu-pal stood up and called out, "Warriors of Tibet!" Silence came over the men as they looked to the General standing with his large ornate silver cup of chang beer held high. "You brave warriors have run off the Chinese thieves and shown them we are the lords of Kan-chou!"

The room exploded as the men stamped and cheered. Klu-pal raised his hand for silence. "This trade route oasis is the domain of our Emperor, Trisong Detsen," he called out, causing the men to settle and listen to his words. Waving his arm in a gesture to the merchants sitting at the table, he said, "These merchants pay taxes to our great Emperor. Therefore, you must respect his domain and not molest any in this town nor their merchandise." With a stern expression, Klu-pal continued, "I give you warning. Do not think you can molest any woman here either. If you are invited you may enjoy yourselves, but only if invited. If any report comes to me that a woman has been violated or any merchandise stolen, you will lose your head!"

Murmurs of agreement rumbled through the men. Klu-pal waited for a moment, then ordered, "Each general will choose men as sentries tonight." Then, with a final raising of his cup, he concluded, "Those of you not on duty can drink yourselves into a stupor if you choose. You have earned it!"

The men cheered as Klu-pal sat down. With joy they all ate and drank, recounting the battle, telling their stories of killing and of surviving. They joked and laughed until they all staggered to their camps and fell fast asleep.

8

Sitting cross-leg on a cushion in front of his felt tent, his thick coat of sheepskin sheltering him from the cold, Senge watched as night turn to day. The cold night's black sky, awash with stars like crystals, now turned from gray to pink to red in the sky to the east. White rays appeared, shooting into the sky from behind the hills in the distance, becoming brighter and brighter. First a glint, then a sliver and finally, golden rays spread across the valley and engulfed all in light.

Holding his silver cup of tea in his hands, Senge contemplated the amazing fact that he was alive after the frenzy of killing just the day before. Never allowing himself to get drunk after a battle as other men did, he sat sober, appreciating the life around him. Chirps of the morning birds fluttering about filled the silence. Dark wisps of smoke from the battlefield fires, burning the corpses of the fallen, stained the clear perfect morning sky. Though the air was acrid with the smoke from the field and campfires, he took pleasure in the feeling of his breath passing in and out of his lungs. Most men wanted to forget the blood, the screams, the fear, the lust. Senge wanted to remember and he did not want lose the clarity and sharpness of his mind and senses through drunkenness.

Besides, he thought, *only a fool lets himself become vulnerable by being drunk.*

Images of Ketu and his death remained in his thoughts, the pain of his loss still gripped his heart.

Now that morning had arrived, he had to decide which of the string of six horses he had remaining, those he had brought with him on this campaign, he would ride to the morning assembly with all the generals. Having deciding on his older red-dun gelding, he stood up slowly, stretching the stiffness from his back muscles. The pain in his back assailed him as he swayed back and forth to loosen the tightness. He winced in pain from the angry black bruises on his thighs and left side. Limping to the pile made by his saddle, blanket and bridle that lay in front of his tent, he picked up the lead-rope. Feeling the first rays of sun warm him, he set off for the herd grazing next to the encampment of the Tibetan forces.

"Yes, these are fine, fine horses indeed," General Klu-pal said to Prince Mune who stood next to him. Though still a boy of thirteen springs, Prince Mune carried himself like a man, his lean strong form exuded confidence being the eldest born to Emperor Trisong. He felt it his duty to represent his station with nobility as they strolled along, admiring the captured Tang horses tied for their inspection. The group of generals following them nodded in agreement.

Turning to his lieutenant, Klu-pal ordered, "Bring the stallion."

The lieutenant turned and obediently ran off.

"This one is fine, is she not?" Klu-pal said to Mune, stopping in front of a white mare. He reached out and stroked her strong neck.

"She is fine," Mune replied, taking a step back to admire her conformation. He rested his hand on the gold hilt of the royal sword he wore on the belt of silk tied around his robe of fur-lined silk. The green garudas of the pattern on the robe danced on the background of gold as he moved. Under the wolf-fur hat he wore, his long black hair was tied back, its mass reaching his waist. "She has a gentle eye. I do like mares, they are very sensible and have great endurance," he said in admiration.

The men's attention were drawn by the return of Klu-pal's

lieutenant leading a fine stallion, its golden coat shimmering in the morning sun. Stopping before them, the lieutenant handed the lead-rope to General Klu-pal. All in attendance murmured their approval of the fine horse who stood before them. He was a hand taller than their Tibetan horses and lean, not stocky, making him look regal. Many of the Tang cavalry horses were taller than those of the Tibetan cavalry. Mune stooped to run his hand up the straight leg, coal-black from hoof to the knee, then turning a golden color to the shoulders and body of the horse.

Looking up at Klu-pal, Mune said, "Fine legs, this one is truly great."

The horse shook his black mane and swished his black tail, then raised his head, pulling lightly on the rope.

With a slight bow, General Klu-pal handed the lead-rope to Mune, saying, "He has a very intelligent eye. He is a prize."

Looking over the shoulders of the generals in front of him, Senge appreciated the fine conformation of the stallion. He could see why Mune would want everyone to see the fine horse he claimed as his prize.

Turning to the assembly, Mune called out, "Is General Senge here?"

"Yes, I am here!" Senge answered, as he stepped from behind the men and bowed to the Prince.

Admiring the horse, Prince Mune said, "This stallion was the property of the Frontier General. He is battle-trained and is of fine stock. What is your opinion of him, General?"

Senge strode to the horse's side. Stroking the stallion's neck, he ran his other hand along the strong back and well-formed flanks. "He is very fine. A fine prize for you, my Prince. You must be well pleased. Beautiful golden color, as well," Senge said.

"I must be well pleased? No, General Senge, it shall be you who is well pleased," Mune laughed, as he held the lead-rope out to Senge, "as he is yours."

Senge froze in confusion. "Mine?"

"It was reported to me that you lost your fine horse to a Chinese sword," Mune said, still holding the rope toward Senge. "Therefore, you shall receive a fine horse in return."

Understanding Senge's hesitation, Prince Mune assured him, "You have served your King Pelgyi and my father Emperor Trisong well. You are a fine general, General Senge, and an even greater warrior. It is my discretion to divide the treasure from this battle. I have no doubt that the Emperor would agree with my decision that you shall have this horse as your prize. I am sure this fine horse will serve you as your Ketu did."

Slowly, Senge took the rope into his hands and bowed low to Prince Mune. "You are very generous, my liege."

Mune smiled, then turned and walked down the line of horses with Klu-pal and the other generals in tow.

Standing alone in amazement, Senge beheld the finest horse he would never have even dreamed to have as his own.

The undulating rumble and jingle of the army caravan marching along the wide worn track of the trade route broke through the silence of the cold morning. The Tibetan invasion of Chang-an was successful. With ease, the Tibetan army rolled over the Chinese defenses. Now the long line of wagons loaded with the goods taken from the battle at Kan-chou and Chang-an were making their way back to the palace of Emperor Trisong in Lhasa. Many of the men had traded the fine war accouterments they had received, as payment for their service to the Emperor, to the merchants for silver or for items for which they had more need. Cheerfully, the warriors rode in columns in front and behind the wagons. Many had new armor, new bows, new spears, new horses.

Klu-pal's army and two other general's armies were heading west to check on the other towns on the trade route controlled by the Tibetan Emperor Trisong Detsen. Then they would turn south, returning to the Yarlung Valley and Lhasa.

Astride his new horse, whom he named Skamar, meaning star,

Senge felt tall, enjoying the easy gliding walk of his stallion. He had spent all of his free time working with the stallion during their stay at Kan-chou. Delighted by Skamar, who was smooth and fast and had learned Senge's cues quickly. The war horse had performed fearlessly in the battle at Chang-an; Senge was well pleased.

Drawing in the fresh cold morning air, it felt like cool nectar filling his being. Senge and his men were quite content after receiving their share of the booty. King Pelgyi would be pleased with the many wagons loaded with treasure bound for Karchen, Senge was sure of this.

The men were content and happy as they marched this morning. They were warriors, this is what they loved and lived for. To fight and win for their King and their families, making Tibet secure and prosperous. They were undisputedly the most powerful army of the land, making Tibetan Emperor Trisong Detsen ruler of the most powerful Empire in Asia.

9

Tsogyal opened her eyes sleepily. Gray light in the room told her dawn had arrived. Burrowing under the thick sheepskin blanket, she snuggled deeply into the softness of the large cushion she slept upon. Soft breathing, of her sisters in their beds, was the only sound in the room they all shared.

Her stomach rumbled, announcing her hunger. She wondered if yogurt would be served for breakfast. *I hope so*, she thought. She decided she would ride Lungta this morning after breakfast, since she was so hungry. *Then writing and reading lessons*, she mused.

A stiff cold morning breeze whipped across Tsogyal's face as she rode Lungta beside Chudak. Leaving the palace, they trotted along the road leading to the valley and the river. Not far along the road they were faced with a procession of many warriors, wagons and a herd of horses, forcing them to urge Lungta and Goba up the hillside. There, they watched in wonderment as the entourage rumbled and jingled past them. Lungta stamped and whinnied at the herd of horses kept in a tight mass by many riders enclosing them. Many in the herd whinnied and neighed in answer to her calls.

Tsogyal and Chudak watched the visitors amassing on the plain below the palace walls.

"Who are they?" Tsogyal asked Chudak.

"I do not know, Princess, a Lord or a King of another realm must be visiting your father. I do not understand why they need so many provisions, however."

Trotting off their perch, Tsogyal breathed in the thick cold air. Then she enthused, "Let us race to the place on the river, Chudak."

Chudak rolled his eyes. "Perhaps we should go at the trot for awhile so the horses can warm up?"

Tsogyal nodded, "Yes, of course. But later we will race?"

"As you wish, Princess," Chudak affirmed.

No longer concerned about the gathering mass of men, wagons and horses, they trotted toward the river. The morning sky was deep blue with thick dark clouds piling on the mountaintops.

King Pelgyi sat upon his throne, his agitation rising, as Prince Wangchuk, of the small Kingdom of Zurkhar, addressed him. "Your Grace, I have brought three hundred horses, two hundred mules and fifty wagons of ivory, silk, gold and tea for the hand of your daughter, the Princess Tsogyal."

Pelgyi looked beyond Wangchuk at the loud thudding of Prince Zhonnu, of the small Kingdom of Kharchupa, striding into the hall. Stopping at the side of Prince Wangchuk, Zhonnu bowed to King Pegyi, saying, "King Pelgyi, I have brought three hundred of the finest war-horses, two hundred and fifty mules and forty wagons filled with spices, tea, silk, gold and silver for the hand of your beautiful daughter, the Princess Tsogyal."

Pelgyi fidgeted as he sat cross-legged on the high cushions that made his throne. Absently he tapped his fingers on his knee. "I have three beautiful and accomplished daughters," Pelgyi answered. "Dechen, my eldest daughter, would make a fine wife, as would Nyima my second born. You may choose which of these daughters you would desire."

Prince Wangchuk bellowed, "No! It is the Princess Tsogyal I desire. Prince Zhonnu may have one of your other daughters."

Clenching his fists, Prince Zhonnu stepped forward. "I desire only the Princess Tsogyal. I will have none other."

Abruptly, Pelgyi slid from his perch and stood, glaring at the men below him. "I will think upon this. You may make your camps below my palace in the valley beside the river. There you will await my summons." Then he turned and quickly left the hall.

Zhonnu looked menacingly at Wangchuk, then turned and left the hall. Wangchuk gritted his teeth, waving to his attendants to follow as he turned from the empty throne and strode out.

Standing on the roof of the palace, Pelgyi observed the movements of the two camps below. Sensing movement behind him, he turned to see his wife, Queen Getso, walking to him from across the terrace. Coming to his side, she took his hand in hers.

"What will you do, husband?"

Sighing, Pelgyi looked into her eyes, then turned to gaze down at the gathering,

"If I give Tsogyal to Wangchuk, Zhonnu will war upon us. If I give her to Zhonnu, Wangchuk will never rest until he avenges the dishonor we have shown him."

"But what of your decision to keep her for the Emperor?" Getso inquired. "Why can you not tell them neither may have her?"

As she spoke, they both noticed two forms on horseback in the distance galloping across the valley. "Chudak and Tsogyal," Pelgyi confirmed. "Look at her, she is wild. She is too savage for the Emperor, he will never want her."

Pelgyi stroked his mustache, watching the pair racing along in the distance as he pondered aloud to Getso, "Both Princes Wangchuk and Zhonnu have fine palaces. Both are in good grace with the Emperor. Either can give her a good life and we will benefit from the alliance." Turning to Getso, he cursed, "Yet, they leave me no way to choose, they both arrive on the same day, offering the same amount for her hand in marriage."

Considering the wagons and horses in the valley below, Pelgyi considered. *It would be beneficial to have them. Senge will come back from Kan-chou with treasure, but how much treasure,* he wondered? *How many horses were lost in the fighting? The horses below look fine indeed. The treasure would be a good addition my coffers,* he mused.

Suddenly, Pelgyi thought of a solution. "We will give the decision to Tsogyal herself!" Pelgyi declared to Getso.

Getso shook her head in dismissal. "They will say you are weak to allow her the decision," she warned.

"I think not, as it will be my decision to grant her the choice," Pelgyi said, a smile of triumph spreading over his face. "How can the loser blame me if she does not desire him? He will look weak and pathetic to complain. Yes, this is the way," Pelgyi said, thumping his fist on the top of the terrace wall. Turning to leave, Pelgyi said, "When Tsogyal returns, bring her to me. We will tell her together "

Then he stopped and turned back. Placing his hands on Getso's shoulders as he looked down into her eyes, he assured, "It will be well, my love, all will be well. She will have a good husband and live a fine life."

Then he turned and strode away. Getso could see he felt relief by the light bounce in his steps.

"I will have neither of them!" Tsogyal cried as she stomped around the room. "Please, I have told you I do not wish to be married. I wish to be a yogini and practice the dharma. If I am married, I will be chained to my husband and his requirements of me. Oh, please, Mother, Father, please send them away."

Pegyi and Getso sat in shock at the tantrum Tsogyal was displaying.

Pelgyi admonished Tsogyal, "There is no one better than either of these suitors. You could end up with no one wanting you at all."

Getso added, soothingly, "Both these lords have fine palaces. You will have Lungta with you and you will find new companions to ride with. You can study the dharma as a Princess wife."

Fists clenched to her sides, tears running down her face, Tsogyal stood staring at her parents in disbelief. Crying out in a moan, she fell to her knees before them. Clasping her hands together, she pleaded, "Please! Please hear me, I do not want to marry anyone, I want to be free."

At a loss, Pelgyi and Getso looked at each other.

"Free?" Getso asked, "Daughter, what do you mean?"

Choking on her tears, Tsogyal looked up at her mother. "If I go with one of these men, I become his chattel. I will sink into the prison of samsara never to be able to escape worldly existence," she sobbed, burying her face in her hands.

Standing abruptly, Pelgyi paced across the room in agitation. Turning to look down at his daughter, he implored, "Tsogyal, either of these Princes would give you a fine life." Becoming more angry, he continued, "You are being unreasonable. You are an insolent daughter to me and to your mother. You must marry and you will marry. You should be glad I am not sending you to China or to Hor! If you will not decide which of these men you will accept, then I will!" Pelgyi shouted, overcome by anger. Pointing toward the doorway, he yelled, "Now go to your chambers until you are summoned by me."

Shocked by her father's outrage, Tsogyal knelt frozen, staring at her parents.

"Guard!" Pelgyi called out.

The guard, standing outside the royal chambers, rushed in, "Yes, sire?"

"Take the Princess to her chambers and make sure she does not leave. I will summon you when to bring her to me," Pelgyi ordered.

Moving to Tsogyal's side, the shaken guard gently took her arm, lifting her to her feet. Weakness overtaking her, feeling powerless, Tsogyal sank into grief allowing herself to be lead away.

The rush of anger draining out of him, Pelgyi paced back and forth, stroking his mustache, muttering to himself, "Ungrateful child. Now what to do?"

Sitting in stunned silence, Getso watched as her husband paced back and forth.

At a loss, turning to look down at her, he pleaded, "What shall I do?"

Getso looked down at her hands folded in her lap, answering, "I know not."

10

"I have made my decision," King Pegyi announced as he stood in front of his throne addressing the morning gathering of Prince Wangchuk, his minister Jamyang, and Prince Zhonnu with his minister Shantipa.

"My daughter has told me she wishes to marry neither of you," he declared.

Shocked, the assembly of men looked at each other in incredulity. Anger rose in Wangchuk, his face growing red and hot.

Pelgyi held up his hand, "I have decided for her. You have both made it clear you do not wish either of my other daughters. So what am I to do?"

Zhonnu broke in, "You shall give her to me or you shall have war!"

Glaring at Zhonnu, Wangchuk cursed to Pelgyi, "You shall give her to me or you shall never rest! I will torment you. I will attack your trade caravans. I will ambush your troops!"

Pelgyi stepped forward. "Silence!" he commanded, holding his hand up. "My answer to you both is that I have decided on a competition."

Wangchuk and Zhonnu looked perplexed. "What do you mean, a competition?" Zhonnu growled. "Between Wangchuk and I?"

Pelgyi held in his anger at Zhonnu's interruption and continued, "I will send the Princess Tsogyal out of the palace along with a caravan of her chattels and provisions for her travel. He who places his hands on her first, thus capturing her, wins her. You must both agree to this and that the loser will hold no grudge and seek no revenge, but will acquiesce to his loss and leave in peace. If you do not agree to this, I shall give her to neither of you. And if you cause me trouble I shall take my grievance of your actions toward my kingdom to the Emperor, Trisong Detsen." Looking from Wangchuk to Zhonnu, Pelgyi asked, "As men of honor, do you agree?"

Wangchuk looked at Zhonnu, a smile growing over his face as he answered, "I agree."

Zhonnu calculated. "Our ministers may act for us as well?" he queried.

Pelgyi considered. "Yes, your ministers do represent you, so if their hands capture the Princess, it is the same as yours," he said. Then raising his finger he added, "Yet only one of your ministers."

Zhonnu nodded firmly, "I agree."

"Very well," Pelgyi said. "The Princess shall be sent out when the sun is high in the sky. I shall have a line marked upon the ground showing the place you and one of your ministers must stand, equal to each other. The one who captures her must take her away immediately and your men must remove your camp and leave tonight. The loser must leave on the morrow," King Pelgyi announced, then he turned and briskly walked out of the audience chamber.

Standing on tiptoes, Tsogyal leaned out the small window of her room, looking down at the courtyard below. It had been three days since her argument with her parents. Under guard, she was forbidden to leave her room. All of her meals were brought to her. Now, in the early morning light, she saw wagons and men running to and fro below her room. Hearing the door open, she spun around to see her sister Dechen enter the room, the door shutting behind her.

"Oh, sister," Tsogyal ran to her. "What is happening? Are the Princes Wangchuk and Zhonnu leaving?"

Dechen looked grave, "Little sister, I do not know what is happening. Father as sent me to dress you in your finest silks and all of your jewels."

Sinking onto a cushion, Tsogyal groaned. "Oh, that does not sound good."

Just then a servant entered the room with a tray of food and tea. Looking from Dechen to Tsogyal, the woman placed the tray on the low table and left the room without a word.

"You must eat, then you must get dressed," Dechen commanded. Not able to hold in her feelings any longer, Dechen broke into tears. "Father is very angry, I have never seen him like this." Falling to her knees next to Tsogyal, Dechen pulled her little sister into her embrace, hugging her fiercely. "Oh, Tsogyal, I do not want you to go," Dechen cried.

Releasing Tsogyal, Dechen stood up and paced as she wiped the tears from her eyes, trying to compose herself. "Little sister, you must eat, then we must dress you."

Clouds were gathered in the sky, obscuring the sun at its zenith. Princess Tsogyal's belongings and provisions for her travel hung on the backs of a caravan of twenty horses and mules who stood silently along the road outside of the palace walls, their heads hung low.

Wangchuk and Zhonnu waited too, with their ministers at their sides. The assembly of warriors and onlookers came to attention at the loud creaking of the opening of the palace gates. There, in the open gateway, stood the small solo figure of the Princess dressed in fine silks of gold, red and malachite. Though the day was gray, all could see the twinkle of the gold and silver which held the turquoise and coral beads of her necklaces and a belt. With her eyes cast to the ground, not wanting to look at those in attendance, she walked out into the cold beyond the palace walls, then stopped. A gasp rose in the assembled crowd at the sight of her, she was exquisitely beautiful. Then Tsogyal looked up. There, not far, she saw Lungta being held by Chudak. The sight of their familiar forms, the two beings of her world that brought so much joy in her life, lifted her spirit from the deep darkness she felt. She started toward them as a rush of activity from the gathered crowd stopped her. She stepped back at the sight of four men running toward her. Startled, she looked at Chudak. He did not move toward her, his hands gripped Lungta's reins, a grim look on his face. Then the men stopped running toward her. Instead they started yelling and fighting with each other.

Wangchuk was bellowing at Zhonnu's tight grasp on his arm, stopping his progress toward the Princess. With a quick move, Zhonnu tripped Wangchuk and threw him to the ground. Shocked by this, Wangchuk's minister, Jamyang, flew at Zhonnu and began punching him. "Leave him, get the Princess!" Wangchuk yelled at Jamyang, as he pushed himself up from the ground.

Meanwhile, Zhonnu's minister Shantipa, whose way was clear, ran straight for Tsogyal. Tsogyal looked to Chudak, her eyes pleading for him to come to her aid. He stood frozen, shaking his head to convey to her that he could not protect her. Seeing a large boulder at the side of the road, Tsogyal ran for it in fright of this man rushing at her, a look of grim intensity on his face. Crouching behind the rock to shield herself from his approach, she wrapped her arms around the cold stone. Arriving in front of the large boulder, Shantipa reached around, grabbing her by her hair, and yanked hard. Tsogyal screamed, releasing her hold, grabbing at his hand to stop the pain.

As he was attempting to lift her to her feet, he growled, "You are now the property of the Prince Zhonnu of Kharchupa."

Tsogyal let go his hand and encircled her arms around the boulder, holding tightly, bearing the pain.

"No!" she screamed. "I will not."

Shantipa let go Tsogyal's hair and grasped the back of her silk robe, pulling with all his might. "You will go, you are the property of my master now," he grunted.

He pulled hard, amazed at the tight hold the small Princess had on the rock. Then he felt the silk robe tear. He pulled even harder, ripping the garment, exposing her back

Tsogyal was shocked at the icy fingers of cold air on her naked back. She held tighter to the rough surface of the boulder, her arms aching. Prince Zhonnu strode up to the pair, carrying his short horse-whip.

"Your father decreed this competition. I have won you, you are mine now. You will be my wife. Let go at once or you will feel this lash," Zhonnu said, wiggling the leather straps in front of Tsogyal's face so she would know what pain would come if she did not release her grip.

Tsogyal gritted her teeth and tightened the hold onto the boulder. "Beat this body if you wish. For if I cannot use my human existence to gain enlightenment, then I might as well be dead," she said, as tears welled in her eyes.

Zhonnu held out the whip toward Shantipa. Shantipa took it, a look of satisfaction spreading across his grim face. He turned and looked down at the shivering girl, her naked skin exposed. Feeling a stirring of pleasure rising in him, he raised the whip high, then lashed down hard across Tsogyal's back. Tsogyal's scream drowned out the gasps of all who stood gathered to watch. White-hot stinging pain coursed through Tsogyal's body. Warm wetness dripped down her side.

Then, Tsogyal began to feel light, that all this that was happening was just a dream. Words poured from her, strong and clear like the sound of a gong. "Prince of Karchupa, look how you waste your precious human birth. Your evil actions do not make you a man. Though you are of noble birth and are powerful you have not the intelligence to desire even one day of wisdom. Your evil actions and karma make you less than human. Why should I be a wife to such a man as you?"

Glaring at Tsogyal, Shantipa cursed, "You shameless girl, how dare you speak to the Prince like this?" Shantipa struck Tsogyal's back again, the leather edge like a knife, cutting another gash though her fine skin. "Your beauty has caused Prince Zhonnu to desire you beyond good reason," he growled as he whipped her again. "You may be beautiful on the outside, but inside you are hard as this stone. You will be the Prince's wife." He gritted his teeth as he whipped her again and again, cutting her back with each stroke.

Zhonnu grabbed Shantipa's arm stopping him. "Enough, she has fainted," he ordered.

Just then King Pelgyi came running through the gate, Chudak right behind him. Stopping in shock at the sight of his daughter's body hunched behind the boulder, her back bloody with lash marks, he fell to his knees by her side. His hand covered his mouth in horror at the sight of her.

"Oh, my child, Tsogyal," he gasped. Wanting to touch her, he stilled his hand, realizing how damaged her back was.

Standing up, he bellowed, "Who did this!?"

Then he saw the whip in Shantipa's hand. Enraged, Pelgyi grabbed the whip, tearing it out of the minister's grasp. Shaking with anger, he slashed it across Shantipa's face as he cursed, "I shall beat you to an inch of your life, you wicked man."

Shantipa staggered back and hunched over in shock at the searing pain. Holding his cheek, he felt hot blood ooze between his fingers. Pelgyi held the whip high for another strike, his rage boiling. Zhonnu grabbed Pelgyi's arm, staying the whip. "The Princess refused to come with me though had I won her. My minister had my permission to collect my property."

Wrenching his arm from Zhonnu's grasp, Pelgyi shook the whip at Zhonnu. "You did not have to beat her! How could you destroy such innocence and beauty?"

Ignoring the King, Prince Zhonnu turned and summoned his warriors who were standing by watching. "Come, put the Princess on her horse, we are going now."

Turning back to Pelgyi, Zhonnu grabbed the whip out of King Pelgyi's hand, sneering, "I will tame her and make her a good wife."

Two warriors ran up to Tsogyal and picked her up, careful not to touch her bleeding wounded back. Another warrior led Lungta. They laid the battered body of the Princess over her saddle on her stomach and tied her so she would not fall. Hot blood dripped down her sides, soaking into the red felt of her saddle. As they led her away,

Tsogyal opened her eyes in a daze. There, she saw Chudak in the distance. He was kneeling on the ground looking up at her, his face wet with tears.

"Goodbye, Chudak, my friend," she whispered. Then all faded into darkness.

11

Prince Zhonnu's caravan halted on route back to Kharchupa at Drakda. Rab-ten, a healer and wife of one of Zhonnu's warriors, was brought into Zhonnu's large round felt tent. A fire crackled in the hearth as she looked down at the bloody wounds inflicted on the young girl's back. Smoke hung at the high roof, making its way out of the smoke hole. Shifting her felt-booted feet on the carpets covering the hard ground, she held back a gasp of horror, keeping herself composed. Prince Zhonnu knelt by the Princess's side, his hand hovering inches over her damaged back, afraid to touch the cut and bloody flesh. He looked up at the healer. She was tall for a woman, his own height, strong of body with a pleasant handsome face.

"You must heal her," he commanded.

Rab-ten heard the pleading in his tone. Kneeling next to Zhonnu, she inspected the torn flesh. "My Lord, these injuries are very bad, she is very weak." Looking at him, she said, "You must stop the march to Kharchupa and allow her to rest so she can heal. I fear she will not survive if we do not stop."

Anger swelled in Zhonnu's chest. *The minister beat her too hard,* Zhonnu thought. *She may die. That idiot may have killed my Princess.* Zhonnu stood up and looked down at Rab-ten. "You, and only you, will stay with her here in my tent. Let me know what you need to heal her," he ordered. Staring down at the bloodied body of the Princess, he said, through gritted teeth, "You must heal her."

Rab-ten's head was bent as she thought. Then she counted on her fingers. "I will need my medicine bundle, my herb bags, my mortar and pestle." Looking at the small flickering fire in the hearth, she added, "I must have more wood for the fire. Also, butter, tea and water and she needs more furs for her bed."

Zhonnu nodded threw the tent flap open in a rage, ducked through and was gone.

Rab-ten sighed as she took in the wounded body that lay before her. "You poor dear girl," she whispered. "What a beast that Shantipa is."

Days later, Rab-ten's gentle fingers patted a healing poultice onto the Princess's back. This she applied each day. Cold wind swirled into the abode as Zhonnu opened the tent flap, stepping in. The scents of campfires, horses and men followed behind him.

"How is she today?" he demanded.

Not looking at him, Rab-ten answered as she continued her work applying the poultice to Tsogyal's back, "My Lord, she is healing but is still very weak, she will need more time."

"How much more time?" Zhonnu asked, impatiently.

"I cannot say the exact amount of time," Rab-ten answered.

Zhonnu paced back and forth in what space there was in the tent, saying, "It has been four days. My men are growing impatient. I need to occupy them."

Looking up at the Prince, Rab-ten did not hide her scorn as she suggested, "Perhaps the Princess would grow strong if she had fresh meat to replace the blood she has lost."

Stopping, he looked down at the Princess laying on her stomach on the bed of furs, amazed he had not thought of this. "Yes," he said, "that would be good for the men. I will send out hunting parties. Let them bring in as much game as they can, then we will feast. The men can hunt and we will feast until the Princess is well and can travel."

Turning away, he was gone, a rush of cold air stirring the flames of the fire in the hearth as the door flap fell closed. Just then Tsogyal started to stir and groan. Rab-ten placed her hand gently on Tsogyal's head. "Be careful, Princess, do not move too much or you will open your wounds."

Tsogyal whispered weakly, "Where am I?" Shifting her eyes to take in the woman kneeling next to her, she croaked, "Who are you? Where is my father?"

Lowering herself to speak softly, Rab-ten answered, "Princess, I am Rab-ten, a healer for Prince Zhonnu. You are in his encampment. Your father is in his palace. We are camped here in Drakda waiting for you to heal." Then she asked, "Would you like some water?"

Closing her eyes, Tsogyal nodded slightly. Rab-ten got up, walked across the tent, picked up a flask of water and poured some into a silver cup. She brought it to Tsogyal, kneeling beside her. "Here, Princess, if you can raise yourself slowly, I will help you drink."

Tsogyal slowly raised herself onto her elbows, pain stung along her back. "Oh," she cried, "it is so painful."

Rab-ten held the cup to Tsogyal's lips, lifting it slowly as Tsogyal sipped.

"It will be some time until the pain is gone, Noble Daughter," Rab-ten assured her, "but you will heal. The men are hunting for meat. Fresh meat will give you the strength you have lost. Do you think you can stomach some butter tea?"

"No, I think not," Tsogyal groaned as she lay back down.

"Princess, you should try to drink some tea, to give you strength," Rab-ten said as she stroked Tsogyal's head.

"What am I to do?" Tsogyal whispered to herself.

"Do? Princess, what do you mean?" Rab-ten asked.

"I have been kidnaped by that beast, Prince Zhonnu, to become his wife. Yet, I have no desire to live my life with him," Tsogyal choked, closing her eyes against growing tears. "I cannot go back home. I am weak now. I have nothing."

Rab-ten sat back on her heels. "Noble Daughter, the Prince is not a bad man, he can be managed," she assured. "It is true the Minister Shantipa is a very bad man. Yet, I have heard Prince Zhonnu has ordered Shantipa never touch you again. Indeed he has commanded Shantipa never even look at you. The Prince was very angry at him for whipping you so hard." Placing her hand gently on the back of the Princess's head, stroking her hair, Rab-ten added, "Your father has given Shantipa a scar that he will wear forever in shame."

Tsogyal opened her eyes and looked at Rab-ten. "My father?"

"Yes." Rab-ten nodded. "He avenged your injury at the hand of Shantipa."

Tsogyal looked at Rab-ten, whispering, "You are kind, Lady. It matters not. I wish to be free, married to no man." Then the tears welled up in her eyes and she cried softly.

The strong pungent and sweet scent filled the tent as Rab-ten sat pounding the healing herbs in her mortar and pestle. The soft thump, grind, thump, grind, and the soft crackling of the fire in the hearth were soothing sounds, as was the soft breathing of Tsogyal deeply asleep. As Rab-ten toiled she wondered why this young Princess was so against marriage to the Prince. *He is not so bad a man and his palace is very fine. She will have a good life and be the future Queen of Kharchupa,* she mused. Rab-ten smiled, thinking of her husband, Jigme. *He is a good man and a fine warrior,* she thought. Rab-ten nodded to herself as an idea formed. *I will teach the young Princess about men and how to control them, while we wait for her to heal,* she thought. Suddenly it occurred to her, *perhaps she loves another?*

Tsogyal's groan brought Rab-ten out of her reverie. Getting up from her work, she went to Tsogyal's side. "Princess? Are you in pain?"

Tsogyal turned her head, looking sideways at Rab-ten. "Yes, but I wish to rise, can you help me?"

With Rab-ten's strong hands as an aid, Tsogyal rose to a sitting position on the bed.

"All is spinning," Tsogyal groaned, holding her head, her back stinging hot pain.

"Perhaps, you should lay back down," Rab-ten advised, "Would you like poppy tea for the pain?"

"No, let us wait, it will stop," Tsogyal pleaded, "I do not want the poppy tea, I do not like how it clouds my mind."

As they waited with Tsogyal sitting and Rab-ten kneeling in front of her, holding her shoulders to keep her steady, Rab-ten admired the strength of this young Princess. *She is not spoiled like so many other Royals*, Rab-ten thought, *a sign of good parents. King Pelgyi and the Queen must be good rulers of Karchen*, she mused.

"It is becoming better now," Tsogyal announced. "I can sit unattended. Is there butter tea?"

"Yes, Princess," Rab-ten answered as she got up. Stooping at the hearth, she put a lump of yak butter and a bit of salt into Tsogyal's silver cup. Then poured the thick black tea from a pot where it had been simmering for hours into the cup and stirred, making a thick butter tea.

"How many days have we been camped now?" Tsogyal asked.

"Seven days, Princess," Rab-ten answered as she stirred.

Handing the cup of hot tea to Tsogyal, Rab-ten knelt and sat back on her heels.

"Princess, is the tea to your liking?"

"Yes, it is good," Tsogyal replied after taking some sips. Then she looked at Rab-ten who was looking at her with a look of bewilderment on her face.

"Is there something you would like to know, Healer?" Tsogyal asked, resting the cup on her knee.

"Oh, I am sorry, Princess, I did not mean to..."

"It is alright, Rab-ten," Tsogyal chuckled, then grimaced at the pain that seared across her back. "May I call you Rab-ten?"

"Why, yes, of course, Princess," Rab-ten said in surprise. Never had a Royal asked permission to call her familiar.

Tsogyal inclined her head. "You wish to ask me something?"

"Yes, Princess, I am perplexed why you feel so strongly against marriage. Is there another that you love? Is that why?" Rab-ten asked.

Tsogyal thought for a moment, then answered, "Yes, there is

another. Though the other is not a man but a goal. Prince Zhonnu and marriage to him stand in my way."

"A goal?" Rab-ten asked, bewildered.

Nodding, Tsogyal continued. "A great goal. Rab-ten, have you heard of the teachings of Lord Buddha?"

Slowly shaking her head, thinking, Rab-ten answered, "Well, yes, I have heard of the Buddha's teachings from Nepal but I do not know much of it. I only know that which is the way of all of our people, of the Gods of the mountains and waters and the Bonpo priests. Are these teachings of Lord Buddha the way of the people of Nepal?"

"Many of Nepal follow the teachings of Lord Buddha," Tsogyal explained, "but the Buddha's teachings are not of one people but are for all people. The teachings are profound and lead the way to ultimate freedom, to enlightenment, to Nirvana. Rab-ten, my goal is Nirvana."

"Nirvana? Where is Nirvana?" Rab-ten asked

"It is a realm where there is no suffering or desire, a place where one is always content, always happy, but greater than just happiness," Tsogyal answered, becoming very animated.

Tsogyal's excitement piqued Rab-ten's interest. Leaning forward, she asked, "Where is the road to this land called Nirvana? "

"You travel to Nirvana when you find a master to show you the road and how to travel upon it. I wish to find such a master. Do you see why being married to Zhonnu will get in the way of my finding such a master and never allow me to travel down the road to Nirvana?" Tsogyal pleaded.

Rab-ten nodded. She was overcome with affection for this young Princess and intrigued by this place called Nirvana. She did not understand why she felt so strongly that she wanted to help this girl in some way. *Something about this young Princess is different, she seems to radiate a light,* Rab-ten thought. *Something like light, like adventure.*

"I must escape this camp," Tsogyal announced. "I must get away from here."

Rab-ten stared at Tsogyal, shocked by her decree. "Where will you go if you could escape Zhonnu?" she asked.

Tsogyal looked down, thinking, then looked at Rab-ten. "I cannot go home, I have no home. I do not know. I will travel until I find a teacher of the Buddha and study with him." Tsogyal looked anxiously into Rab-ten's deep dark brown eyes. "Can you help me escape this camp?"

Startled by this entreaty, fingers of fear began to crawl up Rab-ten's back. Looking wide-eyed at Tsogyal, Rab-ten shook her head. "No, I cannot. It is too dangerous," she whispered. Trying to shake away the fear that gripped her, she got up and walked to the hearth and sat. Her back turned to Tsogyal, she began pounding the poultice again. They were silent for a long time with only the thumping and grinding of the pestle upon herbs in the bowl. Rab-ten did not understand why tears were welling in her eyes. She wanted to help this Princess and she did not understand why. It would be great danger to her, yet she felt she must do this. *It would be possible*, she mused, *I can do this. I must do this.*

She stopped her pounding and stood. Going to Tsogyal, she knelt before her.

"Yes, Princess, I will help you," Rab-ten declared.

Tsogyal felt a surge of relief and excitement. "Call me Tsogyal. From now on, you are my spiritual sister."

Rab-ten was surprised to find she did not feel dread any longer, only excitement and a great feeling of happiness. Tsogyal reached to her and hugged her, ignoring the pain shooting along her back as she did so.

12

Sitting up drinking butter tea, Tsogyal could hear the yelling and singing of the drunken men outside as she tore a bite off the chunk of cooked deer meat she held in her hand. The men were all gathered around the fire a good distance away from Zhonnu's tent where Tsogyal and Rab-ten stayed. Prince Zhonnu came once a day to see Tsogyal's progress in healing.

At the door flap, looking out, Rab-ten turned and hissed, "Tsogyal, lay down quickly, he is coming!"

Minutes later, Zhonnu brushed through the tent door to see Rab-ten tending a meat stew on the fire. Tsogyal lay seemingly asleep on her stomach on the bedding of furs.

"Well?" he asked. "Is she better? When can we leave this place?"

"Your Highness." Rab-ten got up and walked over to stand next to him, looking down at Tsogyal's prone figure. "She is healing, but slowly. She had lost so much blood, it is taking a long time. I believe it would be best if we could wait longer. I am trying to get her to eat so she will grow strong. Yet it is difficult for her, she is so weak. I fear if we leave too soon, she will die along the way. Or if she becomes more ill we may have to make camp again in a less suitable place," Rab-ten pleaded, her hands clasped in front of her face to accentuate her worry. "She is a fragile Princess, My Lord."

Sighing loudly, Prince Zhonnu looked down at Tsogyal's sleeping body. Then he glared at Rab-ten. "We have been here almost a fortnight. I will not wait much longer. Three more days, then we leave for Kharchupa. I will take my chances with her health. We will stop again only if we must." Then he was gone.

Rab-ten ran to the door flap, watching until he was out of sight. "He is gone," she whispered.

Tsogyal sat up and stretched. Standing up, she walked slowly around the tent.

"It is settled then, I must go tomorrow night," she declared. "Can all be ready?"

"Yes," Rab-ten assured her, "the men have been hunting every day and drinking every night. They sleep like dead men in a drunken stupor. I have walked around camp every night to observe the watch and even those men are no longer vigilant; they sleep at their posts. I have checked Lungta every day to see where they keep her and how they tie her at night. It is always the same. I know where your saddle and bags are. No one is concerned about her or your things. Before the dawn, when all are still asleep, I will fill the bags with food and water for your journey. Have you decided where you will go?"

Tsogyal paced, thinking. "I will go to Nepal, that is south of here," Tsogyal mused aloud.

Shaking her head vigorously, Rab-ten advised, "No, Princess...I mean Tsogyal, you cannot go south yet, as that is where Kharchupa is. You must go in another direction at first."

Rab-ten got to her knees on the floor, pulling Tsogyal beside her. Drawing lines in the dirt, she explained, "Here, this is the road to leave the camp when you are away on your horse."

Looking sideways at Tsogyal, she asked, "Do you know how to find the north star?"

Tsogyal nodded. "Yes, I can find it."

"Good," Rab-ten said. "Here is the road we came in on, you must take this road back, it goes north." She made another line. "And here the road is met by another. Your horse will want to go east, as that is the way back to your father's palace. She will want to go back home.

Take the way west and then, finding the north star, you can choose your way further north, if you wish to go that way. Or you can go further west then south, but you must find the passes over the mountains into Nepal. You can ask at villages and find a scout to lead you."

With a concerned look, Rab-ten warned, "Sister, you must be careful who you choose as a scout, for you may be robbed. Or worse."

Rising to her feet, Tsogyal paced, thinking aloud. "I will just get far away from this camp on the road west, then decide my way later."

Rab-ten rose and took Tsogyal's hand. Looking into her new sister's eyes, she pleaded, "Tsogyal, are you sure about this? It is very dangerous to be traveling alone, there are very bad men on the road and it is so cold. I am so worried about you."

Tsogyal squeezed Rab-ten's hand. "My sister, you have been so kind. I must go, don't you see? If I do not go tomorrow night, then I am trapped forever as Zhonnu's wife in his palace."

Releasing Tsogyal's hand, Rab-ten nodded sadly.

"All is ready," Rab-ten whispered as she entered the tent.

Keeling down on the floor she folded up the edge of the carpet and began to draw a map in the dirt. Tsogyal huddled next to her.

"This is our tent here," Rab-ten explained, drawing a circle, then more circles, then a line. "You will go around the back of these tents, this way. Lungta is tied here." She drew an X. "I have saddled her and your bags are filled with food and water, no one has noticed them. The men are all in a drunken sleep. This is your time to flee!"

Tsogyal studied the map, memorizing the picture of it. Then she rubbed out the image in the dirt.

Rab-ten asked, "Do you remember the way on the roads we made maps of?"

Tsogyal nodded, "Yes, I remember."

"I want you to take this," Rab-ten walked over to her bed and from her bundle took her thick sheepskin coat. Bringing it to Tsogyal, she held it out to her.

"I can't take your coat, Rab-ten," Tsogyal protested. "You need it."

"You need it more. I will find another somewhere in camp. Tsogyal, you must accept this. The only clothes I could retrieve out of your wagons were your brocades and silks. Zhonnu would not even let me get your felt boots out, only your slippers. I could not protest or he would have been suspicious. Your clothes are not warm enough, you will freeze. Please take it."

Reaching to take the coat, Tsogyal said, "Thank you, Rab-ten, you are so generous and kind."

Then Rab-ten reached into a bag at the side of the tent, pulling out a pair of old worn boots. "Here, take these," she said. "I had a pair of old boots I had brought. If you are found, no one will know they were mine."

Tsogyal took them, sitting to pull them on. Then she stood, looking down at her feet. "They are a bit big but will serve well," she said.

Pleased, Rab-ten circled around Tsogyal to help her on with the coat over her silk robes. Then she stopped, asking, "Where are your jewels?"

Tsogyal pointed. "There, under the furs of my bed. You take them. I have no need of them."

Rushing over to the bed and pulling out Tsogyal's jewel necklaces and belt, Rab-ten gasped, "Yes, you do need them. You need barter. How do you think you will eat? How will you pay your scout?"

Carefully, Rab-ten placed the jewels over Tsogyal's head and fastened the belt around her waist under the sheepskin coat. She held up a piece of the jewelry in her fingers. "You will need to break pieces off to trade for food and other items."

Tsogyal nodded her understanding.

"Cover the jewels with the coat, here is a belt to tie it tightly," Rab-ten said, as she tied a cord around Tsogyal's waist. Tsogyal looked down at her lumpy figure.

"Now, I must tie you so they do not suspect you of helping me," Tsogyal declared.

Quickly crossing to a pile of spare cords laying at a side of the tent wall, she rummaged until she found a length and approached Rab-ten. "Lay down here on the floor, I will tie you."

Rab-ten shook her head at Tsogyal. "Tying will not be enough. It must look like you hit me and I fell, then you tied me."

"Hit you?" Aghast, Tsogyal looked at Rab-ten. "I cannot hit you!"

Taking Tsogyal's hands in hers, Rab-ten assured her, "My sister, you must. If Zhonnu thinks I helped you escape, he will have me beheaded. For my own safety, you must hit me and hit me hard." She turned to the hearth and picked up a piece of wood, handing it to Tsogyal. "Hit me with this, at the side of my head. Here, I will kneel by the fire like I am stoking it," Rab-ten explained as she knelt down.

Tsogyal felt the weight of the wood in her hands. Looking at the back of Rab-ten's head, she worried, "I have never hit anyone, what if I kill you?"

Rab-ten looked around and up at Tsogyal. "Hit me on the side so it makes a mark. I will be ready for it so you will not kill me. Hit me hard, Tsogyal, for my life, hit me hard. Then do not think, just tie me tightly and run; remember the maps."

Turning back to the fire, Rab-ten braced herself for the impact of the coming strike. Tsogyal raised the wood and stood frozen, tears starting to cloud her eyes. Feeling Tsogyal's hesitation, Rab-ten encouraged, "Hit me now, sister, for my life and for your freedom. I will be fine, it will only be a bruise."

Tsogyal held the wood up ready to strike. Frozen, she hesitated, she could not bring herself to act. Rab-ten continued fervently, "If you cannot be strong now and do this, then you should not go. For if you do not have the strength for this, then you do not have the strength to be free."

Hearing Rab-ten's words, Tsogyal knew that her old life was forever gone, she must do this. She swung hard, the wood hit the side of Rab-ten's head and cheek. The sound of the thud made Tsogyal sick. She watched the healer fall to the floor on her side; a red mark on her face and ear. Stealing herself against her rising emotions, Tsogyal grabbed the rope and tied Rab-ten's unconscious body.

Rising, Tsogyal ran to the tent flap and peered out. All was silent. She looked back at Rab-ten's form laying by the hearth. "Make her well, keep her safe," she prayed. Then she fixed the maps in her mind and stepped out into the cold night.

13

Master Padma sat upon a cushion contemplating the three men seated before him. The wooden door of his small hut rattled from a gust of wind outside. Nestled in a brushy crag on the steep ravine of the hermitage at Chimpu, the stacked rock walls of the abode withstood the strong cold wind that howled up the mountainside swirling the falling snow.

A fire flickered in the small hearth, giving little warmth to the room. Bundled in their sheepskin robes, their fox-fur hats removed, the three men included a Tibetan, his hair in one long braid down his back, a long mustache following the line of his grimace. Padma noticed a slight shiver from the man. The journey through the wind and snow had taxed him. Next to him sat a man from India, with light skin and fine features, the thick sheepskin robe swallowing his slight build. And lastly, Padma's gaze fell to the third man, older than the rest, with hair tied up in a top knot and a white long beard; yet his skin was clear, not wrinkled as one would expect. His eyes had a sparkle that Padma liked, he was from Nepal, of that Padma was sure. The strong odor of wet sheep's wool and fox-fur hats mingled with the peppery woody scent of sandalwood incense smoke that clung to the ceiling, slowly finding its way out the smoke hole.

Though seated, the Tibetan bowed from his waist and began,

"Master Padma, I am Kasa, translator of the scriptures of Lord Buddha. I and my colleagues here," he motioned with his hand to include the two men seated next to him, "are in the employ of Emperor Trisong Detsen and have come to you at his behest."

Kasa reached into the bag by his side, pulling from it three bowls made of solid gold. Laying them before Master Padma, bowing his head in reverence, he explained, "Emperor Trisong requests your presence at the monastery in Samye, where he resides at this time. You are well-known to him as a great master of the highest teachings of the Lord Buddha, the way of Tantra. He requests instruction by you."

Kasa nodded to the two other men seated next to him. They each pulled three solid gold bowls from their bags. Spreading them before the Tantric Master, they bowed their heads before him.

Padma lowered his eyes, his gaze resting on the glittering array of the nine gold bowls.

Nodding slowly, he said, "Very well, I shall journey to Samye to see the Emperor two days hence. I wish you three to go ahead of me and inform the Emperor of my arrival."

The men exchanged looks of alarm. Kasa asked, "Do you not wish to travel with us for protection?"

"Protection?" Padma inquired, his lips curving up in an expression of amusement.

"Master," Kasa implored, "the Bon Minsters have complained to the Emperor that you should have been driven out of Tibet, to Thokar. These are dangerous men, they fear you, they wish to slay you. Bon Minister Tsenpo has many warriors, he knows you are here in Chimpu."

Padma looked at each man in turn, his expression solemn. "I am aware of these men and their intentions. In what way can you three protect me? You are clearly not warriors."

Kasa shifted on the carpet laid on the hard ground of the dirt floor as he explained, "Master, we are sent by the Emperor." Gesturing in the direction of the door, he went on. "We have two warriors as escort who await us outside. With us all as witness, they will never harm you in our company."

Padma considered this, then he said with finality, "Do not fear for my safety. I will arrive at Samye in two days. I wish you to go ahead of me, you shall leave on the morrow."

Gazing at the men, their expressions showing confusion, Padma continued, "There is an empty abode just up the path from here, you may stay the night there. I believe there is wood there, stacked ready for use." Smiling, Padma assured, "I will follow a day after you have gone."

The translators looked at each other with apprehension, then each rose to his feet.

"As you wish, Master," Kasa said as he bowed.

The two other men followed Kasa's example, bowing low. Then they turned and filed out of the hut.

Silence returned to the room as Padma contemplated the images appearing in his mind's eye. There he saw warriors. He felt their desire for his death.

Crouching behind a boulder, high above the steep ravine trail that was the only pathway from Chimpu to Samye, Minister Tsenpo waited to spring his ambush. Looking up into the clear blue sky, he was pleased the wind and snow had stopped on this day. *The mountain God is assisting our cause,* he mused, *having calmed the wind so our arrows will fly fast and true.*

He was at first perplexed, when the day before, his scouts observed the entourage of translators and their escort returning down the mountain path without that beggar from the country of Oddiyana they call Padma. He was sure Padma had refused their request. *Refuse a request from the Emperor?* he had pondered. *Something is amiss.*

Then, that very morning, his scout had arrived back from Samye with the news that Padma was to arrive there this very day. He gazed now, where, along the side of the ravine, his warriors lay in wait, holding their bows relaxed yet ready. They all watched the rocky trail leading down from the heights of Chimpu hermitage to Samye Monastery, which lay on the valley floor next to the Tsangpo river.

Just as he was wondering how long they would have to lay in

wait, he saw appear in the distance, a figure. He was tall and lean, dressed in a woolen robe of natural color, making him blend into the boulders along the trail. His red sash and red felt boots were the only easily visible sign of him in the distance.

Tensely, the men waited for Padma's approach. They all watched as he strolled down the rocky trail, getting closer and closer to their position. As he came closer, they could see his long dark hair was loose, flowing over his shoulders. When he finally came into range, they could see his sliver of a mustache and his short beard. The time had come. Minister Tsenpo tensed as his archers slowly rose up, some on their knees and others standing. Even if Padma saw them now it was too late for him, he could not escape.

"I have him!" Tsenpo whispered to himself, thumping his fist on his knee.

Still, the warriors remained silent as they held their bows up, ready to draw in unison, when given the command to loose their arrows. Tsenpo opened his mouth to give the command when a strange sound engulfed them, silencing him.

Hung, Hung, Hung, the sound rang like a bell reverberating louder and louder though the canyon.

Though their ears were ringing, the warriors held to their bows. Disciplined, they fought to stay focused on the figure of Padma approaching, waiting for the command to end his life. Then, to their astonishment, the Master erupted into flames. Tsenpo fell back in horror. Gasping in shock, the men all looked at each other, confirming if they all had seen the same sight. Then, the flames that engulfed the figure of Padma shot high into the sky, filling the sky with roiling black clouds. Their bows lowered, now forgotten in their grasp, the warriors looked up, gesticulating as they shouted out in fear at the unusual appearance of black clouds in what was only moments before a clear blue sky. Out of the turbulence of clouds, a figure rose up the size of a mountain. The men fell back, some falling hard to the ground on their backsides, at the appearance of what was clearly a demon. Its skin was a fiery red. Three fierce eyes looked down at the warriors, its mouth gaping open with bloodied lips curled back exposing long fangs. Its yellow hair, a writhing mass entwined with snakes, blew up and away from the beast's snarling face in the howling wind of the churning black clouds. Around its neck hung a garland of severed heads, blood and brain dripped from the gruesome appendages. A tiger skin covered its loins. Its right hand was raised up above its head holding a black iron vajra scepter. In its left hand, the demon grasped a huge black scorpion.

With a powerful thrust, he threw the scorpion to the earth. When it crashed into the rocks of the hillside, it burst into thousands of scorpions. The blanket of black forms, their tails arched high, stingers as big as spears, scurried up the ridge toward the warriors. In pure panic, the archers dropped their bows and ran to escape. Tripping over each other, some becoming entangled in their bow strings, they clawed and climbed over bushes and rocks to get away from the stinging insects. The men fled upward to the top of the ravine, then reaching the top, they slid and jumped down the other side into rocks and brush, crashing through and over any obstacle to get away.

In minutes the ridge fell silent. The warriors were gone. In another moment, the demon faded away as mist into a clear blue sky. Only Minister Tsenpo remained, crouched behind the boulder. He cursed the men. Though he knew they had no way of seeing, as he finally did himself, that all was merely an elaborate apparition created by this talented master from Oddiyana.

Guru Padma looked up to where Tsenpo was crouched. He raised his hand in a wave. Tsenpo snarled at the impudence of this man. Padma strolled on with a smile on his face as he chuckled. Then he laughed, the sound of his mirth echoing off the walls of the ravine.

It is a fine morning and a beautiful land, he thought, as he walked on toward Samye.

Emperor Trisong felt the cold stone floor on his forehead as he prostrated to the tall figure standing before him in the doorway. The Emperor's luxurious golden and red silk robes splayed around him as he lay prone on the floor. Rising to a kneeling position, hands held out in supplication, Trisong implored, "Master Padma, I have prepared a great feast in your honor. You know the way to enlightenment, without one having to abandon desires and suppress the passions. I beseech you, teach me this so I may attain enlightenment in this lifetime and reside forever in Nirvana."

Master Padma crossed the room to sit on the glittering silk brocade cushions set out for him. He noticed all of the servants had been dismissed, the room only contained himself and the Emperor. He realized Trisong would not want it known he had bowed before anyone, let alone this foreigner who was dressed in simple garb. Padma gestured for Trisong to rise and sit next to him.

Servants appeared as if silently summoned and set plates of food down before the two men. More servants appeared, carrying platters of food and pots of tea. Placing these before Padma and Trisong, they bowed deeply as they scurried backwards out of the room. Padma picked up a dumpling filled with spices and meat. He bit into it, the aroma and flavors exploding into his senses as he chewed slowly.

Looking over the food laid out before them, he replied, "Emperor, I can see you are sincere in your request for teachings. However, you are not ready for the Tantric mysteries."

With shocked surprise, Trisong asked, "Not ready?"

Padma took up a cup of hot tea and sipped, the exquisite warmth sliding down to his core.

Shaking his head slowly, he explained, "You must purify your mind by practicing the Mahayana path first. Practice this whole-heartedly for one full season, then make your offering to me again. If you appear ready to me, I will instruct you in the Tantric teachings. However, if you have not practiced earnestly, your mind will not be ready; I will know this and will refuse you again."

Trisong, mouth agape in disbelief of what he was hearing, insisted, "I do not want to be given a lesser path."

Padma set down his tea and looked into the Emperor's eyes. "Your Highness, the Mahayana is by no means a lesser path. It is in fact a great path. Indeed, many have attained Buddha-hood by this path alone. I require this path for you as it will purify the defilements of your mind and make you ready to receive and actualize the Tantric teachings."

Picking up another dumpling, Padma gazed at it, considering. "If your mind is not ready, I can give endless teaching, yet it would be like trying to fill a leaky vessel. No matter how much I pour in, you will understand nothing," he said, then took a bite of the tasty morsel.

Trisong willed himself to remain calm. Forcing himself, he bowed his head. "I see. As you instruct so I shall do, Master," he said solemnly.

"Very well. Is it true the great adept Santaraksita is here at Samye?" Padma inquired.

Trisong nodded. "Yes, he is here, as a translator of the scriptures, just arrived three days ago. Do you wish to see him?"

Padma, nodded his head. "Yes, call him here now to join us. I wish you to know that you are very fortunate to have him here. I know Santaraksita, he is a master of Mahayana. He shall instruct you."

Trisong sat considering, then said, "I see. Then I shall employ him and follow his instruction. In one season hence I shall offer to you again, Master Padma."

Calling out to the servants standing outside the doorway, Trisong commanded, "Call Master Santaraksita here."

They could hear the scurry of feet running down the hall and away.

With a gesture toward the food, Trisong added, "Well then, let us enjoy this feast. Tell me of your travels."

14

Tsogyal shivered, clasping the front of her robe to close it tighter. The night was cold and clear. Though only half full, the moon was bright, lighting their way. She and Lungta had been traveling for hours, the moon crossing the sky before them. Yet, it all seemed timeless to Tsogyal. Feeling Lungta becoming weary, Tsogyal dismounted, to give the horse a rest from carrying her. Lifting the reins over Lungta's head, Tsogyal pressed on, leading her mare. She could feel the wet cold of the ground seep into the thin soles of the old boots she wore.

Away, just get far away from those men, was the *mantra* in Tsogyal's thoughts and desire. She was driven by a primal urge, like a deer fleeing from wolves.

Her escape from the camp had been surprisingly easy. All was as Rab-ten had said. Leaving Zhonnu's tent, Tsogyal moved quickly and silently finding Lungta, saddled and ready. The mare had nickered softly when she saw Tsogyal approach. Tsogyal blew gently in the mare's nostrils to quiet her. Then she untied the reins and in a swift fluid movement into the saddle, woman and horse stole away like smoke on the wind.

Three days later, Tsogyal and Lungta made their way up a large valley heading north, where clouds hung low, hugging the steep hills. They had spent the previous days in sheltered canyons of rocks and trees along the way, staying hidden from possible search parties. Traveling only in the late afternoons and through the nights, when the roads were empty, they avoided the curious eyes of travelers.

Now, she could feel that Lungta was weary. She needed rest and time to graze; they had to stop. Through the gray gloom, Tsogyal could make out a grouping of boulders on a hill rising in the distance. Wearily, she trudged in their direction with Lungta in tow, thinking they could hide there, spending the night. There they would be hidden. Lungta could graze all night long and Tsogyal could rest.

As they approached, Tsogyal noticed the group of boulders were not natural, they looked as they had been positioned in this place in a large circle. Leading Lunga in between two of the boulders, Tsogyal placed her hand on the large rock and looked up at its size, its surface rough and ancient under her hand. Stepping past the stone to the inside of the circle, Tsogyal looked around her at the massive forms as the mist grew thick around her. Unease crawled up Tsogyal's back as she felt how small and all alone she was. Swallowing back the rising fear that urged her to reconsider her choice at fleeing Zhonnu and placing herself alone in the wilderness, Tsogyal steeled herself against the thoughts that threatened to assail her.

Suddenly Lungta's head rose up. Her ears alert, she nickered.

"What is it?" Tsogyal whispered, fear now squeezing tightly.

To her amazement, a black horse stepped into the circle of stones. Regal, his head was raised, looking at them. His eyes were large and wide. *Like Lungta's*, Tsogyal thought. His coat was shiny black, like a raven's wings. His black mane and tail were thick and luxurious. In awe of seeing him, fear gave way to wonder.

Moving very slowly, Tsogyal led Lungta, approaching the stallion. Extending her hand toward him, she cooed softly, "Who are you, my beauty? My, you are quite a handsome one."

The stallion stood stiff-legged, ready to spin and bolt if these two strangers became a danger to him. He was interested in Lungta and so held his ground.

"Where did you come from?" Tsogyal asked softly. "What is your name?"

"His name is Poso," came a voice from the right of Tsogyal.

Startled, she turned to see a man leading a gelding, which was saddled with saddlebags, enter the circle between two of the standing stones. She could see he was not Tibetan. He was of medium height with long black hair in many braids. A thin mustache and a small beard framed a pleasant expression. Tsogyal wondered at the circle patterns embroidered on his thick silk robe, inside each circle was a beast that Tsogyal had never seen a design of before. The raw silk sash at his waist held a curved sword in a decorative scabbard at his left side. A dagger, its hilt glistening silver with inlaid colorful stones, was held at his right side. His boots were made of leather, not felt, with cords tied around them to hold them tight. Leggings of wool were tucked into the boots. His skin was light. *He is very handsome,* Tsogyal thought. Under the piece of cloth banded around his head, there was a twinkle in the soft brown eyes. This told Tsogyal he was a lighthearted sort of man.

Tsogyal stepped back. "Who are you? You speak Tibetan?"

"I am Abaka, and, yes, I speak your language. The better question is who are you and what is a young woman doing here? Are you alone?"

Tsogyal grew wary. "I am not alone. I have many warriors, an army, just behind me, they are coming soon."

Abaka smiled. "An army? Well, I must beware to not offer you offense, Noble Daughter."

Tsogyal became tense. "How do you know... I mean, what makes you think I am a Noble Daughter?"

"Well, Noble Daughter, a common girl would not have an army at her back, now would she? What is your name?" Abaka asked, stopping just a few steps away from her. His gelding lowered its head and began grazing.

Tsogyal realized this man probably had no idea she was now a fugitive.

"I am Princess Tsogyal, daughter of King Pelgyi. I am out riding about. Where are you from? You are not Tibetan. Why are you here with this stallion?" Tsogyal inquired, trying to sound authoritative.

Abaka looked Tsogyal up and down, an expression of

amusement on his face. Taking in the incongruity of the dirty sheepskin robe she was wearing, with fine silk robes peeking through, and the tattered worn felt boots, his expression turned to concern.

"Princess, would you like to sit and have tea with me? I will tell you all about myself and Poso," Abaka said as he gestured to the place they stood. "Here, I have a cook pot." He turned to the bags behind his saddle. "We can make tea here and rest."

Tsogyal hesitated, thinking perhaps she should mount Lungta and get away. But Lungta needed to rest and to graze, and tea would be very nice, she considered. Besides, if he were a bad man she was sure she would have sensed it.

"Your mare is not in season so she will be safe to graze with Poso," Abaka assured her as he untied a rolled rug from the back of his saddle and, with a flourish, unrolled it and laid it on the ground. Then he gathered more items from his saddlebags and knelt placing chunks of yak dung in a small pile and began making a fire. "We will tie my gelding here with us, the others will remain close. Please sit, Noble Daughter," Abaka implored, gesturing to the rug he had placed on the ground.

Soon, Tsogyal was holding her warm silver cup that Rab-ten had thoughtfully packed for her in her saddlebags, filled with sweet dark tea. Leaning against Lungta's saddle on the ground at her back, she sipped appreciatively. Tsogyal felt content, gazing at Lungta, free of the saddle on her back, nibbling on the thick grass near Poso. The circle of stones felt as they held her safe from the outside world. A wave of fatigue washed over her. She steeled herself not to give in to sleep. She turned her gaze from the horses to Abaka; he was studying her.

"Well?" she asked, "you will tell me of yourself now?"

With a bow of his head, Abaka began, "Noble Daughter, I am Abaka from west and north of this land. I come from Ferghana. My family is of the Turkic lands."

"Why are you here in Tibet?" Tsogyal inquired.

"Poso is a fine stallion of Ferghana stock. I am bringing several such to the Emperor Trisong Detsen. When the Emperor sees the fine horses I have, he will want many more for breeding."

Tsogyal became interested. "Ferghana? Are there masters of the teachings of Lord Buddha in Ferghana?"

Abaka was surprised by this question. "I do not know of any Buddhists in Ferghana, though there may be some. I follow the Manichaean teachings.

"Manichaean? I have never heard of this. Is this of a God or a great enlightened being?" Tsogyal asked.

Abaka sat up straight, amazed at the question from this girl. "Princess, you have asked a question that will take much to answer. But to answer simply, the truth of existence and the world was brought to my people by the prophet Mani, thus Manichaean."

Tsogyal nodded thoughtfully.

Abaka continued, with concern in his tone, "Princess, it is plain you are not just riding about. I know of the Kingdom of Pelgyi, it is days from here. And I am sure your army is lost." Leaning forward, he entreated, "You may trust me. In my land women are revered, no man would ever harm a woman. You are safe with me." With a sweep of his hand, he asked, "Why are you here alone, days from your father's kingdom, dressed in a commoner's sheepskin coat covering fine royal silk robes and wearing old worn boots? As well, riding upon a fine Ferghana mare that clearly has carried you faithfully farther than she would like."

Tsogyal looked into this man's kind eyes. She could see he was sincere.

Looking at her feet, the sole of her boot now split open, cold air chilling her foot, she said, "I will tell you but only if you make an oath to keep my secret as yours."

Abaka studied the young woman sitting before him. His decision made, he drew the dagger from its scabbard in his belt.

"Very well, I will make an oath with my blood to you, Princess Tsogyal. Your secret is my secret," he declared as he drew the dagger across his forearm making a cut, blood springing from the wound.

Alarmed, Tsogyal rose to her knees reaching out to try to stop Abaka. "No, please do not harm yourself," she exclaimed.

Abaka laughed. "Now you have my oath. So, Princess, tell me why are you here."

Tsogyal sat back and studied Abaka for a moment. Defying the feeling of hesitation, she said, "Very well." To her dismay the words tumbled out, telling Abaka everything:Her father giving her to Zhonnu; the beating; Rab-ten's help; her search for a master.

At the end of her story, Abaka's jaw was clenched. Clearing his throat to release the tension, he got up and slowly walked to the end of the circle. There he stood, gazing out between two of the large stones into the distance beyond; deep in thought.

Tsogyal sat motionless, she picked up her now cold tea and sipped what was remaining. Abaka turned and walked back to the fire. He picked up the pot and gestured to Tsogyal, asking if she would like more. Tsogyal held out her cup.

Filling it, Abaka spoke. "Princess, I am touched by your tale of woe. I am sorry for your father, for I am sure he is now in great pain. However, you cannot go back to him. You can rest assured that I will not tell anyone. I am a foreigner and so I do not care about laws or decrees by any King, or Emperor, for that matter, of Tibet. Princess, you need more than my silence, you need my help." With a slight bow of his head, Abaka offered, "I will help you if you will allow me."

Tsogyal choked on the sip of tea, hearing Abaka's last words. "Help? How?"

Abaka continued, "I have a friend here in Tibet, a farmer who lives near here. I will bring you to him, you can stay with him and his family while I complete my business with the Emperor. Then, we can decide where you can go. Is this acceptable to you, Princess?"

Tsogyal could not believe what she was hearing, Sitting up, she declared, "Yes, Abaka, yes, this would be very good." Turning her attention to Lungta, who was grazing contentedly, she asked concerned for the mare, "When will we go? My horse needs rest"

Abaka nodded his head. "Yes, your horse needs rest. I have a camp up over that ridge there. This mischievous Poso left our camp. I am traveling with two other men and six more horses to bring to the Emperor. You will stay in my tent tonight, there you will be safe and your mare can rest," he assured her.

He began gathering the tea-makings, saying, "We will return to my camp now.   I will tell the men I have found my farmer friend's wayward daughter. We will leave on the morrow for the farm. Do not speak a word to any of my men, act submissive. Do you understand?"

Tsogyal nodded. "Yes, I understand."

Rising, she, put her silver cup in her saddlebags then lifted her saddle and carried it with the blanket to Lungta, saddling the mare while she nibbled the grass.

Abaka packed his pot and tea into the saddlebags on his gelding. That done, he walked over to the grazing stallion and placed a rope around his neck. He led him to his gelding and mounted. When Tsogyal was mounted and ready, Abaka led the way out of the circle of standing stones.

15

Tsogyal hugged Lungta's neck in the stall below the farm house. Lungta shared the space under the house with two other horses, two sheep and four goats. It had been several weeks since Abaka left Tsogyal in the care of Nawang, his wife and three sons.

Hearing the sounds of the family preparing for their day, she looked above at the ceiling which was also the floor of the house. Nawang had many more horses and several yak on his farm, these stayed in large stone corrals outside the farm house walls. The family raised barley on many acres.

When Abaka first brought Tsogyal to the farm, the farmer looked suspiciously at this young girl. The two men talked inside alone, leaving Tsogyal and Lungta inside the walled courtyard below the two-story building. Abaka's men waited outside the walled enclosure with Abaka's stallions for the Emperor, not knowing what was going on inside.

Finally, after what seemed a long time to Tsogyal, Abaka and Nawang came out of the house, climbing down the ladder into the courtyard.

Abaka looked at Tsogyal and said, "I will return, wait for me." Then he opened the wooden door in the stone wall and was gone.

Nawang approached Tsogyal and Lungta. "You are welcome

here in my home. We will call you Yeshe while you stay with my family. I will tell my family you are betrothed to Abaka. and that he will return for you."

Tsogyal nodded.

Nawang continued, "You must act as a common girl and help my wife, can you do this ?"

Tsogyal answered, "I expect no special treatment."

Nawang smiled. "Very well, I will take you to my wife."

Since that day Tsogyal helped milk yaks and goats, boiled tea for butter tea, helped prepare food, mended clothing, mucked the stalls, remaining quiet and subservient while doing so. She was glad for her mother having her learn so many things. No one suspected her of being a Princess.

At first, Tsogyal almost retched at the dirt and grease covering everything in this farm house. The food was greasy, the farmers did not wash their hands that they ate with. It was very new to Tsogyal who just assumed everyone lived as she did in the palace. Yet, she remained steadfast, waiting for Abaka to return, knowing she needed his help. Nawang never discussed her plans, nor even spoke to her more than he must.

Tsogyal had hidden her silks and jewels in her saddlebags when in Abaka's tent the night she stayed in his camp by the circle of boulders. He had brought her into his camp and quickly hustled her into his felt tent so his men would not get a clear view of her. There he searched in a bag then pulled out a small robe made of thick cotton and a pair of felt boots.

"Here are some clothes more suitable for a commoner," he said. "And some boots. You should take those silk robes off and hide them away." Leaving Tsogyal in his tent, he spent the night sleeping next to the fire under the stars wrapped in a sheepskin blanket.

Now in the farmer's home, she wore this same robe every day and the sheepskin coat Rab-ten had given her. When she was not doing the many chores delegated to her, she spent every minute she could with Lungta, hidden in her stall.

It disturbed her how few clothes Nawang's wife had and that the boys wore the same robes day after day. She was uncomfortable herself wearing the same cotton robe; it becoming more and more soiled.

Then, in the late afternoon after many days had passed, Abaka returned. He rode into the farm alone, leading his gelding into the courtyard through the wooden door. Tsogyal held herself back from rushing to him, anxious to be away from the farm and to know where they would go next. So forcing herself to be patient, she waited, acting demurely as he had instructed.

After greeting Nawang, the two men went into the house and sat for a long time talking and drinking tea. Tsogyal sat with the wife, making the evening meal. After the family ate, Abaka gestured to Tsogyal to accompany him to the roof of the house where they could talk in private. Abaka brought two cushions onto the rooftop terrace, inviting Tsogyal to sit.

"They are looking for you," Abaka began.

"My father?" Tsogyal guessed.

"Well yes, Pelgyi has his troops out covering the countryside. I have heard Zhonnu spent many days searching all of Karchen, looking for you. He gave up and has returned to his palace in Kharchupa. However, he has left several of his warriors to continue searching."

"Can we go to Nepal?" Tsogyal asked.

"Nepal? Why do you wish to go to Nepal?" Abaka queried.

"Did I not tell you I wish to find a Buddhist master to study with?" Tsogyal replied, a bit irritated. "There are masters in Nepal. I wish to find one."

Abaka sat back. "Oh yes, you did mention that. I did not realize you had your sights on Nepal. No, now is not the time for you to be traveling about. Your horse, for one thing, stands out, and, with you astride her, the story of you and your whereabouts will travel quickly. The Emperor is aware of your disappearance as well."

"What am I to do?" Tsogyal groaned, leaning forward pressing her hand against her forehead.

Abaka leaned forward as he whispered. "Are you sure you would not just return to Prince Zhonnu?"

She shot a look at Abaka. "No, never!"

Rising to her feet, she paced. "Is there someplace other than here I can go and hide until they give up looking? I do not want to impose on these people any longer."

Abaka nodded. "Yes, you have to leave this house. Nawang and his family are in danger now if you are found here. I have spoken to Nawang about a plan I have. Though I had hoped you would have decided to return to Prince Zhonnu instead. Since you are steadfast in your desire and I have made an oath to help you, here is my plan..."

They set out in the morning, Tsogyal riding a dun gelding, Abaka upon his red bay gelding and Nawang's son, Richen, upon a grey gelding. Lungta was being led by Richen. She was fully saddled, her saddlebags were empty. They traveled for two days staying clear of the roads that would have travelers who might take notice of the group.

On the second day by the Tsangpo river, Richen prepared to leave Abaka and Tsogyal. He would take Lungta with him.

Tsogyal sobbed as she hugged Lungta's neck.

Abaka tried to console her. "She will be fine. Richen will lead her up that valley." He pointed to the valley that lay open across the river to the south. "There is water and much grass. She will, no doubt, be found by one of your father's search parties, so near to the palace as this valley is. Then she will be lead back to her home. Or she will wander back to the palace. Either way, she will be cared for and they will have no idea where you have gone. They will search a long time in the mountains of that valley looking for you, when you will be far away in another place."

Tsogyal tried to be strong, as Lungta, led by Richen, crossed the river, getting smaller and smaller until they disappeared from her view. She felt her heart was being ripped from her chest, she was sure she could not bear this loss.

Abaka placed his hand gently on her shoulder. "I understand, she is part of you. You must let her go if you wish to be free." Taking up his reins, he urged his mount forward, calling over his shoulder, "We must go now quickly, lest a search party find us and I lose my head."

Tsogyal looked through her tears at Abaka's blurry form riding onward. She looked once more to the empty place Lungta had been. The urge to forget all, to run after Lungta, to get her back, over came her. *Go to Kharchupa. Become Zhonnu's wife. Someday be Queen. Just bear it. I could have Lungta.* The thoughts raced through her mind. She looked to Abaka, who had stopped and turned, gazing at her, sadness on his face.

"You can change your mind. We can retrieve Lungta, then I will lead you to Kharchupa," he called out.

Tsogyal shook her head. "No! We will go to the hiding place you spoke of."

Abaka sighed and nodded. Turning his mount, he continued onward.

Willing herself, Tsogyal tapped the sides of her mount and followed.

They continued east, following the Tsangpo river for two more days. Then Abaka dismounted and looked up a canyon. He mounted again and they traveled to another canyon, Abaka searched the canyon entrance with his eyes.

"What are you looking for?" Tsogyal asked.

"I am looking for the signs that this is the ravine we will travel up. And, I see now that it is. We will lead the horses up until they cannot continue. Then we will tie them and continue on foot." Abaka dismounted and started leading his horse up the rocky terrain, leaving the river.

Tsogyal dismounted and followed, leading her horse. They walked for what seemed to Tsogyal to be a long time, then the terrain became very steep. With the horses no longer useful, they emptied their saddlebags into sacks they would have to carry. With these slung over their shoulders, they climbed for the remainder of the day. Then Abaka stopped and looked up another ravine.

"Up there," he pointed. "The cave is there."

Tsogyal looked up the rugged and desolate place. "Can we climb up there?"

Abaka looked at her and nodded. "You go first. In case you slip, I will stop your fall."

Tsogyal sighed, then began her ascent.

"If you have changed your mind, I will take you to Kharchupa and the Prince?" Abaka suggested.

Tsogyal glared back at him. "Never."

They climbed up the rocky terrain, slipping at times, causing rocks to tumble down the steep mountainside. Abaka watched as Tsogyal made her way up the steep trail. Then she disappeared into the side of the mountain.

Abaka entered the cave and looked with pity at the form of Tsogyal slumped on the dirt floor. Her head in her hands, she was weeping.

He knelt beside her. "You will be fine here. I know a boy in the village near here. I will arrange with him to bring you food."

Looking at the crumpled sheepskin coat Tsogyal held in her lap, he asked, "Was that left here?"

Tsogyal nodded, tears sliding down her face.

"Good, a gift for a gift. I was concerned when you gave Nawang's wife your only coat," Abaka scolded.

Tsogyal wiped the tears from her face, calming herself. "She needed it."

"So do you, Princess," Abaka replied as he began unpacking the bag he carried.

"Here, I have brought you more things," he said as he unpacked the bag. "A pot, a brick of tea, a large flask of water, butter, dried meat, a flint and dung chips. There is plenty of wood on the hillside for cook-fires, but these chips can be used for a fire tonight. There is a spring that flows all season up the ravine, so you will have all the water you need. You will pay the boy who brings you food with pieces of your jewelry."

Then he laid his dagger before her. "You may need this, Princess, if there are any animals that challenge you."

Tsogyal gazed down at the knife, eyes wide. Then she looked up at Abaka as he stood.

"It is late, I must go now to get the horses and return to Ferghana," he said, looking down at her. "I will return when I have brought the Emperor the horses he requested. It will be three or four moons. In that time, having not found you, all will decide you are dead and will stop searching for you. I will take you to Nepal, then my oath to you is completed."

Tsogyal stood up and faced Abaka. "You have helped me greatly. I thank you."

Abaka looked at Tsogyal for a long time. Then he nodded. "I will return, wait for me, Princess Tsogyal." Then he was gone.

Tsogyal could hear the tumble of rocks as Abaka made his way down the steep path. Soon all was silent.

16

She held Lungta's reins firmly in her grasp as they galloped across the valley. Fear crawled up Tsogyal's back, the panting of the wolves behind them growing closer. Tsogyal urged Lungta faster. Feeling Lungta growing tired, Tsogyal pleaded, "Lungta do not falter or they will devour us."

Then, Tsogyal saw a figure in the distance. "Chudak!" Tsogyal yelled, feeling relieved at the sight of her protector.

Yet, he did not move. Riding up to him, she saw that he was slumped over his saddle, weeping.

"Chudak, what is wrong?" Tsogyal asked in alarm.

He looked up, not responding to her, looking right through her as though she was not there.

Clutching the hilt of the dagger, Tsogyal woke suddenly, shivering in the cold dark. Curling her body, she pulled the sheepskin coat tighter around her and covered her ears against the howling of the wolves outside. In and out of dreams, memories of Shantipa's beating assailed her. Her back twitched at the images coursing through her mind. The howling of the wolves woke her out of her dream-state, chasing away the images of Shantipa. Still she shuddered at the murky presence of evil that remained in the memory of him. Shifting her position, the cold hard floor reminded her of where she was. She prayed for morning to come, trying not to hear the whistling of demons on the cold wind outside. Shivering, she closed her eyes. Overcome by fatigue she slid down the dark passage into a dreamless sleep.

Tsogyal opened her eyes to the pale morning light that filled the cave, relieved that morning had come. Closing her eyes, the need for more sleep pulled her into a murky state of half-waking, half-dreaming, as she remained curled tightly against the cold and fear that assailed her every night of the five nights she had now spent in the cave. Feeling pressure to relieve herself, she reluctantly sat up. She cast her sleepy gaze upon the rock walls that surrounded her, a cold hard womb. Slowly, stiffly, she got to her feet and walked unsteadily to the cave entrance. Bracing her hand against the cold hard stone, she looked out. To her surprise, all was white, covered in the previous night's snow fall. She picked her way through the rocks and brush to a suitable place. When she was finished, she stood up and looked around at the cold dusting of snow on the rocks and bushes of the ravine around her. Feeling a warmth, she looked down and noticed blood trickling down the inside of her leg. A sudden cramp seized her. Grasping her belly she bent over waiting for the pain to subside.

"Oh, drat," she cursed. It was her moon-cycle of blood.

She made her way back into the cave and pulled her silks from her bag. Taking the dagger she cut the beautiful robes into pieces. She folded several into thick pads, then made a piece to bind one of these between her legs to contain the ooze.

Shivering, she sat and pulled the coat tighter around her. Grief tormented her as she held her head in her hands. She missed Lungta terribly and was worried about what may have happened to her. *Is she alive or could she have died, all alone? It is my fault, I betrayed her, my beautiful friend. I left her alone, I abandoned her!* The thoughts assailed her. She missed her mother, the way she was both graceful and commanding as she made sure all was as it should be in the palace. She missed her sister Dechen, sweet and reassuring, and Nyima, always scolding her. This idea made her chuckle. The laugh felt good. Hunger gnawed at her, she fantasized what she would have for breakfast if she were home. Then decided to stop thinking of these things, as it was making the hunger worse.

"Make tea," she ordered herself, standing to get the fire started. Taking a handful of dried grass from a pile she had collected and placed in the corner of the cave, she knelt before the small fire pit and placed the grass in the middle. Striking the flint, sparks jumped into the tinder. After a few strokes, the grass burst into flames. She placed small sticks from a stack she had ready beside the fire pit, onto the small fire, feeding the flames. Then she placed larger sticks on the small fire, making the fire grow larger. Deeply concentrated on this task, images of her father entered her mind. A lump formed in her throat as tightness clutched her chest. Pain grew around her heart as the clench of grief grew tighter. Tsogyal stood up, trying to release the searing pain that gripped her; the betrayal of her by her father. Grief turned to anger as the thoughts continued. Not being able to bear the pain of the strong emotions changing from grief, to shock, to dismay, to anger, she paced around the small room of the cave.

"Father, how could you have given me to such a terrible man!" she muttered aloud to his image in her mind. "I told you I did not wish to be married!" she yelled, as the anger rose and rose in her chest.

"Why would you not simply respect my wishes!?" she ranted, tears welling in her eyes as the pain of anger turned to a flood of grief. She paced and paced, trying to relieve the discomfort of the emotions coursing through her. Then she noticed the fire was losing fuel, she ran to it and fed the flames with more wood. Concentrating of the task, the strong emotions fell away, bringing relief. She picked up the tea flask, which held tea prepared earlier and, finding it empty, she cursed. Over the past several days she had drunk it all. Now she would have to prepare more before she could have her tea this morning.

"I should pay attention to these things," she scolded herself. Hearing her sister Nyima in her words, she could not help the urge and burst out laughing. As the mirth grew, Tsogyal danced in a circle, laughing harder and harder, her arms wrapped around her belly, bending over as the laughter turned to pain. Heaving and choking, she forced herself to stop. Gasping for air, bringing herself to calmness, she noticed the flickering flames of the shrinking fire and added more wood. Sitting in a state of dismay at the range of emotions she had just experienced, she watched as the fire grew large. Placing the pot of water on it, she broke off a small chunk from the tea-brick Abaka had given her and plopped it into the water. It would need to simmer for a long time to be strong enough, then poured into the tea flask to make butter tea over the next several days. After a few minutes, she took the pot off the fire to pour herself a cup of weak tea.

"This will do for now," she spoke aloud.

The warmth of the cup in her hands was a comfort. She noticed she was running low on food and tea, this made her worry whether Abaka had been able to arrange for a boy to bring her more. Sitting on a cold stone set by the fire, she ate her breakfast of weak tea, dried apricots and walnuts. She wondered if she should ration what she had remaining. Fear gripped her as she considered what she would do if no one came. Stoking the cook fire, she left the pot remaining to simmer the tea and determined to not let fear paralyze her. She decided she must busy herself.

Getting up, she went out to collect fire wood. After that was done, she swung the empty water flasks onto her shoulders and climbed down the trail, setting out to find the spring. The snow was not deep, only a few inches. Stumbling down the cave path and then up the ravine, she found the spring bubbling up out of the ground. While she filled the water flasks, she looked around her. All was still. An uncomfortable feeling began to climb up her back, a tightness clutched her chest. She felt alone, fear and dread rising in her body. Stealing herself against an outbreak of emotion, she concentrated on her task. When finished, she hoisted the bags to her shoulders and looked up to the ridge of the ravine. Then she froze. A wolf, silhouetted against the sky, was looking right at her. Heart pounding in her chest, she walked quickly to the path leading back to the cave. She felt the wild eyes on her back. Gritting her teeth, images played in her mind of the beast hurling down the ravine and pouncing on her, tearing out her throat, devouring her. Casting a look back, the way was empty. She broke into a run, the primal urge to flee was too strong.

Then, she stopped suddenly at the sight of a figure coming up the ravine whence Abaka and she had arrived. Bags hung from his shoulders. Carefully, he picked his way across and around the rocks on the trail. He looked up and saw her.

With a wave of his hand, he yelled, "Hello, I am Jalus. I am sent by Abaka. I come with your food."

The feeling of relief caused Tsogyal's legs to go weak. She waved back and waited for the boy to reach her. Stealing a glance over her shoulder, she could not see the ridge where the wolf had stood. She hoped the beast had not followed her. When the boy caught up to her, they both scrambled up to the cave. Arriving at the cave entrance, Tsogyal stopped and turned to the boy. He was just her same height and very thin, but strong. Relief turned to fear as she considered, he could overpower her, if he desired to.

"Here," she pointed to the ground just in front of the entrance, "place the bags here. I will carry them inside."

Jalus looked at the young woman, surprised by her demand.

With a shrug, he said, "As you wish," and laid the bags down. Then he sat on a rock near the cave entrance to rest.

Tsogyal looked through the bags. She was happy to see butter, salt, barley flour, dried meat, and more tea. She looked up at Jalus. "Thank you for bringing this to me. I will give you payment for the next time you come."

Ducking into the cave, she went to her bag and pulled her jeweled necklace from it, glancing over her shoulder, to make sure the boy had not followed her inside. She snapped off a piece of heavy silver holding a turquoise stone. Feeling the weight of the small object in her hand, she walked outside the cave.

Holding it out to Jalus, she asked, "Is this enough to buy more food for me?"

Jalus stood up, taking the precious article in his hand. Inspecting it, a smile came over his face. "Yes, this is very good. I have brought enough food for a fortnight, thus I will return with more food in fortnight from this day."

He turned and left, picking his way back down the trail. Tsogyal watched him go. He began singing to himself. Sitting down on the rock, she listened to the song diminish, until silence returned.

The sun was high in the sky as Tsogyal sat at the entrance of the cave, looking out at the blue sky and the view. Snow lightly dusted the rocks and bushes of the ravine, though much of it had melted. This was the only time of day the sun shone on the cave. She held a cup of hot butter tea in her hands. It had been ten days since Abaka brought her here. She tried to keep busy, but there was not much to do. She felt sad and alone. Fear constantly assailed her. She could get through the days, but the nights were torture. She wanted to be back home riding Lungta. She missed her terribly and worried about her, wondering if she was safe. She missed her life writing and reading scripture with the Buddhist teacher.

"I am here because I want to find a master," she said aloud, reminding herself. "I must be strong and wait for Abaka."

She lay her head against the cold rock of the entrance doorway. The sun warmed her body, relaxing her. Feeling very sleepy, she yawned. Closing her eyes, she sighed and relaxed against the hard stone. Moments later she was sound asleep.

Dechen's graceful hand held the delicate paintbrush as she painted exquisite lines of gold on the sky. Strokes of the brush painted green and blue on the clouds. Sweeping line by line, the figure of Goddess Sarasvati finally emerged fully-formed in all of her glory. Musical sounds of mantras filled the space. Her hands in the gesture of a mudra, she floated down to Tsogyal, who looked up at her in awe. Stepping onto the ground before Tsogyal, she motioned to follow her into the cave. Amazed, Tsogyal got up and entered the cave after her. To her surprise, Sarasvati was sitting on a lotus made of clear crystal light raised from the floor. She gestured to Tsogyal to sit on her cushion of sheepskin coat. Tsogyal obeyed and looked, in wonder, at her visitor. The Goddess was dazzling, dressed in flowing glistening robes made of rainbows. Her face, hands and feet were pure white light.

Sarasvati spoke, her voice sweet and soft, "Princess Tsogyal, why do you waste your time here in this cave?"

Tsogyal was puzzled. "I await Abaka, he will bring me to Nepal to meet a master," she explained.

Sarasvati looked at the girl, her eyes filled with love. "You do not have to wait to begin practice. It is true, your destiny is to meet a powerful master. Yet, until that event arrives, you should use this time of solitude wisely."

"How?" Tsogyal asked

"Meditate," Sarasvati answered.

"How do I meditate? Our teacher in the palace never gave us instruction in meditation."

Sarasvati held out her hands in a gesture of giving. "I will teach you."

Tsogyal's eyes went wide. "That would be wonderful, as I want to learn."

"To begin, sit in a cross-legged posture, your back straight. Look at the floor just in front of you, your eyes relaxed," Sarasvati instructed.

Tsogyal adjusted her posture.

Sarasvati smiled. "Very good, now breathe in slowly, feel the breath as it enters your nostrils, feel it travel down inside of you all the way the base of your belly. When you exhale, concentrate on the breath at your nostrils. Follow the breath in and out. When thoughts arise, ignore them and they will dissolve. You will notice your mind will try to distract you by creating more and more thoughts. Ignore these and they too will dissolve. This is the beginning teaching. Do this every day for several hours. When you are ready, I will return to teach you the next step."

Then, before Tsogyal's eyes, Sarasvati began to dissolve into space. As her form became lighter and lighter, she spoke again. "Worry not for Lungta. She has been found and is now in your father's stable. She is healthy and well cared for."

Tsogyal awoke startled. She looked around her, the dream remained so vivid in her mind, she was sure it had just happened before her. Yet here she sat at the entrance of the cave, not inside. Warmth filled her being, with it a feeling of contentedness she had not experienced for a very long time. She gazed out at the sky; it sparkled. Looking out at the view before her, the ravine was alive. The forms of rocks and bushes were distinct, the muted colors exquisite. A melodious song reached her ears. It sounded familiar, yet she could not remember the pleasantness of it before. Then it struck her, it was the song of a wolf calling in the distance. The howling echoed through the ravine again, filling her with wonder at its primordial beauty.

Lungta is safe, she had been told, relief filling her. Knowing now what she was to do, the instruction feeling as a great gift in her hands, she got up. As she did so, she placed her hand on the rock of the entrance, feeling its cool solidity. She turned and looked out again, all was simply wondrous. *Why,* she thought, *had I not seen before how beautiful this all is?* She felt as if she had been blind and now could see. On light feet, her heart full, she entered the cave, placed her cup by the fire, then sat on her cushion of sheepskin coat. Crossing her legs, she settled her eyes and concentrated on her breath entering her body. It felt like nectar.

17

Nawang scrutinized his wife as she milked one of their many goats. The morning was cold, dark clouds filled the sky.

"You should not wear that silk cloth Abaka's woman, Yeshe, left here," he scolded.

"Why should I not?" his wife asked in protest. "Yeshe gave it to me, along with this fine warm coat." She nodded, remembering the quiet young woman. "What a kind one she was."

"It will bring us trouble. Take it off and put it in a special place inside our home," Nawang demanded.

"Father!" Nawang's son yelled, as he ran up to them. He turned and pointed. "A rider is coming."

Nawang looked where the boy was pointing and saw a man on a horse, alone and trotting up to the group of them. When he was close, Nawang could see he was not Tibetan.

"*Tashi de lea,*" the man greeted in Tibetan.

"*Tashi de lea,*" Nawang replied, looking up at the stranger who stopped his horse before them. The long robes and head scarf identified him as from Arabian lands.

The man looked at Nawang's wife, his eyes settled on the silk around her neck.

"What a beautiful family. Does your daughter not help with the milking?" the stranger inquired.

Nawang's wife looked up at him, then replied, "We have no daughter."

His eyes widened. "I see, I am sure one day you will," he said, with a slight bow of his head. Then he addressed Nawang. "My name is Ahmed. I have a matter of importance regarding which I wish to speak with you."

Nawang hesitated, then in an instant, made his decision. "We can talk in my home. Will you leave your weapons outside with your horse? My son will look after them."

Ahmed dismounted. "Very good," he said as he handed the reins of his horse to Nawang's son. He took his sword and dagger from his belt and laid it on the rock corral wall. The two men disappeared through the wooden door into the courtyard. Nawang led the Arab up the ladder and into the sitting room.

"Would you like tea?" Nawang offered.

"No, thank you. I think it best I come directly to the reason for my coming here," Ahmed said.

Nawang gestured to the two cushions. "Very well, please sit and be comfortable."

Settling himself on the cushion facing Nawang, Ahmed said, "I travelled with your friend Abaka from Ferghana on his last visit. I assisted him in bringing stallions to your Emperor Trisong. Not far from here we camped by the circle of large stones. That night Abaka brought a young woman into camp." Sitting up straight, stretching his back, he continued. "He told us she was your daughter and so we brought her here. I waited outside with our other men." Placing his hands on his knees, he said, "Now, I come to this house and I find you have no daughter and your wife wears a fine silk. Where did she get that?"

Nawang stared back at Ahmad, his face expressionless.

Ahmed smirked. "You may sit there and say nothing, yet I am very sure the young woman Abaka brought here was the Princess Tsogyal who has run away and is sought by Prince Zhonnu and by her father King Pelgyi." Waving his hand in dismissal, Ahmed went on. "Abaka tried as he might to hide the identity of the Princess. However, the daughter of a farmer such as yourself would not ride a fine mare of Ferghana stock and with a royal saddle. This I could see plainly."

Ahmed leaned forward. "I know she was here. Where is she now?"

"I do not know," Nawang replied, keeping his voice steady. "Abaka took her, I know not where. He said she was his betrothed." He shook his head. "To my knowledge she was simply that. If she was as you say, then I had no idea she was the Princess."

Ahmed stroked his beard. Then his voice grew stern. "Should I go to King Pelgyi and to Zhonnu and tell them my story? What do you think will come of you and your family for hiding the Princess?"

Nawang protested, "If she was the Princess, I knew not. What harm could come to an ignorant farmer?"

Ahmed looked in astonishment at Nawang. "What harm? I will tell you what harm. You will lose your head, your land will be forfeit and your wife and sons will end up beggars on the road. Do you really think they will believe you were unaware of her identity?"

Nawang sat stone-faced.

Ahmed leaned forward and spoke softly, "I have no desire to destroy you and your family. I only want to find the Princess. Tell me were she is and I will tell no one of her stay here. I will protect your secret. No harm will come to her, she will simply be returned to her rightful owner; her husband."

Nawang sank in his cushion. "Will you take an oath on your silence?" he queried.

Ahmed straightened his back. "Yes, I will take a blood oath. However, if I find you have lied to me, the oath is null."

Ahmed smiled, his ruse had worked. *Unbeknownst to Nawang,* Ahmed thought, *I have no intention of telling anyone about this farmer and his role in Tsogyal's escape. Abaka would be very angry if he knew I'd betrayed his secret and cost his friend's life. Abaka is no man to cross. As well, at times, we are business partners, and good ones. However, by the time the Princess is found and in royal hands, no one will remember the man who told of her whereabouts. I will fade away from here like steam from the cooking pot and will be back in Ferghana, my saddlebags heavy with gold and silver.*

Ahmed sat astride his horse on the edge of the Tsangpo river. *The place must be near here,* he thought, looking at the ravine leading up the mountains from the river. *But which one?* Urging his horse to the entrance of a ravine, he pondered the rock and brush. Frustrated, he scolded himself, *remember the landmarks, what did that farmer say?* His attention was drawn to movement in the distance on the river bank. Waiting, he could make out a figure heading toward him. Casting about for a place to conceal himself, he dismounted and led his horse around a group of bushes clustered by a ridge of rock. Tying his horse, he quietly crept around the brush until he could see. It was a boy, carrying bags on his shoulders. The boy pulled at the bags and strained; they were heavy, Ahmed could see. The boy turned up the ravine Ahmed had been scrutinizing. Waiting for the boy to get ahead of him, Ahmed followed at a distance, staying concealed. He followed the boy for hours, climbing higher and higher. Then the boy took a steep path away from the ravine. Ahmed followed cautiously behind, taking care not make any sounds, such as loosening rocks which would reveal his presence. Hiding behind a large rock on a bend in the path, Ahmed stopped as he watched the boy high above and ahead of him. The boy stopped and let the bags drop to the ground. He heard the boy speak. Then, to Ahmed's amazement, the girl Abaka had brought into camp so many weeks ago came out of a wall of stone. *The cave,* Ahmed confirmed, *that farmer was telling the truth after all.* Turning silently, Ahmed made his way carefully back to his horse. Mounting, he smiled. *A prize,* he congratulated himself, *information, what an easy prize.* Turning his horse, he kicked it into a canter.

Prince Wangchuk considered the Arab sitting before him. "Of what do you wish to speak to me?" Wangchuk inquired, irritably. In truth, Wangchuk did not like Arabs, he did not trust them. Though they were allies of Tibet in battle, Wangchuk considered them opportunistic rather than loyal. For this reason he was wary of them in any dealings.

"I have information for you," Ahmed bowed, standing before the Prince, "for a price."

Wangchuk, squirming with impatience, asked, "What information can you possibly have that would be worth a price to me?"

Ahmed still bowing, explained, "Prince, I know the whereabouts of the Princess Tsogyal."

Stunned, Wangchuk sat staring at the Arab. Then he leaned forward. "How do you know this?"

Ahmed stood straight. "If you will allow me, Prince, I will explain. However, I will need a promise of payment for my trouble. Say, one bag of gold coin and two of silver?"

Wangchuk gestured to a cushion. When Ahmed was seated, Wangchuk asked, "Why do you come to me? Why not go to Zhonnu?"

Ahmed smiled. "You are an honorable man. Zhonnu could not hold on to her. Now you can claim her. Is this not true?"

Wangchuk stroked his small thin beard, considering, "Yes, I think this is true. I can now claim her. And you are correct to come to me. Zhonnu is a cheat, as he showed on the day of our contest. I will give you one bag of silver. And when I have the Princess in my grasp, you shall receive one bag of gold. That is all I will offer."

Ahmed considered. "It would be more pleasing to me if you would include one of your fine recurve bows of horn and a quiver of arrows."

Wangchuk nodded. "Very well, it will be done. Now, tell me where the Princess is and how you have come to know this?"

Ahmed sat back and held his hands out, his palms up in a gesture of giving. "Through divination, Prince. I consulted an oracle. After the divination, I went to the place indicated and saw her with my own eyes. This confirmed the reading. I will show your men the place for you to capture her. When she is in your hands, I expect the final payment. Will you give an oath to this?"

Wangchuk sat back. He did not believe that through divination this man had found Tsogyal. *Well,* he thought, *it matters not.* Wangchuk considered the Arab, then decided he was telling the truth about knowing her whereabouts. "I give you my oath."

Breathing in cool air to the base of her stomach, sensation, life force, peace, flowed up and through her whole being. Breath flowing out, a cool sensation at her nostrils. Breathing in again she was suffused with an exquisite, alive, exhilarating peace. The sensations were almost painful, they were so pleasurable. Thoughts arose trying to distract her, she paid them no attention. Gazing at them with light attention, as though they were puffs of smoke, they melted away. She experimented with them, looking from afar at their manifestation. Sometimes looking hard at them to see how long she could make the same thought remain. It would quiver to escape into another thought, to make a string of thoughts, like beads of a necklace.

Pain in her knee attracted her attention, this she must pay attention to, not wanting to cause damage to nerves. She stretched her legs out on front of her, kneading the muscles along her legs and around her knees. Rising, she walked to the entrance of the cave. She raised her arms above her head and stretched her back. Turning, she walked back into the small room and walked slowly in a circle. Amazingly, she had the sensation that her legs picked themselves up without her lifting them. They rose higher and higher with each step, as though a force under her, from the ground, was lifting each leg. She giggled, it felt funny. She rode the energy lifting her legs as she circled the cave.

A sound caught her attention. Rocks and stones tumbling, from outside. *Jalus?* She wondered, *back so soon?* The jingle of metal on metal, heavy foot falls crunching on the stone of the path. A shadow filled the doorway, a man covered in metal, a sword at his side, stepped into the small space. Behind him another man stepped around the first, filling the space more. A third man looked over the shoulders of the two.

Tsogyal fell back against the wall in incredulity. The strong odor of sweat, horses and leather filled the cave-room. The men looked at her intensely. Seeming frozen, they gazed at her.

Tsogyal broke the silence. "Who are you? What do you want?" she asked, fear seeming to be a feeling outside of her, hovering close, ready to grasp as her own.

The leader bowed. "Princess Tsogyal, we are warriors for Prince Wangchuk. We have come to bring you to him." Crossing the cave to her, his large hand extended, he took her arm in a firm yet gentle grasp. "You are now the property of the Prince."

Unable to bring herself to protest, Tsogyal realized it would be futile, she could not outfight these men. She submitted to their strength. Exiting the cave, she looked down the path and stopped in surprise. Strung along the length of the path, as far as she could see, were no less than thirty warriors in full battle armor.

Looking up at the man grasping her arm, she asked, amused, "So many for one small woman?"

He looked down at her, deciding to answer. "Prince Wanchuk was concerned Prince Zhonnu may have received a visitor telling him of your whereabouts. It appears we are the first to arrive for you."

He gently moved her in front of him and behind another warrior as they carefully escorted her down the path. Though her cotton robes were torn and soiled, her felt boots worn, she was a Princess and as such she was respected by these men.

Tsogyal's steps were still light, she felt the energy raising her up from the ground. The earth had not abandoned her; this she held close, a precious gift.

18

Queen Getso stared out at the distance from her rooftop retreat. She saw nothing. Only the stream of images in her mind's eye held her attention. Dour images of Tsogyal, lost or worse, dead.

"Too long you have been lost. Oh, my daughter, if only I knew your fate," Getso prayed softly, her eyes filled with tears.

Footsteps drew her attention, she turned her head slightly to see who was approaching. Dechen appeared at her side. Her hands clasped Getso's arm.

"Mother, Tsogyal has been found!"

Striding back and forth across the domain in front of his throne, Pelgyi fought to keep his temper in check. Glaring down at the man bowing before him, he said through gritted teeth, "Tell your master that I had no knowledge of Prince Wangchuk finding my daughter until just before you arrived. Indeed, your master knew of it before myself."

Exasperated, Pelgyi continued, "What does he hope to achieve by warring on my kingdom? Go now and tell your master, Prince Zhonnu, my reply to his inquiries and threats."

Pelgyi noticed Getso standing at the doorway, her hands

clasped together tightly. Turning to the still-bowing messenger, he flung his arm.

"Go, I said, and tell your master!"

As the man hurried out of the audience hall, Pelgyi went to Getso and clasped her folded hands in his.

"Wife, Tsogyal is safe."

Getso sobbed. "Where...when?"

Leading Getso to his throne so she could sit, he explained, "Prince Wangchuk found her in a wilderness cave."

Getso looked up at him, incredulous. "A cave!"

"Yes, I know not why she was in that place, nor how she found it. It is so far away. I know not how Wangchuk found her. I only know that she is safe. Now, Wangchuk demands I give her to him. He accuses Prince Zhonnu of cheating in the contest and so declares Zhonnu should not have her. We made an agreement and she belongs to Zhonnu, even though he could not hold on to her. If I am to remain honorable, I have no choice in this. Zhonnu thinks I conspired with Wangchuk to hide Tsogyal and is massing troops for war against us. Wangchuk has promised he will not give Tsogyal back to Zhonnu and is also massing troops to fight to keep her."

Pelgyi turned and took a few strides in agitation.

"Wangchuk has locked her away in his palace to keep anyone from stealing her." Turning back to Getso, he sighed. "These men only think of war."

Just then a servant entered the hall, Pelgyi turned and glared at him. "What now!?"

The man bowed deeply. "Sire, seven ministers sent by the Emperor await an audience with you."

Stunned, Pelgyi asked, "Emperor Trisong Detsen?"

"The same, Master," the servant said as he bowed.

Pelgyi looked at Getso. She nodded, then rose to leave. As she passed him, she reached her hand out to him and clasped his, then quickly released him. Swiftly, she made her exit through the royal doorway.

Seating himself on his throne, Pelgyi took a deep breath to

regain his composure then gestured with his hand as he ordered, "Show them in."

The envoy representing the Emperor of Tibet, dressed in fine silk padded robes entered the hall as King Pelgyi's servants hurried to place cushions for each man to sit upon. The men all bowed before Pelgyi. Pelgyi gestured as he welcomed them.

"Please sit, do you wish tea?"

The minister who had seated himself in the middle answered, "Thank you, King Pelgyi. Yes, we would appreciate refreshment, it was a tiring journey."

Pelgyi ordered the servants, who left quickly to bring tea. The men all waited in silence until tea was brought and all had a fine cup of silver placed before him filled with thick butter tea. Pelgyi nodded to the men.

"Gentlemen, enjoy your tea."

Pelgyi waited while the men sipped appreciatively. When they had set their cups down, servants appeared and filled them again. The Minister seated in the middle folded his hands in his lap, looking up at Pelgyi, a sign he was ready to speak.

Pelgyi asked, "What causes the Emperor to send a delegation to my kingdom?"

"King Pelgyi," the Minister began, "my name is Shen-po. We have been sent by the Emperor as he has been given word that a war between yourself, Prince Wangchuk and Prince Zhonnu is brewing."

Pelgyi shook his head slowly, incredulous. "I have just received these threats this very day. How does the Emperor know of this so soon?"

The ministers looked at each other and chuckled as Shen-po answered, "The Emperor of all the Kingdoms of Tibet and beyond has knowledge of all that goes on in his realm. Especially when Kingdoms under his rule declare war on each other."

Pelgyi leaned forward, his arms resting on his knees, looking intently at Shen-po. "I have no desire for war. Indeed, I have been trying to avoid it."

Shen-po nodded slightly. "The Emperor understands the cause

of this strife between you and the two Princes. The Emperor requests you come to his palace. He wishes you to bring your wife and two daughters. If you do not do so, you will incur his displeasure."

Pelgyi sat back. "I will be happy to do as the Emperor wishes. We will leave in two days. You are welcome to stay here in my palace." Pelgyi called to the servant, "Bring these men to their chambers and arrange an attendant for their needs."

Shen-po stood, followed by the six men at his sides. They all bowed as Shen-po said, "Thank you, King Pelgyi, for your hospitality. We will return to the Emperor's palace on the morrow to inform him of your arrival." Then they all turned and filed out of the hall.

Pelgyi sat back, stroking his mustache, wondering, *bring my two daughters?*

Tsogyal rode a grey dun-colored horse surrounded by an escort of 900 of the Emperor's soldiers. Wangchuk gave her up without a fight when he found the morning brought with it a sea of warriors outside his palace walls. The huge force of the Emperor's was enough to cause Wangchuk to give up his plans of fighting for the Princess. Dressed in fine silks, Tsogyal was escorted by Wangchuk himself through his palace gates to face General Klu-pal.

"I am loyal to the Emperor, let this be known to him," Wangchuk declared to the General, as he offered Tsogyal to him.

"You may declare yourself to the Emperor. He requests you come to the palace immediately," Klu-pal informed Prince Wangchuk.

Taken aback, Wangchuk held his surprise and fear in check. "Very well, I will be happy to go to the Emperor's court. I will leave on the morrow."

General Klu-pal looked down at Tsogyal and asked, "Noble Daughter, are you well? Can you ride?"

Tsogyal looked up at him and simply nodded.

A warrior brought a horse to the Princess. Without a word, Tsogyal mounted and sat waiting. Klu-pal looked at her quizzically, then turned his horse and retreated. Tsogyal fell in behind him. The force followed, melting away from Wangchuk's walls.

In the Emperor's palace, sipping hot tea, Tsogyal felt warm as she relaxed into the soft cushion. Servant women bustled around her. The room was large with beautiful carpets, many sitting cushions and a very large cushion for a bed.

"Princess, I am Sangmu, your attendant." A young woman bowed before Tsogyal. "Are you hungry? Is there anything you desire?"

Though having been bathed and given fine silk robes, Tsogyal felt exhausted. She contemplated all she had been through since the day she had been beaten and taken from her father's palace. Now she felt the full force of the physical toll all had taken on her.

"Is there yogurt?" she inquired in a soft voice, almost a whisper.

Pleased, Sangmu enthused, "Why, yes, Princess, we have very good yogurt." Turning, she ordered a servant to bring the wish of the Princess. Just then the door opened and Tsogyal was surprised to see her mother, Getso, in the doorway.

"My daughter, where is she?" Getso demanded as she swept into the room.

The attendants all parted, gesturing toward Tsogyal, as Tsogyal stood up. Dechen and Nyima followed in after their mother.

"Daughter!" Getso gasped as she rushed to Tsogyal. Taking her daughter into her arms, she hugged her fiercely. "Tsogyal, I have been so afraid for you." She looked into Tsogyal's eyes. "I feared you were dead, that I would never see you again."

Tsogyal was paralyzed, she had never seen her mother like this. "Mother, I am sorry I caused you distress."

Dechen and Nyima came and joined Tsogyal and their mother. They gazed at Tsogyal with wonder at her appearance. Secretly, they had spoken to each other of their surety that she had been devoured by wild animals after she ran away from Zhonnu's camp. Or kidnaped by robbers and sold into slavery in some faraway land. Now, here she was, found in a cave.

Getso, shook her head slowly. "No my daughter, we should never have let that beast beat you. You must understand, your father had no idea Zhonnu would allow that to happen."

"Am I to go home then? Has Zhonnu forfeited his claim on me?" Tsogyal inquired, looking from Getso to Dechen and finally Nyima.

Getso gestured to the cushions, arranged so all could sit. Tsogyal sat, followed by her family. Then, as if remembering something, Tsogyal called, "Sangmu, can you bring tea for my mother and sisters? Yogurt too?"

Sangmu, standing close by, bowed and answered, "Yes, Princess, as you wish." Then ordered a servant to the task.

Seating herself, Getso answered, "Zhonnu has not forfeited his claim on you."

"Why am I brought here, to the palace of the Emperor?" Tsogyal inquired.

Getso answered, "We do not know."

Servants came in the room with trays of tea and yogurt, placing a silver cup of tea and a silver bowl of yogurt before each of the women. Then they bowed and removed themselves. At Tsogyal's side, Sangmu bowed, asking, "Is there anything else you desire, Noble Daughter?"

Tsogyal looked to her mother and sisters, they all shook their heads. "No, that will be all for now, Sangmu," Tsogyal said, with kindness in her tone. Sangmu took her leave to give privacy.

"Little sister, why were you in a cave?" Nyima asked.

Getso looked sharply at Nyima.

Tsogyal smiled. "I will answer, Mother." To Nyima, Tsogyal answered, "Sister, I was meditating."

Surprised by the answer, Gesto inquired, "Meditating? Where did you learn to meditate?"

"I can not answer now, Mother, but I will in the future," Tsogyal assured her.

"Why have we all been brought here?" Dechen wondered aloud.

"I have no knowledge as to why," Getso answered, "but we will soon find out."

19

Three days later Tsogyal was awakened by Sangmu. "Noble Daughter, we are to dress you this morning for an audience with the Emperor."

Tsogyal rose from her soft cushion bed and yawned. "Will there be a meal before I see our Emperor?"

"Oh, yes, of course, Princess, it is being brought now," Sangmu encouraged.

After her meal of tea, yogurt and dumplings filled with meat and spices, Tsogyal was bathed by her attendants. Then they dressed her, draping several layers of fine silk garments of beautiful colors on her strong slender body. Sparkling jewels of gold, turquoise and coral were placed around her neck and her waist. Fine slippers with gold-thread designs adorned her feet.

Sangmu stood back, admiring Tsogyal. "Princess, you are so beautiful. The Emperor will be very pleased."

"It is good of you to dress me for my audience with the Emperor as I have only the clothes I arrived in to wear," Tsogyal said, looking down at the flowing silken colors and glittering jewels.

Sangmu looked at her, bemused. "These are gifts for you, from our great Emperor, Princess."

Then Sangmu clapped, ordering the servant, "Run and tell the

Emperor the Princess is ready. We will arrive to the audience hall very soon." The servant hurried out of the room.

Sangmu gestured to the door for Princess Tsogyal to lead the way, following behind her. Exiting the doorway into the hall, Tsogyal was startled when eight guards took positions around her and Sangmu, four in front and four behind, making their escort.

They walked though hallways and made several turns. Then, they crossed a courtyard with beautiful gardens. The day was bright and Tsogyal realized she had not been outside for many days. Moving down a hallway, Tsogyal could see past the guards marching in front of her, a large doorway coming closer. As they walked through it, the guards in front of Tsogyal and Sangmu parted, taking positions by the door. The space opened into a huge room. The rear guards remained following the two women to the front of the room. They passed many pillars holding the high ceiling aloft. The gathered throng parted before Tsogyal's entourage. Reaching the front of the audience hall, Tsogyal saw Prince Wangchuk, Prince Zhonnu, her father, mother and sisters all standing waiting for her. Her gaze moved upward to the carved throne with a thick brocade cushion. Sitting upon it, cross-legged, was the Emperor Trisong Detsen. He was radiant, in silks of gold, red and blue. His hair was tied back. Upon his head he wore a crown of gold with large jewels of lapis lazuli inlayed around its circumference like shining eyes. A small beard and long mustache adorned his strong serene face. His eyes sparkled when he saw Tsogyal approach. Tsogyal was surprised, seeing the man she had heard so much about all of her life. She had thought, as Emperor, he would be very old. Yet at thirty-one springs he was, in fact, very handsome. The twinkle in his eye caused her to be intrigued by him.

All in the hall stood silently. Emperor Trisong Detsen looked down at the young exquisite woman standing before him. He smiled at her, she felt sincere kindness in his smile. For that moment she felt as they were the only two people in the room.

Trisong turned his attention to the assembly. In a commanding voice, he called out, "King Pelgyi of Karchen."

King Pelgyi walked in a strong even stride to stand next to his daughter. He did not look at her but kept his attention on the Emperor. Tsogyal looked at her father, a wash of pain flooded her. She looked away from him, placing her attention on the Emperor.

Pelgyi bowed. "My liege."

Trisong Detson spoke. "Your daughter has been the center and the cause of upset in three of my Kingdoms. She is legend to have been born with many auspicious signs. I can see now, as she stands before me, that she is indeed sublime and very beautiful. In the interest of peace, I wish you to bestow her upon me in marriage. She is worthy to be my Queen."

The crowd gasped. Getso looked at Dechen and Nyima. Tsogyal looked at her father, shocked by this proposition of the Emperor. Then she looked down, keeping her emotions hidden.

Pelgyi held in his surprise. "My Emperor, lord of the world, strongest of all men! My daughter has been desired by many. I had wished her to be your Queen. It was my error in thinking you would not desire her. It would be a great honor for me to bestow her upon you. As an honorable man, however I must tell you, that I created a contest in which Prince Zhonnu of Kharchupa had won her. I cannot give her, as she is rightfully his property now, though he did cause her to be mistreated and caused her to run away from him. I do know the marriage was never consummated by him."

Listening, Trisong sat stroking his chin, then having made up his mind, he called out, "Prince Zhonnu."

From the front of the crowd, Prince Zhonnu strode forward and bowed low before the Emperor. "My liege."

"Prince Zhonnu of Kharchupa. I have been informed that you allowed this innocent young woman to be beaten by your minister. Is this true?" Trisong boomed.

Zhonnu straightened. "Yes, he did cause her injury. My minister overstepped his authority."

"King Pelgyi, bring your daughter Nyima to stand here before me," Trisong commanded.

Pelgyi turned and gestured to Nyima, to come forward and stand by him.

"Prince Zhonnu," Trisong began, "I think this daughter of King Pelgyi is better suited to you. King Pelgyi, will you agree to bestow her upon Prince Zhonnu?"

Pelgyi's eyes widened as he answered, with a slight bow, "As you wish, my liege. My middle daughter Nyima will one day make a good Queen of Kharchupa." Looking sideways at Zhonnu, he added, "And we will live in peace with that Kingdom."

Zhonnu looked over at Nyima. She glared at him. For an inexplicable reason, this caused him to like her. He could see she was strong and he was pleased as she was also beautiful. *Perhaps,* he thought, *she was the better choice in the first place. I need a strong Queen for Kharchupa, one the people will respect. Not one who will run away and cause me grief and dishonor.*

"Well, Prince Zhonnu," Trisong interrupted Zhonnu's revery, "do you agree to forfeit your claim on the Princess Tsogyal in favor of the Princess Nyima?"

Zhonnu bowed, a smile on his face. "Yes, my liege, your wisdom is limitless, the Princess Nyima is a fine choice for my future Queen."

"Very well, take her," Trisong ordered with a wave of his hand.

Prince Zhonnu turned to Princess Nyima and held out his hand. Her chin held high, ignoring him, she turned and walked to her mother's side. Startled at her impudence, a feeling of glee filled him. He smiled as he followed her. *Yes, she is very strong,* he thought.

Nyima was shocked by this development. It took great effort not to show that she was in fact very pleased with this turn of events. For, when Prince Zhonnu of Kharchupa had arrived at her father's palace, she had found him to be very handsome. She was crushed when he was blind to her, only wanting her little sister Tsogyal. Now she would make him fight to be worthy of her. She would not give in easily, she decided.

"Prince Wangchuk," Trisong called out.

Prince Wangchuk, fear causing hesitation, gathered himself, then walked to stand before the Emperor. Bowing low, he declared, "My liege, I have always been and will always be your loyal Prince of Zurkhar."

Trisong nodded. "I am glad to hear of it. I am however troubled that your desire for the hand of the Princess Tsogyal was so great that you were willing to begin a war. As you know, I demand peace between Kingdoms in my realm."

Wangchuk bowed lower. "My Emperor, Zhonnu cheated in the contest. I witnessed the terrible beating bestowed on the innocent young Princess Tsogyal by Zhonnu's wicked minister. I only wished to keep the Princess from coming to harm in Zhonnu's keep."

Emperor Trisong listened intently, then declared, "King Pelgyi, you have another daughter?"

Pelgyi answered, "Yes, Dechen, my eldest."

Trisong looked over at Dechen, saying, "Noble Daughter, will you come forward and stand next to Prince Wangchuk?"

Dechen looked quickly at her mother, then walked forward, tall and graceful, to stand next to the Prince.

Trisong looked down at Dechen. "Princess Dechen, will you accept Prince Wangchuk as your husband?"

Shocked that the Emperor of Tibet would ask her permission, Dechen looked at Wangchuk. His tall thick figure. His awkward yet strangely appealing features. Wangchuk returned her gaze, feeling his knees go weak. *She is so beautiful and elegant*, he thought. His heart pounded in his chest. He took in a breath, trying to calm himself.

Dechen nodded. "Yes, great Emperor, I will," she said, then turned and bowed to Prince Wangchuk.

"Prince Wangchuk, will you give King Pelgyi the same dowery you offered him for the hand of Princess Tsogyal, now for the hand of Princess Dechen?" Trisong inquired.

Wangchuk looked at the graceful woman standing next to him. "I will give the same and I will give twenty yaks more for this beautiful woman. I will be very fortunate to have her as my future Queen," Wangchuk declared as he bowed to the Emperor.

Why did I not notice this beautiful eldest daughter of Pelgyi's, Wangchuk thought, *she will make a much better wife and Queen than that troublesome younger sister.*

Trisong gestured to Pelgyi. "Is this acceptable to you, King

Pelgyi?"

Amazed by what was transpiring before him, Pelgyi bowed and replied enthusiastically, "Yes, I am honored to bestow my daughter, Dechen, unto the Prince of Zurkhar." He made a quick glance at Getso, noticing the tear that ran down her cheek in happiness.

"Very well," Trisong declared, "there is only one more thing to attend to."

Looking at Tsogyal, he asked, "Princess Tsogyal, you were mistreated by Zhonnu's minister, given serious injury and caused much fear. This in turn gave you the desire to run away, causing you grief and hardship hiding in the wilderness. How can the Prince repay his crime upon you?"

Tsogyal looked at the Emperor, then to Zhonnu. "There are two things the Prince can give me," she began. "I injured a good woman in my escape from his camp. She is a healer and did not deserve this injury. I would like her to be given to me as a healer for your court. Her husband is a fine warrior, I would like him to be given as well to serve you, my Lord." With a bow, Tsogyal asked, "Would this be acceptable to my Emperor?"

Far from expecting this, Trisong was moved. "Are the woman and the warrior here?" Trisong asked Zhonnu.

"Yes, my liege, they are," Zhonnu replied, then turned and called out, "Rab-ten the healer and Jigme the warrior!"

The crowd parted as a strong lean man, wearing leather armor and a sword at his side, strode through the throng. Rab-ten followed in his wake. Finding themselves standing before the Emperor, a man they had only seen from a distance, a figure that was the living embodiment of all that was truly powerful in their world, they bowed low. Tsogyal could see the fading blue black mark that remained of the bruise she inflicted on Rab-ten's cheek.

Trisong looked at the two bowing before him. To Zhonnu, he asked, "What skills has this warrior?"

Zhonnu, looked at Jigme, then up to the Emperor. "He is captain of my personal guard. He is a fine warrior and a smart man. You will find you can depend on him."

"And the healer?" Trisong asked.

"She is skilled," Zhonnu assured. "Her father is a healer trained in the Byzantine tradition. My father's court healer was trained in this lineage going back to your grandfather's time. Rab-ten has this training by her father as well she has training in other traditions as well. She has served me well in healing many warriors, as well as myself, of battlefield wounds."

"Very well," Trisong said, nodding appreciatively to Jigme and Rab-ten, "you are welcome in my court. Jigme, General Klu-pal will find a position for you. Rab-ten, you will be an assistant court healer and attendant to Princess Tsogyal, who will soon be my Queen."

Jigme looked sideways to Rab-ten, a look of great pleasure on his face. This was a great boon to them both. For him to be serving in the great army of the Emperor of Tibet. For Rab-ten to be attendant to the Queen. Rab-ten held in the flood of tears pounding at her self-control with the racing beat of her heart. They could not believe their great good fortune.

20

"My daughter, we are leaving today," King Pelgyi said as he held Tsogyal's hands in his. "There is something I wish to give you before we leave. Will you come with me?"

"Yes, of course, Father," Tsogyal said.

It had been two days since the event with the Emperor. Tsogyal had not seen Emperor Trisong since that day. After her betrothal and that of her sisters, Tsogyal was escorted back to her rooms. Exhausted and overwhelmed, she allowed her attendants to undress her, then she fell fast asleep, only waking to eat.

On this morning, Sangmu awakened her to a request for an audience with her father. Tsogyal had her attendants dress her. She breathed in the cold clean morning air and felt her legs strong as she strode along with her attendants who escorted her to the room where her father waited.

Now, King Pelgyi and his daughter, the future Queen of Tibet, walked side by side through the courtyard of beautiful gardens. Pelgyi looked sideways at his daughter as he took in the scents of the flowers blooming in the morning sun. They proceeded onward to another courtyard. There, seeing her mother waiting, Tsogyal rushed to her and hugged her.

Getso, surprised by this show of affection, held her daughter for a moment then released her. "Your sisters have left the palace with their new husbands," Getso explained. "Your father and I are leaving now."

Looking through the opened gate of the courtyard, Tsogyal could see it led out of the palace. Tsogyal was surprised to see the familiar form of General Senge, mounted on a fine tall golden-colored horse with black legs and long black mane and tail. A line of warriors waited to escort their King and Queen back to Karchen.

Pelgyi walked up to his daughter. "My daughter, I hope one day you will understand that I never meant for you to be harmed. We are graced that all has turned out so well," Pelgyi said. Then he turned and signaled to Senge. In a moment two forms appeared in the gateway. It was Chudak leading Lungta. They proceeded to stand before Tsogyal. Smiling, Chudak proudly held Lungta's lead-rope out to her. Tsogyal stepped forward, taking the rope. She slid her hand along the soft black neck of her mare, as Lungta nickered. Wrapping her arms around Lungta's neck, she felt the flood of relief that indeed Lungta was well and safe. Nuzzling her face into the strong neck, she breathed in the familiar scent of her horse, the scent that was her childhood. Tears welled in her eyes. Lungta curved her head around Tsogyal and nibbled at her hip with soft lips. Tsogyal was overjoyed to have Lungta with her again, images of their racing across the land filled her mind. Yet alongside it, another realization came to her. Turning to Chudak, her heart aching. Tsogyal hesitantly held out Lungta's lead-rope, her arm feeling weak.

"Chudak, my friend, my life has changed. I know not what will be required of me now. I do know that my days of riding free like the wind are most likely over. Please, take my beloved horse and care for her, love her as you would your own. Ride her as I did, she is my gift to you and my gift to her as well. If she is with you and with Goba, she will be with her family, she will be safe and well cared for."

Shocked, Chudak looked at King Pelgyi, then back to Tsogyal. Protesting, he answered, "Noble Daughter, will this not be a great sadness for you?"

Tsogyal slowly shook her head. More secure in her decision, she explained, "Knowing that she is with you, I will forever have her in my heart and what she was to me. She and I are connected. She is part of my spirit. I do not want her left with strangers here in the Emperor's palace, should I not be at liberty to ride her."

She held the rope out to Chudak, her arm strong now with conviction. Looking into her eyes, Chudak saw she was no longer the young girl he once knew. Taking the rope, he declared, "Noble Daughter, I will give her the best of care."

Tsogyal released the rope into Chudak's hand, then realizing she had forgotten something, she added, "Chudak, when you ride her, let her have her head. Do not restrict her with the reins like you do with Goba. A light touch on her mouth, firm pressure with your leg, she is very responsive."

Listening carefully, Chudak nodded, "Yes, Noble Daughter, I will remember these things. You can be assured she will be well treated. But hear this, if you should ever want me to return her to you, I shall, gladly."

Tsogyal smiled, then wrapped her arms tightly around Lungta's neck, breathing in her scent as she whispered, "Lungta, you have been my splendid horse. Chudak will take good care of you, teach him well." Then she released the mare, Lungta's large soft eye gazed at her mistress. Wiping a tear from her cheek, Tsogyal nodded to Chudak, who reached out, stroking the mare's neck. Taking in a deep breath, she then turned away from Lungta as Chudak led her away.

To Pelgyi, Tsogyal said, "Father, I was very angry with you for letting Prince Zhonnu take me." Holding back a rush of tears welling in her eyes, she continued, "I understand now. I forgive you." She reached for her father's hand, Pelgyi took hers in both of his and held it in a strong embrace. Then Tsogyal reached out to take her mother's hand. Looking from her father to her mother, Tsogyal asked, "I will see you at my wedding?"

Getso squeezed Tsogyal's hand. "Yes, daughter, your father and I have to return to Karchen to make arraignments. We will then travel to Samye for the great feast of your wedding."

Releasing her parent's hands, Tsogyal turned to leave. She felt the life go out of her legs as she started across the courtyard away from her family. With a surge of determination, she willed herself to be strong, to walk with grace and show no fear. Her life was new, she knew not what the future would bring.

As he watched his daughter disappear though the doorway, a tear rolled down King Pelgyi's cheek.

PART TWO

21

TWO SPRINGS LATER

Padma felt the swish of air by his ear as the arrow thumped into the bag he had just untied from his pack horse.

Dropping it, Padma ran shouting, "Run! Take cover!" to his companions.

As he slid behind a boulder, he felt something slice by his right shoulder. His three companions fled, hiding behind what boulders they could find. Reaching for his shoulder, Padma found no cut or tear. Relieved, he pressed against the rock as more arrows showered down from the cliffs above. A shriek startled Padma. Looking around the boulder, he saw it was one of the horses screaming in pain as it bolted away, an arrow shaft protruding from its flank. The other horses followed it, all disappearing down the trail.

For a moment a heavy silence lay over them. Then the sounds of pinging and scraping rang out as deadly shafts of wood, sending sharp metal points, showered around the boulders the men hid behind.

"Demons," cursed Gyaltso. "Who are they, robbers?" he called to Padma.

"I think not," Padma answered.

"Then who are they, what do they want?" Zongpa yelled from his hiding place behind a grouping of rocks. Jetsun crouched next to him.

"My corpse," Padma called back.

Jetsun and Zongpa looked at each other incredulously.

Padma continued, "They are Bon warriors sent by the ministers, no doubt. I can only guess my arrival was not kept a secret."

Gyaltso growled, "Well, a fine fix we are in. My bow is on my horse, now long gone. I only have a sword, a lot of good that will do us now."

Jetsun called, "Master, perhaps some magic?"

Padma glanced up at the cliff as he chuckled wryly. With a sigh, he called back, "I will think of something." Yet he scowled, knowing he was too fatigued with travel and that, with the attack fully upon them, it was too late to conjure anything.

A loud thump drew their attention. A warrior from above lay at the bottom of the cliff, an arrow in his chest. A scream sounded from high on the ridge. Padma carefully looked around the boulder to see up on the ridge where the scream had come from. There a warrior's body lay slumped over a rock he had been shooting from. Blood trickled over the rock face.

A thundering sound filled the canyon as a group of warriors came riding into the clearing leading the runaway horses. Padma's companions shivered in fear.

Gyaltso jumped up, his sword raised. "Here, you swine, I will cut you all to pieces," he swore, as he charged out, exposing himself. Padma jumped up and ran out to catch up to him.

"No!" Padma yelled. "It is me you want. Take me."

The warriors fought to hold their mounts still as they looked down at the men running toward them. The lead man looked to the man beside him, perplexed. Before they made a decision to defend themselves from Gyaltso, another warrior rode in and pushed to the front.

"Stop," the warrior ordered Gyaltso and Padma, his horse jigging side to side. "Master Padma, I am Captain Jigme. We are sent by the Emperor Trisong Detsen to escort you to Samye."

Gyaltso stopped, the words sinking in, he lowered his sword.

Padma caught up to him. Looking at each other in amazement at the arrival of these warriors to their aid, Gyaltso chuckled. "Some magic!"

Padma roared with laughter. "Indeed!"

Looking up at the cliff-tops the arrows had flown from, Padma said to Jigme, "We are thankful you arrived just now. Are they all dead or run away?"

Jigme dismounted. Still holding his recurve bow, his quiver full of arrows swinging from his belt, he strode over to Padma and Gyaltso. With a slight bow, he declared, "The Emperor was told by an informant that the ministers had learned of your planned arrival. This would have been the place I would have ambushed you. So, we waited for them. We got three of them. We saw several more running away." With a quizzical look, he inquired, "What is this about magic?"

Padma reached for Jigme's bow. Jigme held it up and allowed Padma to take it.

Holding it up, Padma pulled back on the string. Using all of his strength, the sinew of the string bit into his fingers. The bow creaked as he pulled. The black smooth layer of horn pressed into his hand, holding the bow out straight. His muscles began to tremble. Padma was amazed at how hard it was just to move it only a few inches. At last he could pull no further, he slowly eased the string back to its resting place.

Holding the bow out to Jigme, Padma answered, "This magic! Your powerful bow and strong arm."

Jigme smiled. "Yes, it is a fine weapon," he said as he held his hand out to retrieve it from the Tantric master.

Turning, Padma called to Jetsun and Zongpa, "Come out, all is safe."

Turning back to Jigme, Padma said, "I would like to learn to use this weapon."

Not hiding his surprise, Jigme nodded. "It is a good thing to know. It takes many springs of practice to build strength."

Gesturing, Jigme suggested. "Let us sit and have tea. That was why you had stopped here, is it not?" Jigme said. Looking at Gyaltso, he added, "In the best ambush spot?"

His attention was drawn by the sound of the wind as it began howling across the ridge top. He looked up to the sky. Tendrils of clouds appeared, snaking across the high ridge. A cold wind swept through the canyon. Jigme pulled his fur hat down, covering his ears. Noticing Padma was doing the same with his hat, he considered how this man was not at all what he had expected. He liked him and had not thought he would. Different from other Buddhists from India, this man was brave and strong.

Looking at Padma, Jigme said, "It will snow soon, but there is time for tea. I would be pleased to hear of your trek over the pass from Nepal. After tea, we will proceed to Samye."

Drum, boom, boom, boom. Drum, boom, boom, boom; drum beats reverberated in the courtyard. Then came the crash of the cymbals, reverberating through the throng in attendance. Sixteen dancers whirled around in a circle before the crowd. Their long sleeves, extending beyond their hands like unworldly appendages, twisted and flew as they spun and jumped. They circled and leapt into the air, whirlwinds of colorful legs spinning into the air and twisting down. Their movements animated the oversized colorful masks they wore. Large-eyed, grim faces with sharp fangs of demons. And also of those of powerful Gods. As they spun and leapt, they sang and uttered nonhuman sounds, creating a strangely beautiful and other worldly ambiance.

Emperor Trisong looked at his Queen sitting next to him, admiring her beauty; now sixteen springs old, she was radiant. He placed his hand over hers. Tsogyal did not respond, transfixed by the spectacle before her. Then the last beat of the drum. All fell silent, the dancers stopped, frozen in gesture. All cheered as the performers bowed and walked off the courtyard stage. Tsogyal looked down at her hand covered by her husband's gentle firm grasp. Realizing she had been oblivious to all around her during the dancer's performance, she smiled at Trisong. The love she felt for him filled her with joy. From the time of their marriage two springs he had been a kind husband.

When Emperor Trisong had married Tsogyal, he had dressed

her in the finest silks and bedecked her with stunning jewels of gold, turquoise, silver and coral. Then, parading the new Queen, riding on a fine white Ferghana mare, before the cheering Tibetan people, they traveled to Samye Monastery. There the Emperor feasted and celebrated their marriage for three moons. During this great feast and with great care and gentleness, Trisong introduced his young Queen to the pleasures of love-making.

Two moons into the great marriage feast of Trisong and Tsogyal a Turkish trader of horses arrived. Tsogyal held her face serene as Abaka entered the great hall to bring the news to the Emperor of his return with the Emperor's new horses, which he had stabled in the palace. Introduced to the new Queen of Tibet, Abaka held back his shock, bowing low to the very girl he was on his way to retrieve from a cave and take to Nepal.

Then, days later, on a cold clear morning, Tsogyal was out for a walk through the garden courtyard. To her delight, she came across Abaka.

"My Queen." Abaka bowed deeply.

"My friend," Tsogyal greeted Abaka with a smile. The scent of horses exuded from his clothes, giving Tsogyal a feeling of warmth toward this man. Tsogyal continued, "I am sure you have many questions."

Abaka smiled. "I have met your father, King Pelgyi, a fine man. We shared a meal and much drink. He told me the entire story." With a sheepish grin, he glanced around, making sure they were not being overheard, and whispered, "Of what he knew, that is. Therefore, Your Highness, all of my questions are answered." With a grand sweeping gesture of his arm and a low bow, Abaka declared, "Please be assured, I remain your humble servant."

Tsogyal laughed. "Very well. I accept your allegiance with much gratitude."

New to Samye, during the marriage feasting, Tsogyal wandered around the Monastery finding translators from India, Nepal and China translating texts from the teachings of Sakyamuni Buddha. She wandered into rooms where astrologers studied. She stood and watched Bon scribes copy ancient Bon texts in turquoise ink.

Learning of her presence in the rooms and halls of the monastery, Emperor Trisong had appointed teachers to instruct her in writing and grammar, knowledge of the five arts and sciences, as well as secular and religious accomplishments.

To Trisong's delight, they would sit and discuss the subjects she was learning. She was learning very quickly, to the amazement of all. Tsogyal was delighted with the obvious love of the dharma Trisong displayed. He wanted the Buddha dharma to be the religion of all the people of Tibet. Tsogyal declared her commitment to help her Emperor husband in this.

Now, two wonderful springs having passed, they enjoyed the spectacle of dancers at Samye. Relaxing, Tsogyal sat back as servants arrived, setting dishes of food before her and her husband. "Did you find the dancing enjoyable, my Queen?" Trisong inquired.

"I had never seen anything like it before our wedding two springs ago. Every time I see these dancers it is like being transported to another realm. My father had dancers come and entertain us; my mother and sisters. They were from India and from Persia," Tsogyal explained. "But this is so different. I have never thought to ask you about these dancers and what this dance means."

Bringing Tsogyal's hand to his lips, Trisong kissed it and set it gently down. Sitting back, Trisong brought a cup of tea to his lips, the aroma filled him with pleasure. He took a sip of tea, the warmth soothed him, as did the rich flavor. Placing the silver cup down, Trisong smiled as he remembered what his father told him about these dances.

Then he explained, "My three-times great-grandmother was the Princess Wencheng of the Tang court. She brought the costumes, music, and dances of the Han people to Tibet. My three-times great-grandfather, Songtsen Gampo, greatly admired all of these things. So he had sixteen of our traditional dancers trained in the new art form. He combined the Han-style and our own folk music and dances to entertain the Princess. Since then these dances have evolved, becoming distinct from the Han style. Now they are our own tradition."

"But the masks look like Bon Gods and deities. Why not those of our dharma?" Tsogyal inquired.

Trisong leaned close so they would not be overheard. "We must pacify the Bon ministers, it keeps them from stirring trouble."

Tsogyal stared down at her food. "When will our dharma be the dharma practiced by everyone in Tibet?"

"It takes time and it takes skillful means," Emperor Trisong replied. "You and I understand and love the dharma. We must make it so everyone can have access to the teachings."

Trisong sat silent for a moment, then continued, "Your instructors have told me of your swift understanding, not only the sciences, but the teachings of Lord Buddha."

Tsogyal looked at him and nodded. "I love the teachings. They make sense. I love learning new things."

As the thought just occurred to him, Trisong declared, "I think you, my Queen, should be steward of the Buddha dharma of Tibet." He sat back, mulling this idea. Then, decision made, he stood and called out over the din of conversation of all assembled in the courtyard, "Silence."

A hush fell over the people as they looked at their Emperor in anticipation.

With a sweeping gestured toward Tsogyal, he called out, so as to be heard by everyone, "Hear me now. I name the Queen Tsogyal, from this day forward, the custodian of the Buddha dharma in Tibet. Your Queen has shown great adeptness in her understanding of these teachings and she has great love of the dharma and of the Tibetan people."

Those in the courtyard sat stunned, not knowing what to do. The Bon Ministers Lugung Tsenpo and Takra Lutsen looked at each other in disbelief from across the space of the yard. Five Buddhist translators in attendance called out a cheer. Then Rab-ten stood and cheered. The crowd, following their example, all cheered as well.

Trisong sat, smiling at Tsogyal who looked around at the cheering crowd, amazed at her husband's decree. Leaning over to him so he could hear her over the roar, she said, "Husband, I shall not disappoint."

Making their way to meet at the courtyard doorway, Ministers Tsenpo and Lutsen ducked out and walked quickly side by side away from the din. Finding a quiet place, they turned to each other.

Tsenpo hissed, "The Emperor makes the Queen steward of Buddha dharma?"

Lutsen looked around, making sure they were alone. Waving his hand in dismissal, he said in a low voice, "Do not be concerned. It means nothing. That Indian vagabond Padma is by now dead. The Emperor will fall back. The Queen can dally in her study room as long as she wishes, it means little."

22

"My Queen?" Rab-ten said as she bowed before Tsogyal, who was sitting at a low table writing with great care; the fine paintbrush sliding over the parchment.

Looking up, Tsogyal smiled. "How many times must I ask you not to bow to me? We are spiritual sisters."

Sheepishly, Rab-ten whispered, "I do not want others to become jealous that I have a special relationship with the Queen."

Tsogyal whispered in reply, "I think by now everyone knows of our friendship. However, you are probably correct, it would be better to be discreet."

"You would like an audience with me, Healer Rab-ten?" Tsogyal said, in a raised voice.

"The Emperor requests you to come to the shrine," Rab-ten reported.

Tsogyal looked up at Rab-ten. "Now?" she asked.

Nodding, Rab-ten said, "Yes, it is his request."

Setting her paintbrush down, Tsogyal looked longingly at her work, not wanting to leave it. "Very well," she sighed.

General Klu-pal listened attentively to the Emperor's instructions as they sat on cushions leaning over the low table studying at the map before them.

"I wish you to ride into Bodh Gaya." Trisong placed his finger on the map. "This is where the Buddha Sakyamuni sat under the bodi tree and awakened. You shall obtain relics from this place and return with them for our new shrine, now under construction," Trisong directed.

Klu-pal looked at the map painted on a parchment scroll. Pointing, he said, "Here, in the Northern part of India, is the realm of King Dharmapala. I do not know how much of a fight he may give us." Looking at Trisong, he added, "It matters not, we will crush him if he does not submit."

Trisong nodded his approval as he rolled up the map and handed it to Klu-pal. Standing, he inquired, "How long will you need to assemble the force you require and take command?"

Taking the map, Klu-pal rose from the cushion and began pacing, absently, he tapping the rolled map lightly against his leg, as he considered his answer.

Turning to Trisong, he said, "It has been a moon since our return from the last campaign. The men are bored, eager for a new campaign. I will take the troops I have with me here and ride to the palace. From there, I will arrange all and send a messenger with my report and time of departure."

"Very well," Trisong said, pleased. "Include a list of all the provisions you will be taking from the palace stores in your report."

Clapping the General on the shoulder, Trisong escorted him to the door. "There are important relics there. They will be a great boon to our new shrine, great indeed!" Trisong said with exuberance.

Klu-pal smiled, then as it occurred to him, he asked, "Are the builders still having trouble with the southern walls under construction?"

Trisong's smile turned to a frown. "Yes, they are. There are demons and demigods, those against the Buddha dharma, that come in the night and shift the ground so the walls built during the day fall to rubble."

Klu-pal nodded sympathetically. "How can you fight such an enemy?"

Looking in the direction of the monastery under construction, Trisong said, "I have sent for a powerful master. He will deal with the trouble."

Klu-pal's face went hard. "Will the price not be too high?"

Trisong looked at Klu-pal quizzically, then understanding he assured. "No, no, he is a good man, not a sorcerer."

"Ah," Klupal said, relief softening his features, "very good." Then with a bow, he said, "With your permission I will take my leave."

Trisong's smile returned. "To your success, General."

Walking swiftly with Rab-ten in tow on route to the shrine where Trisong had summoned her to meet him, Tsogyal came out into one of the courtyards and looked up into the sky that opened up above them. White clouds as big as mountains floated slowly by in the deep blue sky. Suddenly Tsogyal stopped, causing Rab-ten to move quickly to her side so as not to collide into her, and stood gazing into the sky. Slowly, an expression of triumph spread over her face as she exclaimed, "There, do you see, Rab-ten? The clouds do not change the sky!" She spun as she looked up in exuberance.

Perplexed, Rab-ten looked up, then looked at Tsogyal. "Well, yes, they do, my Queen, they make it dark and bring sleet and snow."

Turning to Rab-ten, Tsogyal pointed up, saying, "Yes, they do affect the sky, but the sky remains the sky no matter. It is the same as the mind. Thoughts are a part of the mind, yet they do not disturb the nature of the mind. The clouds do not disturb the nature of the sky." Tsogyal looked at Rab-ten expectantly. "Do you see?"

Tapping her finger against her chin, her forehead crunched in thought, Rab-ten nodded hesitantly. "I think I understand." Then exasperated, she admitted, "No, I do not really understand. I think I should meditate more, then I will understand."

Tsogyal grinned at her friend. "Yes, you should!" She laughed, taking Rab-ten's hand in hers they continued on their way.

As Tsogyal and Rab-ten hurried along, they could hear the thudding of many footsteps and the ting of metal on metal become louder and louder. Turning the corner around a building, the two women stopped suddenly, finding themselves facing a wall of men in armor marching toward them.

Seeing the Queen and her escort, General Klu-pal held his hand up, calling a halt.

"Make way for the Queen," he called out.

The troops of leather-and-metal-clad warriors stopped, then parted like a chasm, bowing as they made a path for Tsogyal and Rab-ten to pass through.

General Klu-pal bowed as he addressed Tsogyal. "My Queen," he said. Then he straightened, standing tall.

Tsogyal stopped before the General who towered above her. "Are you off to battle, General?" she inquired.

Klu-pal smiled down at Tsogyal. He liked this Queen, she had spunk and feared no one. "Indeed, my Queen. We go for relics to make Samye a great monastery."

"It is my wish that you harm as few as possible, General," Tsogyal said in a firm voice.

Klu-pal considered. "When the force is large, the prey submit quickly and few are harmed. Our force is large, strong and well equipped. I think we will have no trouble with the North India King."

"Very well. Good day, General," Tsogyal said, with a nod of approval.

Before proceeding through the warriors, Tsogyal looked at the men standing before her and said loudly so all could hear, "You are all fine warriors. You are in my thoughts. Please return to us safely."

Nodding to Rab-ten, they proceeded on, gracefully walking through the passageway of men, leaving them behind.

Entering the great shrine, her eyes adjusting to the darkness illuminated by the flickering of many butter lamps, Tsogyal saw Trisong sitting on a cushion. To her amazement, he was sitting lower than another man seated before him on cushions piled higher. Trisong rose and held his hand out to Tsogyal. Rab-ten bowed and moved to the back of the room in deference. There she stood silently watching the Emperor introduce Tsogyal to this stranger.

Rab-ten heard the words: "My Queen, this is the great Tantric Master and my Guru, Padma."

A movement in the back of the room, near where she stood, caught her attention. She felt him before she saw her husband, Jigme, silently move to her side. He did not look at her but kept his gaze on the Emperor.

"My Guru, Padma," Trisong said as he bowed slightly, "I present to you my Queen, Tsogyal."

Tsogyal stepped forward and, following her husband's example, bowed to the Indian master.

Padma gestured. "Please, sit. Let us become acquainted. I understand Queen Tsogyal you are the steward of the Buddha dharma in Tibet. With whom have you studied?"

Tsogyal sat still and straight on her cushion as she answered, "My mother, Queen Getso of Karchen, brought teachers of the Buddha dharma from China and Nepal, who would give instruction of translated texts for myself and my sisters. I have received teachings with my family from the Abbot Santaraksita when he visited my father. Here in Samye, I receive instruction from the Abbot Santaraksita, when he has time, as well as other translators from India and Nepal. Recently I have had some instruction from a Chan Master from China. And lastly, I have received instruction in meditation by a Goddess who visited me while I was hiding in a cave in Onphu, before I was brought to my husband, the Emperor. I practice her instruction everyday and have not wavered in it."

As Tsogyal recited her experience to the man sitting before her, she was overcome with feelings of great attraction to him. She could feel his power fill the room. Her attraction to him was more than the fact that he was handsome and well-formed to her eye. Lean and muscular, like a panther, he sat relaxed, yet his body alert. When she finished, Padma looked interested.

Tilting his head in amusement, he asked, " A Goddess? What Goddess visited you?"

Tsogyal answered unhesitatingly. "The Goddess Sarasvati."

Trisong sat looking incredulously at his wife. "You never have told me of this. How do you know it was Sarasvati? Did she tell you her name?"

Turning to look at her husband, Tsogyal answered. "My sister Dechen had painted her form years ago. I have never forgotten her, it was the same Goddess."

"Did she visit you when you were asleep at night or was it during the day? What did she teach you?" Padma asked, with a more serious expression.

"I was cold, I was afraid. I could not sleep, the wolves howled at night. She came from the daytime sky at the doorway of the cave where I had fallen asleep in the sun. She came and entered my cave. She explained the basic technique of following the breath and watching thoughts arise and fall. When she left me, I was no longer afraid. I followed her instructions."

The room fell silent. Tsogyal looked up at Padma quizzically, "Who are you?" she inquired.

Padma smiled, looked into Tsogyal's eyes as he answered, his voice reverberating in the room. "I am the Buddha who is Lotus-Born, possessing the precepts of highest insight. Skilled in the fundamental Teachings of Sutra and Tantra, I elucidate the way of the Buddha without confusion. I am the dharma which is Lotus-Born, possessing the precepts of progressive practice. Though outwardly I look as a common man dressed in simple garb, meditating in caves as a simple yogi; inwardly I am the highest of Vajrayana yogins. My knowledge is higher than the heavens."

Stunned by his reply, Tsogyal, overcome by emotion that she could not hold back nor explain, slid off her cushion and knelt before Padma. Bowing her head, she entreated, "Great Master Padma, if it is true you are a Buddha, I must tell you I love the Buddha dharma. It has been my aspiration from my earliest springs of age to find a master who will guide me in practice of the true dharma. Please consider my plea to you now. Will you accept me as your student, as you have accepted my husband?"

Looking into his eyes, Tsogyal felt kindness and strength. Then all the room disappeared from her sight, replaced by an image before her eyes. It was a disk, red and blue and gold with all the forms of her ego. She could not explain what she was seeing, yet it was revealed as a knowing in her mind. In another moment the image was gone, replaced by the Master still looking into her eyes.

Tsogyal gasped. "I just saw a mandala of my ego!"

Trisong looked astonished. "A vision? You just now had a vision? How do you know that was what the vision was?"

Tsogyal shook her head slowly from side to side, thinking, trying to bring the image back. Helplessly, she looked at Padma. "I do not know how I know. But I do know that is what I just saw before my eyes. It filled the room."

Padma nodded slowly. "It is so. That is what you saw. To answer your request, I will not accept you as a student now. I am sure one day you will be more than a student. Until then, I request you continue in your practice."

23

A million stars shone as bright lanterns in the crystal black sky above Samye. Master Padma recited a mantra in a steady cadence. With each magical word, he danced a small circle, lifting each felt-booted foot high, then placing it upon the ground, tracing a geometric pattern in the dusty earth before the rubble that was to be the south wall. Masons, once again, had toiled to build this wall and, once again, it had fallen to rubble, two days before.

Padma leapt and spun, his long silk robes twirling as he drew a design with his feet into the top layer of soft dirt covering the hard ground. As he chanted and stomped, he swung his arm, tracing a pattern in the air with his magical dagger held firmly in his fist.

This dagger was very powerful. Padma had it made to his own design for his work alone. The blade was not one blade but three together, cast of strong bronze, symbolizing the cutting through and destroying of the three root poisons of ignorance, greed and hatred. The three blades, making a triangular shape, also represented the element of fire. Fire was a necessary element used for wrathful activity in Padma's work in subjugating demonic forces. For demonic forces are strong, therefore only a wrathful force in turn can overpower and subjugate them. To this triple blade, Padma had the metal craftsman attach a handle made of solid gold, symbolizing the powerful light of the sun, made into a casting of a snow lion and a dragon twisted together. Their claws and teeth bared, pressed into his hand now, raised high in the cold night air.

In his other hand, he held his damaru, double-headed drum, which he had made by his own hands. He had found the necessary parts for the drum by searching in villages for news of children having recently died. In one of the villages, Padma recovered the decayed bodies of a boy of sixteen and a girl of twelve springs old in the charnel ground. Because they were at the onset of puberty their remains were very powerful. He was also most pleased to find these two children because one had been devoured by a panther, the other by the venom of a snake bite, adding to the power of their skulls for his special work. Taking the skulls from the remains, Padma then cleaned and cut the craniums, making perfect clean bone bowls. These he attached together, crown to crown, by drilling two small holes into each, then tying them together with sinew. Then Padma took the attached craniums to a silver smith, who worked a silver band between the crown junction of the drum, thus holding the two skull bowls more firmly together. Into the silver band were inlayed turquoise, lapis lazuli and coral and two small rings were attached to either side.

Then Padma obtained the raw hides of two monkeys, once swinging and scurrying in the trees of the jungles of Nepal, killed for their meat. After soaking the skins and removing the hair, Padma cut them to size, then punched sixteen holes into each with a small thorn. Then he stretched them over each of the bony bowls. Cutting off a lock of his own long hair, he tied the drumheads fast. As they dried, the rawhide shrank over the bowls with a tight grip. Next, he needed two strikers to make sound from the two drumheads. Searching the shores of a lake, Padma found the skeleton of a water bird. Taking the bones of its feet only, he wrapped them into two pieces of cloth, then he soaked the small bundles in hot wax. Once cooled, these made two hard balls. He attached each of these balls to a string of silk, tying each one to the two small rings on either side of the drum's silver band.

To this double-headed drum he fastened a handle of elephant ivory. Carved deeply into the smooth whiteness of the handle were the Sanskrit letters of Padma's own magical mantra.

Whirling side to side, back and forth, the balls struck from drumhead to drumhead, with the twist of his wrist.

Clack, droom, clack, droom, clack, droom, now the sound split the cold silence of the darkest hours before dawn.

"Come to face the one greater than you! Oh, demon that destroys the walls of this great Samye. Come, show yourself to me," Padma called out as he danced the pattern in the earth.

Clack, droom, clack, droom, clack, droom, the sound reverberated with his call.

Under Padma's dancing feet the ground began to tremble. Loose stones of the broken wall clattered as they fell and rolled.

Padma kept dancing while he looked to the wall. As the ground still shook, Padma was amazed as a mist rose out of the ground, rising high and wide, carrying with it the stench of rotting corpses.

Clack, droom, clack, droom. "Come, show your self. I have no fear of you," Padma growled, as the mist rose above him, looming. Then it became more and more solid. Wisps turned to hair, surrounding two heads forming on a wide neck. Both faces glared down at the small dancing figure below it, its eyes bulging as it snarled through long bared teeth as long and sharp as lion's fangs, dripping with blood.

Clack, droom, clack, droom, clack, droom.

Its shoulders grew wide as the mist expanded, its muscles bulged. Its skin was rippled over the huge arms. In its right hand it grasped the mass of hair of a dangling bloody severed head, in its left a curved sword, blood dripping. Skins of humans, the hands and feet still attached, were draped over its body, and tied around its loins. Its legs, forming out of the rising mist looming high above Padma's shrinking form, were as huge as ancient Banyan tree trunks. Its feet, as large as the ships that sailed on the Bengal seas, stomped, shaking the earth. More stones of the remaining wall shook loose, causing the entire wall to fall to rubble.

A voice like rolling thunder, spoke. "Who are you, little man, to call to me? I will crush you, you insolent bug."

The wave of stench of rotten corpses and feces that emanated from the beast became overpowering, causing Padma to choke. Steeling himself, he did not miss a step as he danced his geometric pattern. Clack, droom, clack, droom, clack, droom, his drum sounded with each twist of his wrist, his dagger waved with the swinging of his arm.

Drawing in a breath of the putrid air, Padma stopped dancing and stepped aside, revealing the geometric image he had drawn into the earth with his dance. Pointing down at the geometric pattern, he called out to the beast looming above him, "Look at this, you figment of imagination, you conglomerate of superstition and ignorant thoughts. You are nothing. You are not even as substantial as mist in the night."

Furious, the demon roared at the sky, reaching up with its gnarled hand to grasp a star to throw at Padma. When the beast looked down at Padma, it saw the glowing geometric shape that Padma had danced into the earth. Padma saw the reflection of the mandala he had drawn in the demon's four eyes. Stunned by the sight of the mandala, the beast froze, its heads tilted, trying to comprehend the image. Seizing the moment, Padma ran up to the demon and sank his dagger deep into its toe. Roaring in incredulity, the demon tried to pick his foot up to crush Padma. To the demon's amazement, the Phurba dagger held its toe fast to the ground; it could not move. Then Padma, using his magical ability, caused the rubble of stones from the destroyed wall to levitate and multiply, building a wall around and around the demon. Higher and higher the wall built itself, until the demon was encased in a prison made of the stones of the destruction it had wrought. Only its toe remained exposed, the dagger holding it fast. High above Padma, at the top of the prison wall, there was a small window only large enough for the demon to see out with one eye. Roaring and screeching, the demon struggled inside its prison.

Padma danced and called to the demon. "Demon, insubstantial and now impotent, you will be trapped forever in this stone prison unless you submit to me."

The walls shook with the loud booming of the demon's body struggling inside against the rock, its growls and curses were thunder in the night. Padma winced at the screech of claws, scratching over stone. Yet, try as it may, the walls held fast, they were too strong for the struggling clawing beast.

Padma danced his pattern as he waited for the demon to realize it could not escape.

Clack, droom, clack, droom, clack, droom, Padma's drum cut through the cold night as the struggling of the demon slowed, then finally, ceased.

The demon whimpered and moaned, "You are a great vidya-dhara. I cannot free myself. What do you want? What must I do for you to set me free?"

Padma stopped his dance and looked up to the window. He called out in answer, "Demon, look again at the form I have created in the earth from my dance."

Padma could see in the small window of the prison wall, the demon's eye swivel to look down at Padma. The eye widened as he saw Padma reach down with his arms wide, wrapping them around the geometric pattern he had danced into the earth. Raising it up, it became a three dimensional mandala made of light. It was in fact the mandala of Samye monastery, depicting the main temple in the middle as Mount Meru. The other buildings, making up the remainder of the mandala's forms were shown as the continents and sub-continents of the universe.

Holding the mandala up high so the demon's eye could see it, Padma called up to the demon, declaring, "You will vow to protect this treasure. Samye is now yours to protect. You will help to build it and keep all destructive forces away. You will also hold in your hands the precious Buddha and Tantric dharma to protect. Will you vow to be the protector of these treasures forever?"

The demon's voice was clear through the thick walls. It rang out in the shimmering cold of the darkness before the grey of dawn that would soon arrive. "You have my vow and my allegiance. Samye will forever be protected by me. The Buddha and Tantric dharma will also be forever under my protection," the demon assured.

Satisfied, Padma released the mandala and watched as it rose higher and higher. Reaching the window, it stopped for a moment, spinning slowly around and around, shimmering and sparkling. Then it floated into the small window and dissolved into the demon's eye.

Moments later a ray of white light shot out of the window above piecing the darkness. Satisfied by this sign, Padma strode to the demon's exposed toe, wrapped both hands around the hilt of his dagger and pulled hard, freeing the demon. The stones of the prison walls loosened and tumbled away, down to the earth. Padma looked up at the transformed demon. A strong handsome face with long flowing mustache, looked down at him. Mandalas of rainbow colors spun in his eyes under heavy eyebrows. Gone were the fangs, in their place now rows of straight white teeth, like conch shells. Long black silky hair spilled over the huge muscular shoulders. Gone too, were the skins of humans hanging from him, now robes of beautifully-colored silks adorned his form. He held a recurve bow in one hand, a quiver of golden arrows hung from his side. In his other hand, he held a beautiful shimmering sword. In his wide sash of woven gold and silk threads of light, was a long knife in a jeweled scabbard. His once bare and ugly feet wore now covered in luxurious felt boots embroidered with gold threads in the forms of clouds. Emanating from his form was the scent of flowers and sandalwood.

The subjugated demon spoke, his voice now deep and soothing, "I am grateful to be given these great treasures to protect. Those faithful to the dharma and to Samye need no longer have fear of me." Then raising his sword in threat, he added, "Yet those who threaten my treasures, of Samye and the Buddha and Tantric dharma will be cut down by me."

Padma said, "I name you, Pehar Gyalpo, the worldly protector of Samye and all of Tibet. I make you the supreme protector. All demons I bring to subjugation shall be under your command to protect Tibet and the dharma."

Pehar Gyalpo bowed, as he answered, "It will be so."

Then the protector faded to mist and slid back into the earth. Padma felt a gentle warm breeze caress his face, then the cold of the night returned, his body shivered with the chill.

Exhausted, Padma walked over to his sheepskin robe that he had placed on the ground before he began his dance. Lifting his fur hat that lay atop the robe, he pulled it tiredly on his head, then wrapped the warm robe around his shoulders. Sinking exhausted onto the ground, he closed his eyes, crossed his legs and rested his mind in the stillness of the night before dawn.

Gradually, the sky turned lighter and lighter. Feeling the warmth of the sun's first rays on his face and seeing the brightness through his eyelids, he roused himself. The smoke of the cooking fires from Samye's cook house and the aroma of barley and tea on the morning breeze attracted his attention. Opening his eyes he rose stiffly to his feet. Realizing how hungry he was, he made his way to find his breakfast.

Tea would be very nice, he thought, *yes, a nice cup of tea. I wonder if they have honey?*

24

"Honey on yogurt? Yuk!" Tsogyal exclaimed. The turquoise and coral beads braided in her hair glistened in the morning sun as she shook her head, recoiling in disgust.

"You should at least try it," Padma encouraged, as he held out the bowl of amber honey.

"It is really very good," Rab-ten assured, as she wiped a bit of honey from her lower lip.

Skeptically, Tsogyal held her bowl out to Padma as he leaned forward dribbling honey over the top of the remaining yogurt in her bowl.

"Stop, that is enough," she ordered, holding her hand up. Her gold rings sparkled as they caught the sunlight.

His eyes crinkled at the corners in mirth, Padma removed the stick, thick amber glistening from its carved form, and returned it to the honey bowl.

Taking a tiny bit of the white yogurt with the amber sweetness dribbled on top onto her tongue, Tsogyal grimaced, waiting for the taste to confirm her preconception. Gradually her face changed as the flavors saturated her senses. She took more onto her tongue, letting it melt in her mouth. Her eyes widened. "Mmm, that is very good," she exclaimed.

At this, Padma burst into a roar of laughter, stamping his felt boot on the ground and slapping his knee. Rab-ten bent over, giggling, causing her bowl to slip from her hands. Tsogyal watched with stunned awe as Rab-ten, grasped at the miscreant bowl as it danced precariously on the tips of her fingers then took flight. Miraculously she caught the bowl in midair, keeping the contents from spilling into her woven chuba apron of reds and blues, that she wore on front of her blue wool robe. At this, Padma laughed even harder, his eyes shut tight as he wiped at the tears rolling down his cheeks into his mustache. Tsogyal, beset by hilarity, set her bowl next to her on the stone bench and wrapped her arms around her waist as she bent over, howling. Her silk robes of green and gold, with a gold silk belt at her waist, glistened in the morning sun as she heaved in mirth. Rab-ten, her bowl now held firmly in her lap, giggled, her eyes closed, shaking her head back and forth. Her long black plait hanging down her back swayed, the colorful ribbons that were braided-in danced in the brightening sunlight.

"You see? I said you would like it," Padma gasped. "You should trust me more." Then pointing to Rab-ten, he added, "and you should trust your friend, Rab-ten, who has shown us the breadth of her many skills."

Trying to settle herself, Tsogyal gulped, "Yes, you are correct, Master Padma." Not able to hold back her mirth, her laughter took over again as she looked at Rab-ten. "That was marvelous!" she exclaimed.

Struggling for composure, Tsogyal picked up her bowl and looked down at the yogurt remaining in it. Holding it out to Padma, she asked, "Is there more honey?"

It had been seven days since Padma's subjugation of the demon. As the trio sat in Samye's courtyard in the morning sun, they watched the workmen gathering to begin the day's work on the once-troubled part of the monastery. To everyone's surprise, the morning after Padma's confrontation with the demon, the wall was standing, built higher than the day before. Now the work went quickly. The mornings that follow-ed a day's work, once met with rubble and ruin, now stood as left the night before, ready for continuation. The men were no longer afraid and worked contentedly, building to the plans drawn and overseen by the Abbot Santaraksita.

"You are feeling well today, Master?" Tsogyal inquired.

"Yes, my Queen," Padma confirmed as he stretched, luxuriating in the warmth of the sun on his black felt wool robes. He noticed Ministers Tsenpo and Lutsen walking at the far end of the courtyard, glaring at him, as they made their way to their destination. As Padma watched them, he felt their fear and hatred wash over him.

"I was concerned when you slept for three straight days," Tsogyal continued.

Turning his attention to Queen Tsogyal, Padma smiled, "Yes, it takes much energy to subdue a demon as was that one. However, I am rested now and fine."

"Can I get you more tea, Master?" Rab-ten offered.

Holding his hand up, Padma answered, "No, I am content."

With a perplexed look on her face, Rab-ten asked, "Master Padma, I have a question."

Turning his attention to Rab-ten, Padma nodded for her to proceed.

"My father told me demons are not real," Rab-ten began, "yet, many people believe in them. I hear terrible stories about demons. These stories frighten me. My father said these are just people's superstitions. He had many talks of this, with his teacher of medicine from Byzantium. Yet the stones of the wall were in rubble the next day here, how can this be explained? Did some people come in the night and destroy the wall and call it demon's work? Emperor Trisong had men guard the walls, they would run back in fear saying the ground shook and they saw demons. You confronted one seven days ago. I do not know what to think anymore. Are my father and his teacher wrong?" Rab-ten asked, looking intently at Padma.

Listening with interest in Rab-ten's question, Tsogyal added her own inquiry, "And, why did the demon only cause destruction to that one place being built?"

"The demon was created by beliefs," Padma explained.

Tilting her head quizzically, Rab-ten looked at Tsogyal, then at Padma, not understanding.

Padma went on, "Perhaps this wall was first built by a mason who did a poor job. That same night the ground shook, causing it to fall to rubble."

Looking up and seeing the ministers were now gone, Padma continued, "Or, perhaps the wall was vandalized and a story begun about demons being the cause. Whatever the original cause, the thought arose or was placed in all who heard of it as the cause being a demon. These thoughts, all concentrated on that spot, grew very strong and determined, filled with passion and emotion. This was the birth of the demon."

Beginning to understand, Rab-ten ventured, "You mean the demon was created by the people here?"

"By the concentrated thoughts and beliefs of people here and any who had heard of it and also believed in it, thus sending their thoughts to breath life into it," Padma corrected.

"So the demon was not real," Rab-ten confirmed for herself.

"The demon was very real," Padma corrected. "It was created, fed and lived. Once it was created and its energy directed, by the fears of those that created it, it enacted exactly that which the creators feared the most. I had to re-direct its energy to positive actions. Now it is an ally of Samye instead of a destructive force," Padma explained.

Tsogyal nodded, "So, as long as there is hope and fear, people will create demons?"

"Yes, evil is created and fed by negative thoughts and beliefs. By attachment to strong negative desires and fueled by strong emotions feeding these desires. By not understanding the true nature of the mind. By not taking to heart the reality of the impermanence of all things. Understanding that the content of thoughts are not substantial, they are simply the activity of the mind. That emotions created by thoughts are simply energy. Negativity must be redirected to positivity or demonic forces will seize upon it," Padma answered.

Rab-ten perked up at this last statement, "Demonic forces will seize upon people's thoughts? So demonic forces are real?"

Taking the last sip of his tea, Padma set his cup down and pondered this question, "It is complicated. There are demonic energies that exist, and, as well, they are fed by people's energies and thoughts. It is hard to explain in words something as complex as this subject." Then looking from Rab-ten to Tsogyal, he instructed, "To understand these complex metaphysical realities, it is better to experience them through meditation."

The morning growing warmer, he slid out of the arms of his robe and tied them around his waist, exposing his richly-colored under-silks of red and gold. The chink, chink, chink, of the masons' hammers filled the void of silence as Padma contemplated. Stroking the teardrop of beard at his chin, Padma thought for a moment, then he continued, "It is important to be happy, to cultivate happiness. Not for the purpose of fulfilling desires, but for a more important reason. People who allow themselves to be in a state of unhappiness invite demonic forces into them. These forces feed on their negativity. Eventually this evil rules their being, their thoughts and actions become demonic. And most importantly, at the moment of death, one's last feelings and thoughts must be positive. As this will determine to a large degree what the next incarnation will be, a Hell Realm or a better rebirth."

"Even for a practitioner?" Tsogyal asked, as she set her empty bowl down beside her and took up her silver cup of tea.

"Oh, especially for a practitioner!" Padma exclaimed. "You see, at the moment of death a practitioner's thoughts are very powerful. A negative thought at the moment of death for a strong practitioner can create a very strong demonic force. Very difficult to subjugate."

Padma picked up his cup and looked into the empty vessel. Setting it down, he said, "So even if the life is difficult, one must find the good, be grateful for what is good, cultivate positive thoughts and actions." Padma stretched, reaching his arms up and arching his back. A crack and pop sounded, as his spine adjusted. Relaxing, Padma looked at Tsogyal and Rab-ten and smiled. "Besides, a life of appreciation and happiness is much better and more enjoyable than wallowing in anger, hatred, self pity and other such negativity."

Rab-ten and Tsogyal nodded, looking in wonder at Padma. They all fell silent, contemplating his words. The perfume scent of flowers in the garden wafted over them. They listened to the sounds of the workers' hammers, click, clink, clink, on rock, from the distance.

Padma picked up his cup, looked into it, then set the empty cup down. "Queen Tsogyal, I understand you have learned to write and copy texts?" Padma inquired.

Breaking out of her thoughts, Tsogyal answered, "Yes, I can write and I read scriptures as well."

"I think it would be a good if the account of my subjugation of the demon here at Samye was written down for history and for knowledge. Would you be agreeable to scribe this account?" Padma asked.

Excited by the offer to hear firsthand from the Master of his subjugation of the demon, Tsogyal enthused,"Yes, Master Padma, I would very much like to scribe this account. I think it would be beneficial as well to write of our discussion here, this morning. Do you agree?"

Nodding, Padma smiled. "Yes, both would be good to retain on parchment. When would you like to begin?"

Tsogyal stood up. "Right now, if you wish. We can go to my study," Tsogyal declared. Turning to Rab-ten, Tsogyal inquired, "Lady Rab-ten, would you like to accompany us?"

Rab-ten stood and bowed. "Thank you, my Queen. I have work I must attend to this morning. I have herbs that I must prepare for medicine."

"Very well, I shall read it to you later," Tsogyal assured her.

Padma rose, stretched and picked up his cup. Tsogyal turned and headed for her study, Padma in tow.

Over her shoulder, she assured Padma, "I will send for tea when we get settled to work." Then she mused aloud, "And maybe some yogurt with honey at midday."

25

"Ha, ha!" Emperor Trisong urged his stallion, already at the full gallop. It surged ahead as Abaka's stallion thundered up alongside. The men looked at each other, grinning from ear to ear. Then they both looked to the figure disappearing ahead of them. Her body lay crouched low, black braid whipping in the wind, the quickened hooves of the white mare she rode upon taking wing up the rise of the hillside.

Abaka yelled to the Emperor, over the thunder of hooves, "Your Queen rides like she is upon the wind!"

"It is that white mare Tsogyal rides, she is spectacular," Trisong shouted, trying to be heard over his horse's hooves pounding the earth.

Falling back to dodge around an outcropping of rocks, Abaka then commanded his horse to catch up to the Emperor. Gasping, he called out, continuing the conversation at the full gallop, "Yes, the mare is fine, Sire, but these stallions are every bit as great. It is the Queen, she has a method of getting the most speed from her mount."

Trisong, undulating with the strides of his steed, looked over at Abaka, now his Master of Horse. Comprehending, he nodded.

Up ahead, Tsogyal leaned over her racing mare's neck and called out in pure glee, "You are as fast as a ray of moonlight shimmering across the night sky. You are splendid!"

Coming to the top of the rise, Tsogyal slowed her mare and wheeled her around to watch Trisong and Abaka galloping behind to catch up to her. Beyond them the troops of the Royal Guard with General Klu-pal in the lead, followed at the canter. Squinting, her eyes roved the vast plain over which she and her new mare Dawa, meaning Moon, had just passed. Huge white clouds tumbled across the intensely blue sky, their dark shadows spreading across the land. She could make out the small dark shapes of the many men, horses and mules packing the Emperor's traveling capital in the far distance as it slowly progressed to their next camp, one of many camps for the Emperor's summer tour of the Northern part of his Tibetan empire. The line of mules struggled under the weight of the rolls of felt, that when assembled, would make the Emperor's tent the size of a palace. Many more mules carried food, cooking utensils, rugs, bedding and all other comforts for the Emperor's entourage. Behind them, yaks and sheep were herded along, for food and wool, and a herd of horses for remounts.

Dawa stamped her feet, puffing clouds of mist from her nostrils, as Trisong and Abaka, slowing their mounts, cantered up to her. They circled around her, their stallions jigging and prancing. Settling their horses, they joined Tsogyal in admiring the vast view that tumbled away from them.

To Tsogyal, Trisong exclaimed, "You are the fastest rider I have ever seen, my Queen. In all the battles I have been in, I have never seen any ride as you do."

Looking at Abaka, Trisong asked, "Have you, Master of Horse?"

Abaka shook his head. "I have not. Not even in my home country of Ferghana, where we are the greatest of riders. I know that mare is of the finest stock, but it is not only the mare." With wonder, Abaka inquired, "What is it, Queen Tsogyal? What are you doing to get so much speed from your mounts?"

"Simple," Tsogyal answered, "I give them their heads, and I balance my body to aid their flight. I watch you men, you all urge your mounts forward while holding steady on their mouths. You ask them to go, but then you are pulling them back. You men sit unbalanced, further making flight difficult for your mounts. Do you know all your riders do this? Like men everywhere, they feel they need control and to overpower." Shaking her head, Tsogyal continued, "With horses, this is not necessary. Your men need to learn to become one with their horse, they need to let go and let their horses fly."

Trisong looked at Abaka. "Is she correct about this?" he asked.

"There is more they do to slow their mounts," Tsogyal said as she pointed. "See how some flap their arms. With each flap of their arms, they bounce on their horse, slowing it. And those there, that are pounding their horse's sides with their legs, that slows a horse, it pounds the wind out of them. And there is more. Many more things need be corrected for better flight of their horses."

Abaka considered while watching the men riding up to them, looking critically at them to see what Tsogyal was describing. Turning his attention to Trisong, Abaka replied, "Yes, I see what the Queen is describing. She is correct."

Trisong thought for a moment, then asked, "Can you teach the men this, to improve their speed?"

Abaka looked at Tsogyal, while he replied to Trisong, "I can, Sire. Not only would the method improve their speed, but it would also improve the distance the horses could travel in a day. Would you permit me leave to consult the Queen more on this?"

Trisong looked at Tsogyal while answering Abaka. "Yes, you have my leave. She shall teach you, then you shall teach the men." Rubbing his hands together, feeling on the edge of great possibility, Trisong enthused, "We will ride faster and be the best riders in all the world. This will be of great advantage."

The roar of many hooves, the clang of metal, the slap of quivers and bows against legs and saddles, deafened them as General Klu-pal and his men arrived and surrounded them. The strong scent of horses, men, sheepskin and leather rolled over them. The troops settled a distance away from the foursome, now on the rise overlooking the procession below. Then Rab-ten appeared, cantering up with three guards. These men joined the troops as Rab-ten settled her horse next to Tsogyal and Dawa.

Rab-ten greeted Tsogyal. "My Queen, you are so fast. I could never ride as you do."

Tsogyal smiled at her friend. "If you ever have the desire to learn, I will teach you."

Nodding to Klu-pal, Emperor Trisong said to Abaka,"The General has returned from Bodh Gaya with important relics of the Buddha Sakyamuni, for our stupa at Samye. Tell him, General, how you did so with not one casualty."

Smiling, General Klu-pal glanced at Queen Tsogyal, as he answered. "We rode right up to the palace of King Dharmapala as a great force, well equipped and with many fine warriors. The King, being wise, realized he could not win and would only cause much death needlessly, so he surrendered. We rode on to Bodh Gaya and took what we came for. This King is now a vassal of Tibet. He comes to visit you, does he not, my liege?"

"Yes, he comes with Abbot Santaraksita. He will be there upon my return to Samye. They are working with the translators, translating Sanskrit texts of the Buddha's teachings into our Tibetan scrip," Trisong confirmed.

Tsogyal called to her husband, "King Dharmapala knows the Abbot?"

"Yes," Trisong replied, "Santaraksita was abbot of Dharamapala's own Buddhist university at Vikramasila. The King is a disciple of Haridhadra, Santaraksita's own student. I am sure this is why he was wise and did not fight. We are friends now and the Buddha dharma grows."

Turning to General Klu-pal, Trisong ordered, "We shall proceed to tonight's camp spot and have tea there." Then he asked, "Tomorrow, the district general comes to give a report to me, what is his name? I remember it being General Norbu."

Shaking his head, Klu-pal corrected, "No, Sire, General Norbu was killed this past winter. His captain, Namkang, has succeeded him."

"Do you know him?" Trisong inquired.

"I have heard he is impatient and harsh, yet capable," Klu-pal answered.

"Mmm," Trisong intoned. "Well, I shall meet him on the morrow and see for myself. General, arrange for a secret meeting with a few of his men, his captain included. I will confirm from their accounts how he performs."

Klu-pal nodded, "As you wish, Sire."

"Very well, the day passes, let us go now and mark where camp will be made and have tea. After tea we will hunt. I am sure we will find some antelope. The tents will be set up by the time of our return from the hunt. We will have a great feast tonight!" Trisong said as he turned his mount and kicked it into the trot.

Nodding in appreciation of this order, Klu-pal and Abaka smiled as they turned their steeds and set off following their Emperor. Tsogyal stayed behind, with Rab-ten.

Their horses walking side-by-side, Rab-ten asked, "Where has Master Padma gone?"

"He has gone to Chimpu to meditate. He will return to Samye when Abbot Santaraksita arrives there," Tsogyal answered.

The troops formed behind them, as the procession continued their journey.

26

"It is the most beautiful place I have ever seen," Tsogyal exclaimed, raising herself higher in her saddle upon Dawa as though it would bring her closer to the place that lay before them.

Trisong, Abaka, Klu-pal and Rab-ten, their horses standing side-by-side, all gazed in wonder at the sight. A beautiful lake of lapis lazuli blue lay protected by a ring of snow-capped mountains, their peaks soaring up into puffy white clouds floating lightly upon the deep blue sky. From the lake a stream of crystal water flowed through a beautiful valley. Tall evergreen trees clustered along the stream banks. A large open grassy plain lay between the travelers and the lake.

"It is a sacred place," Trisong said, pointing. "There, a perfect place for our next camp. We have been traveling for three moons now. I have chosen to come to this place so we may rest and enjoy its beauty for a moon."

Their tour though the north had taken them to many places. Tsogyal and Rab-ten were amazed at the land in its many environments. They had never known how vast Tibet was and of the many clans of farming and nomadic people. Her world had been very small, Tsogyal had realized. To see these many places and people gave her a more expanded view of the world and her husband's greatness. She felt grateful to see it all and to be Queen. Yet still she felt a longing. Her travels showed her many places and peoples and as well the truth of suffering and of impermanence.

They spent wonderful days by the shore of this sacred lake, enjoying the great luxury in the Emperor's tent palace at night. Tsogyal and Rab-ten took long walks looking for herbs. Rab-ten would skip in glee when she found an herb she had never seen before.

"I will consult my texts on this one!" she would enthuse.

Sitting side-by-side on a rock close to the water's edge one morning, warm cups of sweet milk tea clutched in their hands, fur blankets across their shoulders, Tsogyal and Rab-ten gazed out on the water, watching the refection of the changing colors of the sky as the sun rose behind the mountains.

"Why have you no children, Rab-ten?" Tsogyal inquired, breaking the silence.

Rab-ten shifted, pulling the fur at her shoulder, bringing it down further to warm her. "I had a child before I met you. A son, he died shortly after birth. When I was called to be healer for King Zhonnu and my husband promoted to be his Captain of the Royal Guard, we decided it would be difficult to serve our King in battles with children in tow. So I take the wild yam you also take, so you will not have children." Sipping her tea, Rab-ten inquired, "Why does the Emperor wish you to remain without children?"

Tsogyal gazed out. "He told me I have a purpose. If I were to have children it would complicate it. He has his Queen, Tse-pongza, and will have more wives. He says they can bear him children. He told me that should my purpose be changed I will have time to have children."

Nodding slowly, Rab-ten wondered, "A purpose? I can see he loves you very much. He laughs with you and has long discussions with you. He respects you. He is not as attentive to Tse-pongza."

Tsogyal shrugged. "And she is jealous. Even now he brings me with him on this campaign and she remains back at the palace. Trisong married her to strengthen the alliance with the Tsepong, an important clan to the Empire. I do not think she would care to come on this campaign in any case. She is soft and does not ride a horse well."

Sitting in silence, they sipped their tea, then Tsogyal asked, "Do you miss Jigme?"

Gazing out at the play of the light of the rising sun on the lake's surface, Rab-ten smiled. "Yes, I miss him. However, I know he is content with his duties for the Emperor. He is very proud to be a Captain and wishes to become a General one day; to lead an army of fine warriors. Though, he does want a son. If I were back at the palace now I would not see much of him." Then, turning to her friend, she said, "Then I would miss you, my Queen."

Tsogyal smiled, as she rose. "Well then, we must begin our day of new adventures in this beautiful place, my friend."

During their stay by this sacred lake, Trisong and Abaka spent time in archery contests, sword practice and hunting. General Klu-pal would join them, when he was not occupied with his men. Trisong and Abaka took Tsogyal and Rab-ten with them exploring the secret places they found, clambering up the mountains around the lake. Klu-pal sent six men to guard them and carry water and food, though well behind so as to give privacy.

The nights were spent in the Emperor's huge tent. Lanterns filled the space with an amber glow. Silk rugs from Persia and China and soft furs were provided to sit and lean upon. The Emperor, Tsogyal and those invited from the traveling entourage, Abaka and Rab-ten always included, sat before low tables. Servants brought in platters of yak meat, dumplings filled with spicy mutton, yak cheese, yogurt, tsampa barley flour and fresh soft bread baked everyday. If the day's hunt was successful, they would lay platters of ibex or deer. Spiced tea and butter tea was served and chang beer.

Dancers entertained, musicians played dulcimers, lutes, flutes and drums. Trisong got up and sang a traditional Tibetan folk song.

Then he danced as the musicians played, the crowd clapping in delight. General Klu-pal played beautiful compositions on his bamboo flute, one he had acquired from India. The lilting melody lifted all in the felt tent into a heavenly realm. Abaka awed the night's guests with dramatic and skilled sword dances, the beat of the drums punctuating his steps as he twirled and leapt with the steel blade.

One evening as the full moon cast twinkling lights across the dancing water of the cold clear lake, Trisong and Tsogyal were out for a stroll along the bank.

"Are you content, my Queen?" Trisong asked.

The strong breeze carrying the cold scent of snow from high on the mountaintops mingled with the sweet smell of the evergreen trees as it rustled through the branches. Taking in a long deep breath of the crisp sweet scents, Tsogyal gazed out at the vista before her.

"You have given me the most wonderful life. How could anyone be unhappy?" Turning to look up to him, she continued, "Yet, I feel a longing. That I have a journey I must embark upon."

Trisong placed his hands on her shoulders and pulled her close to him, encircling her in strong lean arms. His heart swelled with his love for her. Then he gazed down into her face, her beauty illuminated by the moonlight. Looking deep into her dark brown eyes, he assured her, "I understand. I have the same longing. Only Master Padma can show us the road upon which to travel."

Her eyes widened. "Yes," Tsogyal whispered," the road to Nirvana."

Trisong released her and she turned to gaze out upon the reflection of the moon on the lake surface. Looking up at the moon, then at its reflection on the water, she intuited this had meaning. Profound meaning, yet she knew not what.

She continued, "Since our marriage I have been enthralled by my life with you, my husband. I have seen so much of the world I did not know existed. I live in luxury and pleasures. I am learning the

Buddha's teachings. I am blessed to study with the Abbot, the translators and, most of all, to be in the company of Master Padma. Yet, there remains a gnawing feeling that it is not enough, that I am missing something. It niggles at me constantly now. I meditate, yet I feel I cannot go deeper unless I do something, yet I know not what I must do."

Trisong placed his arm around her side and pulled her closer to him. He whispered, "I know what you need, my Queen. We both must take this journey and to do so we must leave all behind us."

Tsogyal looked at him inquiringly. Trisong smiled at her. "You will see. We stay here one more day then we return to Samye."

27

Sunlight filtered through the open windows of the audience hall. Its rays illuminated the throne sitting upon a raised platform. Glittering along the outlined form of the carved hardwood, were countless inlayed jewels all sparkling as the morning light brought their colors to life.

Padma entered the hall to see Emperor Trisong prostrating before him. Alongside the Emperor, Queen Tsogyal also prostrated. Padma was dressed in his ceremonial silk robes. His under-robes were blue adorned with silver embroidered clouds. A emerald-green silk sash was tied at his waist. Over this he wore a red robe, adorned with gold-embroidered snow leopards, that lay open, flowing as he moved. He wore felt boots with golden leather cut-outs in rounded patterns of clouds, the green felt beneath showing through. His long black hair was gathered and tied at the top of his head in a round knot.

"Master Padma, I thank you for accepting my invitation," Trisong said as he bowed to Padma. Gesturing toward the throne. "If you will please sit upon this throne made for you. I implore you to accept my offerings."

Padma glided across the room, mounted the platform and settled himself upon the silk brocade cushion-seat of the jeweled throne. Removing his boots, he crossed his legs in a lotus posture. As he straightened his back, he looked down at Trisong and Tsogyal. Just then, the sun shone brighter through the windows, its rays illuminating his form. Trisong and Tsogyal both gasped at his bright presence and the omen it portended.

Trisong clapped, summoning servants. Entering through the side doors, they carried platters of food. Bowing low, they set them down before the platform as offerings. Leaving, they returned in a short time with more platters. The room filled with the aromas of momos, seared mutton and yak meat and spices. So much food was brought that the servants had to stack trays of food upon trays already placed, making a mountain of food offerings.

Trisong knelt before Padma, his knees resting on a thin cushion as he placed a silver tray before him. "This tray represents all the lands of my empire, of Tibet. Even now my armies conquer more lands making my empire even more vast. In the lands to the North, we now take Hami, thus giving us more control of the ancient trade route, that which brings trade goods from the eastern end of the world to the western end of the world and back again. Warriors of Tibet ride through the lands to the south, making the King of Northern India our vassal. My warriors ride over passes and mountains, taking more lands to the East. The soldiers of the Tang Emperor shudder and run as we roll over their armies and control cities that were once theirs and now belong to Tibet. To the west we gain more and more ground fighting the Arab Muhammadan armies, the only real force that challenge us, yet we prevail. My great armies conquer all who lay before them, there are none greater than the warriors of Tibet!" he proclaimed.

Upon the middle of the shining tray, Trisong set a piece of solid gold. Looking up at Padma, he said, "This represents the four districts of the central part of Tibet and Tsang." Placing a solid gold piece on the right side of the tray he explained, "This represents the eastern part of my Empire, China, Jang and Kham." He placed a gold piece at the bottom of the tray. "This represents India and Bhutan." On the northern quadrant of the tray he placed a gold piece. "This represents Hor, Mongolia and the Northern Plains." And placing his last gold piece, "This represents the three regions that now belong to Tibet to the West."

Sliding back, Emperor Trisong prostrated to Master Padma as he spoke, "Master Padma, I offer you my empire." Then raising himself, Trisong reached for another tray, this of gold, and placed it next to the silver mandala tray. Upon this gold tray he placed a large stone of pure turquoise.

Prostrating again, he said, "And this represents Queen Tsogyal. I offer my Queen to you, Master Padma. She is a woman of the greatest beauty. She is most sensual and is most gratifying. As you are acquainted with the Queen, you well know, Master, how intelligent and skilled she is. She is a true gift and a great sacrifice for me to give, as I have a great and deep love of her."

Hearing this, Tsogyal froze. Her heart started to pound as what had just been declared by her husband sank into her consciousness.

Trisong's continuing entreaty broke Tsogyal's racing thoughts. "Oh, great Guru, Precious one," he went on, "I offer everything within my power. As all creatures, men and Gods, in every form and at all times, are held by you in your great compassion. I request you grant me the great instruction through which I will attain Buddha-hood in this lifetime. All the other teachings are the lower paths and require many lifetimes to attain enlightenment. Grant me the extraordinary teaching of the Tantra, that which only you have the secret knowledge and attainment of." Ending his supplication, Trisong began prostrating.

Padma gazed upon the prostrating Emperor, then he looked at Queen Tsogyal.

His voice echoed in the hall as he spoke loudly for his words to be heard and his meaning clear. "I, Padmasambhava, known to you as Padma, spontaneously appeared on this earth in this time, projected as a ball of light from the Buddha Amitabha. I appeared on a lotus blossom in the great lake Dhanakosha, in the land west of here known as Orgyen. I am awakened, as the previous Buddha, Sakyamuni. I transcend the law of cause and effect. I am holder of the very Secret Mantras, Tantra, Dzogchen, Agama and Upadeha, teachings." Looking down at Emperor Trisong, he continued, "I have the world already within my power. Your material gifts, though vast, do not suffice. I cannot break my sacred vow. I cannot barter the great teachings for wealth, nor even for the gift of the high power of the Emperor."

Spreading his hands wide, he explained, "If I take the wealth you offer and give my teachings to you, both I and you will die and fall into the Realms of Hell." Shaking his head slowly, he went on, "Your offering is great and vast, your purpose however is improper. You see, the only real requirement for the great Tantric teachings to be bestowed is that the recipient be a suitable vessel. Tantra is as the Snow Lions milk; a pure elixir. This elixir can only be held in a pure golden jeweled bowl. Pour this elixir into any other vessel, and the vessel would break, the elixir lost."

As he completed his response, both Trisong and Tsogyal, gazed upon him. Padma's form began to waver, like ripples on water. Superimposed over his sitting form, another form took shape. Its head was large, its color blue, a great wheel was clutched at the top in its fangs. Its great clawed hands held the sides and the bottom of the wheel rested between its knees. Within the wheel was a mandala. The mandala depicted many figures and the many forms of karmic existence and delusions. The actions that lead to being trapped in the cycles of suffering and rebirth after rebirth, never achieving the wisdom to free one's self from pain and suffering.

Seeing this mandala vision before them, only reaffirmed Trisong's and Tsogyal's great desire for the teachings, the practice which would place them both on the path to liberation through wisdom.

Slowly, the form dissolved before Trisong and Tsogyal. They looked at one another in astonishment. Realizing they both had seen it, Trisong nodded in understanding and Tsogyal wept. A tightness formed in Trisong's throat as he realized the close psychic connection he shared with Tsogyal.

Overwhelmed, Trisong fell to the floor and cursed through tears. "What a cruel karma! I am the most powerful Emperor on this earth, yet I am not a fit recipient for the teachings?"

Padma bid Trisong, "Please calm yourself and listen to me. The Secret Mantra is secret not because it is immoral nor has any defect, it must remain hidden from those of narrow-mindedness that practice on the lower paths. You see, your wealth is not a fit offering, though it shows your resolve. You have intelligence, intuitive insight and a broad mind. I am sure you will not altar your faith nor renege on your vows. I have seen you attend to me, your Guru, with great devotion."

Padma stared down at Trisong, then gesturing toward Tsogyal, he said, "Your offering of your Queen shows your true resolve and strength. The Queen Tsogyal is a woman of good family, she is faithful, beautiful, skillful in her dealings. She has excellent insight. She is kind and generous to all she meets. A woman who has all of these attributes is very rare. This makes her suitable to become my consort. For a being such as I, free of any desire, free of the aberrations of lust, a woman possessing the required attributes as Queen Tsogyal does, is a sacred ingredient of the most advanced form of Tantric practice. The presence of such a woman is required or one will never reach the full ripening and full freedom of the mind." Sitting back, his hands clasping his knees, he went on, "There are many practitioners of Tantra in this land of Tibet. However, very few reach the final fruit of the practice. In light of this, since you have shown your sincerity, I have this moment decided you should be given the opportunity." Padma held his hand out in a gesture of giving, as he declared, "Emperor Trisong, I accept your offering of the Queen. I have no need nor desire for your wealth nor of your empire as I seek not mundane power. To you I will open the door of the Secret Mantra and reveal the path you desire to travel upon."

Looking up at Padma, Trisong's face was wet with tears of happiness, streaming down his face.

For Tsogyal, the room was spinning. She was stunned, trying to grasp all that was happening. She was now given to Master Padma. She had dreamed to be a student, but a consort was more than she could have asked for. Yet now she was also no longer Queen of Tibet, no longer wife of the Emperor. Her mind struggled, grasping at the meaning, trying to slow down all that was changing so quickly in her life. Breathing to slow her thoughts, Tsogyal tried to take stock of her situation. She had longed for more, to go deeper. She had in her heart wanted to be disciple of the great Master of Tantra. Now she was to be his consort. It became clear to Tsogyal that Trisong had not given her away as a gift to Master Padma, but he had given her a greater gift. Realizing this, she looked up at Padma to see him gazing at her. Meeting his eyes, she felt a great calm overtake her. The knowledge filled her that she would be set solidly on the road to Nirvana. Then pure joy poured into her being, like nectar. *Yes, I want to go with you,* she thought, her love for him now free to swell in her heart. Padma smiled as he nodded his acceptance of her.

Tsogyal looked at Trisong, who met her eyes. His eyes swam with the emotions of joy for the thing he had longed for and was now granted, mixed with losing her whom he loved so dearly.

"Thank you," Tsogyal whispered to him.

Trisong nodded, his eyes filled with his love for her.

28

Swirling wind stung Tsogyal's face as she climbed higher and higher on the path to Chimpu. Looking back along their trail of footsteps in the snow leading from Samye, she adjusted the strap of the large heavy bag slung across her shoulder as she took in the realization that her old life was really gone. Breathing hard to catch her breath, the cold air stung her chest as a drip of sweat rolled down her side under her wool felt tunic. She turned to look up the path at Padma's trudging figure, his sheepskin coat had one sleeve slipped off his arm and hanging to his side to cool him. The falling snow dusted his thick fox-fur hat as his wool felt boots sunk a hand's width into the snow that covered the trail. Padma adjusted the bag slung across his back as he climbed higher ahead of her. Continuing her march along the path, stepping over white mounds of snow-covered rocks, the memory of Rab-ten flooded Tsogyal's mind.

"You are leaving?" Rab-ten asked, stunned. "You are no longer Queen?"

"Yes, it is true. I am now consort of Master Padma," Tsogyal confirmed.

Rab-ten turned away in shock. "I will never see you again?" she asked, tears beginning to push behind her eyes.

"I am sure we will see each other again. I just do not know when," Tsogyal answered.

Rab-ten suddenly turned to face Tsogyal. "I want to come with you. Can I come?" Rab-ten implored. "I do not want a mundane life. I want to go with you and practice the dharma too. I can be your attendant, your healer. Surely you will need a healer in the caves?"

Tsogyal took Rab-ten's hands in hers as she spoke gently, "Sister, think about what you are asking of me. You must ask Master Padma if he will accept you as a student. You must ask the Emperor if he will release you. And what about your husband?"

Realization dawning, Rab-ten straightened, asking, "Do you want me with you?"

Tsogyal laughed. "You are my spiritual sister. Of course, I would love for you to come and enter the practice with me," she declared. Shaking her head, she added, "However, it is not my choice."

Wiping tears from her cheeks, Rab-ten settled herself. "You are right. I must find my own way to be with you and the Master."

Now on the trail far from Samye, Tsogyal tripped and stumbled, her body lurching forward as she struggled to regain balance and keep from falling. She looked up the trail to see Padma waiting for her. Catching up to him, she looked to where he pointed as he said, "There, see up that ravine? We are almost there."

Tsogyal could only see a steep tree-and-bush-covered ravine, now dusted with white, green leaves peeking out from underneath the growing weight of the falling flakes. She heard the rush of water falling down the slope, but could not determine its whereabouts. She nodded without comment as Padma turned and led the way. After what seemed a long time to Tsogyal, they arrived at a small level area in front of a wall of stacked stones against the brushy hillside. Padma stepped up to a wooden door set into the wall of stone that Tsogyal could now see was a small hut built against the hillside. Next to the door, an opening was made as a window, a wooden shutter covering it. Sliding the door's latch sideways, Padma opened the door inward and stepped inside. Tsogyal followed him, then stood inside the doorway looking around the abode. She could see that the stone walls were not a hut but were built to make a small room extending the size of a small cave that fell back into the hillside. She looked up to see that the roof of the extension was made of wood planks then covered in stone and earth.

Padma pointed to a place at a back wall of the cave where there was a cushion that lay upon a rug. A low table was placed in front of the cushion. "You can sleep and meditate on that cushion, that is your place. I will make tea," he said.

Tsogyal looked around the rock cavern, the smell of earth rose from the floor to meet her. The smallness of the cave's walls pressed in on her, making her feel cramped. Images of the high ceilings and spacious rooms of Samye and the great palace of one thousand rooms in Lhasa filled her mind as she laid her bag next to her cushion. She noticed a butter lamp sat upon the small table. A cold rush of wind with flurries of white flakes blew through the doorway, chilling her.

Stowing his bag containing his ceremonial silks into a cubby-hole chipped out of the rock, Padma instructed, "Push the door shut." Then he knelt, placing yak dung into the fire pit at the front in the extended part of the cave.

Tsogyal reached for the wooden door and pushed it shut, then slid the wooden latch dowel into a metal ring, holding the door fast. She went back to her cushion and sat. Her body began to shiver. Pulling her sheepskin coat from her bag, she put her arms through the thick sleeves and settled the wooly mass around her. Feeling warmth sink into her, she began to relax. Looking up at the natural rock of the cave, she remembered her time alone when she ran away and lived in such a cave. Looking at Padma, his back to her as he toiled at the fire, she wondered how the two of them would live in this small space.

The yak fuel alight and hot, Padma placed a pot onto the fire, that he had filled with pre-made tea he carried in a water bag. Most of the smoke from the fire pit went out a flue, yet some hung at the ceiling. The smell of tea began to fill the room and Tsogyal realized how hungry she was.

Handing her a cup of butter tea, Padma assured her, "Here, this will fill you and help you get warm. We will eat in a few hours. After tea I will initiate you."

Tsogyal froze. "Initiate?" she asked, not able to hide a tremble in her voice.

Padma stood looking down at her and smiled. "One day you will be my consort in the highest Secret Tantra of union. However, you must attain a higher level of practice before you will be ready." Kneeling before her, he assured her, "I will instruct you in preliminary practices and I will give you a meditation schedule. By initiation I mean I will give you empowerment to help you progress in your practice. I will also ordain you a Bhiksuni, which is a female practitioner in the monastic order."

Relieved, Tsogyal looked down at the cushion she sat upon. It was big enough for her to sit on but not to lay stretched out on. "Do I sleep here, on this cushion?" she inquired.

Padma took up his cup of tea and settled himself cross-legged on a small rug next to her. Then he answered, "You will be meditating in sessions throughout the night. When you do sleep, it will be sitting up. You may lean against the wall behind you. Until you get more used to it, you may curl up on this cushion." Seeing her eyes go wide, he placed his hand on her knee, assuring her, "I know, it sounds strange but you will become accustomed to it, then even enjoy it. I will teach you to raise your inner fire, that will help your practice and help you to be more comfortable."

Rising, he went to the back of the cave where a shelf was cut into the rock, withdrawing a thick brocade wrapped item. He placed it on the small table in front of Tsogyal's cushion. Taking the butter lamp to the fire pit, he lit it with a flaming stick, then placed it on Tsogyal's table. The soft light filled the corner. Unwrapping the brocade, Tsogyal saw it was a text made of many sheets of parchment, each two hands long and a hand's width wide. The stack was held together by two boards, one atop and one on the bottom, all wrapped in brocade and tied with a cord of silk.

He settled himself upon the floor as he explained, "You have studied many texts during your time at Samye. You understand the Four Noble Truths; that life is suffering, that the origin of suffering is attachment, that the cessation of suffering can be attained, that there is a path to the end of suffering. This is very good." Placing his hand on the text he laid on the table, he instructed, "In-between your meditation sessions, I wish you to read and understand this sutra on the provisional truths, the laws of karma and what you should renounce and what you should cultivate. After you are finished with this text, I will give you more texts to study. I will clarify any points you wish to discuss. When you have shown you are ready for the next level I will instruct you."

Tsogyal sipped her tea then reached out her hand out to touch the text. She noticed her hand shaking. *All has been so fast*, she thought. Then a realization washed over her. Sitting up straighter, she looked at Padma, his eyes intent on her face. Letting her breath out, feeling her confidence rise, she said, "I have lived in palaces of stone and luxury, yet those palaces will one day crumble to dust. Now I am on the path to something which is eternal."

Padma nodded. "Yes," he affirmed. Then looking around at the rock walls, he added, "This is our palace now." Looking into Tsogyal's eyes, he declared, "And here we will soar."

29

Music drifted up and up into the sky, the waves of sound enveloping a vulture as it soared in a circle, looking down at the mass of people gathered in Samye's courtyards celebrating the beginning of the new season. Dancers spun and twirled to the rhythm of drums and horns. The audience of men paid little attention to the dancers, their heads lowered to one another like closing flower pedals to hear their conversations beneath the cacophony of sounds. Trays of food were carried by servants prepared in the great kitchens of the monastery. Children chased each other with screams of delight. Women dressed in their best colorful tunics and robes, their hair woven in many small braids decorated with turquoise, coral and large amber beads, stood in circles with beaming smiles, giggling as they whispered gossip and confidences.

Minister Lutsen strolled around the perimeter of the crowd like a father watching his many children. Noticing Minister Tsenpo in the distance, he adjusted his course to meet him.

"I have not seen the Queen, have you?" Lutsen said as he sided up to Tsenpo.

Tsenpo, scanning the crowd, answered, "No, I have not seen the Queen, she is most likely in her study."

"On this day of celebration?" Lutsen became insistent. "I have not seen her for weeks. I have seen the Emperor, yet not his Queen. Some-thing is amiss."

Tsenpo looked at Lutsen, as it dawned on him, he confirmed, "Come to think of it, I can't remember when I last saw the Queen. You are correct, something is amiss, the Queen is usually present in the courtyards or at least seen walking the grounds."

Both men needing no words, turned and walked swiftly to find the Emperor's head minister Goe.

Finding Minister Goe giving orders to a servant, Lutsen demanded, "We wish an audience with the Emperor." The deep lines of his stern face glared at Goe.

Goe sent the servant on his errand and turned, looking from Lutsen to Tsenpo. His face soft and serene, Goe replied, "Gentlemen, what is the matter, why the stern faces? Today is a day for celebration, yet you come to me demanding to have audience with the Emperor?"

Tsenpo stepped forward, saying, "Minister Goe, please forgive our haste, it is due solely to our concern. We wonder what has become of the Queen as neither of us has seen her in a very long time. We request you alert the Emperor that we wish an audience as soon as he will see us, so we may ask him. Will you arrange it?"

Bowing, Minister Goe, acceded, "Yes I shall. Enjoy the day, Ministers." Then he turned and strolled away.

Bowing before Emperor Trisong, Minister Goe explained, "I can't hold them off for much longer, Sire. They ask me every day. It has been a fortnight since their first request, they are deeply suspicious." Looking up, Goe advised, "You will have to tell them what has become of her."

Sitting cross-legged on his throne, Trisong tapped his knee with his fingers, deep in thought. Coming to a decision, he sighed, "Yes, you are correct, Minister Goe. Tell them I will see them on the morrow after midday meal." Then as an afterthought, "And arrange to have all the ministers present."

Eyes raised, Goe bowed, repeating, "All the ministers. As you wish, Sire."

The next day, Tsenpo and Lutsen walked briskly to their audience with the Emperor. Entering the audience hall, they were stunned to see all the Bon Ministers assembled. They took their place at the front of the audience hall with the other ministers. Across from them were assembled those ministers that followed the Buddha dharma. All assembled had curious looks upon their faces in wonder at this strange assembly.

Entering from the royal door at the front of the audience hall, Emperor Trisong was dressed in his finest regalia of silk robes, sash, gold-thread-embroidered felt boots. His long raven black hair showered over his back and shoulders under his felt hat with a band of gold inlayed with large oblong lapis lazuli stones. The gold of the crown glittered as shafts of sun light shone into the hall through the windows, the wooden shutters lay open to let in the light.

Seating himself upon his throne, Trisong raised his hand. The room was completely silent in anticipation. Deciding to simply tell what was so without preamble, Trisong announced, "Ministers, I have gathered you all here to announce I have given Queen Tsogyal to the Great Master Padma of the Buddha dharma to be his consort."

A murmur rose in the hall, then an incredulous Lutsen shouted, "Sire, you gave Tibet's Queen to that vagabond, that spell master, from Indian? Are you possessed of a demon?"

Tsenpo stepped forward, his face contorted and red, flinging his arm sideways, shouted, "Lord Emperor, do you throw the lineage of our great Emperors onto the dung heap? Do you cast our great traditions of centuries into the river to be swept away and lost forever?"

Shaking his head in disbelief, Bon Minister Gyugyu cried out, "The people of Tibet will fall into great sorrow when news of this sweeps the land. Please, Sire, reverse this, bring the Queen, Tsogyal, back to your bed."

Then Bon Minister Ringmo cursed in a loud voice, "This daughter of Karchen has ruined her reputation, been nothing but trouble for her family, then her first husband and now you, great Emperor. She will bring disaster down upon Tibet!"

Turning to face the horde of Bon Ministers, Bon Minister Trompa called out, "Listen to me, great Ministers. Though the King has surely lost his mind, if we remain strong we can correct this." Then, turning to Emperor Trisong, Trompa continued, "Oh great Emperor Trisong, do not flay the law and traditions of Tibet. Queen Tsogyal is the best of your consorts, most beloved of the people of Tibet, she is like the daughter of Brama. Restore her to your side. We shall hunt down this sorcerer, Padma, who has bewitched your mind and kill him!"

Shocked at this threat to their Precious Master, the Ministers sympathetic to the Buddha dharma shouted their objections.

Buddhist Minister Pelseng stepped forward with raised hand, silencing all so he could be heard. "Sire, this unspeakable intent upon the great Master Padma, the second Buddha, will not be allowed. These Ministers disgrace you, the great Jewel of Tibet. They oppose your decree that the dharma flourish in Tibet. If they succeed in snuffing the light of the Great Tantric Master, the dharma will wither and die." Turning to face the Buddhist Ministers, he called out, "If we allow these Bon Ministers their way we will also accrue their karma." Then glaring at the assembled Bon Ministers, he continued, "I am willing to take up the sword to ensure that Master Padma and his consort remain safe."

With that said, the Buddhist ministers all called out, cheering in agreement, "We will protect them, we will protect them!"

The roar of arguing voices filled the hall. Master Goe, standing behind Emperor Trisong, stepped forward at a gesture by Trisong to give him counsel.

Bending low, Goe whispered into Trisong's ear so as to be heard over the roar, "Lord Emperor, this may cast the land into anarchy, would it not be wise to come to terms with these Ministers?"

Nodding in agreement, Trisong stood up, arms raised high, yelling, "Silence!"

The room fell silent, all stunned to see the Emperor standing with arms raised.

Trisong took his seat and began. "Ministers of Tibet, there is no greater Emperor than I. My greatness makes you great too. Without me you are nothing, so do not fool yourselves as to your power. Any minister who does not show respect to the Master Padma and especially any who try to harm him or his sacred consort Tsogyal shall receive punishment nine times as severe than that perpetrated by any of you upon Master Padma. My decree is that the Buddha dharma flourish in Tibet. I am the dharma protector. We shall practice the methods and propagate the dharma. Monasteries and centers devoted to the teachings shall be built throughout the Empire of Tibet. Any who disobey my decree shall be punished for opposing the Emperor and his Ministers."

Then, pointing to the Buddhist Ministers, Trisong said in a stern voice, "In your self-centered zeal you harm yourselves. Do not disgrace the Buddha dharma this way by vowing to take up the sword and kill others for your Master. Crimes committed in the name of religion can never be justified. Have you no faith in your Vajra Master Padma? No one can harm him. They have tried and cannot achieve it."

Bon minister Tsenpo implored, "But my Lord Emperor, the country's happiness depends upon Bon. Without the Swastika Gods, who will protect Tibet? To whom can the people of the village clans and nomadic clans pray? We implore you to bring Tsogyal home and exile that foreign devil."

A murmur of agreement rose from the Bon ministers. The Buddhist ministers shook their heads in disagreement of Tsenpo's words.

Trisong looked over the fractured throng. All fell silent as he sat thinking. Then he proclaimed, "I will think upon this and we will meet again to discuss these things and come to an agreement. Until then if you speak to each other of this then do so with civil discussion and not in argument."

With that he rose and stormed out of the hall. The sun, having set behind the mountains, cast all in the hall in a gray light.

30

The air was cold as it entered her nostrils. Breathing in slowly, Tsogyal brought it down to the bottom of her belly. In her mind's eye, she visualized it as white light filling her. Then, through her nostrils, she blew out the air, now filled with all negativity. It was black like smoke, leaving her being. When it entered the outside air, it dissolved away.

Her hands were clear like crystal, her torso was rainbow light. No longer was she made of flesh and bones, her entire body was clear and empty, she was radiant light.

Tsogyal visualized a hollow form, like barley straw. Though flexible, shimmering like shining silk, it was made of light. She concentrated on this hollow channel, the beginning point of it between her eyebrows. From there she followed it over the crown of her head and down inside her body in front of her spine, to a point a hand's width below her navel, at the secret chakra. Then saw in her mind's eye two more smaller channels made of silky light, running one on either side of the larger central channel, at the secret chakra they curved up and into the central channel.

She let go the image of herself as a woman of flesh and bone, now she was a Goddess, pure and beautiful made of light, overflowing with love and compassion for all beings.

Tsogyal concentrated on the chakras within the central channel. The crown chakra at the inside top of her head, she could see was multicolored and a triangular shape. Within this triangular shape was the sanskrit syllable Ham. Upon the letter was a crescent moon shape laying in its side holding a kundalini drop and upon the drop was a nada, a small squiggle point. All of this sat upon a moon disk and was upside down, the nada pointing downwards toward the throat chakra.

The throat chakra was a red-colored ball of light. Within this chakra was the syllable Om sitting upon a moon disk. Upon the Om was the crescent moon, drop and nada all upright.

Tsogyal visualized her heart chakra, a radiant ball glowing pure white. Within this chakra was the syllable Hum sitting upon a moon disc, with the crescent moon, drop and nada all upside down pointing to the navel chakra.

At the navel the chakra was a triangle of glowing red light with the short A syllable, shaped as a tall pyramid, upon which the crescent moon, drop and nada sat, pointing upwards.

Her body shivered as the wind roared up the steep canyon coursing over her body. Dressed in only a cotton tunic, Tsogyal sat upon a rock that was covered in snow. A memory of something Padma said to her floated into her mind, *'Pleasure is necessary for the practice. Those people that are miserable in nature and do not strive to cultivate a positive view can never practice, because having no experience of pleasure they do not understand pleasure.'* Steeling herself not to be distracted, Tsogyal continued her concentration.

The cold wind swirling around her, Tsogyal drew in her breath, seeing it fill the channels on either side of the central channel. It filled the side channels all the way down to below the navel where the channels met with the central channel. Then, she closed her lower doors and swallowed drawing the airs up from below. Simultaneously, she drew the airs from the side channels into the central channel. These airs rushed in stoking the syllable A inside the navel chakra, causing it to glow red-hot. Then it exploded into flames, shooting up through the central channel into the heart chakra. The heart chakra became filled with hot fire igniting the syllable Hum there, causing the kundalini drop to melt, dripping nectar from the nada down the central channel onto the glowing syllable A inside the navel chakra.

The kundalini drops acted like butter dripping onto the flame in the navel chakra, causing it to explode into flames again. Incredible bliss filled Tsogyal as the explosion of fire reached up to the throat chakra filling it with the fiery blaze. Tsogyal let all happen naturally, loosening her grip on the visualization and basking in the exquisite feelings filling her.

Drawing in the cold outside air, Tsogyal saw her ego and self-pity within the airs in the side channels. Drawing this air into the central channel and the navel chakra to stoke the fire, all self-pity and ego was consumed in the flames.

Breathing in slowly again and again, causing the flames to rise higher, eventually the red-hot flames rose from the navel chakra through the channel passing through the heart chakra, though the throat chakra, finally reaching the crown chakra. At the crown chakra, the heat melted the drop, causing the kundalini energy to drip down through the nada. Like nectar, it flowed through the central channel all the way down to ignite the fire source at the navel, causing almost unbearable bliss to fill her being.

Sitting there in the wilderness, on the cold hard mountainside, Tsogyal experienced the intense awareness of non-duality. She could comprehend the entire universal reality without any obstacles.

Warmth grew within her body. Gradually it filled her until she was completely warm, the cold wind felt refreshing to her. The snow covering the rock she had been sitting on had melted into her tunic, saturating it. The inner fire expanded out of the central channel and filled her entire being, radiating out into the world. Steam rose as her tunic began to dry, the stone she sat upon became dry and warm.

Opening her eyes, the view expanded before her, the ravine cascaded downwards into the vast space of the valley and the mountains rising up beyond. Huge white clouds sailed above the mountains in the great distance. All was as if made of shimmering crystal light. Eyes open, the feeling of bliss still present within her, Tsogyal noticed a vision growing within her heart. A figure within a ball of light was growing larger within her. It floated out of her body between her breasts and hung in the space out in front of her. There, the ball of light with the figure within it grew larger and larger. Bliss coursed through her body, but at the same time, Tsogyal was startled at the appearance of this apparition. Then joy filled her as Tsogyal realized she recognized the Goddess within the ball of light, sitting upon a lotus.

Sarasvati spoke, her voice musical and sweet like clear soft bells. "Princess Tsogyal, you are achieving your yogic abilities rapidly, this is very good as your time on this earth in this life is short. I am here to assist you so you may move even more quickly upon your path, thus helping all beings on earth."

Reaching her hand out, Sarasvati touched Tsogyal at the crown of her head, as she spoke, "Your memory is now vast and infallible. You now have clairvoyance, thus having far knowledge of mundane events. You now have divine intuition, a very important tool on the path. So those you meet will gain faith in the dharma, I give you the power of miracles, to be used for good and for propagation of the Buddha dharma, thus helping all beings to realize their Buddha Nature and be freed from the ocean of suffering."

As Sarasvati touched her and spoke, Tsogyal saw within her and felt a cool silvery nectar sliding down from the crown of her head through the center of her being. The nectar caused all of her chakras to glow brightly.

Looking into Sarasvati's kind eyes, Tsogyal heard her speak inside her mind. "Lady Tsogyal, you will write down all Master Padma's teachings, all that happens to him and yourself this life. You shall hide these writings for future generations to find. The Tantric Buddha dharma will not grow steadily here in Tibet. There will be many seasons the dharma is opposed and absent from the people's minds and hearts. Masters will appear in the future to find your hidden teachings, thus helping the dharma to grow again. You, Princess Tsogyal, play a most important role in the dharma remaining here on this earth." As she spoke Sarasvati dissolved, at her last word she was gone.

A ray of sunlight blinded Tsogyal's eyes. Reaching up with her hand, she shaded her eyes. In her mind's eye, Tsogyal saw men coming up the trail intent on her and Padma's cave. Jumping down off the rock to hurry down the path, Tsogyal stopped as Padma appeared running up the trail to get her.

Tsogyal gasped, "Men coming."

Padma stopped, a quizzical look on his face. He turned to look down the ravine. "You saw them?"

Shaking her head, Tsogyal answered, "In my mind."

Padma looked at her, then he looked at the rock she had sat upon. The snow gone, the rock dry, a smile drew across his face. "Very good. Very good indeed!" he enthused. "Come, let us get back, you can tell me all later."

31

Hurrying into their cave, Padma pushed the door shut and sent the latch home. Though still warm, Tsogyal pulled her robe of wool around her and tied the cord belt tight. Padma knelt, stoking the fire, and placed the pot on it for making tea. Sometime later, Tsogyal and Padma, each with a cup of the fragrant liquid warm in their hands, heard many footsteps and the clang of metal-on-metal in the distance. Closer and closer the sounds came until they stopped outside the door. "Master Padma?" a voice called. Then after a few moments, "Master Padma, I come with an important message from the Emperor."

Tsogyal looked at Padma, quizzically. Padma rose to his feet and strode to the door, opening it. Using his body as a barrier filling the doorway, determined to block any who would try to enter the cave, Padma looked out. A wall of grim battle-scarred faces met Padma's gaze. Shock overcame Padma for an instant seeing how many warriors were assembled on the small patio of flat stones outside the cave.

In a calm voice, Padma said, "Give me the message."

A warrior burrowed through the mass of men, his metal-covered leather tunic clanged as he moved, his hand rested on the hilt of his sword hanging at his side.

He stepped right up to Padma. Looking directly into Padma's eyes, he ordered, "Let me pass."

Padma stared back into the warrior's eyes, he could smell the warrior's sweat and the leather of his armor underneath the metal. Padma stepped back out of the way, allowing the warrior to enter the cave. Padma closed the door and waited behind the man. The warrior stood looking around the small rock-enclosed space. When he took off his fur hat, Tsogyal was shocked to see the warrior was none other than the Emperor, Trisong. A smile spread over his face as he gazed down at her. Jumping up, Tsogyal went to meet his outstretched hands.

Her warm hands slid into his cold palms as she enthused, "I am so glad to see you, my Emperor."

Gazing into her face, Trisong said, "You look more radiant and beautiful than I have ever seen you."

Smiling at the Emperor's ruse, Padma gestured to his own cushion. "Please, Emperor, sit and make yourself comfortable. Would you like tea? Why are you dressed as a common soldier?"

Squeezing Tsogyal's hands before releasing them, he turned to Padma, answering, "Vajra Master, I have important news I wanted to bring myself." Taking his sword-belt off, Trisong nodded as he sat. "Yes, tea would be very good."

Tsogyal returned to her cushion in anticipation of what this unusual visit forebode. Trisong gazed around the cave as Padma prepared tea.

Looking at Tsogyal, Trisong said, "It has been a very long time since I have roamed about unnoticed. I rather like it."

Taking the cup of the hot tea from Padma's outstretched hands, Trisong waited for Padma to seat himself upon a small rug, his sheepskin robe folded to make a cushion.

Sipping the hot sweet tea, he sighed in pleasure, the warmth filling him, the sweetness energizing him. "Very nice. It is wonderful to have tea after a good ride then a climb up a mountain." Still holding the cup, Trisong let it rest on his knee. Looking from Padma to Tsogyal he continued, "As you would expect, it was noticed the Queen of Tibet is missing." Looking at Padma, Trisong frowned. "The Bon Ministers have called for your execution."

Shocked, Tsogyal asked, "In open audience?"

Trisong nodded as he answered, "Yes, and in front of the full assembly of the Ministers. This caused quite a row. The Buddhist Ministers vowed to take up swords and bows for your protection."

Shaking his head slowly in sadness, Padma looked at Tsogyal, then to Trisong. "That is very bad news. What has come of this event?"

Trisong sipped his tea. Then he placed the empty cup on a shelf cut into the rock next to his seat. Looking at Padma, he answered, "After several audiences and discussions I have agreed that if the Bon Ministers promise they will end all attempts to harm you, then I will send you to India with a load of gold. And that you shall never return to Tibet."

Turning his attention to Tsogyal, he continued, "And you, My Lady, shall be banished to Lhodrak to live in peace."

Tsogyal looked from Trisong to Padma in shock. "Padma leave Tibet? I go away to live forever in Lhodrak, away from him, and you?" she asked incredulously.

A deep frown on his face, Padma looked from Tsogyal to Trisong. Noticing a slight upturn at the corners of Trisong's mouth, realization dawned on Padma. His frown turned to a smile as he confirmed, "And of course we will do no such thing."

Slapping his knee, Trisong burst out in the laugh he was holding in. "Of course not!" he chortled, "We just need to placate the Bon Ministers."

Tsogyal looked from Padma to Trisong, a smile spreading over her face as realization of Trisong's words sunk in.

Trisong held out his empty cold cup and Padma took it. As he filled it, he listened as Trisong went on, explaining, "If they are not satisfied, they will make it their work to spread rumors far and wide how the Buddha dharma is a religion of wife-stealing sorcerers. Scandalized accusations will make it difficult for the provincial Kings to embrace the dharma and be examples for the people of the villages and nomadic tribes. The people across the country will become confused and fear will cause them to close their minds and remain steadfast in the old religion. Those who embrace the dharma will loose faith." Trisong took the proffered cup. Taking a sip of the hot tea, he rested the cup on his knee, then he continued, "We need time for the dharma to gain hold and to build monasteries and teaching centers. So if the Bon Ministers think they have won and that you are gone and no longer a threat to their hold on Tibet, then they will go back to their duties and think no more upon it. Meanwhile, you and the Lady Tsogyal will go to a secret retreat further away and continue your work here in Tibet."

With a quizzical look at Padma, Trisong inquired, "Do you have knowledge of a suitable place?"

Thinking, Padma tapped his fingers on his chin. Then he said, "Yes, I do know a very good place. It is to the northeast of here, several days journey and high in the mountains, it is very hidden. The place is known as Zhoto Tidro. However, before we go there I think it best we leave Chimpu. There are those who may take it upon themselves to try harm us despite your agreement." Gesturing toward Tsogyal, Padma assured, "I fear more for the Lady than myself. As well, we need to wait for the snows to melt at Zhoto Tidro, so we can reach the caves."

Trisong took on a somber look and nodded. "Yes, I had the same thought myself, fearing for your safety. Perhaps you can go south to the hermitage at Yamalung until the snows melt? This way the ministers, being told you have agreed to my decree, will see for themselves you heading south, affirming you are going to India and the Lady to the east by way of the southern route." Nodding, his mind set on the plan, Trisong declared, "I will arrange an escort of trusted warriors for your travel, as a way of further pacifying the ministers that you are in compliance. But you and the Lady will instead go to Yamalung and stay for a time, until the snows in the mountains decrease. The Bon Ministers can send their spies here to Chimpu and see you have surely left. You will be free and unmolested to continue your meditation at Yamalung."

Padma nodded in agreement. "That is a good plan. However, I do think it important that when it is time for the Lady and me to proceed to Zhoto Tidro, we shall have a secret audience for the Buddhist Ministers, so they do not lose heart thinking we are banished. Knowing we continue in the dharma, their faith will grow stronger."

"Very well," Trisong said. "I will see you off from there as well."

Then, Trisong rose to his feet. Padma and Tsogyal also rose.

As he put his sword-belt on, Trisong nodded to Tsogyal saying, "I have a gift for you, Noble Daughter."

Placing his hand on the hilt on his sword, he opened the door and called out for the gift to be brought forth. A warrior stepped up and handed him a ceramic bowl wrapped in a silk scarf. Taking the bowl, Trisong turned back into the room and handed it to Tsogyal. Wrapping her hands around it, she looked at Trisong with a quizzical smile.

"I will leave several men behind to protect you until you leave for Yamalung. How many days do you request to stay here?"

Padma answered, "We will be ready to leave in two days. Is that enough time for you to arrange an escort?"

Trisong nodded. "Very well, your escort shall be awaiting you in the valley at the base of the mountain. Until Yamalung," he said in farewell.

Turning, he opened the wooden door and stepped outside, then pulled it shut behind him. The brightness of the sunlight blinded him for a moment. He called to his men and arranged for four to remain protecting the Master and his consort. The remainder would return with him the way they had come, down the path.

Trisong stood still for a moment, watching as his men disappeared down the trail before him. Enjoying a moment of solitude, he breathed in a long deep breath of the cold clean air as he gazed at the view from the mountain height down into the valley below and the mountain range beyond. Rays of the sun, now low in the sky, lit up the mountainsides in hues of greens and golds. The valleys and ravines were filled with deep shadows of purple. The sky was painted with wisps of lavender on a canvas of many hues of blue.

A memory of himself as a young warrior, riding fast on his horse into battle, flashed into Trisong's mind. For a moment he felt the surging power of his horse beneath him, his bow held tightly, his arm straight, his other hand drawing the arrow back, his steely resolve to win the battle coursing through him. Striding down the trail, away from the cave, Trisong smiled to himself thinking, *Now I am a warrior to win the battle for the* dharma.

Inside the cave, Tsogyal set the bowl down on the table and unwrapped the silk covering. She and Padma peered down into the vessel. They both let out a laugh, seeing the contents. Within the bowl was gleaming white yogurt with amber honey trickled over the top.

32

The sun's rays were hot on the backs of her hands holding the reins as her horse climbed the steep winding path. Rab-ten fought off the fatigue assailing her. Suddenly she came awake, jolted, as her horse lurched to navigate the rocks dusted with snow on the ascending trail. The river they followed roared as the snow melt brought its waters high. Rab-ten could hear the thump and clink of the boulders and rocks as the freezing water spun and churned over and through them down the ravine. She grew cold as the trail passed beneath high rock walls, casting a shadow on the foursome as they climbed higher and higher to reach the caves of Zhoto Tidro. Looking down, they all marveled, seeing a thick layer of ice still clinging to the sides of the rock walls deep in a section of the river gorge, eternally cold and dark, the sun's rays never reaching its depths.

Riding for days since they left the hermitage at Yamalung, Rab-ten was not used to travel like this. It had been many springs since she lived in a tent and on a horse following her husband Jigme when they were part of Prince Zhonnu's army. *I am still strong,* she thought, *I will become stronger with each day.* Memories of her last time with her husband Jigme assailed her, looping around and around in her mind.

Jigme had looked quizzically at his wife, Rab-ten, when she had asked him to ride out, away from Samye, to a place their conversation would not be overheard. Jigme, however, had consented. In a small valley far away from interested ears, they stood face-to-face as their horses grazed nearby on the sparse grass.

His face grim and hard, Jigme asked in disbelief, "You wish to go with Tsogyal and Master Padma? But you are my wife, you belong with me."

"Now that the Emperor has made you General of the Emperor's Army in the West, you will be gone for a long time. I do not wish to follow your battles into the western lands," Rab-ten protested. "You will be General! You will have no time for me in the west. I will sit in a tent and on a horse while you command your men and have strategy meetings with the other generals."

Waving his arm in the direction of Samye in the distance, Jigme asked, "Are there not great teachers of Buddhism in Samye? If you do not wish to accompany me, then why can you not be content to study with them and remain here?"

Rab-ten's eyes began to fill with tears. "I do not wish to stay here while those I care for most for are now gone from Samye. I have nothing here, I wish to practice the dharma with Master Padma and be with my sister, Tsogyal. "

Calming his frustration, Jigme inquired, "Has Master Padma even accepted you?"

Nodding her head emphatically, Rab-ten explained, "I sent a written parchment explaining my request with one of the escort warriors from Chimpu. Master Padma sent a reply from Yamalung accepting me, but only if you are in agreement."

Then in a soft voice, Rab-ten consoled, "I would never leave you, husband. I am your wife and will always be. There is none other than you who fills my heart. I simply wish your blessing for me to go be with those I care so much for, in your absence."

Jigme's face softened as he looked into his wife's face, now understanding the reason she would not follow him to the West.

Rab-ten stepped closer to him, seeing his expression now softer and his mind opening. "While you are away I will simply be with the Master and Tsogyal in their secret place. You like Master Padma, do you not? You have told me you trust him. Do you not yourself feel an attraction to the Buddha's teachings?"

Jigme stood thinking, then asked, "What of the Emperor, does he know of your desire?"

Rab-ten nodded. "Yes, I have requested leave. He expressed that if you give permission for me to go he will grant it. Being a dharma practitioner himself, the Emperor has a desire to assist all who wish to go into deep practice. Besides, he expressed that I would be helpful in the daily chores to Tsogyal and the Master."

Thinking, Rab-ten then added, "Do you not think it an omen you have just now been granted the promotion you have desired for so long? And what of my dream, to practice the dharma with the Master? Should I not also be granted my dreams and desires in my life?"

It was true, Jigme thought, *it is an omen that one of the Generals of the Western Army had died and the Emperor promoted Jigme to replace him.* Though Jigme knew he had proven himself to the Emperor to be a leader of men and a good strategist in war, so he was a likely candidate. Still, the timing of the event was an omen and it was also true he did like and trust Master Padma.

Jigme, being told by the Emperor the secret of Padma and Tsogyal going to Zhoto Tidro instead of India and Lhodrak, asked, "So, all in Samya will think you have gone with me?"

Rab-ten nodded. "Yes, I will go to Yamalung when you leave for the West. I will stay there until the Master and Noble Daughter Tsogyal leave for Zhoto Tidro and will go with them."

Jigme paced a few strides away from Rab-ten, considering as he looked up at the mountains in the distance, their white peaks glistening in the bright sun. He noticed a large majestic vulture in the distant sky, soaring in circles, spiraling higher and higher on the draft. Rab-ten stood still watching him. She followed his gaze to the flight of the soaring bird and waited. Jigme stood contemplating the soaring bird for a long time. Then turning to Rab-ten, he walked up to her and took her hands in his. His battle-scarred face and hard eyes softened, filling with his love for her.

Looking into her eyes, he brushed her cheek with his coarse fingers as he said, "You shall have your dream, my wife. Go with my blessing."

Holding back the welling of tears, Rab-ten returned to the present as her horse drew up to the group.

Abaka smiled at her. "We have arrived as far as we can go on horseback," he announced. "From here we must go by foot."

Padma walked up to Rab-ten. Looking up at her sitting on her horse, he informed her, "We will set up the tent here for the night and rest. On the morrow we shall proceed to the caves."

Rab-ten nodded, then swung her stiff leg slowly over the rump of her horse. Padma took her by the waist to help her down.

Smiling at her, he asked, "Stiff?"

Rab-ten smiled as she nodded, then let out a groan when she went to take a step. Her thighs seized up in spasms. She massaged her legs then took more steps. She grimaced at the stiffness in her knees. They loosened as she walked in circles.

Looking back at Padma, who was watching her with concern on his face, she laughed. "I am fine now. I am strong." Then standing straight and tall, she inquired, "How can I help?"

Padma nodded. "Very well, let us unpack the mules, then you and Tsogyal can set up the tent and prepare evening tea and our meal. I will help Abaka bring the horses and mules to the grazing area."

Tsogyal dismounted Dawa and fastened the reins to a large rock. She walked over to help with unpacking one of the mules. Rab-ten was relieved to see she was limping in stiffness too.

Hours later, they all sat cross-legged in the felt tent. Bowls of tsampa, toasted barley flour, in their laps and cups of hot tea held in appreciative hands as the wind rustled the tent walls. The horses and mules, content with their hours of grazing on the hillside grass, stood tied and snoozing outside the tent.

"Yes, I have seen a couple of speed-walkers," Padma said in answer to Abaka's inquiry. "They can cover vast distances in a short period of time."

"Why bother?" Abaka asked. "I hear they sit and practice for many springs and for what? Why, a good horse can take you as fast."

"True," Padma agreed, "and you can enjoy the land you pass through on a horse."

"Is that because they are in a trance the entire time they are speed-walking?" Tsogyal inquired.

Swallowing the tsampa he had squeezed into a ball and popped into his mouth, Padma nodded as he took a sip of tea. Then he answered, "Yes, the practice requires total concentration on a distant point. They are aware of the place they begin and the place they end, yet see nothing in between. They also cannot do this speed-walking over rough terrain, best for them on the open plains."

Rab-ten inquired, "I thought this was a siddhi of dharma practice."

"No, it is not a dharma practice, though it is practice of lung, or wind. Anyone who wants to spend many seasons of their life engaged in the practice, with a competent teacher, can achieve it. Though it is not a path to enlightenment," Padma explained.

Taking a pull off the dried yak meat, Abaka chewed. Swallowing, he laughed. "One passed me when I was in the north. He looked ridiculous bounding in leaps, his eyes bugging out, gazing somewhere way ahead of him, murmuring his mantra. He looked like a madman." Shaking his head, he straightened, stretching his back, adding, "It is not noble, like riding a fine Ferghana horse is. I would rather see the world between the ears of a fine horse."

They all murmured in agreement as they chewed tsampa and sipped their tea. A cold wind blew outside the felt tent. The river continued its roaring decent, a millennia of carving the gorge deeper. The full moon sent shafts of light embracing the small black tent nestled between the soaring steep mountainsides of stone as soft laughter arose from within.

33

ℜab-ten sat mesmerized by the swirling water. She followed its course as it plunged over boulders and fell into eddies, then between rocks until it disappeared over the edge and out of sight. Her hand lost all feeling as she held the skin water-bag in the current, the freezing water sliding over her hand. Bringing the bag up, now heavy and full, she tied it closed, setting it down on the shore beside her. Quickly she rubbed her hand dry on her furs, then held them both under her arms. The freezing hand began to grow warm, the sensation almost painful. She heard sounds behind her and turned to see Abaka making his way down the rocks to where she stood.

Arriving, he looked down at the six bags she had filled with water and nodded. "Here, sister, let me help you."

Rab-ten said nothing as she watched him lift three of the bags and start back up the way he had come. Looking after him, she smiled. She was startled the first time he called her sister, not understanding. Then she realized he wanted her to know she was safe with him, he would never offend her. It showed his respect for her and a familial bond as now they were all a family of practitioners. She liked Abaka and thinking of him as her brother made her feel secure in his presence.

Picking up the remaining heavy skin-bags of water, Rab-ten followed, her legs burning as she climbed up the rocks to the path.

Reaching the path, she adjusted the water-skins in her grasp and continued, all the while seeing Abaka's form growing smaller as he made his way up the winding path. Finally they reached a rock-face wall. Hanging from a cave opening far above was a ladder of hemp and wood. Alongside the ladder was a rope, which Abaka tied the water-skins to. Then he grasped hold of the rope ladder, stepping from wood limb to wood limb he rose higher and higher.

Waiting at the base of the ladder, Rab-ten looked out at the view of rugged rocky hillsides descending into the river gorge. She could see their horses and mules, side-by-side all tied to a rope stretching between two boulders, their heads hanging as they napped. They were content now that they had spent the morning grazing with Abaka and Rab-ten watching over them, alert to signs of hungry wolves. Abaka carried his powerful recurve bow of horn and sinew, his quiver of arrows hung from his belt. He also carried his sword sheathed at his side. He gave his dagger to Rab-ten, for her defense should she need it.

She turned her gaze up at the steep rock-encrusted slopes soaring upward, disappearing into the clouds that were wrapped around their tops. As a cold wind whipped around her face, Rab-ten drew her fur collar up higher around her cheeks. The bags at her feet tied to the rope began to rise as Abaka pulled them up into the cave. The rope, now free of bags, dropped and Rab-ten tied her load to the end. She watched them rise and disappear into the rock wall. Then Abaka's head appeared, looking down at her. He waved his hand, motioning her to ascend the ladder.

Grabbing the rope sides, Rab-ten felt the roughness bite into her hands as she pulled herself up with each foot-hold on the wooden steps. The ladder twisted and swung as she ascended the rock wall. At the cave opening, she felt strong hands grasp her by her arms and pull her inside. Looking up, she found herself looking into Padma and Abaka's smiling faces.

"Come, sit, have tea," Padma said. "You have been working all morning."

Rab-ten went to the fire pit inside the cave and sat on a cushion of furs. Padma handed her a cup of warm tea. Rab-ten took in her surroundings. The cave was small at the opening, then it opened to make a good-sized room, where they all sat around the fire. It continued back into the hill, making a smaller room. Rab-ten could see Tsogyal in that room sitting on a cushion of furs, clearly in deep meditation. Though the light was dim, Rab-ten could see her face was serene and beautiful.

"We shall have some discussion for a while," Padma said in a quiet voice.

"Will our talk not disturb Tsogyal's meditation?" Rab-ten inquired.

"No, no, she is learning to not allow distractions. Our discussion will help her in her practice," Padma assured. "Here," Padma said, handing Rab-ten a bowl filled with tsampa, "have something to eat."

Rab-ten took the proffered bowl appreciatively and proceeded to squeeze the flour and fat into balls, then popping one of them into her mouth, she chewed. As she ate, Padma turned his attention to Abaka, who was sitting on the other side of the firepit sipping tea.

"So, have you considered our last conversation?" Padma inquired.

Nodding as he swallowed his tea, Abaka answered, "Yes, I have given your points much thought. The prophet Mani, whose teachings I follow, describes a force of darkness that causes our deeds and actions. That we as beings have no control. However, you say that we have total control of our actions and that we must understand this if we are not to be as a leaf on the winds of karma. In truth, the Mani teaching did run against my nature, to posit such an idea; that it is not myself who acts badly but some other nature that causes such actions within me. However, I have been pondering, how do I know which is true? The prophet Mani or you, Master Padma?"

Listening intently to Abaka's words and feeling his energy, Padma asked, "How dedicated are you to knowing the answer?"

Abaka sat thinking, considering this question. All was silent in the cave. Coming to a decision, Abaka looked directly into Padma's eyes, saying, "I am a warrior at heart. I no longer lust for warfare as I did when I was young. It is not power I seek any longer. Now I seek to know what is truth in life, indeed in existence."

Sitting up straighter and taking a breath, Abaka let it out slowly, then he continued, "If you will accept me, I ask you to teach me that which you know. I have no gold to give you, I have only my solemn promise that I will follow your direction to the fullest, you have my allegiance. I will ask the Emperor for whatever leave you direct I take for my practice. As well, I will stay and help Lady Rab-ten with the chores required for your retreat with Noble Daughter Tsogyal."

Padma nodded as he considered Abaka's proclamation. Then he said, "Gold is necessary in that it buys provisions for staying in places like this for practice. It buys horses and mules for travel. Other than for those basic things, I have no use for gold. I do not require gold for my teachings, I only require those with a pure heart, as you have." Nodding to Abaka, Padma went on, "I see you are a noble man, a sincere man. Your word is as solid as the rock that makes these walls. I accept you as my student."

Abaka smiled broadly, hearing these words. Padma held up his finger, admonishing, "However, I expect you to fully investigate all of my teachings, do not take my word for anything. Faith should not be blindly following a belief. For blind faith is weak and can be toppled easily." Looking from Abaka to Rab-ten, Padma continued, "Faith should be something that grows from reasoned investigation as to its truth. You must test every teaching I give you as to its truth. Reasoned faith is as strong as a banyan tree, never can be felled." Pointing to Abaka then to Rab-ten at their heart center, Padma instructed, "Your Buddha nature lies within, the teachings show the way to recognize it, it is not something fabricated. And your faith in the path must be a reasoned faith."

Padma sat back, his hands on his knees, taking in a deep breath then he let it out slowly. The soft spit and crackle of the fire hummed in the silence. Abaka and Rab-ten sat very still, waiting. Padma closed his eyes for a few moments then opened them looking at his new students.

"Do you have any questions?" he asked, looking directly at Abaka.

Shaking his head, Abaka answered, "No, Master, you are very generous. I will give my service to you and the Noble Ladies, while I am here."

Padma looked at both Abaka to Rab-ten. "I will give you both preliminary instruction for your time here in Zhoto Tidro. Then I will give you practices for you to bring back to your lives when you leave here."

Addressing Rab-ten, Padma said, "You are a married woman, but that is not a distraction from practice, indeed it is an aid to practice. I will show you in which ways this is true. It is good you will remain here with us here for a long time as it will allow you to build a foundation of practice. When the time comes for you to return to your husband, I will give you laywoman teachings so you can continue on the path to liberation."

To Abaka he said, "Abaka, you may return to serve your Emperor and continue your practice while in his service. Please stay as long as you like here with us. I will give you teachings to take with you when you wish to go."

Looking at both Rab-ten and Abaka, he instructed, "In the springs to come we will visit and I will continue to instruct you. You will find time in your future to go on retreats to deepen your practice. Chimpu is a fine place for retreat and is close to Samye."

Rab-ten felt relief flood through her at these words. She loved Jigme and did not want to leave him. She also loved the Master and Tsogyal and wanted to be with them. The Master was telling her she could have both and still be on the path to Nirvana.

Abaka sat transfixed by the words of Padma. He had thought his meager means would never allow him acceptance to the teachings of this great Master. *As well*, he mused, *he did not have to renounce the Prophet Mani, but was free to investigate both teachings and decide himself which was the truth.* He did not want to leave his Emperor. Now he could practice and serve as Master of Horse for the Emperor as well.

"Very well," Padma concluded, "today you both shall find places for your personal practice while here."

Abaka turned to Rab-ten. "Lady, would you prefer to practice in the tent or find a cave?"

Rab-ten answered, "A cave."

"Very well," Abaka said, "I shall remain in the tent next to the horses and mules. I will assist you in locating a cave and help you set all up inside for your practice. Then we can graze the mules and horses for their evening meal."

Looking at his two new students, Padma smiled. "Come here on the morrow, after you both have completed the morning grazing of the animals, and I will give you each instruction. Would either of you like more tea before you go?"

34

She took the proffered delicacy, a sweet plump dried apricot, tartness commingled with sweetness exploded in her mouth as she chewed. Sitting on furs cross-legged in meditation posture, Tsogyal remained rooted fully in the present moment, her senses were heightened. The pleasure of the fruit filled her being like honey poured into a bowl. Tsogyal smiled at Padma as he now offered her a cup filled with fragrant black tea from the mountains of China sweetened with honey.

The sun having just fallen below the high ridges outside of the cave preceded the darkness promising a frigid night. Tsogyal could hear the distant sound of the wind roaring outside the cave. But within all was still. Unwavering, the flames of the butter lamps burned, filling the dark cave with light. The scents of earth and rock, of smoke from the firepit and butter lamps commingled with the gentle scent of sandalwood and herbs of the burning stick of incense that Padma had lit to begin their practice this night.

Moons had passed since their arrival at Zhoto Tidro. Tsogyal had not had contact with anyone but Padma. She was in secluded retreat in the cave. Every several days Rab-ten would see the empty bags of water laying tied to the rope at the base of the cave. The rope ladder had been drawn up into the cave. She would fill the bags with water from the river, then bring them to the base of the cave and retie them before she set out for her own chores and meditation. Padma visited Rab-ten in her cave every few days, giving her instruction and answering her questions. Abaka was gone for a time, having taken the horses and mules to a local farmer in the lowlands were there was more forage, paying the man to care for them there. He would return, bringing more food and supplies before the snows started again. Then they would only have the one horse and one mule to graze. As the snows fell, the grass would become very sparse.

Now, sipping the warm sweetness of the tea, Tsogyal felt it slide down her insides creating a warm glow from within. The sensation was very pleasurable.

"Meditate on the emptiness of these pleasurable sensations," Padma instructed, "recognize pure awareness of mind."

"You are a most sensual and beautiful woman," Padma said softly.

Hearing these words caused Tsogyal to fill with pride in herself, causing her much pleasure. Not becoming distracted she meditated on the empty nature of her feelings, of sensations. Without grasping, she could see beyond the sensations she was experiencing to pure awareness.

Padma nodded in approval of his student's adeptness. After long practice she was now capable of the next step. Gently he began to stroke her leg, his warm touch sending tingles up Tsogyal's spine. He brought his hand up to her thigh, stroking and squeezing gently then more firmly, then gently again.

Tsogyal became flooded with sensations, she noticed desire rising. Recognizing this, she watched it without grasping, in moments it dissolved into pure sensation.

"Meditate on your secret chakra," Padma instructed, "Your secret mandala."

Following his instruction, Tsogyal meditated on her secret chakra at her cervix. She felt Padma's hands caressing her legs, then with his strong finger he gently entered her lotus, the vulva, and gently began to stimulate the veins, awakening the secret chakra.

212

Tsogyal meditated on her secret chakra being stimulated. This was the base of her central channel. Before now, her practice was to meditate on the base of the central channel which came to the chakra below the navel, above this secret chakra. Now she must use this assistance by Padma to awaken and meditate on this secret chakra within her lotus.

As he stirred Tsogyal's inner mandala, awakening it, Padma remained without lust or desire. Through his own practice and attainments he had been purified of these defilements long ago.

Visualizing the chakra at this energy center being awakened, Tsogyal saw in her mind's eye, the central channel arise from this base and followed it to the crown of her head. She saw the energy centers at each chakra point within the central channel. The channels on either side of the central channel appeared in her mind's eye. She drew air into her nostrils, bringing it down the side channels and then drawing it into the base of the central channel at her secret place. Drawing the inner wind into the central channel, bliss began to arise into her being.

Observing that Tsogyal was stable in her meditation, not being distracted by lust and sensation, Padma allowed his vajra to become fully erect. Gently leaving her, he sat back cross-legged on his furs. Aware what she must do now that Padma had seated himself, Tsogyal stood up from her place. Remaining fully in her concentration, she was no longer a mere woman of flesh but a mandala of the lotus. Kundalini energy lay alive and coiled in her base chakra. Looking up at her raw beauty and seeing her not as a woman but as a Goddess, Padma was filled with powerful feelings of pleasure as she approached him.

Swaying in a snake-like dance, the energy moving her body, Tsogyal straddled Padma and settled her lotus onto his flaming vajra, swallowing it into her. Taking command of her lotus throne, Padma held her body close to his, steadying it. Tsogyal straightened her torso to keep her central channel straight for unimpeded energy flow. The chakra at the tip of Padma's vajra, which was the base of his central channel, connected with the awakened secret chakra at the base of Tsogyal's central channel. Now they were in mystical union. Their red-

and-white essences mingled, creating intense bliss as powerful energy flowed through them, making a complete circuit.

After moons of practicing by herself to control the internal winds brought into her central channel, now Tsogyal must use her skills in this new challenge, to control the energy created by this powerful union with her Master as consort.

Padma had instructed her as to what she would strive to accomplish with their union. Steadying herself in the intense waves of blissful energy, Tsogyal directed the energy in her central channel to rise up all the way to her chakra at her forehead. When it reached this chakra, the nectar of her pure spiritual energy purified the passion of anger in her being and with it all traces of habitual action and reaction patterns. From this chakra, the energy flowed down into her throat center. Tsogyal felt it as cool sweet nectar as it purified within her being all the passions of desire. Flowing from her throat down into her heart center, Tosgyal felt the energy turn warm and saw it shimmer like opalescent nectar. The warmth turned hot as the seeds of passion that were inherent in her mind were eradicated. Powerful insight flooded her as to the elements of the path to liberation. Keeping her concentration steady, Tsogyal felt the hot nectar turn warm, then it cooled as it flowed down to her gut center. Here she felt intense visceral and raw bliss as the nectar of pure positive energy eradicated all traces of emotional clinging. Into her awareness the mandala of her egoistic attachment to Padma was revealed to her. Purified by the nectar of the kundalini energy, she was now a transcendent being. This awakened her to the understanding that this energy, once used to fuel her desires, but now having been purified, was being experienced by her now as pure awareness.

In deep awareness meditation, Padma could feel his consort had reached her goal. Gently he lifted her, thus breaking their mystical connection. Tsogyal maintained her concentration on her meditation as Padma helped her to her seat, settling her into a cross-legged position. Tsogyal straightened her posture.

"Now visualize the ascent of this love awareness and remain in meditation upon it as it ascends up your central channel. Remain here until you have reached your next attainment," Padma instructed. Then he silently went into the outer cave-room and settled himself to meditate on the accent of the afterglow of the kundalini within his central channel from their union. He glanced at the butter lamps, now almost extinguished. Rising, Padma went to the cave doorway and pulled the heavy felt covering aside and looked out. The powerful wind swirled and eddied against the steep hillsides of Zhoto Tidro. He listened to the river in its roaring decent through the gorge. Looking up at the bright sky, Padma saw the glimmer of the tip of sun; it would soon rise over the mountainside. His and Tsogyal's mystical practice had lasted throughout the night and most of the morning. He took in a deep breath of the cold clean air. Then Padma released the door flap, returned to his meditation cushion and seated himself. Satisfaction filled him as he considered the progress of his very special disciple.

35

ℜab-ten took hold of the rope ladder and pulled herself up, her arms straining with each step, her foot pushing on the wooden slats. She was pleased to feel how much stronger she was since her last accent up this rope ladder several moons ago. Today she was invited to the cave to see her spiritual sister. She was excited as it had been so long since she had last seen Tsogyal. In the passing moons Rab-ten had spent her days in her own solitary cave in meditation. With each visit by Padma instructing her, she had grown more and more confident in her practice of visualization and meditation.

Now at the top of the ladder, Rab-ten felt strong hands take her arms and lift her up into the rock-walled room. She smiled, looking into Abaka and Padma's serene faces.

"Tea?" Padma inquired.

"Yes, I would love some," Rab-ten answered, suppressing a giggle of delight.

Rab-ten handed Padma her own silver cup then seated herself upon the proffered cushion. Looking around the cave at the walls she had seen so long ago, the scents of incense, tea and roasted barley made her feel warm and relaxed. Glancing to the small back cave-room, Rab-ten thought she would see Tsogyal there in meditation, as she had the last time she was seated in this very same place. Tsogyal was not to be seen there, though not all the room was visible through the opening. Turning, Rab-ten took her cup from Padma's outstretched hands.

"You are looking forward to seeing your sister," Padma said, as a statement rather than a question.

Sipping the sweet and pungent hot liquid, Rab-ten nodded, then answered, "Yes, Master, she has been in retreat so long, I have missed her."

Rab-ten felt a presence behind her and turned to see Tsogyal entering the cave-room. Rab-ten's hand held her cup aloft as she sat transfixed by the sight of her spiritual sister. Tsogyal was slight, and not as toned of body. Rab-ten could tell, as Tsogyal wore only a simple cotton tunic. She moved lightly of step, almost as if she walked a bit above the dirt-and-rock floor. Reaching Rab-ten's side, Tsogyal bent her knees, crouching before Rab-ten, and looked into her eyes. Rab-ten wanted to place her cup down and hug Tsogyal, yet she remained unable to move at the shock of the transformation of this woman she had known so intimately. Tsogyal's eyes were luminous and filled with love.

"Sister," Tsogyal whispered, her voice like a soft warm breeze.

Willing herself to move, Rab-ten placed her cup upon the low table in front of her. Twisting sideways to Tsogyal, who was now kneeling, she held her hands out to Tsogyal who took them in hers.

"Sister," Rab-ten answered. "You look... you are different." Rab-ten struggled, trying to find the words, not able to describe the changes in Tsogyal.

Tsogyal giggled. "Well, I would hope so, Sister, as I have been practicing upon the path shown to me by Master Padma all these moons."

Rab-ten laughed, now a glimmer of her old friend still there. "You look beautiful and so... well I cannot describe it. Are you enlightened now?"

Rising like a wisp of smoke, Tsogyal moved to seat herself upon a cushion, completing the circle of all in the cave. Padma handed her a cup filled with hot sweet tea. The fragrance filled Tsogyal with great waves of pleasure. She smiled at Abaka over her cup, as she sipped the hot steeped leaves.

Lowering her cup, she turned her attention to Rab-ten, answering, "No, I am not fully enlightened. I have reached the first level of enlightenment. There is much further to go." Tsogyal explained, "I am not ready yet for the great effortless practice of Ati."

"Must you continue in retreat?" Rab-ten inquired.

"Yes, I must continue practice in retreat, but I must first go to the Valley of Nepal," Tsogyal answered.

"Nepal?" Rab-ten asked, astonished. "Why must you go to Nepal?"

"She must find a suitable consort and persist in the practice of the mysteries of the Mahayana," Padma interjected. "I am not that consort for her. There is a young man of sixteen springs who lives in Nepal. His name is Atsara Sale. He is an emanation of the Buddha Hayagriva. She must find him and bring him back here, then continue her practice of Tantra with him as her consort."

"Will you be accompanying her?" Rab-ten asked Padma.

"No, I shall not. I am to go to Chimpu. I have several disciples in retreat there who need my instruction. I have been here in Zhoto Tidro a long time," Padma explained.

"How will she find him?" Rab-ten asked, growing concerned.

"He has a mole on his right breast. He traveled from Serling, in India, to the Valley of Nepal. It shall not be hard to find him," Padma assured her.

"But, Master, the Valley of Nepal is many leagues away from here. A moon or more of travel over cold snowy passes. And there are robbers along the way. She cannot go alone," Rab-ten implored.

"I will accompany her," Abaka said, his clear voice sounding very loud in the small room.

Padma smiled and nodded. "That would be very good."

"Well, I am certainly going with her," Rab-ten said.

Frowning, Padma asked, "What of Jigme? Will he not be concerned you have gone to Nepal? You are under my protection. I was considering escorting you to Samye on my way to Chimpu, you can continue your practice there. Or you may come with me to Chimpu if you would like."

Rab-ten shook her head. "Thank you, Master, for your kind consideration, yet I must decline your offer." Looking intently at Padma, she continued, "Jigme is now in a sea of pounding hooves and slashing swords. He will be gone for a long time. I will not sit at Samye or Chimpu, leaving my sister to travel with only Abaka. They will need me. There are robbers on the road. Three of us traveling will be better than two."

Sitting back, Padma considered. "Very well," he said. "We will leave word for your husband with the Emperor that you have gone to Nepal with Tsogyal."

Rab-ten relaxed as she replied, "Thank you, Master. I am sure I will return from Nepal before Jigme has returned from the Western Front. He will not know I had been gone."

Placing his empty cup onto the low table, Abaka said, "I will leave on the morrow for the farm and retrieve our horses and mules. We can buy supplies for our journey on our way south."

Tsogyal rose, retreating into her room. Returning moments later, she carried a bag of gold coins in her hand. Holding the small heavy bag out to Abaka, she said, "Here is gold for what we will need."

Abaka felt its weight fall into his open palm.

36

"Chudak!" General Senge whispered, trying to cast his voice over the expanse of distance as quietly as possible. Catching Chudak's attention, Senge pointed.

There, hidden by rock and brush, was a musk deer feeding on the sparse grass growing on the hillside high above the valley below.

Chudak, standing on the steep slope across from the deer, was in the better position to make the kill with his bow. Keeping himself as still as possible, Chudak raised his bow and drew it back slowly. He aimed at the neck of the buck. Letting his draw-fingers relax, the string slid smoothly over his thumb ring, the arrow's flight straight with such speed it was not visible until the deer stumbled and lurched, then fell in a heap. The wide sharp steel arrow point had severed the deer's spinal cord, killing it instantly.

"By the Gods, what a shot, Chudak!" Senge called out as he stood up from his hiding place behind a boulder.

Chudak smiled brightly, calling to Senge as he made his way to his kill, "The Gods directed my arrow, General."

Clambering over rocks and brush, making his way to the side of the deer, Senge arrived by his youngest sister's husband's side. As he looked down at the fallen animal, Senge shook his head. "That was not the Gods, Chudak." Placing a hand on his young brother-in-law's shoulder, Senge assured, "You are a fine shot, Chudak. You can claim your ability as your own."

Shrugging, Chudak knelt, drawing his knife. "It will be a feast tonight," Chudak said as he slid the sharp blade into the deer's belly, slicing the length of it to remove the innards. The stench of cut entrails, blood and hide filled Chudak's nostrils.

As Chudak worked, Senge cast his gaze over the valley below, admiring the huge white clouds, sailing like the ships he had seen in the Bay of Bengal, on the wind across the deep blue sky. Looking down at the shadows the clouds made moving across the land, dark forms drew his attention. Though the forms were small, he counted three riders leading two mules loaded with supplies. Casting his gaze over the distance, he spotted another group of riders on a hillside. He realized they were observing the travelers. *Bandits,* he thought to himself.

"Chudak," Senge said, keeping his eyes on the robbers.

"Yes, General?" Chudak inquired. He looked up at Senge, who was gazing out at the valley with a concerned look on his face.

Chudak stopped his work and stood up, looking out to see what Senge was gazing at, hot blood turning cold on his hands.

"See them?" Senge murmured.

Chudak searched the valley, then saw the travelers. Looking where Senge was gazing, Chudak then saw the group of men hidden on the hillside.

"Your eyes are sharper than mine. How many thieves do you see?" Senge asked.

"I count seven bandits," Chudak said.

"It will take us some time to reach the travelers to warn them. Perhaps our presence with the three will deter the rogues," Senge said. Then looking at Chudak, he commanded, "We must go now, to the horses."

Looking down at the deer, Chudak felt torn. Senge placed a hand on Chudak's shoulder.

"Better to let the vultures have this deer," he said, glancing up at the sky. "Then let those vultures have those travelers," he said, looking a last time at the bandits as he turned and proceeded to where their horses were tied.   Nodding in agreement, Chudak wiped his bloody knife on the deer's hide, sheathed it, picked up his bow and hurried after General Senge.

"Would you like to visit your parents before we leave your father's Kingdom, Noble Daughter?" Abaka called to Tsogyal.

Riding his fine black Ferghana gelding, Abaka led two dun-colored mules from the rear.   Tsogyal sat astride Dawa.   The mare's white coat, like the shimmering moon she had been named after, contrasted with the royal saddle of red felt. The cantle, overlaid in silver embossed with figures of dragons, twinkled when the sun shone through the clouds above. Behind the saddle, saddlebags of red felt with gold-thread embroidery were full of gold pebbles and coins, gold bowls and food. Beside Tsogyal, Rab-ten rode on a red-dun Ferghana gelding.

Tsogyal urged Dawa, turning her and trotting back to ride next to Abaka.   Rab-ten continued on in the lead.

Reaching his side, Tsogyal answered, "I think not. I would love to see them, but I am concerned that it will take more time as they will wish me to stay."   Then with a wry face, she continued, "Unless they are angry that I am no longer Queen, just a vagrant." Tsogyal laughed, "A vagrant riding a Ferghana Royal mare upon a Royal saddle."

Turning to Abaka, Tsogyal wondered, "I think it is not good I am riding on this saddle, it will bring attention to us."

Looking over at the saddle under Tsogyal, Abaka nodded, "Yes, I should have thought of it. We should have taken it back to the palace and acquired a common saddle. We will trade it at market when we reach Nepal."

Tsogyal smiled at Abaka. "Thank you for all you have done to help me, my friend."

Abaka nodded. "You are very welcome, Noble Daughter."

A rumbling drew their attention. Looking up at the sky Tsogyal asked, "Is that thunder? Is a storm coming?"

Twisting in his saddle, looking behind them, Abaka's eyes grew wide. Tsogyal turned quickly in her saddle and saw them too. A cloud rose behind them as the group of horsemen bore down on them at the full gallop, their hooves as thunder on the wind.

"Take Rab-ten and run, Noble Daughter, I will lead the mules away from you, they will follow me," Abaka called.

"No!" Tsogyal commanded, fear rising in her throat. "Leave the mules, we all will run. They only want the supplies. I have gold, we can buy more later." She looked imploringly at Abaka, terror in her eyes. Nodding, he let the lead rope fall from his hand as they both kicked their horses.

Rab-ten turning in her saddle, hearing Tsogyal and Abaka's raised voices and the sound of thundering behind them, took in the entire situation.

"Run, Rab-ten!" Abaka yelled, as he and Tsogyal came charging up to her. Dawa soon took the lead, charging past Rab-ten, Tsogyal laying low over Dawa's neck. Rab-ten needed no kick to her horse, she held on as her gelding bolted to follow Dawa. Abaka reached Rab-ten's side, and the two of them raced side-by-side. Abaka looked back over his shoulder to see the bandits reach the mules and circle them. *Good*, he thought, *they will leave us.*

Rab-ten's gelding took the lead, frantic to catch Dawa. Abaka urged his mount to catch Rab-ten. Rab-ten looked ahead to find where Tsogyal had gone, only a cloud of dust remained. Then, Rab-ten felt her horse stumble. Instinctively, Rab-ten pulled her body back to aid her horse, trying to lift him up out of his stumble. It was no use, her horse could not regain its footing and fell, its neck outstretched, its legs folding under its body as it skidded onto the ground. Rab-ten felt her body leave the saddle and helplessly slam hard as if the rocky ground heaved up into her.

She lay stunned, her face stinging, dry dirt in her mouth. She tried to move, her arms felt heavy as she forced them to respond. Pushing herself up onto her knees, she remembered their situation. Adrenaline coursed through her, causing all of her senses to return.

Looking up, she saw Abaka arrive and circle his horse around her, his sword drawn.

"Sister, are you hurt?!" he called to her as he looked from her then back to the bandits.

Rab-ten forced herself to stand. On unsteady legs, she stumbled to her gelding, now standing with his head hanging, she grabbed the reins and held them tight.

"They are coming," Abaka said, resigned. "We must make a stand here. Hold tight to your horse, can you mount?"

It was too late, the horde had arrived. Rab-ten felt for the knife she wore in her belt, it was still there. Drawing it from its sheath, she stood, clutching it hard, with her legs wide, toes clenched, tethering her to the ground.

Seven mounted men circled them, their faces hard and menacing. They carried spears and swords.

"Take the mules and leave us," Abaka roared, his sword held high, ready to fight.

Just then an arrow flew into the horde, grazing one of the robber's shoulder. Then another flew in, grazing the flank of a bandit's horse, causing it to shy and bolt. Perplexed, the robbers looked around to see two warriors charging towards them, bows drawn, two more arrows at the ready.

"The other one!" one robber yelled to the others, as he pointed in the direction that Tsogyal had gone. "That one has the Royal saddle!"

As a group, the thieves all bolted away after Tsogyal. Abaka gripped tightly to his sword, watching the robbers leave. Turning to face the next wave of attack from these two new riders bearing down on them, Abaka held his sword high, menacingly, ready to fight Senge and Chudak as they arrived.

Slowing their mounts as they circled around Abaka and Rab-ten, Senge announced, "I am General Senge. I serve King Pelgyi."

"The robbers have gone. You are safe," Chudak called out, intent on Abaka's raised sword. Then, looking down at Rab-ten, as his horse circled around them, he asked, "Are you injured, Lady?"

Abaka lowered his sword, then pointed it in the direction Tsogyal and the robbers had gone. He called out frantically to Senge and Chudak, "Leave us. You must go after them. They are following the Noble Daughter. She carries our gold."

Recalling he had seen three travelers and here stood two, Senge asked, "Your companion is a woman?"

"Yes!" Rab-ten yelled, to be heard. "She is Tsogyal, she needs your help."

"Tsogyal?" Chudak asked. "You mean Tsogyal of Karchen?"

"Yes," Abaka called out, "King Pelgyi's daughter. You must go help her. I will help Lady Rab-ten and we will follow after you. By the Gods, make haste, go now!"

Chudak looked at Senge, trying to comprehend what was being said by these travelers. A look of pure astonishment on Senge's face turned to resolve as he turned his horse and kicked it to the gallop to follow after the bandits. Chudak spun Lungta and loosened his reins, freeing her head. His legs gripped her sides as she raced away, quickly catching Senge, then flying past him, taking the lead.

37

Heart pounding with the rhythm of Dawa's hooves striking the earth, Tsogyal felt the panic of raw fear coursing through her. She was not a woman, she was not human, she was a creature filled with terror running to survive. They were as wolves, after her, their teeth sharp, lusting for her blood. To them, she was nothing more than flesh to devour. They felt no love or caring, they lived to brutalize all those who had the misfortune of crossing their path. They stole, they brutalized, they raped, they killed. They were worse than wolves, they were evil men.

She felt Dawa's terror, that of a prey animal. Dawa, in turn, felt Tsogyal's terror. Following her leader's direction, running as fast as she was able, trusting in Tsogyal to find them a safe place.

Twisting her head to look back, Tsogyal realized Abaka and Rab-ten were not behind her. She faced forward again, agony rising in her as thoughts raced through her mind. *They have been captured. I should go back. No, then they will capture me as well. Will the bandits come after me? Where shall I go? To father's palace? Which direction is the palace?*

Tsogyal lifted her head up, searching for a place to hide. She sat up straighter, pulling on Dawa's reins, slowing her. Dawa pulled up and spun in circles as Tsogyal searched frantically the landscape around her for a place to hide. Feeling Tsogyal's terror and indecision, Dawa began to rear and shake her head. Squealing, she demanded that Tsogyal let her run.

Tsogyal looked about. The land lay wide open with valleys far in the distance. She looked hopefully up to the clouds floating on the wind, the urge to hide so great. Yet, she could not hide there. Looking back from where she had come, she saw the ominous sign of dust wisping in the distance. She swallowed hard, knowing it was the dust churned up by the hooves of the horses ridden by the evil men. They were searching for her. Tears began to well in her eyes, clouding her vision. Wiping them away with the soiled long sleeve of the under-linen beneath her dusty blue robe of thick wool, her breath came in short gulping gasps. Her chest felt tight, her body trembled with fear.

Dawa stamped her hooves and snorted, jigging from side to side as Tsogyal held her reins tight. Casting her frantic gaze once again over the distance, Tsogyal asked herself aloud, "How far can Dawa run?" The answer came as soon as the question. *Not much farther, maybe a few miles. I will kill her if I make her run further. They will catch me, I will kill Dawa,* she thought, her heart sinking.

The wind blew hard, whipping her hair away from her face. She sat frozen and trembling on Dawa. The mare continued jigging and stamping her hooves as she pulled on the reins firm in Tsogyal's grasp, yet Tsogyal was unable to act. There was something she was forgetting, the thought niggled at her, below the surface of her terror. The wind blew hard, then a faint sound came to her ears on the wind, *Om Ah Hum.* She tilted her head, to listen. *Om Ah Hum,* it came again. Her heart began to slow its pounding slightly as she listened. Memory rushed through her mind as she remembered Padma's words to her before she had left him, 'If misfortune befalls you, think of me,' he had told her.

Her voice quavering, she chanted, "Om, Ah, Hum, Vajra Guru Padma Siddhi Hum." Feeling the power of the mantra, she chanted the incantation again, "Om, Ah, Hum, Vajra Guru Padma Siddhi Hum." She chanted it over and over, again and again.

In defiance of her fear, she spoke aloud, into the wind, "I am not an animal. I am a Buddha!"

Turning Dawa, continuing away from the bandits, she kept the mare at an easy trot as she continued her chant. The chanting and steady rhythm of Dawa's trotting hooves calmed her, Tsogyal steadied herself to visualize her Master, Padma. Seeing his form clearly in her mind, she heard a voice from within her. *You are a practitioner. Transform this experience. Remember the dharma.*

Gradually, understanding filled her. Now she knew what she should do. Slowing Dawa to a walk, she reassured the mare in a calm voice, "We are not frightened deer, my beauty. I will protect you. Be calm now."

Feeling Tsogyal's confidence, Dawa calmed, blowing her fear from her nostrils. Stopping, Tsogyal dismounted. Untying the saddlebags, she pulled them free from Dawa's back. The mare shook her entire sweat-coated body under the saddle, then lowered her head and began to graze on a tuft of dry grass.

Kneeling on the ground, Tsogyal cleared the rocks and stones, making a circle of space on the earth. The rumble of many riders sounded in the distance. Pulling the bowls and small bags of gold dust from the saddlebags, she placed them within the circle, making a mandala of them. Then she took the food from the bags and added it to the geometric display. Settling herself, she concentrated inwardly, into her heart. She felt the cold breeze against her face. The sun shone from behind the clouds, warming her as it enveloped her. The thunder of heavy hooves drew near.

Shagdur's face felt tight as he grimaced, galloping his horse hard in the lead to find the rider on the white horse with the red Royal saddle. *We lost the mules, but certainly there is gold in those saddlebags,* the thoughts spun in his mind. He gripped the reins tighter imagining the gold in his grasp. Twisting in the saddle, he looked behind him, wondering if the warriors that attacked them were in pursuit. Only his six compatriots charged behind him, a cloud of dust in their wake. Turning forward, he raised his head to scan the distance. Then, his grimace turned to a sneer when he saw the small figure of a grazing white horse in the distance.

A riderless horse? Must have thrown its rider, he mused. "I have you now," he said aloud, his words lost in the wind. "You will not escape me."

A rush of power filled him. He loved stalking his prey, then the chase and soon the capture. But, this was the moment he loved best, just before the taking, when they could not escape him. His mouth salivated, he licked his wind-dried lips, thinking of the capture soon at hand. Raising his arm, he signaled his men toward the mare in the distance. Directing his horse, he changed course and spurred his mount toward the mare. The men saw the mare and all spread out into a line abreast, casting a net.

Drawing closer, Shagdur saw a form upon the ground, illuminated in a circle made by the rays of sun breaking through the clouds. Slowing his horse as he came closer, he was amazed to see a woman kneeling before glittering gold. *A woman?* he thought, amazed, then delighted. *She does not look injured. She has displayed her gold, what an easy catch,* he thought. He felt a surge of lust and power. "Easy though it may be, you are mine," he growled softly. "I will have your gold, I will have your horse, and I will have you. Then all of my men will have you too."

The bandits slowed alongside of Shagdur, one charged past as Dawa bolted away frightened by the onslaught of riders. He caught her quickly, and leading her, trotted back to the horde. They all sat upon their stamping, blowing steeds, a semicircle before Tsogyal's small form. The gold laid out before her twinkled and glittered. Their faces were hard and grim, sword and knife scars disfigured more than one face.

Shagdur dismounted his horse. Following his lead, all the men dismounted, their capes of fur swirled and flapped in the rising wind, their swords in silver-mounted scabbards, studded with stones of turquoise and corals, swung from their belts. Holding spears with strong hands, their heavy hammered-silver bracelets glimmered in the sunlight.

38

Dropping his horse's reins, Shagdur strode toward Tsogyal. The jangle of his hanging scabbard, the slapping of his whipping robe in the wind, the crunch of his heavy footfalls came closer to her.

Shagdur felt a powerful anger rise in him. *Why does she not run in fear? You ignorant woman, do you not know what I am going to do to you?* Thoughts crashed in his mind, anger rising to a crescendo, he growled out loud, "Fear me, bitch!"

His fists were clenched, eager to grab her and pick her up from the ground into his possession and shake fear into her. He wanted to hear her screams and pleas, begging him to have mercy, his phallus growing harder with each scream of terror. Her terror growing to panic, he would beat her struggling body and violate her into submission and degradation. Then he would watch as each of his men took her over and over again. Excitement rose in him as the images played in his mind. Step by step, he came closer to his prey.

Then, he froze. The light around the woman grew brighter, he shielded his eyes. Trying to look upon the form of the woman, shock rose in him, not believing what he was seeing. Inexplicably, the light came not from the sun's rays above, but seemed to radiate from the center of her form. Turning to look back at his men, he saw them all looking at each other, astonishment on their faces, confirming they were all seeing the same phenomenon. Shagdur took a hesitant step closer to Tsogyal.

The glowing woman raised her face to him, her speech like tinkling bells, "Oh, you seven, you are but a form of enlightenment for my meditation, you are my Yidam. It is fortunate for me to meet you here today, so that I may attain Buddha-hood and fulfill the wishes of all sentient beings to be freed from the ocean of suffering. Let karmic misadventure be swiftly transformed. How marvelous!"

The thieves stood transfixed by the melodious sound of this apparition's voice. They all looked at each other in surprise. She was speaking in their Newar language. As her words filled the men's ears, the ever-present tension that held their bodies and minds in painful bondage fell away like reptilian skin. Their hard faces turned soft. Their yellowed and broken teeth showed as smiles grew over their faces.

Shagdur felt his body relax, all of his muscles let go their tension. He felt emotions drop away. He was no longer angry. Desire no longer nagged at him, he wanted nothing. Having no desire for anything, this moment was all there was. He was filled with bliss. The cold wind blew on his face, the exquisite sensation of it trembled through him. His gaze turned upward to see a bird soaring high on the wind. The beauty and majesty of its form caused his heart to swell. Taking in a breath, he felt his very life force coursing through his entire body. He stopped himself from crying out, the pure pleasure almost intolerable.

Turning his attention to the other men, he could see each was absorbed in his own personal ecstasy. One by one, they stepped closer to Tsogyal.

Bowing low before her, one man asked, "Venerable Lady, of what country are you?"

Tsogyal spread her hands wide, palms up, as she answered, her voice like a melodious song, "My fatherland is Overflowing Joy. Do you wish me to lead you there? Then I will show you that aggression and malice are mirror-like awareness itself. Your minds, filled with hostility and anger are the very source of the energy for radiance and clarity.

Look into this anger that seethes in you. Simply watch it. Do not cling to things as they appear, let emptiness arise."

Silence overtook all as one by one the men knelt down on the ground before her and leaned back on their heels. They were all filled with wonder at the power of this remarkable woman.

"Lady, who are your father and mother?" another of the thieves asked.

Tsogyal directed her smile to him. "My father is the source that grants me all that I may need and wish. Indeed, he is an all-providing wishing-jewel. Worldly wealth are simply mirages, I am not enthralled by these. Thus, I am freed from the mental states of hankering and lust. Looking into them I have realized all-perceiving primordial wisdom. And yet from this energy of desire itself comes clear perception. Do not be attached to this clarity either, by letting go, bliss itself arises."

Looking at each man before her, Tsogyal continued, "My mother is pure all-pervasive light. She is Great Bliss beyond all fathoming."

Distant sounds of rumbling could be heard coming closer and closer. Seconds later Senge and Chudak arrived, their bows raised and drawn ready to kill. Senge's teeth were bared as he braced his bow, looking for his first target. Chudak held his bow steady as Lungta charged around the circle of the kneeling men and Tsogyal. Both warriors could not at first decipher what was happening. Confusion overtook their minds, seeing that all the brigands were kneeling, their heads low.

Tsogyal stood and held her hand up to halt their assault. Chudak gazed at Tsogyal as Lungta raced in a circle around the group. She was seemingly aglow and there were bowls of gold spread out before her. The brigands, all kneeling, some in prostration, heads touching the ground, had no concern of the arrival of Senge and Chudak, they remained in rapt attention, hanging on every word of this Goddess seated before them.

Senge answered Tsogyal's signal by nodding to her, lowering his bow, he moved off a short distance away from the circle of men before her. Chudak followed. Bringing Lungta beside Senge, they calmed their mounts. Senge and Chudak sat mounted, observing this unusual event, ready to move in to protect Tsogyal should the men kneeling before her become a threat. Yet, they were not threatening. This was very strange.

Tsogyal sat down again and resumed her teaching to the thieves.

Chudak leaned over toward Senge as he whispered, "What is happening? What language is she speaking?"

"She is speaking Newar," Senge growled. "These brigands are from Nepal." Anger rose in him that these brigands come into his King's land accosting and stealing from Tibetans. Then looking at Chudak, whose face was contorted in perplexity, Senge shrugged, not having an answer to how this was happening.

Senge stepped his horse up a bit closer, wanting to hear what Tsogyal was saying, perhaps finding the answer to what could have caused these men to surrender. At hearing her lilting voice, his stern countenance softened. Coming closer to Tsogyal, the memory of the oracle Shatri's admonishment filled his mind. *She is no ordinary woman, respect her, protect her.* Looking upon her bright form, seated on the hard ground, Senge felt a lightness come over him as her words reached his ears.

"Look behind jealous thoughts to the true nature of that which energizes them. Detach from envy and resentments, whatever arises is pure. Find the source of a bigoted mind that is quick to judge and hold grudges, there you will experience all-accomplishing awareness. Look into all the activity of the mind to find its true nature. Emotions are simply energy. The mind is active, looking for content to cling to. Do not be confused by the activity of your mind and emotions. Look into them to realize the true nature of awareness and become free from samsara, free from delusion."

Tsogyal sat quietly, her last word trailing off into the void. The wind whistled through the rocks and sparse grass.

Breaking the silence that descended on all of them, Shagdur spoke, his tone pleading, "Noble Lady, will you come with us to our land in the Valley of Nepal and teach your great wisdom to our people there?" The other men's voices rose in agreement.

Nodding solemnly, Tsogyal explained softly, "I must continue on my way with my companions. I am going to Nepal on an important errand, yet I may not tarry there. When completed, I must return here to Tibet."

Just then Tsogyal looked to up to see Abaka and Rab-ten, both mounted on Abaka's horse standing at the near distance outside the circle of brigands kneeling before her. Rab-ten was seated behind Abaka, holding the lead-rope of the mules. Rab-ten's horse, its leg swollen, was tied to the tail of the second mule. Grabbing Abaka's arm for support, Rab-ten swung off the black gelding, a look of concern and amazement on her face. Tsogyal could see there was dried blood and dirt on the side of Rab-ten's face. The front of her robe was brown with dirt. Rab-ten and Abaka remained still and silent, watching the curious event unfolding.

Tsogyal turned her attention back to the seven men before her. "There is a great teacher of this dharma in Nepal. Travel south and east of the City of Kathmandu until you find the caves at Yanglesho. It is less than two days ride, I am told. There you will find the retreat of the disciples of Padma. They will teach you the preliminary practices of the path of this dharma. When the Great Master Padma arrives there, as he will, you will be given more advanced teachings," Tsogyal instructed.

Though disappointed that she refused their plea, the thieves all bowed and murmured their gratitude for this prospect she had given them.

Shagdur called to the man, who, though kneeling, still held Dawa's reins clasped in his hand, "Bring the Wisdom Lady's horse."

Stepping through the throng of men, now picking themselves up off the ground, the man made his way, leading Dawa. He handed the reins to Shagdur who turned and bowed low to Tsogyal as he held out the reins to her. "Your horse, Noble Lady."

Taking them, Tsogyal nodded.

Speaking earnestly, Shagdur looked from Tsogyal to Abaka and Rab-ten, in Tibetan he said, "We will ride ahead of you back to our land and find this retreat of practitioners you speak of. As we travel we will clear the route of any who would harm you."

Looking up at Senge, who was watching all this, doing his best to keep his astonishment from showing, Shagdur continued, "We are leaving this place. We will never return to do harm again. You have my oath upon it."

Senge nodded, amazed that his anger and hatred of this man was gone. He could not explain why. "Very well," he answered, hearing a softness in his own voice he had not expected. Then, trying to affect authority, he continued, "That would be appreciated by my King."

Shagdur turned away and mounted his horse. Obeying his lead, the thieves mounted their horses. All followed behind Shagdur as he rode south, leading the brigands away.

Senge sat upon his mount, Skamar, watching for a long time, the forms of the retreating horde growing smaller until the horizon was empty. He turned to watch Tsogyal as she tended Rab-ten's face, hearing their soft murmurs on the breeze.

"My friend," Tsogyal said, tears welling in her eyes, as she gently dabbed at Rab-ten's wounded face with piece of cloth she soaked with water from the flask.

Rab-ten winced. "It is not so bad, sister. I have healing salve packed." Gently grasping Tsogyal's wrist to stop her administrations, Rab-ten looked deeply into Tsogyal's eyes. "Sister, that was a miracle," Rab-ten whispered.

Shaking her head, Tsogyal explained, "Those men were given the ability to taste their Buddha nature. Experiencing a glimpse of it, they realized the true nature of existence. All material things pale in comparison." Then, looking into Rab-ten's eyes, Tsogyal asked, "You have experienced this in your practice in the caves, have you not?"

Rab-ten nodded, a tear making its way down her cheek. "Yes, sister, it was just a glimpse, yet so powerful."

Amazement brightened her face as Rab-ten whispered, "But I saw the light radiating from your heart. I could not believe my eyes!"

Pouring more water from the water bag to soak the cloth, Tsogyal held Rab-ten's chin up, as she resumed gently cleansing the scrapped skin of dirt and blood. "Keep practicing, sister," she said, smiling, "just keep practicing."

The mandala made of gold bowls, pebbles and coins was now packed away in the Royal saddlebags. The horses and mules grazed peacefully on the sparse grass. Abaka and Chudak struggled with the heavy felt, setting up the tent. Night was close, they would camp on this spot. Senge dismounted and took his saddle and tack off Skamar, settling it all in a pile on the ground, then released his tired horse to graze. Senge's mind was calm and serene as he watched his beautiful horse lower his head and nibble at a tuft of grass. Looking up, he watched for a moment as the sun began its decent behind the mountains, casting the last rays of the day's light over the land. Taking in a long deep breath of the cold air, he let it out slowly, savoring it. Satisfaction filled him as he strode over to Abaka and Chudak, to help with making camp.

39

Lost in thought as he trudged up the well-worn trade route approaching Natu-la pass, Abaka held the reins leading his horse, Batur, meaning warrior, behind him. Tied to Batur's saddle was the rope leading the mules. The cold penetrated the wool wrapped around his hands. Images of the past days filled his mind.

They had stayed in the camp for two days after the thieves left, Abaka massaging his special healing balm into Rab-ten's horse's swollen leg several times a day. When the horse was better able to walk, they led it along as they continued on their journey. Entering the country of Sikkim in the Chimbu Valley, they camped by the river that cut through the valley. There Abaka had Rab-ten's horse stand in the freezing water several times a day.

Now Abaka stopped, taking in a long breath, he turned to watch Rab-ten on the mountain road behind him, leading her horse whom she had named Tashi, meaning lucky. He watched the gait of the horse critically, pleased to see it walked straight and strong, perfectly healed and sound. Then he looked beyond her to the figure of General Senge who was taking up the rear, leading his fine golden mount. Senge, clad in a thick sheepskin zhuba, his sword-scabbard swinging with each step, constantly cast his hawk-like eyes about for any sign of potential danger. Turning, Abaka looked ahead of him, watching Tsogyal and

Chudak as they walked side by side, leading their horses, one white, one black, like the moon and its shadow.

As Abaka took in a long deep breath of the cold air, tasting the scent of distant snow upon it, he remembered how grateful he felt when the two warriors, General Senge and Chudak returned to travel with them. For the day after the event with the thieves, Senge and Chudak had left their lonely camp, returning to the palace of King Pelgyi. There they informed King Pelgyi of his daughter's whereabouts and destination. Queen Getso stood beside her husband, her eyes filling with tears, as Pelgyi granted Senge and Chudak's request to accompany the trio on their journey, to keep them safe. They had caught up with the trio three days after, their saddlebags full of provisions and gold given by King Pelgyi for their travels. Abaka had felt great relief at sight of the two men cantering up to them on that day. The event with the first band of thieves was remarkably averted, but he saw only too well that he alone was not enough to keep Tsogyal and Rab-ten safe.

Turning now, Abaka continued leading Batur behind Chudak and Tsogyal who were in companionable conversation as they made their way along the rocky road. Abaka smiled, hearing the sounds of their laughter.

"Yes, it is true," Chudak assured Tsogyal. "Your sister Nyima is a strong Queen in Kharchupa. She has surely tamed that beast, Zhonnu. I have heard that she is the true ruler of Kharchupa and Zhonnu as well!"

Tsogyal burst out laughing, then chortled, "I am not surprised my sister Nyima rules Kharchupa!"

Chudak gulped back laughter as he continued, "I have heard it said Zhonnu adores her."

They continued chuckling as they stepped over stones on the pathway. A strand of Tsogyal's silk-black hair, having come loose of her braid, blew about her face by the wind, now becoming stronger.

Then Chudak said, his voice now serious, "And that minister that beat you. He is gone. Exiled from Kharchupa in disgrace. He was told if he ever set foot near the Kingdom he would spend his days in hard labor in chains."

Astonished, Tsogyal looked at Chudak. "Really?"

"Yes," Chudak confirmed. Then he added, "I have heard from many that the people of Kharchupa love your sister Nyima. When Zhonnu is away on campaign, she rules with strength and compassion. She allows no corruption by any ministers. The people feel her love for them. The Kingdom grows more and more prosperous because of her influence."

They walked in silence for a time, the wind growing stronger and colder.

Tsogyal inquired, "And my elder sister, Dechen, have you heard any news of her?"

Bracing against the cold wind, Chudak's stern countenance changed to a bright smile. "Yes, she carries her second child now. The people of Zurkhar love her as well. Many comment on her as a most regal Queen. Some say she is not human at all, but a Goddess come down from the mountains. General Senge has told me Prince Wangchuk has become a much more confidant commander of his troops and his Kingdom. All know it is Dechen's influence on him. She is his confidant, it is her wisdom he listens to."

Tsogyal nodded and smiled, remembering Dechen as she seemingly flowed rather than walked along the corridors of her father's palace. And how her voice was soft when she spoke, always giving wise council. *Maybe she is a Goddess*, Tsogyal mused.

"And my mother? How is my mother, Chudak?" Tsogyal asked.

Chudak's face took on a solemn expression as he answered, "She fairs well, yet there is a sadness in her. I think she misses her daughters. You all left her so quickly."

A tear began at the corner of Tsogyal's eye, the wind drying it before it could slide down her cheek. "Does she speak of me?"

"She worries for you, Noble Daughter," Chudak answered.

"She does not understand I have chosen my path, it was not forced upon me as some may think. One day I will visit her and explain my heart to her. I only wish I could take her pain away," Tsogyal said, looking at Chudak walking beside her. He looked back and smiled.

Just then Tsogyal and Chudak became aware of the sound of crunching hooves behind them. Turning they were met with Abaka, Rab-ten and Senge riding up to them.

"Look," Senge said, as he pointed.

They looked up to see huge dark clouds amassing around the peaks of the mountains in the direction they were traveling.

Chudak shook his head slowly. Grimly, he said, "The mountain God is becoming angry. I have heard this mountain is a most angry mountain."

"Yes, a storm is coming, we must hurry to get over the pass," Abaka confirmed.

"Perhaps we should make camp here and wait?" Tsogyal asked.

"We could be trapped here for weeks waiting for the pass to clear and become passable again. No, we must get over the pass now," Abaka warned.

Chudak went to Lungta's side and slipped his felt-booted foot into the stirrup and swung upon her back as he said, "The horses are well rested, we can go more quickly now."

As Tsogyal mounted Dawa, she listened to General Senge speak to Abaka. "Abaka, you know this route better than I. You take the lead, I will bring up the rear."

Nodding, Abaka untied the lead-rope for the mules from his saddle, tossing it to Chudak as he passed him, then rode to the lead. Senge nodded to Chudak as he let the troop continue ahead of him. Chudak waited for Tsogyal and Rab-ten to get ahead of him, then he fell into place behind them.

"We must travel swiftly but not race, the horses will need their strength in the cold," Senge called out, being heard by all.

Tsogyal pulled her fur hat down against the howling wind. Dawa struggled, lifting her legs high, pulling out of the deepening snow, to take each step. They all needed to dismount, the snow was too deep now to ride the horses. Tsogyal felt numb but forced herself to act. She pulled up gently on Dawa's reins, stopping her. Willing her leg to move, she pulled it from the stirrup, then raised it back over the mare's rump to dismount. As she tried to lower herself down, she fell backwards into the snow. Stunned, she felt a grip on her arm. She looked up into the stern face of General Senge as he lifted her to her feet. His fur hat and mustache were white, covered with snow, he looked like a man made of ice.

"Noble Daughter, are you able to walk?" he asked, concern in his voice.

Shivering, Tsogyal answered, "Yes, I am able. Please, hand me Dawa's reins?"

Senge grasped the reins laying loose on Dawa's neck and flipped them over her head. Handing them to Tsogyal, he assured her, "Just keep moving, we will get through this storm, Lady. I will be right here behind you."

Dazed, Tsogyal turned, following in the path cut through the snow by the others, ahead of her. Each step took much effort, the cold a heavy weight on her, leeching the energy from her limbs. *Just keep moving*, she encouraged herself. *Good, now take another step.*

After what seemed like timeless agony, a voice came out of the white gloom ahead of them. "Here! I see the marker. We are at the top of the pass!"

It was Abaka calling out, Tsogyal realized. Relief filled her. But she knew there was still more distance to go before they could make camp. They had to get down the other side out of the storm.

Looking ahead of her, she saw the snow-covered forms of the mules with Chudak pulling hard on the lead-rope. Their loads causing them to balk through the deep snow. They bellowed in protest. Rabten was leading Tashi and Lungta ahead of Chudak, they too were struggling along, Tsogyal could see. The snowfall began to increase. It was so great, their footsteps filled with snow seconds after their foot left the spot. She could not see Abaka and Batur, but could hear him calling out encouragement to all of them.

Each felt a surge of energy as they passed the marker showing the top of Natu-la Pass. Though exhausted, Senge and Chudak trudged off the trail to make an offering ceremony to the mountain God at the stone cairn marking the crossing over the pass. They did not want to anger the mountain God any more than it was now. Tsogyal and Rab-ten, numb and tired, struggled onward following Abaka. Rab-ten took her place behind Abaka as he continued to lead them onward, going down, then up again, then downward. As the sky darkened, Rab-ten wondered when they would stop.

"This is good, we can stop here," Abaka's voice called out from the distance.

Relieved at hearing his call that they could finally stop, Rab-ten followed his trail, eventually coming into a stand of trees on a flat place by a cliffside. Trudging up to where he was standing, she saw Batur tied to a tree. She was delighted, realizing the cliff sheltered the place from the wind and the snow; the ground was lightly covered in white. Glancing about, she led Tashi and Lungta to a tree and tied them. Soon the others all straggled in.

"This is very good," Senge said, the last of them in behind Tsogyal and Dawa.

Abaka and Chudak were already unpacking the felt from the mules. Rab-ten busied herself unpacking the yak-dung they had brought for cooking fuel. Tsogyal tied Dawa and helped Rab-ten. Unpacking the mule with barley flour and butter, Tsogyal then fed each horse a few handfuls.

Soon, they were all huddled inside the shelter of the dark yak-hair felt, a small cook fire in the middle, a cup of hot tea held gratefully in cold hands. Too exhausted to speak, they silently chewed tsampa, barley flour rolled in butter, and sipped their butter tea. Outside the tied horses hung their heads, sleeping. The wind continued through the night, blowing snow-flurries above and around the sheltered cove.

40

Senge could not believe the changes in the land of this country. Winding down the trail from the cold snow camp, they quickly left the snow behind them and traveled through evergreen trees for two days. Now, after twisting around and up and down, however descending in altitude, they were in a jungle. A cacophony of sounds came from the canopy of trees above them. The chatter of monkeys, the songs of birds. Sweat slid down Senge's back and chest, soaking the thin robe of silk he wore, as he rode Skamar through the jungle plants. He looked up, marveling at the leaves, twinkling shades of green backlit by the sun. His gaze fell upon a group of flowers of bright yellow and blue. Reaching out to one, he was astonished when they all lifted and fluttered away. Not flowers at all, but beautiful butterflies. The group ahead of him were all stopped and dismounted by a stream. Halting, he dismounted, listening to Abaka's words of caution.

"The water is good to drink, yet there are leeches, we cannot bath in it."

Tsogyal and Rab-ten groaned, their bodies sticky with sweat, a sensation they were not accustomed to.

Senge led Skamar to drink, then knelt beside the water, scooping handfuls over his face and head, drenching his shoulder-length hair, allowing it to trickle cool down his chest, soaking his robe. He sighed and shook his head, the spray of droplets flung from his hair glittered in the shafts of sunlight reaching them through the tree tops. They all heaped handfuls of the cool water over their faces and heads, the coolness washing down their hot sweating bodies. Their whoops and gasps of delight echoed in the trees.

"Why did we come this route?" Senge inquired to Abaka. "Would it have not been easier to enter the great Valley of Nepal by way of Kodan?"

Tsogyal answered, "The Master Padma wanted me to travel through this country. He said I will return here in the future, so wanted me to learn of it. We will return to our homeland from Nepal by way of Kodan."

Shifting his gaze to Tsogyal, Senge nodded, saying, "It is a strange country, this Sikkim. We were not long ago in evergreen trees looking upon snowy mountains. Now we sit in a jungle like that of India."

Abaka spoke through the water washing down his face over his lips, "Yes, and we will be in the evergreens this night and all will have a bath, as I have a friend, a farmer, we will stay with."

Rab-ten asked, in amazement, "Abaka, is there any country you do not have a friend?"

Tsogyal and Rab-ten chuckled, as Abaka looked up, thinking, then answered, "No, Sister, I can not think of one."

"This country is difficult to travel," Chudak chimed. "Not like Tibet. There you look across the distance and go. Here you look across the distance and must twist and climb endlessly to arrive at your destination."

Standing and stretching his arms up, arching his back, soft pops could be heard as Abaka agreed, "Yes, it is a small country, yet it is made of many steep hills and ravines, high mountains, few large valleys like Tibet, making travel difficult."

"Beautiful country. I have never seen so much green, so many beautiful flowers," Rab-ten said, as she reached out, touching one of many beautiful orchids growing by the stream.

Murmurs of agreement came from all as they led their horses across the stream, then mounted. The clop and thump of the horse's hooves echoed in the trees as they set off up the path.

They reached Khecheopari Lake after their stay at the farmer's house. The beauty of it was so great they decided they would like to linger there, staying two days. Traveling the route from there, they all were amazed as they ascended through a lush rainforest filled with flowering trees and orchids. Calls and songs of birds of all kinds echoed in the canopy of trees. They marveled and pointed at small brown-faced bears staring at them from high on limbs.

The horses at first balked when they attempted to cross a spectacular bridge spanning a cascading river. Abaka's magic with horses saved them as he taught each how to cause the horse to step upon the wooden planks and follow along calmly. After the first, more bridges appeared, built and maintained by the people of the villages; as this was an important route to the north and must be kept passable. The horses crossed each bridge now willingly and without concern.

Days later and much higher in altitude, there were seven snowy peaks always in view as they climbed the rock path to a cliffside. All looked up at the opening in the wall of rock. The wind whistled as it curled around the cliff rocks.

"Bakhim Cave," Tsogyal announced. "We will rest here for three days, then continue across the Singalila range into Nepal."

They all dismounted, the men unhooking their bow quivers, filled with arrows, from the saddles to have them if needed. Their swords hung from their belts.

Fastening Dawa's reins to a large rock, Tsogyal climbed up the rocks placed as steps leading to the opening of the cave. Rab-ten and Abaka followed behind her. Stopping at the entrance, Tsogyal motioned to Rab-ten and Abaka to stop beside her as she whispered, "Master Padma wanted us to come to this place. We must make sure no one is here now in practice before we make camp. I will go in first alone to be sure."

Tsogyal slipped inside as Rab-ten and Abaka waited. A moment later, Tsogyal returned to the entrance and motioned as she said, "We may enter, no one is here." The others followed her inside, all pleased they were able to enter and practice in this sacred place. Tsogyal sat upon a rock and settled. Rab-ten and Abaka sat too, they all quickly fell into meditation, the peace of the cave and the energy of its centuries of use affecting them.

The scrape of footfalls upon rock and scree from outside reverberated in the cave room, a moment later, Senge and Chudak entered. They stood for a moment looking around the cave walls, taking in its size, then casting their sight on the threesome sitting around the room on rocks placed for the purpose. Tsogyal opened her eyes and looked at them. With a smile and welcoming gesture, she bid them sit with them. Chudak looked at Senge, who crossed the room, stepping around the cook-fire stones placed in the middle of the room to a flat rock placed along the wall. He sat, crossed his legs and leaned his back on the wall, his hands resting on his knees. Chudak followed behind Senge and sat on the floor of the cave next to him. He crossed his legs while looking at the figures of Tsogyal, Abaka and Rab-ten, their eyes closed, their faces serene and soft. He looked up at Senge, whose face was stern, his fingers tapping his knee. Chudak tensed, seeing Senge's agitation. Then Senge rose and left the cave. Chudak felt torn for a moment, then resolved to follow the General. As he began to rise, he glanced at Tsogyal, her eyes were open, looking at him. Her gaze stopped him, he sat back down. Smiling as she spoke to him in a quiet tone, Tsogyal said, "You may stay, Chudak. We will not be here long."

Whispering in response, Chudak answered, "The General wants to make camp."

Tsogyal nodded as she whispered, "Yes, I understand. We have time. We will all help in a little while. Rest, Chudak, feel your breath as it passes into your body."

"My breath?" Chudak asked, perplexed.

Nodding solemnly, Tsogyal answered, her voice low, "Yes, sit with your back straight, breath in slowly and feel the air enter your body and travel down to your belly. Sit upon that rock, it will lift you a bit helping the air travel through you."

Sitting upon Senge's abandoned rock, Chudak crossed his legs, then took in a long breath. Then he released it. He let himself relax and took in another breath, this time more slowly. He kept his attention absorbed in the feeling of it as it passed through his nostrils, inside his throat and into his chest, then finally it filled his belly. Letting the air leave him, he payed close attention to all the sensations as it traveled through him and was released. Relaxing more he continued, enjoying the feelings of pleasure growing as each breath made its way into his belly center and out again.

Senge strode up the path away from the cave. Reaching a flat spot, he stood looking at the peaks of the sacred mountain of Sikkim. The farmer they had stayed with told them the name, Karchenjunga. He gazed upon the multiple snowy peaks he could see so clearly. Though the mountain was far away, it rose so high above the earth it could bee seen clearly from the spot he stood upon. He looked for a place to sit, glancing back at the cave to see if Chudak and the others had come out. The cave entrance was empty, all still inside.

"Waste of time," he grumbled to himself. "Just sitting in caves. Life is so full, and so much to do and to see."

He let out his breath, thinking he might as well relax and enjoy gazing upon this great mountain until the others come out of the cave, then they will make camp.

The Gods of that mountain must be powerful indeed, he thought to himself.

Images of Abaka's friend, the farmer they had stayed with, passed through his mind as he sat. The house built of large timbers on a rock foundation, roof of thatch and bamboo walls. The woman sitting at a loom belted behind her back as she fed strings of color-building patterns with each course. *That man was a rich man,* Senge thought. His house was large, built in a large clearing and having several out buildings. Log corral stocks were filled with many pigs. He had told them, as they all sat eating a fine tasty meal of curry vegetables, rice, lentils and mutton, that he also had many more sheep and yak which were herded for him in Tibet by a shepherd he paid. The shepherd would return the herds before the snows to be slaughtered, the meat salted and sold or traded.

His daughters were very beautiful, Senge mused. Visions of his own wife, Michewa, passed through his mind. Her large dark eyes, her strong beautiful face. He felt sadness at having been gone from Karchen so much these past two springs. He had not seen his daughter, Senge-mo, in so long he did not know if she was well or how much she may have grown. Grim-faced, he coughed back the tightness of sorrow that tried to force its way out of him, threatening tears. Getting up from the large rock he sat upon, he forced himself to return to the present, taking a few steps, then resting his vision on the mountain before him, rising massive in the distance. The cold breeze pushed wisps of the hair away from his face. A screech echoed in the distance. Senge searched the expanse to see a falcon soaring in the distance before him. He gazed admiringly at the magnificent bird as it soared and rose on the eddies of cold air. Picking up his bow, he braced it beside his knee, bending it while he wrested the string into the nock. He held the bow out, admiring its form and weight. Taking the string in his fingers, he pulled it slowly, drawing it back. The bow slowly flexed as he pointed it toward the mountain. The pleasure of the strain of his muscles filled him. Images of sending arrows straight and fast flying into the great mountain filled his mind. Then after holding the string in his grasp for a moment, he slowly returned it to its resting position. The image of Abaka's bow came to him. *Fine inlay of gold, beautiful bow and powerful and Abaka was skilled with the bow*, Senge thought in admiration. Shaking his head in disgust, he said aloud, "A fine warrior like him wasting time sitting in a cave."

The sound of crunching and skidding of stones under foot-falls broke Senge's thoughts. He turned to see Chudak bounding up the path to him. Senge noticed Chudak's steps were light.

"We are ready to make camp, General, " Chudak announced, a smile of pure joy on his face. "Princess Tsogyal and Lady Rab-ten will be staying in the cave for the remainder of the night. Abaka will help us with setting up camp, then he will prepare their food and what they need."

Senge's firm expression softened as Chudak spoke. Chudak's lightness and joy was infectious.

"Very well," Senge said as he passed Chudak, taking the lead back down the path. Then he stopped. Turning to Chudak, Senge said, "It will not take long to make camp." Raising his bow in the air he announced, "I think there is enough daylight to go on a hunt for our meal. What do you think, Chudak?"

Chudak's smile turned even brighter as he enthused, "Yes, General, a fine idea." Passing Senge on the trail to run back to camp, he announced, "I will retrieve my bow and tell Abaka, surely he will wish to come."

41

Clang, clang, clang. Morning bells niggled at the edge of his sleep. Rumbling of wagons and calls of passers by in the street outside assailed him, awakening him. Opening his eyes, Chudak looked up at the ceiling above. It felt strange to have the wide open sky blotted out by a roof over his head. Turning on his side, he pulled his zhuba, which he used now as a blanket, over his head and tried to ignore the clamor of the streets outside, longing to sleep more. Voices and laughter burrowed in from outside his door. It was no use, throwing the zhuba back, he sat up and held his head in his hands, covering his ears to mute the noise. How he longed for the silence of the mountains they had traversed, wanting to trade this jarring barrage of sounds from the streets outside for the sweet chatter of the jungles of Sikkim. Images of the jungle paths canopied with flowering trees filled his mind. He would never forget that beauty and longed for it now. The hillsides terraced with green crops of many kinds, the memory of the heavy sweet scent of the green plants filled his mind as he now breathed in the fetid air. Opening his eyes, he stared down at the dirt floor of the room in this inn.

After leaving Bakhim Cave they had traversed the Singalila mountains to the small village of Taplejung. Abaka, never failing as their guide, found the well-traveled path that led from east to west across Nepal bringing them here, to the town of Bhaktapur through the southern gate.

Now Chudak's stomach rumbled. He tied his long hair back with a thong of leather. Fumbling behind him on the woven mat, he found the water flask and lifted it high, sucking the last of the warm liquid. From the small table by the bed, he picked up the string of turquoise and coral beads from which hung a locket of silver and lapis lazuli, fitting it over his head. The beads clattered softly as they came to rest on his chest. The cool presence against his skin of the locket, containing a lock of his wife's hair and his son's baby tooth, made him feel better.

Standing, he lifted his sheepskin robe from the bed, groaning at the tightness in his shoulders and back as he struggled into it. His sword, in its silver-and-leather scabbard, hanging from his wool sash-belt, chinked as he tightened the belt around his waist. Sliding his sheathed dagger into the tightly-cinched sash, he tested it to be sure it rested securely. He thrust the empty water flask into the front fold in his zhuba, pushing it around to his back. Picking up his silver cup and bag of silver coins, he placed them inside the same fold of his robe. Pulling his fur hat onto his head, he reached for his bow quiver leaning against the wall. Shouldering it, he stepped to the door and opened it. Morning light blinded him for a moment as he stepped out into the courtyard. He paused to let his eyes become accustomed to the light. Looking up at the sky to gage the weather, he was glad to see few clouds. Crossing the courtyard, he came to another door. Placing his ear to the rough wood, he heard voices. *Good, they are awake*, he thought.

"Noble Daughter?" he called out.

The voices stopped and a moment later Rab-ten opened the door. "Chudak," she said, welcoming him with a smile.

He noticed she was wearing her chuba apron over her robe, signifying her status as a married woman. Its stripes of green, blue and ocher were clean and bright.

"I am going to the livery to relieve Abaka and General Senge. They will bring food to you from the market for your meal. Is there anything else you need?" Chudak inquired.

Rab-ten looked back at Tsogyal, then turning to Chudak, she said, "We will go to market, as soon as I finish braiding the Noble Daughter's hair. Let Abaka and the General know we will be in the marketplace, they can find us there at one of the food stalls. We will bring food to you at the livery."

Chudak nodded, replying, "Very well, Lady Rab-ten."

The door closed gently behind him as he turned away. He searched for the direction to the inn's privy. Remembering where it was, he made his way to it, feeling glad this inn had such a convenience, as the idea of being so exposed in an alley disturbed him. Moments later he strode out of the courtyard through the doorway leading into the street. The sun rising over the buildings shone into his eyes, blinding him. Shielding his eyes, he paused, looking around him. Gaining his bearings, he headed for the livery, bringing the memory of the route into his mind. Feeling groggy, he steeled himself to wake up and be alert. Suddenly, he was surrounded by children, all holding hands out, chiming, "Baksheesh, baksheesh."

Their rags and old oversized robes were torn and dirty. The overpowering stench of their filthy clothes and unwashed bodies rolled over Chudak. Disgusted and irritable, he pushed through them growling, "Begone, I have nothing for you."

Their dirty grim faces looked at Chudak's back as he strode away. Then their attention turned in unison toward another man walking along the street, like a flock of birds they hurried to flutter around him.

His face fixed in a stern expression, Chudak strode purposefully, remembering the turns that would bring him to the livery. Fear on their faces, the townspeople passed him with lowered eyes as they scurried along the walls of the buildings, allowing him as wide a birth as they could manage, not wanting to make eye contact with him less they bring a warrior's attention on them.

Smoke of coal-and-dung cook-fires hung in the air, becoming thicker as he walked. He looked to where the street he traveled ended and could see some stalls of the marketplace. Finally, he spilled into a mass of people and wagons, stalls of vegetables, grain, silk, furs, weapons, salt and all manner of items. The odor of rotten vegetables mingled with the smells of animals, hides, dung and sweat. Passing a doorway, he was assailed by the stench of urine and feces. He held his hand over his face, trying to keep from breathing in the thick smokey air of the cook-fires filling the enclosed space of the market square. He cast his gaze about looking for the street that would take him out of the square to the livery. Finding the landmark he had memorized, a chipped corner of the roof of the building at the street entrance, he hurried, anxious to free himself from the press of people, the noise and stench.

The sound of his footfalls on the hard-packed earthen street became louder as the noise of the market receded from him. Relief filled him at seeing the two forms of Abaka and the General far down the street. He could see they were in conversation, their heads tilted toward each other as they strolled along toward him. As he reached them, they looked up, recognition alighting their faces.

"Chudak!" Senge greeted, a rare smile on his face.

"General," Chudak answered, as he came up to them. Stopping, he nodded his greeting to Abaka, as he asked, "Did you sleep well in the livery? Are the horses, mules and our supplies safe? I am on my way to stand guard over our property."

Glancing at Abaka as he answered, Senge chuckled. "No Chudak, no need. I am secure in the knowledge that our belongings will be quite safe and well-cared-for. You come with us now."

Looking unsure, Chudak looked from the General to Abaka. Abaka broke into gay laughter as the two men resumed walking, Chudak falling in next to them.

Chortling, Abaka explained, "The General, while displaying his fine and well-balanced unsheathed sword, assured the livery master that if our animals were un-cared for and any of our possessions molested or found missing, the General would sever the livery master's head and display it upon the livery door." Continuing, Abaka assured Chudak, "Of course we assured him, he would be well-paid, and in silver, for his fine service."

Senge chuckled. "You should have seen the poor man's face, he was terrified."

With a guffaw, Abaka said, "It was marvelous, the General had the most fierce look on his face as he held his sword up in the shaft of light coming through the doorway. It shimmered, looking as though it had a life of its own." Placing his hand on his chest, he admitted with a laugh, "Why, it even frightened me!"

Amazed more by the merriment of General Senge than the ruse played on the livery master, Chudak looked from Senge to Abaka in awe. Unable to help himself, his dour expression melted, Chudak felt himself relax, he chuckled, then joined in the laughter, glad to be back in the company of these men.

Clapping his hand on Chudak's shoulder, Senge boomed, "And how are the Noble Daughter and Lady Rab-ten this morning?"

Shocked by Senge's boisterous gesture, Chudak froze for a moment, collecting his thoughts, then he answered, "The Ladies will meet us in the market for our morning meal."

"Tea," Abaka said as he rubbed his hands together, a dreamy look on his face. "A nice cup of tea would be just fine."

"Meat," the General enthused. "Nicely seared lamb and a few momos." His mouth watered at the thought.

Chudak's stomach rumbled. "I liked that curried dal and rice your friend in Sikkim served us, Abaka. Will they have that here?"

"No doubt, my friend," Abaka confirmed. "We shall find you some."

Soon they were surrounded by the chatter and rumble of the marketplace. Passing stall after stall, Chudak took note of what items were being offered for sale.

Abaka scanned the crowd, then said, "There they are."

Following his lead, they came up to Tsogyal and Rab-ten who were huddled together in front of a stall filled with baskets of red berries. They overheard Rab-ten as they stepped up to them.

"Gogi berries, these are very good. We should buy some to take with us," Rab-ten said as Tsogyal looked at the hard red berries held in

Rab-ten's hand. Feeling a presence behind them, they turned to see the men standing, looking over their shoulders.

"Ah, good morning," Tsogyal greeted. Noticing Chudak was with them, she inquired, "Is all well with our supplies?"

Chudak answered, "Yes, I do not need to guard them. The General has...well, has..." Chudak searched for the words to explain.

Abaka broke in, "The General has motivated the livery man to guard our possessions with his life, if need be."

"Motivated?" Tsogyal asked, perplexed.

Rab-ten looked up at Senge, a wry look on her face, as she said, "My husband, General Jigme, had a way of motiving men."

Chudak and Abaka chuckled. Tsogyal looked at them quizzically, not understanding.

Returning the berries to the basket, Rab-ten took Tsogyal's hand as she turned to proceed to the next stall. "Our supplies are safe." Looking over her shoulder to look at the men following behind, mirth on their faces, she added, "I will explain later, sister."

"Perhaps we should all find what we would like to eat from the food stalls then meet up at the Temple Square," Tsogyal suggested. Then thinking, she added, "Ask whom you meet if they have heard of a youth named Atsara Sale. He is from India, Serling. I think he is sixteen springs old or thereabouts."

The men listened nodding. Speaking for them, Abaka said, with a slight bow, "We will do so, Noble Daughter."

Smiling, Tsogyal said, "Until we meet at the Temple Square. Have a fine meal, gentlemen." Then she turned and walked away with Rab-ten.

Abaka lifted his nose, sniffing the air. Pointing in a direction, he said to Senge and Chudak, "I think we shall find the General's meat this way."

Strolling through the stalls, Rab-ten asked Tsogyal, "What would your desire be this morn, sister?"

"Mmm, I would be grateful for some yogurt and tea. Do you suppose we can find yogurt here?" Tsogyal asked.

Rab-ten considered, then answered, "Oh, yes, we will find yogurt here. I would like some too. I wonder if we can find honey?"

Tsogyal's eyes brightened. "Oh yes, that would be very good."

42

"He is a servant of a citizen here, a merchant trader," Abaka said as he sat upon the short wall of the Temple Square. "We were lucky, we talked with the merchant at a meat stall. He suggested we ask the town butcher who knows most of the townspeople. He was not far from here so we went to question him and, sure enough, he knows the boy. He explained that the merchant's wife has bought meat from him for many springs. She used to come to his shop herself for fresh meat every few days. The boy was always with her and would carry her purchase home. Now that the boy is much older, the mistress sends the boy to buy her meat."

"The butcher said the boy is due there today. We can wait at the butcher's shop," Senge suggested, "then we will follow him to his mistress's house."

"We shall go now then," Tsogyal said, as she jumped down from a low wall she sat upon.

The smell of blood and raw meat became strong as they drew closer to the butcher's shop. Unlike the market merchants, this butcher had a small stone building with a large courtyard in the back that held the sheep, pigs, chickens and goats. Arriving at the door of the shop, the group looked around for a place to sit, choosing the doorway of the building across the street. Hours slipped by as they watched citizens come and go from the shop.

"How did you know this Atsara Sale would be here in Bhaktapur?" Chudak asked, breaking the silence.

"Master Padma told me he saw in a dream that Atsara lives in this town. He did not know the boy was a servant, though," Tsogyal answered.

Their attention was drawn to a figure walking up the street heading for the shop. He looked strong and lean, from a distance they could see he was a young man that could be sixteen springs. Tsogyal rose from her seated place and strode toward him, the others followed a bit behind so as not to frighten the young man into thinking he was to be accosted.

Seeing a young woman approaching him, the young man slowed his brisk step. She was beautiful, he could see. He felt an instant attraction to her. He stopped as she drew near to him.

Tsogya greeted the young man in his Newari tongue, "Good day, I am looking for Atsara Sale, are you he?"

A look of surprise on his face, Atsara answered, "I am he. Who is looking for me and why?"

Looking up at him, Tsogyal took in his handsome features. His teeth were straight and white. His skin was red-brown and clear. He had thick black wavy hair. He wore a robe of raw woven silk. Opened at the chest, a large mole was revealed. This was the mark Padma said to look for to confirm he was the same Atsara.

"I am Tsogyal, come from Tibet. You were seen in a dream of the great Tantric and Buddhist Master Padma. You are meant to come away with me and join me in spiritual practice."

A look of pure astonishment on his face, Atsara said, "What?"

Smiling, Tsogyal said, "I can see this would seem a strange thing. But it is true, I am as I say. At the direction of the great Master Padma, I have come for you."

Atsara looked down at the young woman, her silky black hair with turquoise and silver beads braided in. She was not Nepali, he could see that instantly, she wore the distinctive Tibetan style of robe and jewels braided in her hair. Her air of confidence and the sense that she was from a wild and distant place attracted him. She was exotic, like no other woman he had ever met. Looking into her eyes as she spoke to him, he saw his future, a door being opened, and all he need do is take a step; accept what was being offered.

Atsara let out a breath, feeling dizzy. He turned and leaned his back against the wall of the building for support. His face turned up, his eyes closed, he shook his head slowly as he said, "I do not believe this is happening."

A wave of resolve washed over his features. Opening his eyes, he glancing quickly at the butcher's shop door as he said, "Lady, we must sit and talk, but quickly, I may not tarry, I must return to my mistress in due time."

Looking beyond Tsogyal up the street, a look of concern came over him as he noticed Senge, Abaka, Chudak and Rab-ten standing looking at the pair from a distance away. The men looked imposing with their swords and daggers upon their belts. And slung on their shoulders, quivers holding recurve bows and arrows at the ready. Their faces were stern, focused on him.

Following his gaze, Tsogyal assured, "They are my traveling companions, have no fear."

Looking down at this unusual woman, Atsara asked, "Your warriors?"

Tsogyal smiled, "They are friends, be not concerned. They are here to protect, not to harm."

Looking back where he had traveled from, Atsara said, "My Lady, please come this way, we can sit there." He gestured to a doorway.

Allowing Tsogyal to seat herself, Atsara glanced back at the warriors and the woman watching them. Then he stooped close before her to look into her eyes. In a low voice so no one could overhear their conversation, he said, "I have been secretly studying the Buddha dharma for two springs. My teacher told me he had a dream. In the dream he saw a Goddess seated on a lotus come and take me away from here to high snowy mountains. Are you that Goddess?"

Tsogyal looked intently at Atsara as she answered, "I am a disciple of Master Padma. I am a practitioner of the Buddha's teachings and the yogas of Tantra. I am a yogini. I am the one your teacher saw in his dream. You are to return to Tibet with me and practice with me in the great sacred caves of Zhoto Tidro, in the snowy mountains of Tibet. There in solitude we will practice the highest yoga Tantras, the highest of Buddha's teachings together." Then with a quizzical look, Tsogyal asked, "Why must you practice the Buddha's teachings in secret?"

"I am a servant, my life belongs to my mistress. She believes in the old religion, the Bonpo gods. She has no interest in the Buddha's teachings," Atsara said. "I can not go with you unless you ransom me from my mistress," he added.

"Why?" Tsogyal inquired.

"My mistress owns me, I was sold into her service as a slave," Atsara explained.

"A slave?" Tsogyal asked, incredulous, "I had thought you a servant in employ, not a slave. How did you end up a slave to a family here? Are you not from India?"

Gazing into this beautiful woman's dark brown eyes, finding her intoxicating, Atsara explained, "I was stolen from my parents by a Hindu sadhu when I was nine springs old. He brought me here, far from my homeland, and sold me to a citizen of this city. The Nepali man bought me to serve his wife, my mistress, as he travels much. I have been in the service of my mistress for seven springs now."

Tsogyal rose, considering all she had been told. Looking down at him, into his eyes, she asked, "Do you wish to come with me?"

Atsara stood up, nodding emphatically as he kept her gaze. "Yes, of course I do, My Lady. It is my dream to leave this place and practice the dharma. Truly, this is my wish."

"Very well, I will ransom you. Go on your errand now, we will follow you to your mistress's house," Tsogyal said.

Atsara bowed as he said, "I look forward to your arrival, My Lady."

Then he turned and trotted up the street, disappearing into the butcher's shop.

Tsogyal walked briskly to her companions, their eyes fixed on her. When she reached them Rab-ten asked, "Well?"

"It is surely him. We must follow him to his mistress's house and ransom him," Tsogyal explained.

"Ransom?" Abaka asked. "He is a slave?"

"I thought maybe an orphan who was a servant in trade for care," Rab-ten said.

"No," Tsogyal answered, "stolen as a young child from his parents by a Hindu sadhu, brought here and sold into service."

With a wry look, Abaka said, "I guess this sadhu was not satisfied with the results of his begging bowl."

"I wonder at the price to ransom him?" Chudak chimed in.

Brows furrowed, Senge thought of his young daughter, the idea of her being stolen caused anger to rise in him. Images played in his mind of finding this sadhu, of pounding his fists into him, destroying this evil man with his bare hands.

Dispelling the images in his mind, Senge growled, "That is, if they will sell. They may not wish to free him."

43

Regal, she stood tall, looking down her nose at Tsogyal. Dressed in fine robes of silk, the many silver and gold bangles around her wrists clattered and tinged as she gestured with her hands. Her hair was braided in many small braids that swung as she shook her head in dismay.

"You wish to buy Atsara?" Mistress Bhandari asked, incredulous. "Why?"

"The great Guru Padma as sent me here to ransom him. It would be favorable for you to let me buy his freedom," Tsogyal answered, as she stood upon the front stoop of the merchant trader's house.

Tsogyal looked resplendent in her finest silks and necklaces made of lapis lazuli, turquoise, coral and amber with silver and gold. She had brought along these clothes and jewels, wrapped safely and carried by the mules, for just such an audience. The gatekeeper of the merchant Bhandari's home let her in unquestioned as her rich attire presumed her a guest of the mistress of the house.

After her meeting with Atsara at the butcher's shop, Tsogyal had sent Senge and Chudak to follow Atsara to his home. Meanwhile, Tsogyal, Rab-ten and Abaka returned to the inn to dress. Senge and

Chudak returned to the inn with the knowledge of the location of Atsara's house.

"Guru who?" Mistress Bhandari asked.

"Guru Padma from Tibet, Mistress. He is a master of the Buddha dharma," Tsogyal answered.

Looking Tsogyal up and down, as Tsogyal spoke, Mistress Bhandari said, "I can see you are Tibetan and as well a Noble one of high birth."

Looking over Tsogyal's head to the three warriors and Rab-ten standing inside the courtyard at the gate, Mistress Bhandari added, "And with warriors at your back."

Stepping back, holding the door open, Mistress Bhandari gestured to Tsogyal, "Come in Lady, have some tea with me and we shall talk."

Looking over Tsogyal, to Rab-ten, she added, "And bring your attendant lady in with you. I am sure she would rather not be left alone standing in the courtyard with those men."

Tsogyal turned and motioned to Rab-ten to come. Delighted, Rab-ten scurried to the door, bowing slightly to the Mistress as she entered behind Tsogyal.

Entering the large foyer, Tsogyal and Rab-ten could not help themselves gazing about in wonder. The ceiling was high. Tall pillars, with intricate carvings of birds and animals, trees and plants around them, held the ceiling aloft. The space felt light and airy. Following Mistress Bhandari into the next room, they were amazed anew. This room was huge. Many more carved pillars held this higher ceiling aloft. The walls were carved screens of wood. The intricate carvings made openings so light came through from the other rooms of the large house. Beautiful Persian and Chinese silk rugs richly covered the tile floor. Upon these rugs, large beautifully-embroidered cushions lay about the room and around a large low carved round table placed in the center of the room. Tsogyal and Rab-ten could not believe the large pots at the corners of the room and beside the doorways filled with beautiful plants, some with small trees, making the room like sitting in a garden. Beyond was a large doorway, its carved doors now open, leading out to an inner courtyard. The view into this inner courtyard revealed many more beautiful flowers and green plants in large pots.

Mistress Bhandari smiled, watching the awe on the faces of her two guests. Gesturing to the cushions, she implored, "Ladies, please have a seat. Would you like tea?"

Nodding, Tsogyal answered, "Yes, that would be delightful," as she seated herself upon a cushion. Rab-ten followed, seating herself.

"Neema!" Mistress Bhandari called, then seated herself across from Tsogyal and Rab-ten, adjusting her silks around her, her bangles tinged and sang as she did so.

A moment later, a strong-featured handsome young woman entered. Her skin was smooth, the color of coal, her black hair short with tight curls. Bowing, she asked, "Mistress?"

"Tea, Neema. And bring some of those tasty cakes I like. The ones with the almonds."

"Yes, Mistress," Neema said, bowing she left the room.

Tsogyal and Rab-ten glanced at each other, having never seen skin so black.

Fixing her gaze upon Tsogyal, Mistress Bhandari asked, "How long have you been here in Bhaktapur?"

"Only two days, Madam," Tsogyal answered. "I have come from Tibet for Atsara."

Looking perplexed, Mistress Bhandari asked, "How do you know of Atsara and why do you wish to purchase him?"

"My Guru, Master Padma, had a dream in which he saw Atsara and that he lived here, in this town. He is required for sacred purposes," Tsogyal explained.

"Sacred purposes?" Mistress Bhandari inquired.

"Yes, Madam, sacred purposes," Tsogyal answered, her tone suggesting that would be the extent of her explanation.

"Mmm..." Mistress Bhandari intoned. "I must tell you, though Atsara is a servant, he is like a son to me. As well, we paid a great sum in gold for him, we will not free him," Mistress Bhandari explained.

Just then, Neema entered with another servant, carrying trays. The Mistress fell silent as the servants placed a platter of yellow cakes on the table. Then they placed a porcelain dish and cup in front of each lady, with a silver pot they filled each cup with dark tea. They placed a bowl of honey on the table, a small ladle of ebony wood for serving lay in the rich amber. The aroma of sweet cakes and fragrant tea filled the room. Rab-ten had to steel herself to keep from bouncing on the rich brocade cushion, so filled with expectation at the tasty cakes and tea before her.

When the servants left the room, Mistress Bhandari gestured to the food, saying, "Ladies, please help yourselves." Then, as she reached for a cake and placed it on the small plate in front of her, she continued, "However, if you are inclined, you may stay here to be with him. You may both stay here in my service."

Tsogyal froze in motion as Mistress Bhandari's words sank in. Steeling her composure, Tsogyal continued lifting one of the cakes from the platter and placing it on the small plate in front of her. Rab-ten did not speak Newari, yet inexplicably understood what the lady was saying. Though shocked at the idea that Tsogyal and herself remain as servants in the Bhandari household, Rab-ten followed Tsogyal's example, calmly placing her cake before her. Sipping the tea, then taking a small bite of the cake, Tsogyal was filled with pleasure at the explosion of the sweet honey and almond flavor of the cake. The sip of tea that followed was divine. Quietly they all chewed and sipped.

Breaking the sounds of chewing and sipping, Tsogyal said, "This cake is delicious. What is this flavor and these nuts inside? It is wonderful."

"They are called almonds," Mistress Bhandari answered. "They come from the Far West. From a place by a sea, I cannot remember the name. My husband is a trader, bringing many unusual items from his travels. These almonds are very tasty. Neema makes very good little cakes from them; my favorite."

Tsogyal and Rab-ten continued chewing, the sounds of their delight at the sweet flavors and light texture of the cakes filling the room. They both reached for their cups and sipped the dark sweet tea.

"The tea is exquisite," Tsogyal remarked.

"Oh, yes," Mistress Bhandari exclaimed, "also one of my favorites. From some province of China. Oh, I cannot remember the name. My husband comes home with all these names of places." Waving her hand dismissively, the clatter and ring of her bangles accentuating her words, she said, "I cannot remember them."

"Atsara has fine features. He seems a higher caste than that of a slave caste," Tsogyal said, looking over her cup at Mistress Bhandari.

A look of confusion coming over her face as she reached for her cup, Mistress Bhandari froze. Sitting back, she stared at Tsogyal. Then she answered, "Why, of course, he is of the slave caste."

"How do you know? He was taken as a child, stolen from his parents?" Tsogyal inquired.

A stony look on her face, Mistress Bhandari answered, "My husband was assured he was of the slave caste by the man who sold him to us."

"Assured? By a thief?" Tsogyal inquired, her head tilted in question as she gazed at Mistress Bhandari. Then she added, "He was stolen from his parents."

A flush of red heating her face, Mistress Bhandari looked down, adjusting her silks around her. The chatter of a bird outside echoed through the silence of the room.

"Yes, it is true, he was stolen from his parents," Mistress Bhandari said softly. Looking up at Tsogyal with hard eyes, she continued, "And look around you to where he has ended up." She gestured with a wave of her hand around the room. "His parents were most likely poor. But no matter, he was stolen and for sale. And if we did not buy him then who would have? He may have ended up a slave to a camel driver, or a butcher, or who knows?"

Looking from Tsogyal to Rab-ten, lowering her voice, Mistress Bhandari continued, "He may have been sold as a slave to man with unnatural desires or to a brothel."

Her anger rising, Mistress Bhandari steadied herself, taking a breath. Looking fixedly at Tsogyal, defiance in her tone, Mistress Bhandari declared, "We saved him. We gave him a good home. We have educated him. Why, he can read a goodly amount of sanskrit now and is being tutored to write as well. We have been told by Atsara's tutors that he is very quick, very bright. My husband speaks of hiring an Arab tutor to teach him numbers and sums."

Tears welling in her eyes, Mistress Bhandari straightened, composing herself. "He has grown to be a good boy and will one day be a good man."

"He is a man now," Tsogyal said gently, "and you were good to save him. I meant no disrespect. What a fortunate boy he was to have ended up here, when he could have otherwise met a terrible fate."

Adjusting her seat, looking down as she settled her silk robes around her, Mistress Bhandari declared, "This is Atsara's home, yet you arrive here speaking of taking him away. I tell you he will not wish to go."

Feeling great compassion for this good woman, Tsogyal said, "He is a special man. He needs to move on now, to do more with his life. I assure you, Mistress, he does wish to come with me."

Startled, Mistress Bhandari said, "What? What do you mean, he wishes to go with you? How do you know?"

"I met him on the street and asked him," Tsogyal answered.

Confusion on her face, Mistress Bhandari asked, "The street, where?" Then realization followed. "Oh, I see, when he went out on an errand."

Mistress Bhandari reached for her cup. Noticing it was empty, she called, "Neema!"

Entering swiftly with a pot in her grasp, Neema filled her mistress's cup, then filled Tsogyal and Rab-ten's. Bowing, she turned and hurried out of the room. Tsogyal and Rab-ten gave each other a knowing glance; all the servants would know of this conversation before the day was done.

Sipping the hot fragrant tea, Mistress Bhandari sat in contemplation. The room was peaceful and airy. Birds chattered in the courtyard. A cool breeze wafted through the room, on it was the moist scent of flowers and green plants.

Mistress Bhandari weighed her options as she sipped her tea. This Tibetan is a woman of high birth and has arrived on her doorstep with warriors. Atsara was grown, he could not be kept locked in the house. These Tibetans could simply meet him on the street and take him or he could run away with them never to be seen again, if indeed he wished to go. *Stolen once, stolen twice*, she mused. Realizing what she must do, Mistress Bhandari cleared her throat.

"Very well," she began. "I will speak with Atsara. If indeed he wishes to go, I will sell his freedom to you. We payed five ounces of gold for him. He is worth twenty times that amount now. I want one hundred ounces of gold in payment for him."

Rab-ten gulped back her shock. Tsogyal nodded, saying "I have gold. I will come back for him in two days."

Placing her empty cup on the table, Tsogyal waited until Mistress Bhandari had finished her tea, then she said, "Thank you, Madam, for the tea and fine cakes."

All rose. Mistress Bhandari glided to the foyer, Tsogyal and Rab-ten followed. A servant boy entered and reached up, grasping the iron ring on the door. Pulling it, the large heavy wooden door opened. Bowing once to Mistress Bhandari, Tsogyal and Rab-ten walked out into the outer courtyard. The metal ring clanged as the door thumped closed behind them.

44

They knelt in a circle on the floor of the inn room, all looking down at the gold that lay upon the cloth before them. Senge sat upon the woven mat bed.

Shaking his head slowly, Abaka said, "We have only twenty ounces of gold."

"Oh," Tsogyal said, disappointed. "I thought we had more."

"We will need to save some to return home," Rab-ten added.

Looking up at Rab-ten's concerned face, Tsogyal nodded. "Yes, that is true."

"Maybe we can talk the Mistress down?" Chudak offered.

Senge shook his head, grimly declaring, "From what the Noble Daughter and Lady Rab-ten told us of their visit, this lady will not budge. The Mistress sets the price very high, in hopes you will give up and go away."

"We could just take him and go," Chudak suggested.

Abaka nodded, contemplating this idea.

Senge's eyes brightened as he grunted, "Mmm," considering this possibility.

"No, I think not," Tsogyal said, smiling at Chudak. "We shall buy his freedom so he never has to worry about repercussions. As well, I think it best we do not break the law."

Nodding, Chudak smiled back at her. "Then we need to find more gold."

"I will sell my bow and arrows," Abaka announced, as he rose from his kneeling position, his knees popping as he straightened. "They are rare here, they come from the finest maker of bows and arrows in all of Turkish lands, indeed in all of the world. If we find a rich man, they will bring a good price."

Chudak looked up at Abaka, a gasp of shock uttering from him. Senge looked down at the floor, his head shaking slowly, a look of deep sorrow etched on his face.

Tsogyal stood and faced Abaka. Laying her hand on his arm, she implored, "No, Abaka, that will not be necessary. Some way, in some manner, gold will come to us. It would break my heart to have you sell your bow."

Touched by her gesture, he looked down into her eyes, relenting. "Very well, Noble Daughter, as you wish."

"Let us go out and walk. Get some air and think. Something will happen. An idea will come to us," Tsogyal assured, as she lifted her robe and went to the door.

As they stepped out of the courtyard onto the street, the street urchins scurried toward them, "Baksheesh," on their lips. Recognizing Chudak, the children froze. Looks of terror washed over their faces. Turning in unison, they dissolved away into the ally. Tsogyal turned, looking up at Chudak, a questioning expression on her face. He shrugged in answer. Rab-ten chuckled.

As they walked toward the market, Tsogyal suggested. "Let us find some tea."

The five-some strode onward, making their way through the streets to the market. Those they passed looked at them under lowered eyes with wonder at these two, clearly, Tibetan women with their hair braided with turquoise, coral and amber stone beads within the strands. Their earrings and beautiful necklaces of colorful stones and shinny metal. One wearing a thick silk robe lined with sheepskin. The other wearing the classic chuba apron of bright stripes over her dark thick wool robe. Escorting these women were two Tibetan warriors and one, they would guess correctly, a Turkish warrior; all swords and recurve bows. This was not a usual sight for the people of this town, who see many travelers come through, but few like this entourage. The passersby could not help their glance lingering longer on Tsogyal, entranced by her exotic beauty. Then, noticing the looks of her warriors falling on them, they quickly turned their glances away and hurried on.

Finding a tea stall, they held out their silver cups to be filled with warm green spiced sweet tea. Strolling aimlessly through the market, they sipped from their silver cups, gazing vacantly at the items laid out under tents of cloth and on woven mats upon the ground.

"Let us go to some high ground," Senge suggested, as he gestured to the peak of the snowy mountain that towered in the distance. "We shall find an overlook to sit and think. Breath in some clean air, have the sky open and clear above our heads."

Nodding and murmuring in agreement, all fell in with the General and Abaka in the lead. Chudak followed behind Tsogyal and Rab-ten, as they made their way out of the congestion and noise of the market.

Their pace slowed as they found themselves on the wider road in the more sparsely-occupied edge of the town. They walked with eyes fixed on the snowy mountain looming large in the distance, basking in the pleasure of the sight or with their heads bowed deep in thought, turning possibility after possibility over and over in their minds, searching to find the solution to their problem.

As they walked by a large abode, with high walls encircling more than simply one house, the sound of a woman's scream shocked them all out of their reveries.

"Oh, no! Please no!" a woman's voice cried out. "My son, my son. My son is dead."

Turning, they saw a woman running out of the front gate. They watched in surprise as the woman crumpled onto the dirt road. Shortly after her, a man appeared through the same gate, running after her. Reaching her, he knelt beside her, his arms encircling her. He pulled her close to him as she screamed and sobbed.

Tsogyal strode purposefully toward the pair, Rab-ten right behind her. Abaka, Senge and Chudak all looked at each other, then they followed.

Approaching the pair crumpled on the ground in their grief, Tsogyal asked, "Master, Madam, can we be of any help to you?"

Looking up at the two Tibetan women standing before them, the man answered, tears streaming down his cheeks, "My son has been slain. He has just died from his wound, struck onto him in recent battle. You can do nothing. I would wish you a Goddess and could bring my son back from death."

Noticing the open door in the wall to the estate, Tsogyal turned from the pair and hurried inside. Rab-ten hesitated for a moment, then followed Tsogyal, catching up with her as she passed through the doorway.

"Show me to the boy," Tsogyal ordered the servant who approached them, trying to stop their entrance. Confused, the servant just stared at these two strange women coming through the front door of the house.. Their unusual appearance, clearly foreigners, added to his dismay.

"Show them!" a voice ordered, from behind them.

Tsogyal and Rab-ten looked around in surprise. The master of the house was standing right behind them, having followed them in from the street. Glancing through the doorway to the street, Rab-ten saw Abaka with the mistress of the house grasping his arm, she was still sobbing as he led her along gently. General Senge and Chudak followed behind the pair.

Confusion turning to understanding, the servant boy led the way. Tsogyal and Rab-ten entered the room shown to them, stopping for an instant to take in the scene. A boy and two women were kneeling on the floor, their bodies bent, their hands covering their eyes, sobbing. They knelt around a mat at the center of the room. Upon it lay the body of a young man. He wore only a loin cloth. The wafting smoke of burning incense churned as Tsogyal and Rab-ten quickly went to the body laying on the mat.

"Aside, move aside," Rab-ten ordered.

Looking up at the entrance of these two women, the grief-stricken family members simply obeyed, moving away from the mat quickly.

At first glance, it was clear the young man's body looked strong, his muscles well-developed. He had a ghastly wound under his rib cage, that Rab-ten could see had festered, yellow puss oozing from the edges of the torn flesh.

"This wound had not been treated properly," Rab-ten said softly, as she and Tsogyal knelt beside the body.

Looking up at the ceiling of the room, Tsogyal closed her eyes for a moment. Then opening them, she looked at Rab-ten, asking, "If I can bring him back, can you heal him?"

Brows furrowed in confusion, Rab-ten whispered, "What? What do you mean, if you can bring him back?!"

"We have very little time," Tsogyal whispered, urgently. "Can you heal him if he is alive again?"

Rab-ten placed her fingers on the flesh at the edges, around the wound. She could feel his body was still warm, the flesh still hot where she touched. Lifting the edges slightly, inspecting it, she answered, in a whisper, "Yes, it is possible. The rotting is not too far inside. But he died from this wound." Then thinking, concentration hard on her face, she looked up at Tsogyal, whispering, "If he has a strong will to stay when he comes back, then yes, I can. I know how to help this wound heal."

Senge and Chudak stood against the wall inside the room by the doorway, observing all that was happening, their faces grim. They had seen many men die this way.

Watching the two women kneeling beside his son, the master of the house asked Abaka, who now stood beside him, "Can they bring him back from the dead?" Then feeling himself sway with grief, the master said, with a groan, "I would give anything to have my son back."

Hearing the master's words, yet his attention glued to what Tsogyal and Rab-ten were doing, Abaka said, absently, more to himself than meaning to answer, "One hundred ounces of gold?"

Looking at Abaka in shock, the master said, "One hundred ounces of gold!"

Abaka looked back at him, surprised his words had been heard. The master of the house grabbed Abaka's arm, imploring, "One hundred ounces of gold? Why, I would give ten times that amount for my son to live again!"

Tsogyal placed one hand on the young man's chest, at his heart, then her other hand upon his forehead, at the third eye point. She felt his forehead still warm and damp under her hand. Looking up at the ceiling, she closed her eyes and sank into deep meditation. The room fell silent.

45

$\mathfrak{S}$enge's felt boots pounded the earth as he strode away from the house. He gazed ahead toward the snowy peak, yet he saw nothing.

"Sorcerous!" he muttered. "Witch!" he said aloud, in horror, his heart pounding with each footfall as the rage billowed within him. His bow quiver thumped his back, his sword slapped his leg as he strode onward, fists clenched against the clawing that traveled up his back. Talons of fear threatened to clasp his mind in the iron grip of panic. Trying to get free of it, yet controlling his urge to run, he lengthened his stride.

"How could I have been serving a sorcerous all this time and not seen it before?" He scolded himself, trying to shake the pricking claw from the back of his neck. "By the Gods, I have been taken for a fool."

With a rueful laugh, trying to loosen the lump forming in his throat from turning to tears, humiliating him, he said aloud, enraged, "Leaving my King! Traveling afar, to keep this woman safe. Thinking all the while that she is an innocent. Was I bewitched?"

"General!" a voice called from behind him.

The claw tightened, he quickened his stride. He would not look back.

"General Senge," the voice was at his side. Glancing sideways, he saw it was Abaka, falling in beside him, his strides long, his breath quick and deep.

"General, what is the matter?" Abaka asked, between gasps of breath, alarm in his voice.

Senge stopped and turned to face Abaka. Pointing back toward the great house with the walls surrounding it, Senge spit out the words, "She is a sorcerous, a witch!" Swinging his hand to pound his chest, he shouted, "And I am a fool!"

Abaka stared at him, uncomprehending. A gust of wind swirled around them as confusion turned to understanding. Abaka slowly shook his head as he said, "No, General, she is no sorcerous, she is a yogini."

Senge glared at Abaka, his anger molten. "What is the difference? She brings back the dead!"

"General, listen to me," Abaka implored. "There is a great difference. The Noble Daughter is not what you are thinking." Steadying his voice, not allowing it to quiver and betray his shock at seeing the General in this state of fear and anger, Abaka continued, "Sorceresses and witches use magic. They sell their life force to be in league with a God or demon or with spirits to gain power for selfish ends. A yogini of the Buddha dharma is much different. A yogini is sworn to good deeds, she is moved to action by a great and deep compassion for others. She attains siddhis, powers, from her practice of the methods of the dharma and uses these abilities to benefit beings. It is by the development of herself that she attains these siddhis, not by bargaining with outside beings."

Senge shook his head in disbelief, growling, "She brought a dead man to life. I have never seen such a thing. She must be in league with a powerful god or demon."

Gesturing toward the mountain, Abaka said, "General, let us walk, I will explain further."

The fire in his body growing cool, the talon's grip loosening its hold at the back of his neck, the lump in his throat spit out with his words, General Senge, took in a long breath. Letting it out, he grumbled, "Very well."

Abaka kept the pace slow to calm the General further as they walked silently side by side toward the great mountain.

A thought occurred to Senge. Before Abaka began speaking again, Senge asked, "Do you mean she is a white witch, a good witch? Is she a shaman?"

Shaking his head in answer, Abaka explained again patiently, "No, General, she is no witch at all. She is not in league with an outside being. She is not ruled by such a thing. She is not a shaman either, traveling to deep otherworldly realms. She is ruled by a deep compassion for others, not for self-aggrandizement or to control or own others."

Exasperated, Senge asked, "Then what force did she use to raise that man from the dead if not a God or a demon?"

Abaka answered, his voice deep and gentle. "I do not know exactly how the Noble Daughter did what she did back there," Abaka said, lifting his chin to indicate the walled estate they had just come from. "However, I do know the teachings she has been studying and practicing. She develops and then uses the energy of the light, of the goodness within, to do good deeds. She has taken a solemn oath that all she gains from her practice is to be used to help sentient beings."

Abaka was silent for a moment, gazing at the snowy mountain, watching clouds forming around its peak. Then in a quiet voice, he added, "More importantly, I know the heart of this woman and I can tell you I have no doubt she is pure goodness."

Relaxing his clenched jaw, Senge stopped in his tracks. Noticing the General had fallen behind, Abaka turned to him with a questioning look.

Senge looked at Abaka, his stern expression made hard deep lines in his face. "Abaka, you are a warrior. Your father rode with my father as allies in the battle at Talas and other battles as well." Thumping his fist on his chest in the salute of a soldier, Senge went on, "That makes us brothers-in-arms." Dropping his hand to rest on the hilt of his father's sword, feeling the cool smooth shape of the carved design under his fingers, Senge continued, "I trust you as a man of your word. So tell me, warrior brother, are you absolutely sure about her?"

Nodding solemnly, Abaka answered, "I have no doubt of her, my brother."

Gazing up at the snowy peak, seeing it now that his vision was clear, Senge felt his courage return to him. He took in a long breath, tasting the scent of distant snow on the cold air, then slowly let it out. The claw slid away from his back like a silk scarf.

Turning away from the snowy peak, Abaka gestured with outstretched hand toward the house. "Let us go back, General. We must finish our business here. Later, I am sure, the Noble Daughter will explain to us how she was able to help that young man come back to his body to live again." Rubbing his hands together, Abaka added, with a smile. "I, for one, am looking forward to finding out how she did that."

Senge looked at him, a smile smoothing the hard lines that had etched his face. Placing his hand on Abaka's shoulder, he squeezed it saying, "You remain a brave warrior, my brother; fearless."

Turning, they began back, walking along in matched strides.

"Abaka," Senge asked, "why do you follow her?" Stopping, he turned to look at Abaka, then continued, "I came as a favor to my King. I know her as the Princess of Karchen. Even though she was once a Queen of Tibet, I am here at the bequest of my King and to help my brother-in-law, Chudak, who feels himself her protector even still. I am here as a warrior in liege to my King, to protect his family." Senge grew quiet for a moment, weighing if he should mention the oracle's directive, that he should protect her. And, he thought, *respect her.* Deciding not to mention that, he went on, "Why does a warrior, a great a warrior as you, a warrior of the Turkic lands, follow this young woman and serve her. And, why do you waste your time sitting in caves?"

Abaka listened to the General, a slight smile on his face. He pondered for a moment, how to answer. Then he began, "General, I, as you, have been in many battles. I, as you, have seen much blood and watched many a man die at the edge of a sword. You are a warrior to protect your King and in service to your Emperor to ensure his rule and the freedom of your country from outsiders that intend tyranny over your people. I have fought for the same reasons, to keep our lands in the control of our own rulers, free from plunder by outsiders. We both fight to stop the Chinese and others who wish to come into our lands and take them for their own. And we fight for our Kings to acquire new lands to make our people prosperous."

Abaka made a gesture that they resume walking, as he continued, "I have seen a great deal of this world, buying and selling great and beautiful horses to Kings and Emperors." Taking in a long breath, then letting it out, Abaka explained, in a tone of resignation, "But now I am getting old. I think there is more to life than battles and trading for profit." Brightening, he continued, "There is another land to which I wish travel now. The road is hidden and mysterious, the way exciting, a great adventure. As well, a man need not be young to travel this road."

"What land is this you speak of?" Senge inquired.

"Nirvana," Abaka answered. "I wish to travel the road to Nirvana. However, it is not the destination that I am most set upon. Rather, it is the road itself that intrigues me. My travel so far upon this path has amazed me at how rich the landscape of the inner world is. It is a new frontier for me."

Intrigued, Senge asked, "Where is this road you speak of?"

"The road can be in a cave, in a jungle hut, anywhere there is peace and quiet to practice. However, one needs a guide, to find one's way and I have found that guide," Abaka answered.

They came to the door in the wall of the estate. With a perplexed look, Senge said, "Perhaps we can speak of this another time." Placing his hand on Abaka's shoulder, he repeated, "Another time, brother."

Stepping through the doorway into the estate, they saw a servant run from the room where the risen man was. Voices of laugher and joy could be heard emanating from the room. Hearing footfalls behind them, they turned to see Rab-ten and Chudak burst through the doorway from the road. Chudak stopped as Rab-ten hurried past them, heading toward the room, clutching a wrapped bundle.

"General," Chudak greeted.

"Chudak," General Senge replied, "what is happening? Where did you and Rab-ten just now come from?"

"We had to run to the marketplace," Chudak said, between gasps of breath. "Lady Rab-ten needed healing herbs for treating the man's wound." Glancing toward the room, Rab-ten had disappeared into, Chudak added, "I must go, to see if I am needed."

"We will accompany you," Senge said.

Entering the room, Abaka and Senge took in the sight. The wounded young man lay on his mat, his mother and father at one side, tears streaming down their faces, sobbing with disbelief and joy. The mother held her son's hand, stroking it. Tsogyal was sitting on the other side, speaking to the young man in a quiet voice as she held his other hand. The young man's face was turned to Tsogyal, his eyes open. Senge and Abaka could see he was struggling to stay awake and listen to the words Tsogyal was saying to him. Rab-ten was giving orders to two women servants.

"You must crush these in a pestle, then add ...." Looking up, she noticed Abaka and Senge standing watching her. Chudak stood near them, waiting for direction. "Wait here," she ordered the women. Crossing to the men, looking up at Senge, she said, "General, I need my bag from the inn. I have my healing balm there. Can you retrieve it?"

Senge listened attentively to Rab-ten, then he answered, "Yes, my Lady, I will go now."

"You shall bring all of your belongings from the inn," the master of the house said, as he stepped into their circle. "You will all stay here in my house. I will have rooms prepared for your stay and a place for your horses and mules in my stables."

Chudak stepped forward. "If you do not need me here, my Lady, I will assist the General."

Rab-ten nodded. "Yes, Chudak, that would be very good."

Senge and Chudak hurried from the room as Rab-ten turned to Abaka. "Abaka, will you oversee that these women follow my instructions properly?"

"Yes, Lady Rab-ten," Abaka answered, as he followed her to the two servants. He listened attentively as she instructed them in the preparation of her medicine. When they all hurried out the room, Rab-ten knelt next to Tsogyal.

"Sister, do you need anything?" Rab-ten inquired.

Tsogyal looked at Rab-ten, fatigue burning her eyes. "Water, for myself and this young man," she whispered back.

Rab-ten withheld a gasp of shock at seeing how drained Tsogyal was. Fearing Tsogyal might collapse at any moment, Rab-ten rose quickly to her feet. "I need water and food," Rab-ten exclaimed, looking around the room for a servant.

Noticing the servants were not understanding Rab-ten's plea, the master of the house shouted an order to a servant standing by the door as he pointed to Rab-ten, "Assist the Lady!"

With the servant as her guide, Rab-ten hurried toward the kitchen, her voice trailing away from the room. "I need water and some food. Something light and nourishing. Do you have soup made? And we need tea. We must hurry!"

46

"Where are Chudak and the General?" Rab-ten asked Abaka, as they approached the door.

"They were exercising the horses early this morning," Abaka answered. "They will arrive shortly. It is fortunate that..... Oh, I keep forgetting his name. The master of the house?"

"Dana Ayu," Rab-ten reminded.

"Yes, that Dana Ayu, has such a large barn to keep our horses and mules here with all of his horses," Abaka said. "And his son? Sister, please remind me of his name."

"Naga," Rab-ten answered, as she turned to hand Abaka the bowl she carried.

Taking it, Abaka waited anxiously as they stood before the door to Tsogyal's room. It had been three days since she had taken to bed, exhausted. Since the day she had brought Naga from the doorway of death, back into this life again.

Rab-ten reached for the door handle.

"How is she?" Abaka asked.

Rab-ten stopped and looked over her shoulder, answering, "She is still weak, but much better. She asked to see us all, so I think she must be feeling strong. If she falters though, I will ask everyone to leave."

Abaka nodded his agreement.

Opening the door slowly, Rab-ten stuck her head in. "Sister, are you ready to see us?"

"Yes, please enter," Tsogyal answered, her voice raspy and weak.

Just then, the slap of footfalls and jangle of a scabbard came quickly from behind Rab-ten and Abaka. Turning, they were met with Chudak hurrying up to them.

With a gasping breath, Chudak said, "Good, I am not late. The General is coming, he will be here shortly."

Taking the bowl from Abaka, Rab-ten led the way inside the dim room.

"Chudak, can you open the shutters?" Rab-ten asked as she went to Tsogyal's bedside.

The room brightened with the creak and clatter of the wood shutters pulled free from the window jam. Cool fresh air poured into the large room. Now all could see Tsogyal clearly, in her bed of large cushions. Wearing a silk robe, she was covered with woolen woven blankets. Her long black silky hair hung down around her shoulders. Her sunken eyes revealed her continuing fatigue.

Placing the bowl on a small table at the bedside, Rab-ten asked, "How are you this morning, Sister?"

"I am feeling better," Tsogyal whispered.

Feeling movement, they all looked around as Senge quietly entered the room. Tsogyal smiled at the sight of him. Noticing her gaze upon him, he nodded his greeting.

"Good ride, General?" Tsogyal inquired, her voice cracking with the effort of speaking aloud.

Senge's grim expression turned to a smile as he answered, "Indeed, good to be upon my horse."

"And how are the other horses and mules?" she asked, her voice straining.

"They are well, Noble Daughter. The livery here is large with space for turnout," Senge answered.

"General..." Tsogyal pushed herself higher on her cushions as she asked, "Would you be so kind as to exercise Dawa? If you have time."

"I will, Noble Daughter. I have time today, it will be a pleasure," Senge assured.

Looking up at the men, all standing, looking down at her supine form, great looks of concern on their faces, Tsogyal gestured to the several large cushions that lay about the room.

"Please, gentlemen, take a seat and make yourselves comfortable."

Seating themselves, the men waited expectantly.

"Rab-ten, can you ask the servants to bring us all tea?" Tsogyal asked. Looking at her seated warriors, she added, "And food?"

"Already have done so," Rab-ten answered.

At her words a knock sounded from the door. Chudak jumped up and opened it to reveal four young men servants with trays. Fear showed on their faces as they looked up at Chudak, who stepped aside from the doorway. With furtive looks at Tsogyal, they scurried to a large low table set at the side of the room, setting their trays down upon it. The aroma of curry and seared meat filled the room. Other aromas of spices and rice made everyone in the room realize how hungry they were. Chudak could hardly sit still, his stomach tight with hunger. Senge looked at the array of food, delighted to see momos piled high on a plate.

Keeping their gaze cast down, the servants set small low tables, carved with intricate designs of leaves and elephants, birds and monkeys, that had been stored at the edge of the room, before each who sat upon a cushion. Then, they set a plate filled with an assortment of the food before each man.

Abaka looked down at his plate, now set on the colorful painted and lacquered table before him. He breathed in the spicy scents. Picking up a momo, he bit in. The savory juices of the perfectly-cooked meat, mingled with the spiced vegetables and starchy outer shell, exploded in his mouth. He could not hold back his exclamation. "Mmm," he intoned.

Senge looked up, noticing the servant standing before him with a silver pot of tea. Understanding, he reached into the pocket made by the fold of his robe and produced his silver cup, setting it down on the table with a soft clunk. The servant poured, the hot liquid silently filled the cup. The servant proceeded to Abaka and Chudak, who did the same.

Their task completed, the young servants glided out of the room, stealing a last glance at Tsogyal as they closed the door silently behind them.

A feeling of dizziness washed over Tsogyal. She laid back a bit deeper into the cushions waiting for it to pass. Within moments it had gone, but left a renewed weakness in its place. She took a deep breath and let it out, the coolness of the morning air revitalizing her. Feeling a bit better, she decided she must get out this day and walk. She must get her strength back. Looking over the room of men, eagerly eating, she smiled to herself, a sense of great gratification at being able to provide a meal for these honorable men.

"Noble daughter, can you not eat?" Rab-ten asked, breaking Tsogyal out of her reverie.

Looking at the food on the plate, placed on the table next to her, Tsogyal felt her stomach begin to roil.

"I think this food is too heavy for my stomach," she answered. Looking at the bowl Rab-ten had placed on the table, Tsogyal asked, "What is this you have brought?"

Remembering the bowl, Rab-ten put her plate down as she chewed a bite of curried dal with rice. "I brought this for you, sister," she answered, picking up the bowl and setting it in Tsogyal's lap.

Gazing down at the white yogurt with amber honey trailed across the top in swirling designs, Tsogyal smiled. "Oh, thank you, Rab-ten, this will be very good."

The smacks of chewing and breaths of sipping filled the room. A woman's voice calling and a man's voice answering trailed in through the open window from the courtyard outside.

Soon all the plates were empty. The men sat back on their cushions. Chudak went about the room, the large pot of hot tea in his grasp, refilling everyone's cup. Seating himself, Chudak sat back, basking in the satisfaction of the fine meal, sipping his tea.

Setting her empty bowl on the table next to her bed, feeling the strength of the nourishment quickly filling her, Tsogyal said, "I am sure you all are wondering how what happened with Naga was possible."

Looking at each of her friends seated around the room, she was met with intent eyes upon her, waiting anxiously for her next words.

"Mostly it was timing," Tsogyal began. "If we had been even twenty footfalls later it would not have been possible."

As Tsogyal explained to all seated before her, she went back into her memory, reliving the experience over again. She and Rab-ten entered the room with Naga laying upon the mat. At once, Tsogyal sensed a presence above her, hovering at the ceiling. Kneeling beside Naga, she closed her eyes and set herself to concentrate fully. In seconds the feeling of the presence grew very strong in her awareness. It was there, floating above them all. She knew this was the young man's spirit looking down at the scene below him.

Telepathically, she asked, *"Do you wish to stay in this life or to go to your next life?"*

His face appeared in her mind. It was contorted with fear, as the answer came. *"No, I wish to stay in this life. I am not ready to leave. Please, can you help me? I am floating away. I want to get back into my body."*

Tsogyal held his consciousness with her mind, as a rope, to hold him near his body longer. *Stay*, she said to him in her thoughts, *hold to this rope of my mind. Travel it back.*

She placed her hand on his chest above his heart and her other hand at his third eye. Keeping herself from being distracted, Tsogyal began to direct the energy of her life force to circulate around her body as a loop, from her base chakra at the point she was seated upon, to her crown chakra. Up her back and down her front. As the energy built in strength, she then brought it to swirl around each breast. Using all of the energy she could muster and her focus, she brought the strengthening energy down through her hand at Naga's heart point. She circulated it into the young man's body through his heart and out into her other hand at his third eye point. Around and around she circulated her energy into his lifeless body, filling it with her own life force.

"It was something I learned from Padma," she explained,

pushing herself up straighter on the cushions. "We practiced it for many hours when in the cave at Chimpu. It is an ancient practice from the Taoists. They called it circulating energy, it is used for healing. I used it to bring life force, chi as the Taoists call it, back into Naga's body so his consciousness could return. I poured all I had into him, then kept circulating it through him."

Looking around the room, into each face she had come to know so well, she continued, her voice rasping from the effort at the telling, "I myself was amazed when I felt his heart leap under my hand and begin to beat again. I drew his consciousness down from the ceiling through my intention and felt a jolt at his third eye. His consciousness had come down into his crown chakra, yet the awareness was felt at his third eye. This was why I kept the crown chakra clear, by not placing my hand there."

Tsogyal turned her attention to the men seated around her. Abaka and Chudak looked at her, their faces frozen in awe. She noticed the General, his head bent, staring into his cup of tea, deep in thought. His face was deeply lined, his mustache turned down.

"So you see, if we had been any later, Naga's consciousness would have floated away and been gone. I could have done nothing," Tsogyal explained. Then she added, "Of course, without Rab-ten's assurance that she could heal him if he returned I would not have attempted it. To bring him back and have him die again would be cruel to all, himself as well as his family. Better to die just once."

Tsogyal looked at Rab-ten. "How is Naga this morning?"

"He is doing well. Very well. I think he will be up and walking in a few days. The wound is healing, now that it is being treated properly," Rab-ten answered, becoming animated at her success.

Looking at Tsogyal, Rab-ten said, "I am more concerned about you, Sister. What you did for Naga took much of your own life force."

Nodding, Tsogyal said, "Yes, I had no idea of the toll it would take on myself. I had never done such a thing before. But, I remember Padma warning me of the toll some efforts take. Now I understand what he meant."

Dizziness returning, Tsogyal laid her head back onto the

cushion, as she said, "But I am glad to have done it. Naga is returned, his family are happy and we have the gold we need to ransom Atsara, and more."

With an expression of concern, Rab-ten patted Tsogyal's arm as she declared, "You should rest Sister. We will go now."

Tsogyal rallied, asking, "No, not yet. I need to start walking, to get my strength back. Can you help me to walk out in the courtyard today? "

Chudak answered, "I will help you, Noble Daughter," then added, "I mean, I will help Rab-ten help you."

Senge drained his cup and secured it in its place in the fold of his robe. Rising, he inquired, "Abaka, would you like to ride with me? I will go now and exercise the Noble Daughter's horse."

"Yes, that would be good," Abaka replied, as he got to his feet, his eyes fixed on Tsogyal.

Togyal looked around the room as all were preparing to leave. Then she said, "Rab-ten, you should go with them. You have been here by my and Naga's side for days. You need to get out. Chudak can help me and the women servants too. Take Tashi and go with them. Go for a good gallop."

Looking at Abaka, a smile bloomed on Tsogyal's face as she pictured herself on Dawa, the two melded as one, racing across the land. "Horses need a good gallop. Isn't that right, Abaka?" she asked.

"It is true, Noble Daughter," Abaka laughed, "indeed they do. Nothing like a good gallop!"

The sound of Abaka's laugh untangled the atmosphere of intensity in the room. They all began to chuckle and smile, the simple lightness of joy lifting their hearts.

Feeling a surge of energy fill her, Tsogyal announced, "Chudak, I am ready to go for our walk now."

47

The chatter of monkeys echoed from the trees above Atsara as he sat astride his horse, its hooves making a slow steady clip-clop beat on the path. He strained his neck to look up at the dark forms, scurrying from tree to tree, backlit by the sun amongst the sparkling shimmering green of the leaves, high above in the canopy of trees.

At first it was strange for him, riding a horse. He had never done so before. Fearing he would fall, he held tight to the pommel of the saddle and gripped the horse's sides with his legs.

"Just sit and relax into the movement of your horse," Abaka had instructed him. "Keep your heels down in the stirrups yet allow your legs to be loose. And if he shies or bolts, become like a sack of rice on his back."

Indeed, he had never even been out of the city boundaries of Bhaktapur. *Well*, he thought, *that is, since he was taken from his family by the sadhu and traveled many days to his new parents*. That surprised him, as he gently swayed with the rhythm of his horse's gait, to think of them that way now. Now that they were gone. Now that he had left them, forever. He had always thought of them as his master and mistress. But now, riding his horse behind Tsogyal and Rab-ten, Abaka in the lead with the General, Chudak behind him holding the lead rope of a string of three mules, his memories of leaving Mistress Bhandari passed through his mind, as the many trees in this lush forest passed by him now. It seemed as the distance from Bhaktapur grew so did his memories. Drawing in a breath, taking in the damp scent of leaves mingled with the faint sweet fragrance of flowers, he tried to bring himself into the present, to stop the flood of memories. To no avail, they continued washing through him, unabated.

Mistress Bhandari had struggled to hold her composure when she had brought him to Tsogyal and Rab-ten. Her eyes were still swollen red with her tears. He did not see the gold that was paid for him, but knew it had changed hands.

After Tsogyal's first visit, Mistress Bhandari had called Atsara to her and asked him if he wished to go.

"Yes," Atsara had said. "I do, Mistress, I wish to follow the path of the Buddha's teachings."

"But, Atsara, you can study the Buddha's teachings here in Bhaktapur," Mistress Bhandari pleaded, tears beginning to well in her eyes. "You do not need to go. Why can you not stay?"

"I must go, Mistress. My future is with these Tibetans, to go to the snowy mountains for deep study and practice," Atsara had explained, tears filling his eyes, feeling her pain.

He did not tell her of his teacher's dream, for fear of the repercussions that may befall the old Buddhist from Master Bhandari, who would certainly be angry that his servant had been in secret meetings with the teacher without his knowledge.

Atsara was moved by Mistress Bhandari's pleas. He was shocked to realize that they both had loved him. Now, he felt deep sadness, that he had not understood their intentions. He had seen them as his master and mistress, yet they had given him so much.

"I will come back and visit, Mistress," he had said, wanting to console her, to assuage his feelings of guilt for causing her to shed so many tears, for him. "I promise, one day I will return to visit."

Mistress Bhandari just sank into a cushion, buried her face in her hands and wept.

"You think of your home, now gone?" The question came from Vasudhara, who rode next to Atsara.

Atsara looked at him and nodded, wiping quickly at the tears in his eyes.

Vasudhara's lined face showed him to be a man of forty springs. Yet, his strong body was more like that of a younger man.

"Thoughts come and go. That is the energy of the mind. Do not attach yourself to them, watch them. Watch how your emotions change with each passing thought. They are wisps of mist. They are simply energy," Vasudhara instructed. "Life is birth and death. Many deaths and many births in one's life. Your old life has died, like the life before that one, when you were a small child with your parents. You see? Meditate upon this."

Wiping another tear before it could fall, Atsara answered, "Yes, Master Vasudhara."

Vasudhara looked at him, considering. Then, in a gentle tone, he added, "I do not mean that you should negate that which you feel; that would be nonsense. What I mean is to look into the rise and fall of your thoughts and feelings to understand their true nature. Do you understand?"

"Yes, Master," Atsara replied. A shiver went through him as he pulled his wool felt robe tighter around him, the day was cold.

He wondered why this sorrow befell him now, it had been a moon since he left the Bhandari household. At first it was so exciting, leaving Bhaktapur with Tsogyal and her entourage. They had gone to Kathmandu where Vasudhara, a spiritual son of Padma, resided. Tsogyal had wanted to visit with this adept to receive teachings from him. Traveling to the outskirts of the township of Kathmandu, they proceeded through the forest of thick trees to the base of a hill. There stood an attendant, who, for a small piece of silver, would see to the care and protection of their horses and mules and their baggage. They climbed up the steep trail, so steep that in places there were stones laid as steps. Finally arriving at the top, Atsara had looked around him in awe, for built in the forest of trees were an array of small shrines and temples surrounding a large stupa; its dome and spire of stacked disc shapes rising high above the treetops.

The loud chatter of the many monkeys looking down at them

assailed the entourage. Atsara had never liked monkeys, their loud chirps and shrieks and how they would raise their lips showing rows of sharp teeth. He tried to ignore their presence all around him, the agile beasts scurrying from tree to tree, on the temple rooftops and sitting irreverently on the heads of the statues of Lord Buddha.

A man in a simple robe appeared welcoming them. Other visitors ignored them as they passed, their heads lowered in peaceful contemplation. Their guide led their entourage to a small temple made of stone with Sanskrit letters painted on the walls. Waiting outside the temple they all peered through the doorway, seeing a statue of a Goddess inside. Her hands frozen in a mudra pose, her granitic eyes filled with compassion as they looked out upon the world. Flickering butter lamps and offerings of fruit, rice and flowers were arranged before her cold stone figure.

Vasudhara appeared out of the darkness of the interior of the temple dressed in a simple cotton robe that fell to his sandaled feet. Stepping out of the doorway, he was followed by a waft of sandalwood smoke, damp stone and rotting fruit. With hands folded, he bowed, greeting them in the Indian manner. "Namaste," he said.

At the appearance of Vasudhara, their guide silently melted away, leaving to attend his duties.

Bowing, Tsogyal said, "Namaste, Master Vasudhara, I am Tsogyal, consort of Master Padma."

His eyes widening, Vasudhara bowed again deeply to Tsogyal, beseeching her, "Yogini, consort of the great Padma, will you grant me teachings?"

Tsogyal bowed in return, answering, "I will share all understanding I have attained and methods I have knowledge of." Then looking quizzically at Vasudhara, Tsogyal inquired, "What lies within this temple?"

Vasudhara glanced back toward the dark doorway. "There is a great and powerful Tantric adept and magician who is locked in a chamber built far below us," he answered, pointing toward the ground. "I share in the duty of bringing food to the locked doorway, sliding it trough a slot."

"He is locked in? Why?" Atsara asked.

Turning to look up at the tall handsome young man, Vasudhara answered, "It is his wish to remain in solitary meditation and Tantric practice. The door remains locked so no one will ever disturb him. He has been in there for many, many springs." Turning toward Tsogyal, he added, "Master Padma has visited him here. Padma is the only person he has allowed in to see him."

Days later, while Atsara walked along the path that circled around the base of the stupa with Tsogyal and Vasudhara, Tsogyal had asked Vasudhara to teach Atsara what his practice would be as her consort.

During one of their teaching sessions, seated next to a large statue of Lord Buddha, Atsara told his new teacher the story of his ransom, of the warrior brought back to life by Tsogyal. Vasudhara listened in amazement at the telling as the they sat on a stone bench under the tall trees.

Tsogyal invited Vasudhara to accompany them to Yanglesho so he could continue to instruct Atsara. For at Yanglesho resided a great yogini, Sakya Dema, also a consort of Master Padma. As well, Jila Jipha, also a disciple of Padma, was there in practice. Vasudhara was delighted to be traveling to this sacred power place of refuge.

"Stop!" a voice called out from the jungle ahead of them, startling Atsara out of his reminiscing. "Who goes there?" the gruff voice demanded.

Abaka and the General pulled up on the reins to halt. Skamar and Batur's heads were raised, their ears alert, as they fixed their attention on the two warriors that stood in the road before them, their recurve bows with nocked arrows held at rest, ready to raise and loose if need be. Skamar stepped back with a snort. Senge urged him forward next to Batur.

Tsogyal called from behind Abaka, "It is I, Tsogyal, consort of Master Padma. My friends and I wish to visit with Sakya Dema and to practice at Yanglesho."

Seeing Tsogyal and Rab-ten, the two warriors dropped to their knees, bowing their heads in prostration, their bows lay at their side on the ground. In unison, they said, "Please be welcome, Dakinis. We shall escort you to the sacred place."

Rising, they took up their bows and turned to lead the way to the caves. Senge looked at Abaka, perplexed by this display of reverence.

Abaka shrugged, having no understanding of it himself. Then he whispered, "They look familiar, have we seen them before?"

Stroking his long mustache, Senge mused aloud, "Yes, they do seem familiar. Yet, I know not from where."

Tsogyal turned to Vasudhara who rode up beside her. "Why do they bow to Rab-ten and me and call us dakini?"

"They are practitioners as well as guards here no doubt. They practice kriyayoga, the outer Tantra."

"Outer Tantra?" Rab-ten asked.

"Yes," Vasudhara explained, "they project dakini, that which is the reality of emptiness, onto all women. They worship all women as sacred; as dakini."

Following their escort, the way led down a winding path deeper into the thick forest. The soft sounds of the rush and tinkle of water falling and flowing over rock echoed through the forest ahead of them. After a time, they spilled out into a clearing where the trees were set wider apart. Tall pillars they held up the green canopy high above covering and protecting the space. It was a temple of wood, leaves, earth and emerald light. Its incense the heavy aroma of mossy damp earth. Following the path that took them alongside a flowing stream, they admired the lavender, yellow and white orchids that lined the shore. Further up-stream they came upon a large pond made from a circle of stones, hand-laid to capture the water pouring down from a waterfall. The crash of water echoed through the trees as it tumbled over the cliff side filling the pond. Water poured over the edge of the overflowing dam continuing down forming the stream that passed by them. Beyond the pond were stairs, carved into the rock, that led the way up to a wide ledge at the base of the cliff wall. A few large trees grew on the ledge at one side of the cliff, shielding some of the rock face from view. At the top of the rock faced cliff, the forest continued on to cover the steep mountain that loomed high above. Their gaze was fixed upon the twisted rock formations, carved by nature, in the cliff face.

"They look like snakes, writhing down the cliffside," Atsara said.

"Yes, turned to stone," Vasudhara answered.

A woman, who had been kneeling by the pond with a water jug, stood watching their entrance with interest. Now they all noticed her. She wore a simple robe of white cotton that fell to her bare feet. Her loose black hair flowed over her shoulders, reaching to her knees.

The warriors went to her and prostrated. "Sacred Dakini, Sakya Dema, we have escorted the dakini, Tsogyal," they announced.

Smiling, she walked toward them, her jug left by the water's edge. Tsogyal urged Dawa past Senge and Abaka and dismounted, handing Abaka Dawa's reins as the woman approached.

Her hands held out, the woman said, "Greetings Sister, I am Sakya Dema. You and your friends are welcome here."

Looking into the woman's deep brown, kind eyes, Tsogyal took her hands and answered, "My sister in Tantra, it warms my heart to meet you. Thank you for your welcome."

Turning, Tsogyal gestured toward Chudak, saying, "I have brought food and supplies for you and those practicing here."

Chudak squeezed Lungta lightly on her sides. She obeyed stepping forward, the mules following the tug on the lead rope. All parted, allowing him through.

Sakya Dema smiled in delight seeing the large loads each mule carried. "Oh, Sister, you are so generous, thank you," she enthused, squeezing Tsogyal's hands, then releasing them. "We certainly are in need of more food and supplies here." Placing her hands on her cheeks, she exclaimed, "This is wonderful."

All attention turned to the sound of the light clacking of sandals on stone. A young man was making his way down the rock stairway. He wore a long thick padded-silk robe over pants made of woven wool. Though the green and red colors of the robe were faded, the dragon designs were still visible. Striding lightly, he arrived by Sakya Dema's side.

"Tashi de ley, I am Jila Jipha," the man announced. "Your

reputation precedes you, Yogini Tsogyal. What is this about the raising of the dead?"

Surprised, Tsogyal glanced at Sakya Dema, asking, "How did you hear of that?"

Smiling widely, Jila Jipha said, "On the wind, Dakini, on the wind."

Looking up at Abaka and Senge, Jila Jipha said, "You must be tired from your journey, please dismount. I will show you your lodgings for your stay."

A man walked up and stood behind Jila Jipha. He was dressed in a long cotton robe of a natural off-white color. His hair hung loose over his shoulders, his beard was thick. On his feet he wore simple sandals.

Jila Jipha, turned to him, ordering, "Shagdur, have your brothers take our guest's horses and see that they are cared for."

Bowing, Shagdur answered, in a whisper, "I would be grateful to do so."

Abaka and Senge looked at each other in disbelief. Dismounting they handed the reins of their horses to the warriors who stepped up, answering Shagdur's summons. Shagdur took Dawa's reins. He turned his gaze to Senge and Abaka. They looked into his deep serene eyes, not able to hide their amazement at the change in him. His face once hard with anger and malice, was now soft with peace. Even his scar looked as it had faded. The corners of his mouth turned up in mirth, seeing the expressions on Senge and Abaka's faces.

He bowed to them, saying, "It does my heart good to see you both again. The power of these great teachings have changed my world. At last I am at peace and joy fills me every day."

Looking at Tsogyal, who had turned to him, listening to his words, he knelt, saying, "Wisdom Lady, it is good to see you have arrived safely. I honor you." Rising, he turned and led Dawa away, his compatriots following with the other horses.

Tsogyal turned to Sakya in amazement. Sakya Dema said, "Shagdur is a very good practitioner. He had many passions to work with and therefore much power to attain realization. Your gift to him of a moment of samadhi gave him and his compatriots motivation to understand and to practice."

Sakya Dema turned her attention to Rab-ten, who had dismounted and stood in amazement, watching all that was happening. Noticing Sakya Dema's attention on Rab-ten, Tsogyal moved to Rab-ten's side, saying, "This is my dear spiritual sister, Rab-ten. She progresses on the path." Looking into Rab-ten's eyes, Tsogyal added, "Without her I would not be here today."

Sakya Dema bowed, saying, "I am happy to meet you, My Lady."

Rab-ten bowed in return. "It is my great fortune to meet you, Lady."

"Come," Sakya Dema said, gesturing to Tsogyal and Rab-ten, "let us go to my cave. We have much to do."

Then, turning to Jila Jipha, Sakya Dema said, "Brother, we will be occupied for many days."

"Very well, I will see that the others are cared for and that food be brought to you," Jila Jipha replied.

Sakya Dema led the way, Tsogyal and Rab-ten followed. At the side of pond, she stopped to pick up her water jug, then proceeded up the stairs. The men watched as the three women glided up the stairs. The rush and tinkle of running water filled the openness. The sounds of birds and chatter of monkeys sang a chorus, echoing through the temple of trees, water and rock.

As they watched the women disappear into the cliff-face, Abaka whispered, "This truly is a sacred place and they truly are dakinis."

48

Thwack!

"Hah, hah!" the chorus went up from the men.

Thwack!

Jila Jipha pulled back smoothly on the bowstring, feeling the tightening pressure on the ring made of horn that covered his thumb. His first two fingers were wrapped around his thumb holding it in place on the string. These fingers were the strength that pulled the hundredweight of pressure back to his cheek. Letting his fingers relax, the string slid smoothly off the thumb ring, loosing the arrow. Thwack!

"Hah, hah! Again, a direct hit!" Senge shouted in admiration. "By the Gods, Jila, you are a great archer."

The assembled men nodded and murmured in agreement.

"Monkeys, you said?" Abaka asked.

"Yes, monkeys," Jila Jipha answered, as he held out Abaka's recurve bow, returning it to the Turk.

"I do not like monkeys," Senge chimed in. "Disgusting creatures; nasty teeth."

"I would have thought they would have eaten her," Atsara commented.

"But why would the infant of a Queen be left in a charnel ground with her dead mother?" Chudak asked. "Where was the King?"

"I can only guess, as no one knows for sure," Jila answered. "It must have been a case of heir to the throne; this Queen had no sons, only a daughter. Or, perhaps a jealous second wife was cause of the deed."

"So, she is of Royal blood?" Atsara asked.

Jila Jipha looked at him and nodded. "Yes, indeed she is. Yet no one in the Royal Family has any knowledge of her existence. They assume she died long ago as an infant."

All fell silent as Shagdur raised his bow. Aiming at the target made of bundled grass, he let his breath out slowly as he released his arrow. The shot went wide of the center by a hand's width. He groaned, looking at the ground, shaking his head in disappointment.

Turning his attention to Shagdur, Jila Jipha said, "Try again."

Shagdur nocked a second arrow and raised his bow.

"Now quiet your mind. Concentrate on the center of the target, see the arrow there. Relax your hand slowly, let the arrow fly," Jila Jipha instructed.

Thwack!

"Hah, Hah! Good shot!" The men roared. The arrow hit dead center. Shagdur's smile was broad as Senge thumped his back in congratulations.

Senge stepped up to take his turn. Sliding the arrow onto the bowstring as he gazed at the target, he said, "It is remarkable. An infant girl of Royal blood is left to die by her dead mother's side in the charnel ground. She is found by monkeys. They take her, suckle her and raise her." He shook his head slowly. "Remarkable."

The strain in the muscles of his back felt good as Senge pulled smoothly on the string of his bow. Slowly he let out his breath, letting the taut string ease out of his fingers and slide off his thumb ring made of horn inlayed with gold. Thwack! His shot was true, dead center. A smile flowed over his face as the men cheered. He raised his bow, pumping it in the air, causing the men to laugh at his pantomime.

"It is amazing. Many seasons had passed, her living with the monkeys, when she was found in that charnel ground, a grown young woman, by Master Padma. She became his consort and now she is the great yogini, Sakya Dema. What a story," Abaka said, as he watched Chudak take his turn, his bow raised.

All fell silent. Chudak released his arrow. Thwack! The shot went just two fingers right of the center. Chudak turned and shrugged. "I need to practice more, I am getting sloppy."

"Yes, it is fine we can practice here," Senge said. "I was not expecting you would have an archery range here in a retreat."

"It is good to shoot some arrows, keep the body strong, relax from meditation practice," Jila replied. "Speaking of meditation," he continued, turning his attention to Abaka, "are you ready for teachings and practice now?"

Abaka answered, "Yes, I am ready."

Driving his knee into the center of the bow, he released the string from the bow nock. Picking up his bow-quiver, he slid the bow into the leather case. Then he covered the arrows, encased in a pocket on the front, with a flap to protect their feather fletchings.

The sun's rays sparkled down through the trees, patterns of light danced around them.

"Are you practicing with Master Vasudhara today?" Jila Jipha asked Atsara.

"Yes, he said we would be in deep practice for several days. He wanted me to tell you this," Atsara said.

"I see," Jila Jipha said. "Gather what food and water you both will need and bring it to the cave for you and Vasudhara. You know where the supplies are and what to gather?"

"Yes," Atsara replied, as he nodded, "I know what to bring."

Jila turned to Senge and Chudak. "You both are welcome to come with Abaka and me."

Senge shook his head. "No, I will go to exercise the horses now. I do not do well sitting in caves."

Jila nodded, then looked to Chudak. "Chudak?"

Looking from Senge to Jila Jipha, Chudak felt torn, his confusion clearly written on his face.

Senge regarded his brother in-law. "If you wish to go, you should do so," Senge advised.

"You will need help with the horses," Chudak answered.

Placing his hand on Chudak's shoulder, Senge said, "Brother, go with these men if you wish. You will learn something new. We can exercise the horses later. I will practice my sword strokes now. You go."

Chudak turned to Jila Jipha, smiling. "I will go with you."

Senge regarded the disappearing forms of the men. "Hrumph," he said to himself, shaking his head, "sitting in caves, traveling roads to Nirvana. Waste of a good day."

He drew his sword slowly from its scabbard, enjoying the feel of it sliding free from the leather. Holding it up, he admired the way the rays of sunlight shimmered on the dragon etched on its fine blade. Slowly he sliced it through the air, feeling every sinew of his body flex and stretch with the movement. Breathing in, he felt the cool air enter his nostrils and travel deeply into his body, the scents of earth and leaves nourishing him. Releasing his breath slowly, he made another slice in perfect execution of the proper form. His body felt light and strong as he drove his concentration deeper into each stroke.

The monkeys high above in the trees looked down in silence, transfixed, as they watched the form of the man below, dancing with the shimmering blade of light.

49

"And so, you have been here ever since?" Rab-ten asked.

"Yes," Sakya Dema replied. "After Padma found me in the charnel ground northeast of here, he brought me to this place. He taught and practiced mahamudra with me and Tantric yoga. Realization came quickly under his tutelage and in his presence. I like it here and do not wish to go anywhere else. I remain here in practice and teach those who seek my teachings." With a smile to Tsogyal, Sakya Dema continued, "And when practitioners such as Tsogyal or Vasudhara come to visit me, we share knowledge and my realization continues to expand."

"Monkeys?" Tsogyal asked, incredulous.

"Yes, monkeys," Sakya answered. "They saved me, took me in as one of their own."

Rab-ten and Tsogyal looked at each other, shaking their heads.

"Amazing," Tsogyal said.

To Rab-ten, Sakya asked, "And what is your practice now, Lady?"

"I perceive all that arises in my mind as illusion and emptiness, simultaneously," Rab-ten answered.

"Hah," Sakya said, "the union of phenomena and emptiness. How is your practice going?"

"I have had no realization as of yet. However, I do regard the energy of my mind as such and am not as a leaf in the wind of my thoughts any longer."

"That is good," Sakya encouraged. "Tsogyal and I will be practicing a higher yoga than you are capable of at this time. I wish you to remain with us and practice your own practice, ignoring what we are doing. Can you do that?"

Nodding emphatically, Rab-ten answered, "Yes, I can do so." Turning to face the wall, her back to the women, Rab-ten began her meditation. Relaxing into the cushion she sat upon, she gazed at the wall of stone before her, its muted colors of gold and gray danced in the flicker of the light cast by the butter lamps. She breathed in the moist earthy air of the cave. Try as she may, she could not ignore the words of Tsogyal and Sakya Dema behind her. They spoke of careful awareness that keeps proper conduct. Of a mind unbiased, free of pleasure, pain and indifference. The mind a continuum like a river's flow. Fixation upon mahamudra. She marveled at their discussion of fearlessness in the transition into death. Of dzog chen and purifying dream states to enter the sanctum of clear light. They exchanged methods of employing the vital breath's energy to purify the medial nerve. The mystic heat, blazing and dripping.

Rab-ten felt as she could no longer breathe, a lump forming in her throat, she tried to relax, yet the thoughts assailed her, *I will never reach the attainment of these great yoginis. I will never understand what they do. I will never be as good as they are.* A tear made its way from her eye and slid down her check. She was startled out of her thoughts as a hand touched her shoulder.

"Rab-ten?" Sakya's gentle voice said to her.

Turning from the wall to face the women, Rab-ten held in her emotions. "Yes?"

In a gentle voice, Sakya Dema encouraged, "Rab-ten, you are the same as us. We are no different than you. You will attain all. Do not let thoughts of high and low disturb your practice."

Amazed that Sakya Dema and Tsogyal had felt her thoughts, the flood-gates opened, tears poured from Rab-ten's eyes. She struggled to wipe them away, embarrassed at her show of emotion.

"I am still a leaf on the wind of my thoughts," Rab-ten said, embarrassed at her failure before these women.

"No, sister," Tsogyal encouraged, "you see it takes time and practice. Much practice. As you begin to achieve true understanding, your ego will try ever harder to distract you. Ego's purpose is to keep you safe and alive, it strives for survival. It is not a bad thing, just another part of your being to understand and transcend, through practice."

"Yes," Sakya explained, "and now you have a great opportunity."

Rab-ten looked at her, sniffling her tears away. "Opportunity?"

"Indeed. You see, thoughts are the energy of the mind. Emotions are energy too, they are connected. As Tsogyal has said, as you progress the practice becomes ever more challenging. Your thoughts will become more provocative, stirring emotions. That must not be seen as a problem, but a means to progress on the path," Sakya instructed.

"Yes," Tsogyal enthused, "you use that energy, the energy you felt so strongly just now, the energy of competition and sadness, and turn it to look deeply into the thoughts. Drive your concentration using that energy, look into the nature of the connection between thoughts and the energy of the emotions that arise in connection to them."

Rab-ten looked wide-eyed from Tsogyal to Sakya and burst into tears anew. "But Sister, I did not know to do that."

Sakya Dema laughed, "That is why you have a guru, a teacher." Placing her hand on Rab-ten's knee, shaking it gently, her voice soft and sweet, she continued, "No one can succeed without a qualified master to guide them."

"If you had known what to do, you would be greater than us put together," Tsogyal chortled.

Rab-ten looked back and forth between Sakya and Tsogyal, a feeling surging up from her belly, then she too burst out laughing.

"You see?" Sakya said. "First you cry, now you laugh! Do you see how the energy changes?"

Herself now rolling in laughter, Tsogyal gasped, "Thoughts arise and fall away. We laugh, we cry, we love, we hate. Endless thoughts, endless emotions, endless suffering."

"Yet you will become free, Lady, because you have the way and the teachers to show you," Sakya said. Then, thinking, Sakya continued, "How far you progress in this life really is determined by your previous karma. Yet still, you must practice, striving for full enlightenment. You will take all you have gained in your practice with you into your next life. In that life you continue, progressing more in each life until full enlightenment."

"You mean I may not become enlightened in this life?" Rab-ten asked, her laughter subsiding at Sakya's words.

Tsogyal answered, "You may or may not. Yet these practices unravel the bonds of ignorance as you progress. The fruit you do achieve is sweet and makes for a better life, a more fulfilling existence. You lose nothing by devotion to practice and you gain much."

"When you return to your husband you can continue your practice, continue all you have learned from each retreat," Sakya said.

Rab-ten looked in surprise at Sakya, how she read her mind and seemed to know every concern she had.

"When we return to Tibet, I will show you the way to practice while in your home with Jigme," Tsogyal encouraged, then added, "I am always in your life, Sister, and Padma is in your life as well."

Feeling as a great weight had been lifted from her, Rab-ten said, "Well then, I have much to do." Turning, she faced the wall again. Settling herself, she took in a breath, feeling the cool damp air fill her. Closing her eyes, she heard the murmurs of Tsogyal and Sakya resuming their conversation behind her.

"I have received the secret instruction needed in the experience of ultimate reality. The way is to utilize the six lamps, cultivating clear light," the soft voice of Sakya Dema said to Tsogyal.

Rab-ten smiled. Then she looked into the smile, the source of its energy, its nature.

50

Abaka turned in his saddle raising his hand in farewell. The figures of Senge and Chudak were now small in the distance. Abaka watched as both men raised a hand, then they turned Skamar and Lungta and cantered away.

In Karchen now, they had parted ways, Senge and Chudak returning to the palace to serve their King, Pelgyi, Abaka, leading the way to the Emperor's Palace, for Rab-ten to return to her husband, and then onward to Zhoto Tidro with supplies for Tsogyal and Atsara. There they would meet with Padma who was meditating and teaching two of his disciples at Zhoto Tidro. Abaka would help set Tsogyal and Atsara up for an extended period of sequestered practice. Then, Abaka would go with Padma to Chimpu. There Padma would instruct him and he would enter a small meditation hut, built on the hillside, with enough food and supplies for three moons of deep solitary practice. After instructing Abaka, Padma would travel to Lhodrak, taking Batur, Dawa and the mules with him. His route took him past the farm Abaka's friend owned. There Padma would leave the animals in his care with a small bag of silver as payment. He would travel onward upon his horse, Garkan, leading one of the mules with supplies for his own journey.

Deep travel into the inner world, Abaka thought, a smile forming on his face as the thoughts filled him, *on the path to realize the true nature of all that is.* His excitement at the prospect filled his chest.

Abaka would miss the General and Chudak. He reminisced their goodbyes as Batur strode along, avoiding the larger stones on the rocky ground.

Chudak had looked absolutely forlorn, yet tried to put on a brave face, as he stood looking down at Tsogyal.

"Do not be sad, Chudak," Tsogyal had said, looking up to him. "We will see each other again. I am here in Tibet for a long time."

"Yes, Noble Daughter," was all Chudak could manage.

"Please, bid my father and mother my wishes for their good health. Tell them that I am well. Assure them that I have chosen my path, that I was not coerced," Tsogyal pleaded. Then thinking, she added, "And tell my mother I will come to see her, as soon as I am able."

"I will, Noble Daughter," Chudak choked, then cleared his throat.

Turning to Senge, who stood sliding his hand back and forth along the leather of Skamar's reins, Tsogyal said, "General, I am most grateful you came with us and saw us safe."

"It was a great pleasure to do so, Noble Daughter, my great pleasure," Senge replied, his stern face softening, his eyes warm, looking down into her beautiful face. "Should you have need of my assistance in future, do no hesitate to call for me. Unless I am leading a battle for your father, I will come."

Tsogyal placed her small hand over Senge's, feeling the raised scars from his life of fighting and practicing with weapons. Squeezing it slightly, she said, "You are a good and brave man, General. My father is fortunate to have you in his service. And I am fortunate to have your friendship."

Swallowing the lump that rose in his throat, Senge stepped back and bowed. "I wish you a good journey, Noble Daughter."

Abaka played back in his mind his parting words to the General.

Clasping Senge's arm in the solder's grasp of hand to forearm, Abaka said, "If ever you wish to sit in a cave and travel this road we are set upon, find me. I too will be in Tibet for a long time. We shall see each other again, my brother, I am sure of it."

"Indeed, it will be a good day when we do," Senge boomed, tightening his grip on Abaka's arm and slapping Abaka on his shoulder with his other hand.

Abaka considered too, how Chudak and the General were going home richer. Tsogyal had divided the nine hundred ounces of gold she had remaining after Atsara's ransom between all of them. She used her portion for supplies and travel for all of them.

Riding along, in the rear of their small troop, just Atsara, Rabten and Tsogyal now, Abaka played over in his mind all that had happened in Yanglesho. And then, what had happened after they left that remarkable place to return to the land of snows.

Jila Jihpa had given him instruction to deepen his practice. The use of prostrations to soften his ego's hold on his mind. The use of breath to cleanse his inner channels. Blowing out the black air of negativity. Then breathing in the cool white air, filling his being with light. The visualization of himself as the Deity.

Himself as the Deity, he thought now, *not outside himself, yet himself.* Batur's ears swiveled back as Abaka whispered the mantra Jila had given him to recite, "*Om A Ra Pa Ca Na Dhih.*"

Lifting his arm high, he imagined himself holding the double-edged sword that cuts all delusion. Lowering his hand, he reached to pat Batur on the neck, so grateful for this horse who had carried him hither and yon without protest, willingly. *Funny,* he thought to himself now, *I had never considered my horse this way, what Batur may feel.* Compassion rose in him for the cruelty he had seen in his life toward these great beings, horses. He was thankful now for always knowing to treat them well. His heart swelled, with such feeling, such compassion, it hurt. Shaking these thoughts away, he turned his mind to remember the events after their time at Yanglesho on the route home to Tibet.

They had traveled from Yanglesho to Kathmandu to escort Vasudhara back to his temple. A day's ride out of Kathmandu, heading north for the border between Nepal and Tibet, they were stopped by the King of Nepal's troops. The word of Tsogyal raising a man from the dead had found its way to the King's ear. Finding Tsogyal's entourage, the King's guard had taken them to the palace. There the King gave a great feast and pleaded with Tsogyal to remain in his service as High Priestess. Tsogyal refused and demanded he set them free to proceed on their journey home. Finally the King relented, realizing the wrath of such a powerful woman as this yogini may cause him serious problems. With a show of great respect toward Tsogyal, and to save face, he made a great ceremony of releasing them to their journey home.

Now Abaka looked around at the expansive vista around him. The mountains in the distance with their snowy peaks. Huge white clouds sailing in the blue sky. A wind came up and whistled in his ears. He took in a breath of the cold clean air, it was delicious. Taking inventory of his life thus far, *how fortunate*, he pondered, *a good life. And so much more to do*, he mused.

51

ℜab-ten awoke, startled. She turned her head, there was her husband, Jigme, lying beside her, snoring. Turning on her side, she reached for him, her hand softly running the length of the knotted scar that ran across his side. His seed felt sticky between her legs, her organ still warm and engorged with their lovemaking. She shivered, her body feeling the profound pleasure of the power of their release. He had not left his seed inside of her, thus preventing a child. She knew this was hard for him. Yet, he was a most disciplined man. This quality, among so many other qualities he possessed, filled her with pride in him and with love for him.

Playing her fingers over the raised flesh on his side, she considered that she had not concentrated enough, using the pleasure of her release, the moment of no mind, for her practice. Rab-ten smiled, next time she would be more mindful. *Next time*, she thought, as she lay her head on her husband's chest, the steady strong thumping of his heart loud in her ear.

She missed Tsogyal and Abaka, Chudak and the General, even Atsara. *He is a bright young man*, she thought. It is strange, she considered, it was like all she had done, where she had traveled to, was now like a dream. Yet she did have something, a precious thing, that she brought back, to prove it was all real. She had received and brought back with her the teachings she had received. She had met high adepts, she had been instructed in her practice. Tsogyal was with her, if not in body then in spirit. And she would see her again, when she came out of retreat at Zhoto Tidro. She could seek out Padma when he visited Samye, if she really needed help with her practice. Now her friends were gone and she was alone; yet she held the gift of her practice.

"Your husband need not even know you are a practitioner," Sakya Dema had told her. "It is better he not know, better for you."

"Why?" Rab-ten had asked.

"So he will not ask questions you cannot yet answer," Sakya had answered. "If you do not know an answer it will distract you, perhaps shake your faith in your path. Be in retreat in your heart, yet be in the world," she had instructed. "Embrace all in your life and bring it onto the path with you. It is a great practice."

"When you have a profound experience in your meditation, keep it to yourself until you see me or Padma again," Tsogyal had instructed her. "Your light is but a candle now. You need to nurture it. If you tell others of your experiences it would be like giving your candle away. You will lose that light."

And what of having a son or daughter? Rab-ten mused, as she lay now beside her husband, warm and secure in their soft bed, covered with blankets of woven wool, in their small house within the palace enclosure of the Emperor. *What of having children and also being a secret practitioner?*

And then, she remembered, there is the gold to remind her all was very real. Jigme had been most impressed with the gold Rab-ten returned with. Most impressed too, with Tsogyal's generosity toward all who had traveled with her.

And with that gold, Rab-ten thought as she stroked her husband's chest, *I can pay an attendant to care for our child in my absence, when I go to be with Padma or Tsogyal. I can pay from my own gold and serve the Emperor diligently as court healer. I will have a child to teach my healing arts to. It will benefit the Emperor.*

Rab-ten felt Jigme's hand slide over her's and squeeze. His eyes were open now, looking at her.

"I have married a lioness," he growled. "One who travels to all manner of places without her husband's leave. A mind of her own."

Rab-ten raised up onto her elbow to look into Jigme's eyes. "You do not want to be married to a simpleton, do you? One who sits at home and knows nothing of the world? One who waits for you to return from many springs at battle only to nag at you?"

Jigme chuckled. "You are no simpleton, wife." Then reaching for her, encircling her with his arms, he held her tightly to him. "You are a snow lioness, a rare one."

"Husband?" Rab-ten asked. "Would you like a son or a daughter?"

Jigme's eyes widened. "A son?" Releasing her, he lifted himself onto his elbow, to look directly into her eyes. "A son?" Then remembering the pain of the loss of their first child, Jigme wondered aloud, "Try again for a son or a daughter?"

Rab-ten placed her hand on his cheek, feeling the smooth fine hair of his beard. "This one will live, husband, I am sure of it."

The idea taking root, he found himself becoming more excited as he replied, "Yes, wife, I would like us to have a son or a daughter."

Then concern came over his face. "Will the Emperor give us leave?"

"I do not see why not. We serve him and a child will not hinder our service. Indeed, a child will be an apprentice to my healing arts, it will benefit the Royal Family for the future."

Jigme stroked his long mustache, musing aloud, "The Emperor told me, upon my return from our last campaign, that he wishes me to remain here training men in strategy and overseeing the field training for the next few springs." Turning his attention to Rab-ten, a surge of excitement filling him, he said, "I can be here, with you and our child."

"As well, we have the gold. I can pay for a woman to assist me. I will not be alone to care for our child," Rab-ten reminded him.

Jigme looked at her, his eyes swimming with joy. "A child. Rab-ten, we will have a child. I will petition the Emperor this day."

He pulled her close to him. She felt his member against her, risen again, urgent. Rab-ten yelped as he swung her body around and lay atop her, looking into her eyes. She looked up at him, laughing.

"We will make our child now," he declared, anticipating the great pleasure of filling her with himself and with his seed.

Good, she thought, joyfully, *we will have a child. Remember my practice,* she instructed herself. *Be mindful.*

52

A shiver ran through Tsogyal as a gust of cold wind coursed along the rock-face. Pulling her sheepskin robe tighter around her, Tsogyal stood, high up on the mountainside, overlooking the path below. She watched the forms of Abaka and Padma, on Batur and Garkan, leading Dawa, Atsara's mount, and the three mules now free of their loads. Their forms became smaller and smaller as they made their way down the path out of Zhoto Tidro. She and Atsara were now the only ones remaining at Zhoto Tidro, Padma and Abaka being the last to leave.

As she watched them, they stopped, both turned in their saddles to look at her, raising their hands high they waved to her in farewell. Tsogyal raised her hand, waving back to them, her heart heavy. Then, they urged the horses onward and were gone. Snow began to fall, large white flakes, as large as her hand, floated out of the gray low clouds that shrouded the mountains of this sacred place. She stood watching where the men had been, now just a rocky path along the stream that tumbled down the canyon. The snow began to fall with more force, the wind swirling the cold whiteness around her. She looked again to the place the men had been. Now it had disappeared completely, shrouded in the white flurry. Turning, she climbed up the path to their cave dwelling. This cave was hidden away from the others at Zhoto Tidro, a secret cave. The wind blew stronger, howling against the rocky cliff. Stumbling as she reached the doorway, she reached out to catch her fall, grasping the beam of the doorway, the wood felt rough under her hand. A blast of wind hit her back. As it roared in her ears she felt glad for these beams that held the door to the cave opening.

Padma, Abaka and Atsara had built this door onto the cave entrance. They had brought the wood beams and planks loaded on the mules. Toiling for many days, Atsara and Abaka hoisted the wood to the cave entrance. Then Abaka and Padma carefully carved the wood to fit firmly into the rock. Padma laid the flat wood planks together on cross pieces and lashed them tightly with rope, making a fine door.

Remarkable, she thought, as she stepped into the cave and pushed the door closed. Swinging on leather hinges, it fit perfectly into the heavy beams that were wedged into the rock, shutting out the wind and snow. Turning from the closed door, she stood still, allowing her eyes to adjust to the darkness in the cave. In a moment, she could see Atsara, sitting by the fire pit, a glow of small flame lit his face that was rimmed in the fur of his hat. He looked large in his thick robe of sheepskin as he worked, deep in concentration.

Looking up at Tsogyal, he lifted the pot of simmering liquid and asked, "Tea?"

Tsogyal nodded as he poured the thick tea into two silver cups that were side by side on a rock. Seating herself across from Atsara, she glanced at the yak-skin bags, piled along the wall, that were filled with barley flour, butter, salt and tea. Then at the sacks of dried yak dung and the stack of wood that had been collected before the snows; fuel for their fires. She mentally counted the water-skins that lay by the bundles and considered that they would melt snow for water when these were empty.

Taking the proffered cup in her two hands, she sighed as the warmth sank into her cold fingers.

"They have gone?" Atsara asked.

"Yes," Tsogyal replied, "and the snow is falling heavily now."

"They made their departure just in time," Atsara said, "or else we would all be in retreat."

With a fleeting feeling of whimsy at the thought of Padma and Abaka remaining with them, Tsogyal said, more to herself than to Atsara, "We need to be alone, it is good they were able to leave."

They sat, sipping the butter tea, in silence. Tsogyal thinking of her return to Padma here at Zhoto Tidro from her journey to Nepal. She smiled inwardly remembering his pleasure at her success in finding and returning with Atsara. In her mind's eye, she saw his handsome face listening with keen interest in her recounting the details of their journey; the vicissitudes of the road, the bandits, the problems of finding gold, leading the man's consciousness back into his body, back to life.

Talking another sip from her cup, she felt the richness of the thick butter warm her body as she replayed Padma's words to her after she had told the entire account of her journey. "Whatever hardships you suffered are beneficial," Padma had said. "Your struggles purify all kinds of karmic obscurations. The power you used to raise the young warrior from death is a siddhi, a power, that comes of your practice. Yet, it is a mundane siddhi," Padma had explained, then added, "I am glad to see you understand that and have no conceit in regards to the event."

Tsogyal glanced up at Atsara now. He sat gazing into the fire, deep in his own thoughts. She was glad he had progressed so far in such a short period of time.

Padma had instructed them both in their practice and had given Atsara initiation. The power of Padma's blessing and teaching had brought Atsara to a higher level of spiritual maturity, making him equal to the task as Tsogyal's consort. They would both achieve much in this cave retreat, she knew. They were to remain alone in practice for seven or more moons.

The door rattled as the wind grew stronger outside. A deep, long howl filled the cave. Atsara looked at Tsogyal, his eyes wide.

"Wolf," Tsogyal affirmed, answering the question written on his face.

Then another wolf answered from farther away, its howl long, beginning low then climbing higher in pitch.

Glancing at the recurve bow and arrows placed against the hard rock wall, Atsara said, "The first one sounds close."

"Mmm," Tsogyal murmured, following his glance to the bow.

Another howl came, from the one close to their cave. Primal fear crawled up Atsara's back.

Tsogyal considered him, remembering her first time alone in a cave, how the howls of wolves had frightened her.

Setting down her cup, Tsogyal got up and went to Atsara's side. Kneeling beside him, she took his hand in her's and said in a soft voice, "There will be a time when you will hear that sound and realize its beauty. That beauty will fill you with amazement."

Atsara felt her hand squeeze his. His fear subsided.
He laughed at his emotions taking him over.

"Shall we begin our practice?" Tsogyal invited.

Atsara nodded. "Yes, I will light the butter lamps."

Squeezing his hand again, Tsogyal looked up at the ceiling and around at the rock walls that held them in. Atsara followed her gaze, then looked at her quizzically.

"Here, in this cold cave, we will soar, Atsara," Tsogyal assured. "We will soar."

Snow flurried outside the cave, the frigid white piled higher and higher against the door.

PART THREE

53

The ragged edge of the hard glacier inched against the rock scree of the mountainside above Zhoto Tidro. Roaring wind raged over the frigid blue ice. Cold bit at every sinew of Tsogyal's being. Alone, she sat inside the cave of rock. Only a cotton robe hung from her thin form, barely a barrier from the cold. Keeping her concentration, Tsogyal focused on raising the inner heat. Her bony pelvis sat upon the cushion, now threadbare and hard on the rock floor. Her thighs were not much more than skin sagging on bone. Dizziness swarmed inside her head. Steeling herself, she concentrated.

The fire, the inner fire. See the flame, feed it with the winds of the channels. She instructed herself.

Then it began, a slow flicker of warmth, a candle flame inside her being. Opening her eyes, the rock wall before her shimmered. Forms of light danced on the cold uneven surface. The forms transformed into many dakinis, dancing in a mandala on the wall before her. Then the light engulfed her. The naked female beings danced in a circled around her. Their eyes glittered blue, like the surface of a windswept lake, and were open wide with passion. Their long black hair flew wildly around them as they danced. Long necklaces of bone ornaments clattered and swung from around their necks as they lifted her up and up into their dance. The rock and cold faded away.

Tsogyal found herself in a vast landscape. The dakinis set her gently down upon the ground, her feet sinking into the surface. Looking down, she stepped back in surprise, then horror, as she realized she was standing on bloody slabs of flesh. Looking around her, she realized the ground of this land was made entirely of slabs of raw flesh.

Noticing a tree a short distance away, she felt she must go to it, her feet squishing with each step, the bloody mass oozing through her toes. Her attention came away from her feet as she approached the tree. Her mind could not comprehend what she was seeing before her. Trees should have leaves, yet this tree had sharp knives where leaves should be. Tsogyal looked around at all the trees on this landscape, they all had sharp knives of all sizes where there should have been leaves.

Turning away from the tree, Tsogyal looked to the unusually-shaped mountains in the distance. Her hand went to her mouth in a gasp as she realized their unusual shape was due to them being not earth and rock but, instead, huge piles if skeletons reaching high into the sky.

"What is this place?" Tsogyal asked the dakinis who were hovering above her, watching her every move.

"Orgyen Khandro Ling," they replied in unison.

In the distance she saw a palace. Pointing, Tsogyal asked, "Are we going there?"

The dakinis all nodded as they reached their hands down to Tsogyal. She levitated up off the ground and floated with them toward the palace. As they got closer, Tsogyal realized the palace was not made of stone as she had expected. She tilted her head, trying to comprehend what she was seeing, what this palace was built of. Then, as they came much closer, she saw it, not built of stone but of skulls. Yellow old skulls with vacant eye sockets looking out. There were dried heads too, with wisps of hair still attached, waving in the breeze. And also freshly severed heads, their blood dripping over the skulls and heads below them. All were stacked upon each other, in gruesome masonry, making the walls of this palace.

She looked up and around at the dakinis floating with her, their attention fixed on the palace before them. A feeling of great unease gripped her.

Instantly she found herself inside the palace. She had not remembered the doorway she had entered. She was alone now, the dakinis were gone. Standing in a large room, Tsogyal looked at the strange walls around her and up at the ceiling. They were translucent, a soft glow of light coming from behind them illuminated the room. Approaching the wall nearest her, she placed her hand on it, trying to determine what it was made of. Suddenly, realization dawned. She pulled her hand back in shock, realizing these walls were made of stretched human skin. The floor beneath her feet felt solid, she decided she did not want to know what it was made of, so did not look down.

At one wall of the room was a large window with gray light streaming in. Tsogyal walked over to it. Looking out she could see over the lower parts of the palace. She was amazed at how vast it was, with many more structures added to the main body where she stood looking out. She leaned out and looked up, surprised to see more of the palace rising up and up into the clouds. Turning her attention to the distance beyond, she saw many volcanoes leagues away. Then she realized these volcanoes ringed the palace. She looked in amazement as fire shot into the sky from them. She could hear their rumblings and explosions. Rivers of glowing lava flowed down their sides. The sky above them hung heavy with black clouds of ash.

Looking to the base of the volcanos, she made out the shapes of huge vajra scepters made of black iron, standing side by side, creating a formidable fence. Within this boundary, she made out the shapes of large birds fluttering and hopping on the ground. Tsogyal realized they all had bloody flesh hanging from their beaks. She could not decipher what they were eating.

Looking down, directly below her, was a large courtyard where crowds of people were milling about. All at once every face turned up, cold flowers toward a sun. She looked at them in horror, making out disfigured splotchy gray and blackened faces with red glowing eyes all looking up at her. Their blood red lips pulled back in sneers, exposing sharp teeth as thick rough tongues licked out over fangs in their desire to devour her.

No, she thought, *not people, these are demon savages.*

"Illusion," she whispered to herself. "Am I in a place or in a dream?"

Suddenly, the savages turned away, ignoring her as though she was no longer visible to them. Turning from the window, Tsogyal looked across the room to where a doorway appeared. Crossing the room to the doorway, she peered through to see a stairway spiraling upward disappearing into soft glowing blue light. The stairs were made of shoulder blades, the center pole was stacked vertebrae. Grasping the center support, its surface dry and bony under her hand, she placed a foot on the first step, testing its strength. Finding it solid, she took another step, then another, ascended the steep stairs.

Climbing for what seemed like a long time, she finally reached the top. There she came to another open arched doorway made of thigh bones and arm bones. She touched the bones, wondering who would build a palace made of flesh, skin and bones. Passing through the doorway, she found herself in a long hallway. Lavender and red light glowed from behind the translucent walls filling the space with the muted light. She walked slowly in wonder at the light, as she slid her hand along the surface feeling the translucent wall under her fingers. Suddenly she pulled her hand back, realizing these walls too were made of stretched human skin.

Hesitantly, she proceeded onward, fear gripping her. Determined not to let fear paralyze her, she raised herself up, straightening her back, and strode forth with a show of confidence she did not feel. Another open doorway of bones presented itself. This time she walked through it without hesitation, finding herself in an empty room filled with soft white light. She looked around at the walls, made of human skin sewn together, and saw a closed door at the far wall. Walking up to it, she could see it was made of thousands of finger bones lashed together with sinew. Feigning confidence, she reached to push it open. Before her hand felt the boney surface, the door disappeared.

She found herself in a huge hall, the ceiling high above. Tsogyal stepped back in alarm as several dakinis gathered before her with sharp knives in their hands. She watched in horror as they sliced hunks of flesh from their naked thighs and calves, screaming in pain as they did so. Blood flowed to the floor in pools. Others arrived, dakinis holding platters for the severed flesh to be placed upon.

Noticing Tsogyal, the dakinis extended their hands out, bidding her to enter. They parted, making a path so she could pass. Tsogyal walked past them deeper into the space, her feet slipping on the bloodied floor. Forcing her attention away from the dakinis, she looked up toward the center of the room. There she saw a magnificent throne that rose high above all those in attendance. Upon it sat a tall slender woman draped with beautiful gold and emerald glittering silks that pooled around her feet at the base of the throne. Around her long thin neck hung strings of large turquoise stones and silver chains that shimmered, their light coming from within them, not light reflected on their surface.

The Dakini Queen, Tsogyal thought, looking up at her form in awe.

Tsogyal turned her attention away from the Queen and looked around her watching with renewed horror as a dakini next to her gouged at her eye with a spoon shaped silver object, screaming in agony as she did so. Finally, she popped the bulbous mass from her head, blood dripped down her cheeks then between her naked breasts. With great care, the dakini placed her offering upon the platter, already heaped with eyeballs, held out to her by another dakini. Tsogyal stepped back as a dakini passed by her with a platter held in her hands. Bowing, she offered it to a dakini who had sliced her tongue out. Her mouth filling with blood, she placing it upon a pile of tongues stacked high on the platter.

Tsogyal looked all around her in horror as dakinis cut off their ears, their fingers, their feet. She could not comprehend when she watched several dakinis actually sever their own heads with sharp knives, their naked corpses falling to the floor in a heap as other dakinis proceeded to pick up the severed heads, placing them on large platters and taking them away. More dakinis appeared to butcher the headless bodies that lay on the floor, placing the bloody pieces on silver offering-platters. All around Tsogyal, dakinis laid their gruesome offerings on platters. Some offered cups of blood drained from their own cut veins. The dakinis moving through the throng with the platters, ceremoniously placed them before the high throne. The offerings before the throne grew higher and higher as the platters and cups were stacked.

Tsogyal held her spinning head in her hands, sickened at the sight of so much mutilation. She covered her ears to dampen the screams of pain echoing in the great hall. Her gorge began to rise at the stench of blood and of feces from opened intestines.

Attracted by something, she lowered her hands and looked up at the Dakini Queen on the throne. Gazing upon the Queen's beautiful face, framed by long silky black hair that spilled over her shoulders and beyond her knees, released her from her feelings of disgust and fear. Suddenly the Queen's head swiveled to look upon her, glittering diamond eyes, projecting a powerful gaze, bore into Tsogyal.

The Queen Dakini's booming voice echoed through the hall as she asked Tsogyal, "Lady, have you a question for me?"

All fell still and silent. Tsogyal looked around at the dakinis in the room. They stood frozen, staring at her, waiting for her reply.

"I...," Tsogyal coughed, clearing her throat. "I just wondered ...." Tsogyal started again, her throat dry, she swallowed and coughed again. "Why, do you cause yourselves so much pain?" Tsogyal forced out in a rasp.

The Queen of the dakinis tilted her head, looking at Tsogyal quizzically.

Tsogyal continued, her voice hoarse, "If you take your own lives, how is it possible to attain the end of Buddha's path? If you kill yourselves, how can you help others?"

The Queen's smooth skin, the color of the moon, flushed a translucent rose. In a soothing voice, like the sound of flowing water, the Queen answered, "Oh, Lady, you have a procrastinating mind. You must realize that the true Lama is instantaneous unconditional compassion. This Lama is inseparable from your own mind. When you have an experience of ultimate truth, you must offer your understanding instantly, as delay will cause hindrances and obstacles to multiply. If you fail to offer awareness the moment it dawns, procrastinating for even an instant; the merit is lost. In the eons of time that exists, our lives, however long, amount to only a moment. Therefore only a moment exists to celebrate the journey of the path. If you fail to offer this auspicious human body while you have it, your delay will cause hindrances and obstacles to multiply."

The Queen Dakini leaned forward on her throne, her eyes intent on Tsogyal, her voice urgent. "There is only an instant to enter through the doorway of the mysteries. Failing to offer the teaching the moment you possess it will cause hindrances and obstacles to multiply."

A chant rose from the dakinis in the hall, "Hindrances and obstacles will multiply, hindrances and obstacles will multiply, hindrances and obstacles will multiply," sounding like the beating of a heart.

The Dakini Queen turned her gaze to the throngs of dakinis below her. They all fell silent as a red glow appeared at the Dakini Queen's heart center. It began to pulsate growing larger with each beat. Her beautiful silk robes separated and fell away as the red light grew larger. Between her firm milky white breasts her chest opened allowing the sphere of red pulsating light to leave her body. As the sphere of light floated above the Queen, the Queen's lifeless body slumped back onto the throne in a heap. Rising higher and higher, the light grew larger and brighter, forming into a shape. Then all could see it transform into a dancing red yogini. The red yogini was so bright, Tsogyal could hardly look at her as she danced in the air above the corpse of the Queen. Naked, with large breasts swaying and her loose red hair flowing wild around her face, the red yogini lifted her legs high in her dance. As she danced, smaller red yoginis began to emanate from her heart center. Hundreds of small red yoginis floated down from her. Each yogini chose a dakini in the hall and danced before her. Suddenly the Red Yogini Queen snapped her fingers, the sound echoed loud in the hall. In an instant, each small red yogini dissolved into the dakini they had chosen. At the completion of the dissolution, all the dakinis instantly became whole once again. All dismemberment and injury were gone. The blood and stench disappeared as well. Tsogyal looked around in astonishment at the transformation happening before her eyes.

Slap, clang, slap, boom! Loud sounds filled the room. Tsogyal looked to the walls where the sounds came from to see hundreds of doorways appearing all along the walls. The doors flew open, hitting the walls. Slap, clang, slap, boom! Appearing inside each open doorway was a warrior. In unison, each man stepped into the hall from each doorway to stand beside it as guard. The rattle of their chain mail rolled over the throng in the hall. Their long black hair flowed over massive shoulders from underneath eight plated silver helmets with white plume finials waving to catch up with their movement. In unison, each man stamped the butt end of his long sharp spear onto the floor. Boom, boom, boom! the sound echoed in the hall. Then all fell silent as the guards stood at attention.

One by one the dakinis turned and walked to a doorway. There was a doorway for each dakini. Tsogyal watched as the dakinis disappeared into the doorways. Somehow she knew through each doorway was a solitary meditation chamber. When the dakinis were all inside, the doors slowly and silently closed. The warrior guards stepped in front of each door, protecting the space.

Now Tsogyal stood alone in the empty room, the guards standing along the walls in complete silence. She gazed up at the dancing Red Yogini Queen above the throne. The Queen Yogini looked down at Tsogyal, her eyes piecing white light, wild and intense.

A flicker of light appeared above the Red Yogini. It grew larger and larger into a globe of white light. To Tsogyal's astonishment, a familiar face appeared in the globe, it was the face of Padma.

Smiling down at her, in a soothing tone, he said, "Listen to me, Daughter of Karchen. You are too repressed and fervent in your practice. You should use essential elixirs of herbs and shrubs to cultivate the play of your intelligence and restore your body to health." With his last words he faded away.

Tsogyal suddenly felt the weakness of her body and sank down to the floor. She felt a sharp pain as her knees struck the hard surface.

The Red Yogini floated down to her. Tsogyal looked up from her kneeing position, watching the Yogini's approach. The Red Yogini swayed in front of Tsogyal. Then she forced her vagina to Tsogyal's mouth. With no strength remaining to resist, Tsogyal drank deeply from the Red Yogini's copious flow of blood, the warm thick liquid filling her.

"She has awakened," a voice said. "She is drinking."

"Tsogyal?" another voice called, a familiar voice "Tsogyal?"

All was dark. Then the darkness became light and blurred forms became clear as Tsogyal opened her eyes to look into the familiar face looking down at her, a look of deep concern on his face.

"Tsogyal, here drink more," Padma said, his arm holding Tsogyal's starved body up as he held the cup of warm tea to her lips.

Tsogyal drank the hot liquid, the warmth sliding down her center. She felt a surge of strength fill her body.

Turning her head to look beside her, she recognized Abaka kneeling with a pot in his hands, waiting to pour more tea, made of medicinal herbs, into the cup Padma offered Tsogyal. He smiled at her recognition of him.

"Thank the Gods," he said, with a deep sign of relief.

Padma looked at Abaka quizzically and chuckled.

Abaka sighed, "I know, there are no Gods, but I have to thank something."

This made Padma laugh aloud.

Tsogyal looked from Padma to Abaka, confusion on her face. "Where is the Queen Dakini? The Red Yogini? How did you find the palace?" Tsogyal rasped.

Abaka looked at Padma, a question in his expression.

"You are here above Zhoto Tidro, my consort, in the small cave where ice meets rock," Padma answered. "Have you been somewhere in your mind?"

Tsogyal struggled to sit up.

"No," Padma said, "lay down, you are very weak."

Padma removed his arm from under Tsogyal's shoulders and laid her down against the thick sheepskin robe, placing her head gently upon the rolled sheepskin made as a pillow. He covered her with another thick robe.

"Sleep now, my dearest, sleep. We are here with you," Padma said, as he tucked the robe in around her. "We will talk later."

Tsogyal closed her eyes and fell into a deep dreamless sleep.

Looking at Abaka, Padma sighed in relief. "We made it here just in time."

His lips pressed together, controlling the anger rising in him, Abaka replied, "Indeed, but I do wish you would turn the other way so I can get my hands around Atsara's neck for leaving her here alone."

"No," Padma said in a firm voice, "I will not allow it. He is simply not as determined a practitioner."

"He is a weak boy," Abaka growled.

Padma shook his head slowly. "He is not accustomed to the cold, being from southern lands. It is very difficult to be in a place as cold and hard as this."

Then, looking down at Tsogyal's sleeping form with admiration, he said, "She is so strong, so determined."

54

"So you see, I must go back into retreat and give my body, like the dakinis in the vision I had," Tsogyal explained to Padma, as her horse, Dawa, made its way down the mountain path leaving Zhoto Tidro behind them.

Riding Garkan ahead of her, Padma listened intently to Tsogyal's telling of her dream.

Suddenly Garkan stopped, his head held high, looking down the path. Padma saw his attention was on the black forms of two large crows hopping on the path a distance below them.

Squeezing his heels to Garkan's sides, Padma assured, "They are simply crows, walk on."

With a snort, Garkan took a hesitant step forward. Suddenly, he spun around and bolted back up the trail. Padma took hold of one rein and pulled hard to the side, pulling the frightened horse's head around, commanding it to go back down the trail, averting it from pushing past Tsogyal, on Dawa, and Abaka behind her, on Batur, leading the mule.

Man and horse struggled for a long moment, then Garkan acquiesced, proceeding hesitantly down the trail, its attention fixed on the black forms. Spreading their wings, the crows hopped upon the wind and soared away. Lowering his head, Garkan blew out the pent-up tension, then fell into a lazy walk. Padma let out a breath as he relaxed into the sheepskin-covered saddle.

"Your vision was symbolic," Padma called over his shoulder to Tsogyal, in answer to her words. "A healthy strong body is necessary to practice meditation. Certain austerities are helpful, but you must not engage in self-mutilating extremism. Do not mistake proper determination for extremist actions. That would create an obstacle and a hindrance to practice and realization," he explained.

"Another case for having a proper teacher, is it not?" Abaka called from behind Tsogyal, his words cast to Padma's ears.

"Yes, indeed, it is so," Padma called back "It is easy to misunderstand dreams and visions and then to go astray on the path. One needs a guide to traverse the inner paths."

Pulling the thick sheepskin robe more tightly around her, Tsogyal pondered the conversation as she felt Dawa planting each foot solidly upon the path, stepping carefully over the rocks. Placing her hand on Dawa's neck, stroking the mare's soft coat, she said softly, "You are such a dear, taking care of us both on this steep rocky trail."

Sitting back in the saddle, Tsogyal contemplated Padma's words. A gentle steady breeze wafted up through the river gorge they followed alongside. The sound of the rolling rushing glacier-fed stream was a steady hum.

Leaving behind the steep trail from the higher elevation, the land changed, becoming more gentle as they descended to the lower elevations. Tsogyal took in the scents of the trees that now appeared along the path.

Calling to Padma, she asked, "Then what is my next coarse of practice?"

"Well, first we must go to Samye and be received by the Emperor. We will go with him to Chimpu. There I will guide you in your practice. Before you resume practice, however, you must recuperate and build your strength," he called over his shoulder.

"I am grateful you came when you did, Master," Tsogyal said to Padma.

Looking over his shoulder, Padma answered, "As am I. When I

returned to Chimpu from Lhodrak, Atsara showed himself at my hut, explaining he had left your retreat some moons ago. He had gone to Chimpu to practice and await my return. I was truly alarmed that you were alone. However, I could not leave as quickly as I would have liked. I felt you would be competent alone for a time and that a solitary retreat would be beneficial. I had not anticipated that you had run out of provisions. Atsara did not have the presence of mind to determine how much you had remaining, his haste to leave the cold and discomfort of your retreat was so great. Indeed, he marched out of your retreat by foot, his determination was so great to leave that place. He told me you had enough provisions. Now I see he was very wrong. Then word came from the Emperor, requesting both your presence and mine at Samye. With that, I made haste with Abaka to retrieve you." Sighing, Padma added, "It was timely, as I do not think you would have survived much longer."

Not wishing to lay blame and create negative gossip about Atsara, which would break a vow of her practice, Tsogyal averted the subject. "Why does the Emperor request my presence as well?" Tsogyal inquired.

Padma smiled, appreciating her command of herself in not biting into the juicy bait of gossip that dangled before her. "The Emperor Trisong has been practicing the rites of visualization and recitation. All the marks and signs of accomplishment have appeared. This has given him deep faith in the Tantric teachings. He sent messengers to me at Chimpu asking for more profound teachings of Tantra. He wishes us both at Samye to teach his entire court. Then he wishes to go into retreat. And as well for those of his court who wish to go to Chimpu for teaching and practice," Padma explained.

"He wishes me to teach? I am simply a practitioner," Tsogyal mused aloud.

Padma pulled up on Garkan, turning him sideways to look at Tsogyal. Dawa stopped without command.

His eyes narrowed, Padma said, "You, my Lady, are an accomplished adept now. The realizations you have expressed to me show that. Your humility is a further demonstration of your achievements. You have much to teach. Not only that, your presence alone before the Emperor is very important for his courtiers the gain faith in the teachings."

Her eyes wide with surprise at Padma's words, Tsogyal could hear Abaka chuckling behind her. Looking back at him, he was shaking his head, saying, "You do not even realize, you are not the same woman to whom we bade farewell so many moons ago."

"Indeed," Padma chimed in as he turned Garkan back to proceed down the path. "Your friend Rab-ten will be there to help you recover. She knows how to make the elixirs you need."

"She has a surprise for you as well," Abaka said.

"A surprise?" Tsogyal asked.

Chuckling, Padma answered, "You will see."

55

Pungent woody smoke of juniper and sandalwood rose steadily from the burning bowls to the ceiling then thickened, filling the rafters. Golden light of many butter lamps flickered on the walls.

Minister Lutsen sat in deep contemplation.

The door opened silently, a rush of cool air causing the smoke to swirl. Feeling motion, Lutsen looked up to see Minister Tsenpo enter.

Closing the door silently behind him Tsenpo turned to face Lutsen, his tone urgent. "A messenger arrived at court this morning. After his audience with the Emperor, the Emperor arranged for an envoy of a hundred mounted ministers to ride toward Zhoto Tidro to meet Padma and his entourage as an escort. They will arrive here in three days. I questioned the messenger. He said Padma is accompanied by Tsogyal, that Turk and a young Indian sadhu who went with the escort to meet them."

His long dark robe of wool felt swirled around his felt boots as he paced the small room. Driving his fist into his open palm, Tsenpo cursed, "We must stop them."

Sitting cross-legged on a cushion, his hands resting calmly on his knees, Minister Lutsen looked up at Tsenpo. "The Emperor is growing in faith of this Tantra. Yet, how do we stop this Padma?" Lutsen asked. "We cannot kill him, we have tried many times,"

"He is clever, that Padma," Tsenpo growled. "Our greatest shamans have recruited spirits and Gods to banish him, yet he simply turns them to become his own ally. Many a spell and a curse has been placed upon him, yet no malady befalls him. Our warriors have made several attempts to ambush him, yet their weapons do not harm him. He is very powerful. He seems human yet he also seems disembodied." Stopping, Tsenpo looked down at Lutsen, resigned. "No, we cannot kill him. We must find another way."

Shaking his head slowly, Lutsen lamented, "How could this have happened again; the Buddha dharma coming back to Tibet. Our forefathers eradicated this influence after the death of Songtsen Gampo. Now it is back with Trisong as its great patron." Looking up at Tsenpo, Lutsen grumbled, "And even some of our own coven ask for reforms, capitulating to the Emperor's wishes. They wish to abide alongside the Buddhist ministers, even adopting the some of the Buddha's teaching, making changes to our Bonpo way. Our long-held tradition of the Bon shaman teaching will wither and die out."

"As well, our authority governing Tibet will be greatly undermined. We may be cast out altogether!" Tsenpo cursed.

Silence fell over the men as they fell into contemplation of their plight. Tsenpo paced slowly, stroking his long beard, the black streaked now with ever more gray. Lutsen sat staring into space, his long black hair was bound up into a top-knot on his head. The black dragons embroidered on his silk robe of malachite-green danced in the flicker of the butter lamps, though he sat as still as a statue.

Lutsen suddenly sat straighter, his eyes growing bright as a thought grew. "It is true we cannot kill Padma," he said, considering. Looking at Tsenpo, he continued, "Yet, we can kill that harlot, that devil-worshiper, who is accompanying him to Samye."

Blinking down at Lutsen, as his meaning became clear, Tsenpo asked, "Do you mean Tsogyal?"

"Yes," Lutsen answered, a smile growing on his face as the plan began to form in his mind, "Tsogyal, the consort of Padma." Gesturing to the cushion before him, "Sit down," he ordered.

Tsenpo obeyed, seating himself.

Bending forward, Lutsen whispered, "We will outwardly agree to everything the Emperor proposes. Yet, we will make an example of Tsogyal. Her death will show all the weakness of the Buddha dharma. As well, it will send a message to all who wish to follow that teaching that to do so will cause the great displeasure of the Gods. Any who follow it will lose all protection of the Gods, as Tsogyal's death will prove."

"How will we accomplish it?" Tsenpo asked. "There will be many around her as escort."

Nodding as his plan became firm in his mind, Lutsen answered, "When they come through the gates at Samye, an arrow will fly from the wall, seemingly from the Gods. It will pierce her heart. Before the Emperor and all assembled, she will fall and die."

56

Large white clouds sailed in the blue sky. Rays of the sun broke through, sending spears of warmth onto the earth. Emperor Trisong basked in the warm glow of a ray shining down on him as he stood waiting upon the raised platform above the assembled ministers and warriors before the great stupa outside the gates of Samye. A horn was blown from the top of the wall where the sentry stood, alerting all that he could see the cloud of dust raised by the escort Trisong had sent to retrieve Padma, Tsogyal and Abaka. Many colorful banners placed on the walls and hanging from the stupa waved in the wind.

Rab-ten stood in the crowd, her excitement growing in her anticipation at seeing her spiritual sister. Thirteen moons had passed since they had seen each other last. She wondered what Tsogyal would be like now, after so long in retreat.

At last, Padma arrived before the platform upon his horse, Garkan. Dismounting, the sounds of saddles and stirrups jangled as all in the entourage dismounted with him. Trisong descended the steps slowly to meet him, holding a golden pot wrapped in white silk. Stepping before Padma, Trisong bowed, then held out the pot to Padma. Taking the heavy gold pot, Padma held it in the crook of his arm as he unwrapped the silk to see the pot contained fresh white chung beer; a delicacy. Trisong stepped back and fell to his knees onto the carpet placed on the ground, then lay fully prone onto it, prostrating before Padma. His rich silk robes a stunning contrast to Padma's stained sheepskin coat and worn felt boots covered in sand from days of travel.

Completing three prostrations Trisong rose and glanced behind Padma, expecting to see Tsogyal, yet she was not visible. Padma handed the pot of chung to an attendant and untied his trident staff from behind Garkan's saddle. Trisong turned and led the way through the gates into Samye, Padma behind him, then all followed them into the great monastery to the Utse Pagota.

Rab-ten bounced on her toes, searching anxiously between and over the heads of the crowd at the entourage for a glimpse of Tsogyal; yet she could not find her. Seeing Abaka following behind Padma, she waved and called to him. Hearing his name being called, Abaka looked around, his eyes searching the faces through the throng. Then he saw her in the distance and waved back, a smile upon his face.

Atsara, standing next to Abaka, followed his gaze, wondering who had called Abaka's name. Seeing it was Rab-ten, Atsara turned away, his face growing hot with shame. *Lady Rab-ten would have heard of my abandoning Tsogyal*, he thought, *yet she would not know Tsogyal had forgiven me.* Then they turned and were gone, swallowed into the throng following behind the Emperor.

Rab-ten followed behind perplexed. *Where is Tsogyal?* she wondered.

Within the walls of Samye, the entourage were met with grooms who took their horses away to the stables. Trisong led the group to the Utse Pagoda with Padma walking alongside him carrying his tall golden staff that glimmered when the sunlight reflected upon it. Atop the staff was a trident of three heads carved of ivory at the apexes.

The clouds, having parted, allowed sunlight through the square rows of windows at the top of the Utse Pagota. Thick sandalwood smoke reflected the rays creating a translucent mystical ambiance to the interior of the space. Along one wall, the booming of drums began as the Emperor entered. Along another wall, a row of long horns, each as long as a man, blew an eerie wail. Monks with cymbals joined in the cacophony, the ensemble transporting the throng into an ethereal realm.

Once inside, Padma was escorted to a stairway leading up to a high dais, where upon were placed three thrones made of stacked brocade cushions. Following behind Trisong, he made his way up the steep steps. At the top, Trisong gestured for him to sit upon the highest throne of cushions. Trisong took the seat on cushions next to Padma, that made him a head lower than Padma. The third throne, meant for Tsogyal, lay empty next to Padma. There he leaned his ceremonial trident. An attendant appeared, holding golden silk robes before Padma. He took off his dusty fur hat and coat. Taking the robes from the bowing man, Padma slid into them then sat cross-legged on the cushion. Another attendant appeared, bowing, holding out a tray with two silver cups of hot tea. Padma took one, Trisong the other. Nodding to Trisong, Padma took a sip of the welcome thick butter tea.

The music swallowed all sounds of shuffling as those in attendance filed in and found places to seat themselves on the many cushions placed on the open floor of the Pagota.

Queen Tse-pongza, escorted by two Bonpo guards, seated herself in the front row below the dais on a cushioned seat meant for her as Queen, below Padma and her husband, Trisong. Outwardly, she held her expression of calm serenity, yet inside she was seething. She turned her head slightly to the side to see Tsenpo standing with Lutsen along the far wall. A warrior, his bow in its quiver upon his back, stood beside them whispering into Lutsen's ear. Lutsen stood rigid, listening with a grim look on his face. With a slight gesture of Lutsen's hand, the warrior stepped away from them and stood, his back against the wall.

My husband Trisong is a fool. Bowing before this Indian Tantric, Queen Tse-pongza thought to herself, *And now the plan will not be completed this day. Where is that Tsogyal, she must have been left behind. Then why were we not notified by our informants!*

The room fell silent as Trisong stood, his hands raised.

Turning to Padma, Trisong said, in a raised voice so all could hear, "My Guru, I welcome you to court. I have a great feast made for you. I have invited the entire court to share this with us and to have the opportunity to be in your grace."

Padma bowed his head slightly, saying, "I thank you for your generosity, great King."

Still standing, Trisong gestured to the cushion next to Padma, where his trident leaned, asking, "I am curious, where is the Lady Tsogyal? Why has she not come with you? I had wished her presence here. Without her, I cannot fully receive the greater Tantric teachings you have been so generous to present to me."

Padma smiled as he replied, "Oh, Emperor and bodhisattva, my manifestation has the nature of space." Placing his hand on the trident, he continued, "And a space master's magical powers are limitless."

The trident began to shimmer under Padma's hand. A soft gasp could be heard from the crowd. Trisong looked from the trident to Padma, perplexed. Around the shimmering trident, a mist began to form. Padma removed his hand. Like the opening of a cocoon revealing the wings of a butterfly, the mist spread out around the golden staff. The hall was silent, all transfixed upon the magical trident transforming into golden opalescent mist. Then, before the eyes of all, the mist became solid and Tsogyal sat upon the cushions; the trident was gone.

A wave of gasps, of surprise and disbelief, passed through the crowd of courtiers and ministers. Their whispers to each other grew into a loud murmur, filling the room. Minister Tsenpo and Lutsen looked at each other in shock. They turned their attention to the assassin standing near them. He shot them a look of complete bewilderment, having just told them moments before, he had found no Tsogyal in the entourage to assassinate. Then a question formed on his face. Lutsen shook his head slightly, the gesture calling off the assassination plot. The assassin leaned back against the wall, angry and resigned.

Raising his hand, gesturing silence, Padma continued, "The Lady Tsogyal has been here by my side all along. Yet in the minds of all, she appeared as my trident."

With amazement, Trisong asked, "But why hide Tsogyal this way?"

Padma glanced at Tsenpo and Lutsen as he answered, "There are those who wish to undermine the faith in the Buddha dharma, their deadly plots are many. Eventually they will realize they cannot succeed."

Then, looking directly at Trisong, Padma proclaimed, "Emperor, at this moment, in this time, the Tantra has the vital potency of youth. However, in the future, its promise will not be fulfilled. Its practice will be confused and perverted."

Trisong sat looking from Padma to Tsogyal, bewildered at Padma's words.

Padma continued, "This is my prophecy, what I see in the future. To you, my King, I shall give the true teaching. Your devotion to practice is pure, therefore I have no doubt that you will achieve your aim of full enlightenment in this lifetime."

Pleased, Trisong stood and looked out over the assembly of hushed onlookers. Gesturing to Padma, he called out to be heard, "You have all witnessed the power of this great Master."

The throng all murmured and nodded.

Trisong continued, "Those whom now have faith in this teaching may accompany us to Chimpu on the morrow. There we all will receive instruction and those who wish may enter into retreat there."

With a wave of his arm, Trisong gestured to the servants standing at a side doorway. Men and women servants, holding trays filled with many kinds of food offerings, filed in, making their way to the base of the platform. There they laid their platters down and went out of the room for more. The room filled with the aromas of spiced seared meat, curry, dal, roasted barley and sweet fruits.

Queen Tse-pongza's mouth watered at the delicious food laying before her. *The Gods will be angry at this. My husband will bring calamity over Tibet by turning from our Bonpo tradition, offering a feast to this Tantric,* she thought, her fear and anger rising.

Spreading his arms over the display below, Trisong declared, "Now, we will feast."

57

The day was cold, the sky clear blue. Tsogyal and Rab-ten sat outside their retreat hut perched on the edge of the cliff side at Chimpu.

"He is so beautiful," Tsogyal cooed as she bounced little Nam-kha on her knee.

Four moons old, he raised his chubby arms, laughing with glee.

"Brump, brump, brump. You are on a fine stallion, charging across the sands of Tibet!" she declared. "You are riding as fast as the great winds! Brump, brump, brump."

Rab-ten sat giggling, joy filling her as Tsogyal played with her son. She looked at Tsogyal. *So playful, so light, she is changed*, Rab-ten thought.

"Nam-kha, spacious sky," Tsogyal said, ceasing her bouncing to gaze into the round face of the boy. "That is a fine name for the first son of my spiritual sister."

A sudden wave of fatigue washing over her, Tsogyal swayed. Looking into Nam-kha's eyes, she said, "My spiritual nephew, I can play no longer."

Rab-ten took Nam-kha from Tsogyal and called to her attendant, who came quickly out of the hut, taking Nam-kha into her arms.

"Bring a bowl of soup and the elixirs," Rab-ten ordered the attendant. The young girl bowed, taking Nam-kha with her back into the hut.

Tsogyal leaned forward, laying her head on her raised knees.

Rab-ten placed a hand on her back, asking, "Sister, how bad is it?"

"It is not so bad, just the spinning and my stomach turns. It will pass," Tsogyal answered.

"You need to gain strength." Rab-ten assured, "You will be fine. You almost starved to your death, my sister. I would have been very sad and lonely if you had never returned."

Looking sideways at Rab-ten, her head laying on her knees, Tsogyal chuckled, "Then I would have never known of your surprise."

"That would have been the worst. My son would have never known you and you, him," Rab-ten said with a smile.

"Padma gives you lay-person teachings when you are in the palace?" Tsogyal inquired.

"Yes, and I have been able to do short retreats as well, like this one with you," Rab-ten answered.

With a look of concern, Tsogyal asked, "And your husband, Jigme? He does not oppose your being a practitioner?"

Rab-ten waved her hand. "In truth, he does not know the depth of my practice. He is busy with his duties training troops. While he is away during the day I take time to meditate and do my other practices. He is pleased with our son and we are very happy when we share time together. As well, he trusts Master Padma greatly, and Abaka too."

"So, he does not know your level of practice?" Tsogyal asked.

"He knows I receive the Buddha's teachings. However, most all of the court receives teachings now. It pleases Emperor Trisong greatly to have his court become educated to the Buddha's path and to practice. Jigme has no desire to understand what these teachings are. For Jigme, it is well I please the Emperor," Rab-ten explained. "It was you and Sakya Dema who told me not to tell Jigme of my practice. Remember?"

Nodding, Tsogyal said, "Yes, now I do remember."

Tsogyal shook her head looking off into the distance. "This place has changed greatly since I was here last. There are many here at Chimpu now, many huts have been built upon the hillsides."

"Yes," Rab-ten nodded, "why, right now, besides the Emperor, there are over twenty of his close courtiers, there must be at least seven Noblewomen, over thirty acolytes, and many more followers. Why I think right now there are over two hundred practitioners here receiving teachings from Master Padma. Even the great Dzog Chen master and translator, Vairotsana, is here, practicing with his Guru Padma."

Tsogyal scanned the view of the hillside beyond. Several huts were built on the rocky slope. She could see slender wisps of smoke rising from smoke holes in their roofs. Turning her attention back to Rab-ten, she asked, "And you are progressing in your practice?"

Rab-ten nodded again. "Master Padma says I am, though in truth, I do not know."

Looking into Tsogyal's eyes, Rab-ten continued, "Though it is plain to me you have progressed greatly. You are so different, yet the same. There is a presence in you, something exuding from your being; a force. I cannot explain it."

Placing her hand on Rab-ten's knee, Tsogyal said, "I am just ordinary and I have far to go."

"Many here in court have gained much faith in the dharma, due to Padma and to stories of you," Rab-ten said. Then looking down, a look of sadness came over her. "However, some have said bad things. I became worried when I heard people gossiped about you." Looking at Tsogyal, she continued, "They said you were a devil-worshiper and they did not like you being with Atsara because he is an Indian. They call him a vagabond."

"Yes," Tsogyal said, as she gazed into the blue sky above the hillside, "people always think the worst when they do not understand. As well, there are those who wish to destroy all faith in this path."

Rab-ten's attendant came out of the hut with a bowl of soup and a cup of tea. Laying it before Tsogyal, she pulled a small wrapped bundle from her robe. Handing it to Rab-ten she asked, "Is there anything else, My Lady?"

"No, Sonam, that is all for now. We will be leaving for the teachings soon, you will need to watch Nam-kha."

Bowing, Sonam returned into the hut.

Tsogyal picked up the bowl and sipped the soup. The delicate spices and fatty meat broth filled her with a deep satisfaction. "Mmm, Sonam is a good cook," Tsogyal said.

"Yes, she is very good. I can rely on her for many things," Rab-ten agreed. "Save some of the last of the soup," Rab-ten said as she opened the small bundle. "I will mix this herbal elixir in so you can drink it."

Tsogyal held her bowl out as Rab-ten poured some powdered herbs into it. Taking a smooth stick from her robe, Rab-ten stirred the powder in until it was mixed with the soup. Tsogyal sipped the last of the soup with a grimace on her face.

Rab-ten nodded. "Yes it is bitter. Here, have some sweet tea to wash it down."

Tsogyal laid her empty soup bowl down and took up the tea cup. Sipping the tea, she sat back, leaning against a boulder, and relaxed.

Crunching footfalls on rocky ground caused both women to turn. Abaka appeared from the path leading to their hut, his long strides taking him before them. With a slight bow, Abaka said, "Lady Tsogyal and Lady Rab-ten, the Master and the Emperor wish to begin this day's teachings. All are assembling now."

Every space was taken by those in attendance. Padma sat outside, cross-legged, on a pile of cushions. Emperor Trisong sat on cushions to his left and Tsogyal on Padma's right. Eager ministers, monks, courtiers and attendants sat on cushions, boulders and small rugs laid upon the ground.

The weeks of teachings and practice was pure heaven for Rab-ten. She watched many assembled here over the past few weeks filled with joy and exaltation as a result of their practice. Many too struggled with fear and sadness, their doomed egos trying to make them leave this place. Yet they persevered, breaking through to peace and a step closer to realization of their Buddha nature.

Padma sipped his tea as he waited for all to settle and quiet themselves. Soon all was silent.

Kyi-ee, kyi-ee, kyi-ee echoed through the canyon.

Padma looked up to see a falcon circling above them all. He gazed at the soaring bird, its white and spotted gray form against the blue sky. Smiling at the sight, he turned his attention to the throng and began. "Today is the last day I will give teachings to you as an assembly. After today, I will meet with each of you privately and give you personal teaching and practice for your own level."

He took in the attentive faces before him. Some creased and old, some smooth and young. There before him sat Nobles, and Nobles' wives, ministers and monks. None wore jewelry or fine silks, they all wore simple garb as this was a rugged place and their duty was to sit and travel the frontiers of their inner world. They looked up at him, hope and fear was written on their faces. And also trust. Trust in his words, in him as their guide. His heart swelled with his love of them all.

"Now, I wish to give this general advise to those of you leaving in the next few days to return to your lives. Lives filled with the tasks and the distractions of daily living," he said.

Rab-ten sat up straighter, the subject Padma was to speak to felt as a rope thrown to her. As though she hung upon a cliff, fearing to fall into the abyss of samsara. For even though she spoke assuredly to Tsogyal earlier, in truth she feared she was not progressing at all.

Padma glanced at Rab-ten, then looked over the crowd seated before him.

"Dharmata is the uncontrived essential nature, it manifests in countless ways," Padma explained. "Everything is therefore the awakened state. Enjoy the five sense pleasures without clinging, as you would enjoy a plate of fine food. The way of a Buddha's action is non-attachment. Every recollection is wakefulness, since self-existing wakefulness unfolds from oneself. Do not follow whatever occurs in your mind. Let it clear where it occurs; that itself is the awakened state. It is like a water bubble coming from the water, then dissolving back into the water."

Padma stopped speaking, taking a sip of his tea, to let his words sink in. Then he began again, "You are circling through the incessant unfolding of birth, old age, sickness, and death. This is samsara, it is impermanent, it has no substance whatsoever." With a wave of his hand, Padma explained, "It is like magical apparitions, none of these have any substance, since they all occur from your own mind. Understanding this, you experience them, but know they are unreal."

The crowd began to shift in their seats, trying to absorb Padma's words and meaning. Padma looked up, the falcon was gone. He waited as silence fell back over the assembly. Then he continued, his voice deep and clear, "Do not believe that an ego or a self has any substance. A belief in a self is delusion. Your palace or house, children, husband, wife, wealth and belongings are all as objects in a dream. They are to be treated as fantasies, since they are unreal and illusory. All worldly activities are painful in nature. They unfold from you, like the thread from a silkworm's spittle, then they chain you. Give the seal of no concept in whatever activity you do and dedicate your actions as the accumulation of merit. Practice in this way and every action you do becomes a dharma that leads to attaining Buddha-hood."

Looking out over the faces before him, Padma inquired, "Are there any questions?"

Rab-ten spoke out, "Master, do you mean I should treat my son and husband as though they are not real? What of my love for them?"

Padma smiled and nodded, saying to the crowd, "The perfect question and if not asked and then answered would result in a great misunderstanding. This is why one needs a master to give oral instruction."

Padma leaned forward, resting his arms on his knees, and spoke directly to Rab-ten, who sat in the middle of the crowd. "My Lady, you hold them now, in each moment, in your perceptions, according to your desires. You therefore do not see their true nature. Now, your husband and son are fantasies, caught in your delusion. When you realize, through your practice...." Padma stopped and sat up straight, looking over the crowd, thinking. Then he continued, his voice raised, addressing all. "This is an important point. To realize. You see, I can explain all day to you. It matters not, as you must yourselves realize. All my words show the way, what truth is. Yet all that I speak to must become a realization that dawns in your being as your own understanding."

A wave of murmur coursed through the attendants, many nodded their heads in acknowledgement.

Sitting with his back straight, his hands pressed down on his knees, Padma turned his attention back to Rab-ten. "This point you are asking about speaks to renunciation. Your love for them is based on your desires and not from an understanding of their, your husband and son's, true nature. They are transitory in nature. As a method of realizing the truth, look upon them as you would a fantasy. This loosens your tight grip on them. You wish them to satisfy your desires. Your desires are wrapped around them, these are as chains imprisoning them. These chains imprison you as well. This is what you call love. "

Padma stopped, letting his words sink in. Then he continued, "When you realize that mind is a continuum, that karma is a continuum, you will then see them in a true light. When the realization of their true nature dawns and grows in you, as the sun rising over the mountains illuminating all in its light, you will see them clearly. You will understand they are impermanent and they are caught in the wheel of samsara. You will realize a love for them that is more real and powerful than the love you profess now, which is chained by desires; pushing away that which is unpleasant and clinging to that which is pleasurable. True love comes when you are no longer living in delusion."

Padma leaned forward his arms resting on his knees, his voice soft, yet heard by all, "My Lady Rab-ten, when you realize truth, your heart will break as your compassion for all living beings unfolds."

Rab-ten felt hot tears on her checks. She wiped them away with her sleeve, embarrassed to show such emotion in public. She looked at the people around her. Every face was wet with tears.

58

Atsara's hands clasped the cold hard rock to secure himself as he lifted his foot up, the woven sole of his felt boot securing another foothold. The cord of the heavy bag on his back cut in where it crossed his chest. Only a cotton tunic served as a shield between the hard cord and his flesh. He stopped, panting to catch his breath as he gazed upward, deciphering the path through the jumble of rock. Snow began to fall lightly, covering the rocky cliffside with a dusting of white. He lifted the bag over his head and let it drop onto the rocky ground. As he took the sheepskin coat wrapped over the bag, her words flooded his mind, *'We will go south to Bhutan,'* she had invited him.

He chuckled now as he struggled into the warm coat. "Hah! Where it will not be so cold as Zhoto Tidro," he said aloud, between gasps of white breath as he pulled the coat tight and tied it shut with a sash. Taking his fur hat from the bag, he pulled it down over his head as a shiver coursed through him.

Tsogyal had left Chimpu, taking Atsara and a disciple of Padma's, a girl named Dewamo, with her. She wanted to find a secluded place away from Chimpu to resume her personal meditation and Tantric practice. They had ridden southeast out of Tibet into the northeastern part of Bhutan, the realm of King Hamra. Padma had told her of this place, where there were three secluded caves. They rode to the village nearby, paying a farmer there to care for their horses and mule. Having bought barley flour, butter and tea in the village, they loaded these supplies into bags that they carried on their backs and proceeded to find the caves of Senge Dzong. It took two days of searching the area, following a map that Padma had drawn for them, to find the caves. After they had settled each into a cave, Tsogyal had them all search for the medicinal plants this place was known for. Also, they collected the calcite rock. Tsogyal set them all to grinding and preparing the plants and calcite in the manner Rab-ten had instructed her. Thus they made the powdered elixir that she had instructed them all were to add to their daily meal. Now, a fortnight later, they were settled in their caves to practice. Atsara and Dewamo shared the daily chores of bringing water and food to Tsogyal, and to each other on the days assigned. This allowed each a period of uninterrupted practice.

Atsara leaned against a boulder to rest, looking through the falling snow over the rough terrain of boulders and rock with a twisted evergreen tree growing between boulders here and there. Then he froze, noticing a pair of eyes regarding him from the distance. Amber eyes ringed in black seemed to look at him as some creature of rock and snow. The black spots against the white of its coat were one with the shadow and light, of the snow and rock. Atsara instinctively reached to his waist for his dagger, shocked when he felt only emptiness, it was not there. Looking down at the bag, he realized it was inside. Keeping his gaze on the big cat, he slowly stooped and reached inside the bag. Feeling for the dagger, he found it and clasped his hand around the hilt. Then, with a flick of its stripped tail, the great cat turned and was gone. Atsara let out his breath and sank into the stone at his back. After a moment, he pushed himself up and secured the dagger into the belt at his waist. Then he hoisted the bag over his shoulder onto his back. Looking up the steep trail, he sighed as he took another step up the rocky way and began climbing again.

After what seemed like a endless accent, relief washed over him seeing the cave opening ahead. Reaching the entrance, he bent over and called into the cave, in a soft voice, "It is I, Noble Daughter."

Without waiting for a reply, Atsara stepped into the opening.

The darkness of the passage opened into flickering light of butter lamps inside a small room. As he lifted the bag over his head, he looked at Tsogyal, sitting cross-legged on her sheepskin coat. Her eyes were open, staring straight ahead, not seeing out, yet looking inwardly. He took in the sight of her. The swell of her breasts under the thin cotton tunic caused a stirring in him. Stealing himself against the urge, he knelt, laying his bag on the rock floor, and began to empty the contents. Placing a sack of barley flour, a flask of water, a small brick of tea and a bag of butter beside the small cook fire, he berated himself for his lust.

He stole another glance at Tsogyal. She was looking at him now, her eyes soft and clear, resting from her meditation.

"There is no shame in your humanness," she said, her voice just a whisper.

Atsara blushed as he looked into her eyes. *She is so wild, so beautiful*, he thought, then turned his face away trying to dispel the thoughts, the desire, rising in him.

"The feelings and urges are simply energy. We do not want to suppress them, we want to redirect the energy to better use," Tsogyal went on.

Atsara nodded his understanding. Then, wanting to change the subject, he said, "I saw a snow leopard while climbing the path."

"Mmm," Tsogyal whispered, "auspicious."

"Are you ready to eat?" Atsara asked.

"Yes, I will eat some," Tsogyal replied.

Atsara handed Tsogyal a silver bowl filled with barley flour and a lump of butter. He laid the water flask before her. Tsogyal pulled a bag of the powdered herbs and calcite from beside her. As she sprinkled some into the barley flour, she asked, while stirring it in, "How is Dewamo doing?"

"She is practicing diligently in her cave," Atsara reported.

"Mmm, very good," Tsogyal said, nodding, as she deftly rolled a piece of butter into the flour, herb and calcite powder making a ball. Popping it into her mouth, she chewed slowly. After swallowing and taking a sip of water, she continued, "She is learning to do her practice without relying so much on me. That is good, I am pleased."

"Yes, she is doing well," Atsara confirmed.

"And you? How is your cave? Your practice?" Tsogyal inquired.

"The cave is fine. My solitary practice is..." Atsara drifted off, searching for the word, "progressing," he said, finally.

"Do you have any questions?" Tsogyal inquired.

Atsara shook his head slowly. "No, My Lady, it is just in the doing, there are no questions needing answer."

Tsogyal took up the flask and drank. Setting it back down, she said, "You and I will practice together starting tonight. For seven days we will remain together. Tell Dewamo we will be occupied and must not be disturbed. You should return here just as darkness falls."

Thoughts passed through Atsara's mind as he calculated the return down the snowy path to his cave. The hours remaining of light in the day. How much food and water he will need to bring.

"It has begun to snow," he said, looking at her, trying to keep his eyes from roving over her body. Noticing the urge rising in him again, he stole himself to look into it, see it as pure energy, not let it take control of him.

"Mmm," Tsogyal intoned as she chewed another ball of the flour and herb mixture rolled into butter. Taking a sip of water, she swallowed. Looking at Atsara, Tsogyal smiled. "I will see you this night," she said, dismissing him.

Atsara rose to his feet. "Yes, My Lady, tonight," he said, with a slight bow. Turning, he made his way out through the cave entrance. Standing outside, he gazed out at the falling snow and down the rocky path. With a sigh he began down, glad at least the bag across his back was empty, making his decent much easier.

Dewamo sat cross-legged on the edge of the stream, contemplating the water rushing and swirling by her. Her water bags lay near her on the shore, full and ready to be carried back to the caves. She wondered at the element of water and how it related to all the five elements of the universe. She watched how the water rushed over and around the stones and boulders of the stream bed.

"Those hard stones will be worn to nothing in time, by the constancy of the water," she whispered to herself as she absently stroked the sheepskin of the coat she used as a cushion on the ground. The rumble of distant thunder rolled through the canyon. A gust of wind swirling down from the mountains blew her loose long black hair around her face. She pulled the thin woolen robe she wore tighter to keep the wind from swirling inside, chilling her. Chuckling, she thought, *wind can wear away rock too*, considering yet another of the elements.

Crack! The sharp sound came from behind her startling Dewamo out of her revery. Rising slowly to a crouch, she turned to see a large deer standing a distance away, round black eyes looking at her warily.

Oh, you are beautiful, Dewamo thought. Keeping herself very still she took in every detail of the markings of his coat. The buck's nose wiggled, taking in her scent.

"You may drink here, my brother. I will not harm you," she cooed to him.

Suddenly, the dear turned his head sideways. Dewamo could see his body tense, sensing danger. She watched as he sprinted, long strides taking him up the hillside above where Dewamo crouched. Effortlessly, he leapt over the stream, bounced over the rocks that studded the hillside shore and disappeared into the forest. Behind her, she heard the rapid thumping of footfalls coming closer. To her surprise, a man appeared out of the forest from where the buck had come, holding his bow with an arrow nocked and ready to shoot. A quiver of arrows was slung over his back. He stopped suddenly, surprised by her presence there. The man was not much taller than Dewamo, yet his strength was evident in the hard muscles of his forearms holding his bow. Long black hair streaked with gray was tied back framing a hard and angry leathery face. His course yak-hair-woven tunic blended with the rocks, woolen leggings hug over tough bare feet.

"You lost me my buck!" he said in irritation as he released the tension of his bow and removed the arrow.

Dewamo stood, fear rising in her. "I am sorry, I did not mean to disturb anything," she said, her hands held out in supplication.

The hunter looked her up and down. His bristled mustache and beard framed a deep frown. "Who are you? You are not from here," the hunter demanded. Then, with a look of recognition, he sneered, "You look Tibetan to me. Are you Tibetan?"

Dewamo stood frozen. She did not want to answer, she just wanted this man and the fear he caused to leave her.

Then, steeling herself to speak, she said, "It matters not where I am from, I mean no harm. Please leave me in peace."

"It matters greatly!" he growled. Raising the arrow held in his hand, he shook the point at her accusingly. "You Tibetans come here and disturb our land. Can you not find places to be in your own country?" Suddenly concern washed over his face. He looked beyond Dewamo, then glanced up and down the stream with two flicks of his eyes. "How many of you are there?" he demanded.

"It is none of your concern." A voice came from behind the hunter.

Startled, he turned to see Atsara standing behind him. The hunter stepped back. Standing a head taller than the hunter, Atsara was imposing. With a long walking stick held in his hand and a dagger in its sheath held firmly in his sash around his waist, Atsara widened his stance, delivering the message that he would not shrink from a fight to protect himself and Dewamo. The hunter looked Atsara up and down. His bow held in one hand, his arrow in the other. A decision played across his face. Without a word, he turned and strode away, following the path of the buck.

Relief washed over Dewamo as they watched the hunter disappearing into the forest. Looking up at Atsara, she gasped, "Atsara, thank the Gods you came just now. He frightened me." Then realization came over Dewamo. "Has it been seven days? You have completed your retreat with Mistress Tsogyal?"

"Yes, I have," Atsara said, walking over to the water bags. Warily, he looked to the forest where the hunter had disappeared, then bent down and took up the cords, lifting the bags over his shoulder. A roll of thunder rumbled, closer now. Atsara looked skyward, concern on his face.

"There is a storm coming, we should return to the caves now," he said. "Mistress Tsogyal is going to be in a secluded retreat for a moon. We must bring her food and water every few days and leave it outside the passageway. She will see you only this day, should you have any questions about your practice," Atsara explained.

Stepping to stand in front of Dewamo, he placed a hand on her shoulder and looked down into her eyes. "I am glad I came to find you. It is good he knows I am here, that you are not defenseless."

A shiver ran through Dewamo. "I was very frightened by him," she said, as she turned to gather her sheepskin coat from the water's edge. She followed Atsara as they proceeded back to the caves.

"His anger was painful to feel," Dewamo said to Atsara's back. She stopped and looked back at the flowing water, then around her at the rocks and trees. "Sad," she continued, taking hurried steps to catch up to him, "to be blind with anger in such beauty."

59

A clap of thunder rolled through the entrance of the cave as a flash of lightening illuminated the rock walls, overpowering the small lights of the butter lamps.

Tsogyal felt the cold sting of the raw skin of her forehead as she touched it to the ground for the thousandth time. The rain hissed outside as a gust of wind made its way through the entrance. The cold damp air bathed her heated body as she slid on her tender palms, wrapped in sheepskin, to lay prone on the hard rock floor. Sliding back to a kneeling position, she rose to standing.

Touching her folded hands to her heart, she chanted, "From now until gaining full enlightenment," then touching her folded hands to her third eye, "I take refuge in the Lama," then placing them atop her head, at the crown chakra, she completed the chant as she sank her aching knees onto her sheepskin robe, placed to cushion them from the hard floor of the cave, "The embodiment of enlightenment, the teachings and the community of practitioners."

Then she bent and touched her forehead to the ground. Her shoulders screamed as she slid her sheepskin-wrapped tender hands forward, laying fully prone onto the ground. The short cotton tunic was little barrier as her belly and breasts felt the cold hard rock of the uncovered portion of floor. Despite the protest of her lower back, she pulled herself back to kneeling, then she rose to stand straight again.

Tsogyal had been in retreat for a fortnight, prostrating all day and most of the night, pushing through pain and exhaustion. When she was not prostrating, she performed circumambulations in the small cave.

Now, tens of thousands of prostrations later, Tsogyal felt the shift in her, the essence of her being stabilized in the nature of primordial wisdom. She had completed her last prostration.

Staggering a bit, she took up the water flask. The water felt hard as it wetted her dry throat. Sinking down onto her meditation cushion, she enjoyed a moment of stillness and rest. She took inventory of the aching places of her body. A clap of thunder caused her to jolt, an instinctive reaction. A flash of light from a bolt of lightening made the cave bright for a moment, then several cracks followed, bathing the cave in light. At once, dimness returned. She sat transfixed by the power of the storm outside. Feeling the tightness of hunger in her belly, she reached for her bowl. Inside were several lumps of barley flour and herbs rolled into butter.

It was all the food she had remaining until Dewamo or Atsara would come to leave food and water outside her entrance. They may not be able to climb up to her entrance until the storms subside. She took a ball of flour, herb and butter. Rolling it in her hand, she considered if she should fast, saving the food. A wave of dizziness washed over her. She knew she must eat. She bit into the lump, the butter melted, the flour was like chalk, the herbs tasted bitter. Taking the flask of water, she gulped a mouthful, washing it all down. Deciding she would be in an extended state of meditation now for her next practice, Tsogyal sat eating all that lay in the bowl, washing it down with the last of the water. Getting up, she placed the bowl outside her doorway, allowing it to fill with rain water for later. She went to a small cubby hole in the rock wall and pulled a small cloth bundle from it. Lifting a corner of the folded cloth, the pungent fragrance of the medicinal salve held within filled her nostrils.

Returning to her folded sheepskin robe, she sat and rubbed the healing salve onto her forehead, then her knees and palms. The wounds stung with the stimulating herbs.

Aloud, she declared to herself, "Now I will sit here and I will not move."

The skin of her raw knees pulled tight as she crossed her legs into the lotus position, the salve melting in caused them to sting. She fixed her eyes open as she settled into the soft cushion of the robe. With her spine erect, she allowed herself to sink into relaxation. The sensations of her wounded places melted into the sounds of the drip, drip drip, outside the cave entrance. The rain had stopped.

After some time passed, she felt for an imaginary cord holding her up from the crown of her head. Feeling it, she felt it hold her up, as though she hung from the ceiling rather than sat upon a cushion. Tsogyal began to circulate her chi, energy, in a pattern within and around her body. Bringing energy up from the earth and down from the heavens, she commingled it through specific pathways in her body.

Absorbed in deep concentration, she did not react to the rumble of thunder that rolled through the cave entrance nor to the loud hiss of hail pounding the mountain outside. The dim light of day, visible through the cave entrance, fell away to the darkness of night. Tsogyal remained in deep concentration.

The glow of growing daylight illuminated the entrance of the cave. The bowl outside sat covered in a foot of snow. Tsogyal felt a rumble in her stomach. *Hunger*, she thought, then she ignored it. Thoughts of foods she liked entered her mind. Images began to appear before Tsogyal. A bowl heaped with yogurt, amber honey glistening atop it, floated in the space before her. Her stomach ached, the urge to taste the sweetness and feel the fullness of the delicacy began to nag at her. Then, a platter of delicious cakes with almonds floated before her. Another platter appeared, heaped with seared goat meat, causing her mouth to water. Bowls filled with huge juicy apricots joined the feast.

Though her hunger tore at her insides, Tsogyal stole herself to remain unmoved, as she had vowed. The platters and bowls of food remained before her, enticing her to grab for them. Tsogyal considered how to remove these temptations to her resolve. Then, she made a fervent wish that these items before her would become treasures for the future wealth of Bhutan. With her heartfelt wish, giving the food away, the feast disappeared.

Flowers of all types, those she had admired along the paths and roadways on her travels, began to appear, floating around the cave, filling it with their beautiful scents. She ignored the illusions and let not the scent move her to wonder and reach for the beautiful objects. Through her concentration, she transformed them to rocks and stones. They fell heavy to the floor. Stillness returned to the cave, the snow outside falling soundlessly.

Then, a young man entered the cave and knelt before her. Startled by the entrance of this person, Tsogyal almost moved, but remembered that no matter what happened, she must remain still. He was handsome and naked. Tsogyal wondered why a naked man would be out in the snow. Standing before her, she saw his body was lithe and strong. His phallus stood erect as he knelt before her and kissed her neck as he caressed her breasts. His hand stroked her thighs and fondled her soft place.

"I have something very pleasurable for you," he cooed.

Sensations traveled through Tsogyal's genitalia, she felt the urges rising in her.

"Here, milk my manhood," he said, straddling her, thrusting his member against her belly, attempting to lift her onto him.

Tsogyal steeled herself, remaining in concentration that sees all things as illusion. She contemplated this young man without his covering of skin. The metallic smell his sticky bloody corpse caused her gorge to rise. She controlled this urge, realizing once again the fickle nature of the mind when presented with concepts. The young man dissolved away with the whistling of the wind outside.

A beautiful horse entered the cave, she had a shining black coat like Lungta. She was strong and perfectly formed. Her legs straight and strong. She nuzzled Tsogyal, beckoning Tsogyal to leave this cave and ride across the sands, like the wind. Tsogyal could smell the sweetness of her horse scent. Images of riding once again on Lungta's back, free and wild, played across Tsogyal's mind.

You can leave this cold cave. Return to the Emperor. He will take you back. You will have many beautiful horses, with fine saddles. You can ride all day if you wish. You can be Trisong's Priestess. You will wear beautiful silks, eat the best food, sleep on soft cushions in warm rooms. Many will respect and fear you... the thoughts beckoned her.

Tsogyal remained unmoved as she contemplated this beautiful horse before her becoming old and lame, no longer able to carry a rider. She looked into the reality of herself as Priestess, growing old and sick, long white hair falling over her shoulders, a corpse wrapped in beautiful silks that become threadbare and faded. Those jealous of her station and power always looking for a weakness to take advantage of. People who would smile and bow before her, yet when her back was turned, they would be plotting and planning for ways to take her place, to destroy her. She looked into the reality of eating fine foods. When too much is eaten, one becomes sick. Then also the result in the end; heaps of excrement. A profound detachment and distaste for worldly things coursed through Tsogyal. The beautiful horse dissolved away.

A loud clap of thunder rumbled the cave with a flash of lightening. All around Tsogyal the walls of the cave began to fall away, rocks tumbling down around her. She observed her primal urge to run out of the cave to protect herself exploding as panic. Detached, she remained unmoved by the illusion. The cave was solid again. The steady hum of hail replaced the silence of falling snow.

All became quiet and still. A glistening appeared before Tsogyal, a shaft of light transformed into a sharp knife. It floated toward her, its point resting at her eye, threatening to thrust into her. Then, more lights appeared, becoming swords and knives. They danced around her, threatening to stab and cut her. Tsogyal transformed them into a harmless rays of light, then allowed the lights to dissolve into the darkness.

The light at the cave entrance faded to black night, then it glowed again as the new day dawned. Fading to black again, then the light returned. Thunder and rain continued as several days passed, Tsogyal sat unmoved and absorbed.

A shadow filled the entrance of the cave. Tsogyal watched as a snow leopard entered the cave. It stopped at the sight of her, then slowly approached with a low growl. Its sharp teeth bared as it roared inches from Tsogyal's face, its putrid breath filling her nostrils. With tail swishing threateningly, it bunched up, ready to pounce on Tsogyal and rip her throat out. Fear rose in Tsogyal, becoming almost unbearable, yet she held herself steady. "Illusion," she whispered. She transformed the leopard into a musk deer and watched, amused, as it scurried out of the cave.

Small dark forms began to appear upon the walls. First only a few, then they multiplied. Tsogyal heard the scrape of many small hard feet. Sitting unmoved, her eyes open, she saw the ground before her become filled with hundreds of spiders and scorpions. Their numbers multiplied as they scurried down the walls of the cave, crawling toward her. She felt their hard scratchy feet as they climbed onto her knees, then they covered her thighs. They crawled up under her cotton tunic over her breasts onto her neck. They crawled into her ears and eyes, her nose and mouth, they scratched her and bit her, stung her. Trembling with horror, yet determined to remain unmoved, Tsogyal watched them begin to fight and devour each other. The gruesome scene sickened her. Tsogyal could barely hold on. Her body trembled as the sensations of the scratching and stinging threatened to let the scream rising up in her explode into the cave. She held firmly the rising panic that urged her to get up and run out of the cave away from the torment. Then, she watched horrified as a long slithering snake entered the cave at the entrance. Behind it, more snakes followed in its path. The snakes attacked the spiders and scorpions in their path, as they made their way to Tsogyal. The fear became unbearable. Tsogyal searched frantically in her thoughts for a way to dispel these creatures.

Then, a strong compassion for these wicked insects and snakes arose spontaneously in her. *These beings arose in this form due to* karma, she thought, *why should I be frightened? This display before me is but the magical projection of the mind. Are not all actions the issue of thoughts, good or ill? And if so is not all that happens merely thought? Then I shall accept all equally.*

"All of this is the self-glowing light of clarity," Tsogyal proclaimed aloud, as her realization unfolded. "All that happens is but my adornment. I shall remain unmoved in silent meditation."

The cave was empty, the illusions gone. Only the sound of the gentle falling of rain was present. Tsogyal's meditation deepened into a concentration of perfect equanimity, beyond good and evil. Beyond acceptance and rejection.

More illusions appeared. Severed limbs, dripping with blood, floated around the cave. They soon disappeared as Tsogyal saw them for what they were, illusions trying to tempt her to grasp to them as real. Every time an illusion arose then dissolved away, Tsogyal's realization was strengthened. As the cycle of day and night illuminated the cave, then caused it to become black and dark, she remained still of body and mind.

One morning, as the light at the entrance of the cave began to grow in brightness, pure awareness broke forth as Tsogyal's wisdom channel opened. Unshakable faith rose in her being. Tsogyal's enlightenment had dawned.

60

The tall golden spire atop the white dome of the chorten glistened even when the clouds floating across the sky obscured the sun. Irritation rose in Emperor Trisong as he listened to his subject, the Gyu Bon magician Gyaltsen, ask his question as they looked up at the chorten they stood before. This was one of many newly built on Samye's vast grounds. A gust of cold wind whirled through the grounds, causing the stocky muscular Gyaltsen to tug at the slipping bearskin cloak he wore over the long woven un-dyed cotton tunic. A polished bronze disc, the size of the palm of a hand, hung from a red silk cord over his heart. It glinted when the sun's rays peeked through the clouds, striking its surface.

"What are these monuments?" Gyaltsen asked, gesturing to the chorten. "It looks like they are made of heaps of vulture-dropping at the top, rolls of fat around the middle and piles of dog shit at its base," he declared with a smirk.

Blinded for a moment as the sun's rays reflected off the shiny disc, Trisong turned his head to escape the glare as he took control of his rising anger at the impudence of this man.

Patiently, Trisong answered, "These are chortens, symbols of the Buddha's absolute empty being. They are receptacles of the offerings of all beings." Pointing to the top of the structure, Trisong explained, "The spire at the top is constructed of thirteen discs of gold representing the thirteen stages of the dharma. The top of the spire is adorned with the umbrella and crowning ornaments which are symbolic of the Buddha's ideal marks and signs." Gesturing to the forms at the middle, Trisong continued, "These four dome-shapes indicate the boundless qualities." Raising a finger one by one he counted off each of the four. "Loving kindness, sympathetic joy, compassion, and equanimity. Finally, at the base," Trisong gestured toward the structure, "are these beautifully carved lions. They are both vehicle and throne. They represent a treasure house of wealth and wishes fulfilled," Trisong said in completion as he looked admiringly at the structure before them.

"Mmm," intoned Bon scholar Tsalpa, who was standing next to Gyaltsen. Stroking his long black beard that hung down over his black wool felt robe that reached the ground covering his felt boots, he said, "Useless, totally useless."

Trisong felt the blood flush his face hot as his body stiffened; the calmed anger now risen to a suppressed volcano.

Noticing the reaction of Emperor Trisong, Bon scholar Kunga, who made the third of the Bonpo in audience with Trisong, interjected, in an attempt to calm the Emperor, "My King, you have been so gracious granting us, three of your devoted subjects, a private audience. We are most grateful to be here in Samye for this season's Lose Daze festival." Glancing at Tsalpa and Gyaltsen, Kunga bowed slightly to Emperor Trisong as he continued, "Your Highness, we are simply in a quandary that so much hard work and valuable assets have been spent on something such as this, this...?"

"Chorten," Trisong growled through gritted teeth.

"Yes Sire, my gracious thanks...this chorten," Kunga recited, with another slight bow. Holding his hands out, gesturing to Tsalpa and Gyaltsen, Kunga continued, "We are very concerned that our great King is bewitched by this Indian pandita, Padma."

"Indeed!" chimed in Tsalpa.

With a quick irritated glance at Tsalpa, Kunga rushed on, "In this season's Lose Daze festival we wish to demonstrate, as an offering to you, our great King, the superiority of Tibet's tradition, the way of the

Gyu Bon."

Pulling the ever-slipping bear cloak up over his shoulders, Gyaltsen enthused, "Sire, we will provide a spectacle that will call you back to what is great and correct in Gyu Bon. We will demonstrate the superiority of Tibet's great tradition." With a low bow, Gyaltsen oozed, "Oh great Emperor, I assure you, you will be pleased."

Trisong looked from man to man as they spoke. His heart sank at their entreaties. "Very well, show me then," he said, resigned. "Have you brought what you need for your ceremony? Or do you wish for me to provide it?"

"Oh, my King, you are so very powerful and gracious," cooed Kunga, with a low bow, his black silk robe shimmered as the embroidered white snow lions upon it danced with his movement. "We have traveled so far from Zhang-zhung, we could not possibly bring all that would be needed."

"Very well," Trisong clipped, "give a list to Minister Tsenpo, he will see to your needs."

As all three men bowed, Trisong turned without a word and with a composure that he forced upon himself, strode away.

Kunga let out a sigh of relief as he watched Emperor Trisong disappear.

Tsalpa said in a low voice, "This Padma is bewitching our Emperor." Looking from Kunga to Gyalsen, he continued. "This vagabond Padma intends to take control of our Emperor's mind and take the throne for himself, I am sure of it!" he said, pounding his fist into his palm.

Pulling at his long black mustache, Kunga assured, "We will defeat Padma. We will show the entire court the superiority of our way. We will show the Emperor his folly and turn him against this Padma and his Buddha." Turning, he gestured. "Come, we shall find Minister Tsenpo this morn. We must make haste, there is much to prepare. This must be the most powerful spectacle ever witnessed. It shall be spoken of for a thousand springs!"

Tsalpa and Kunga hurried off, yet Gyaltsen lingered behind, letting the two proceed ahead of him. He gazed up at the chorten and thought about the meaning of the structure as Trisong had described. With a quick scan around him, assuring no one was watching, he spat on the lion's face at the base of the chorten. His cloak swirled as he turned away briskly to catch up to his comrades. The snarling lion looked on as the slime slid down its stone face.

61

The eyes of the stag were wide as the men wrestled it to keep it still.

"Here is a stag!" the servant of the sacrifice called out, holding his knife at the ready. A man, denoted as the Purifier Bon, stepped up to the stag with a golden ladle and from it poured water over the animal's back. "Thus he is purified!" he called out, the chain of bells he wore over his shoulder, falling across his chest, chimed and tinkled as he danced away.

Next came the Black Bon, his long black silk robe swaying and glistening as he danced a circle around the beast. The stag's eyes, wild with fear, followed his movements, then flinched when he felt the grain thrown upon its back from the golden bowl the man held.

Nine shamans, their heads circled with crowns of eagle and falcon feathers, danced around and around the terrified stag. Tied to their long cotton tunics were owl feathers to aid them in flight when in other realms. Their chains of bells chimed and clanged as they pounded a beat on the ground with their felt boots. The polished bronze mirror discs they tied to their tunics and wore around their necks glittered and glared in the sunlight; protecting the wearer by repelling negative entities and energy. Holding large round drums in one hand, they drummed with a stick in the other as they twirled and danced.

Thu, thump, thu, thump, thu, thump, thu thump... the drums pounded out a steady constant beat.

"Here is our offering!" the ceremonial slaughterer called out as his knife sliced deep into the stag's neck. It let out a shrill bellow fighting the restraints. Blood poured over the attendant's hands as he held a copper bowl under the wound, filling it with the spurting life blood draining out of the beautiful stag. In moments, the dying animal sank to the ground in a heap, the thud of his head hitting the ground was hardly heard over the cacophony of screams and bellows filling the courtyard of the many other animals being similarly slaughtered.

As the remaining blood of the dead stag soaked into the earth, the entranced shamans called out their questions and listened for the answers which would come to them from the Gods and demons of the beyond.

A beautiful mare, her black coat shiny with the sweat of fear, was forced by ropes before the viewing area where Trisong and the assembled court sat watching the spectacle.

Mune, son of Emperor Trisong, seated to the right of his father, leaned over and whispered, "Father?"

Trisong raised his clenched fist from his knee, and opened his hand as a sign of silence to Mune.

Mune tried to still himself, he did not want to watch what was to come. They did not kill horses for meat in Tibet. As well, as a follower of the Buddha dharma, Mune embraced the tenet of the Buddha, *Thou shall not take a life. Senselessly,* Mune amended, as he had no compunction in taking the lives of his enemies in battle. He did, however, understand the heavy karma that was the effect of such an act. For food, they killed only what was necessary, the larger the animal the better, like a yak, as one life would provide much sustenance. A sheep or a deer at times, yet only for food, not for ceremony. The compassion he felt for this innocent mare being brought before him caused his heart to break and his anger to rise. As he sat, he considered the lives of men who were taken in war and in Tibet's expansion. *Yet, men choose such. These poor creatures are innocent,* he mused, *what makes these Bon think they have the right to collect and kill these innocent sentient beings; all for a ceremony? Then to burn their flesh in fires to their Gods?*

A shaman danced and beat his drum chanting as the attendant poured water over the glistening back of the horse. Shying away from the cold trickle, she struggled. The men holding her, tightened her restraints.

"Here is a beautiful horse!" the ceremonial Bon slaughterer called out. The trembling mare squealed and lunged against the ropes as the sharp blade sliced through the artery in her neck. The fountain of scarlet filled the copper bowl as the mare fell to her knees with a deep moan, then tumbled onto her side, flanks heaving, legs kicking, struggling to flee her fate as she died.

Trisong glanced sideways to Queen Tse-pongza sitting next to him. She wore a look of satisfaction at the spectacle on her face. She was the only one of the court seated around Trisong that did not gasp with disgust and horror at the ceremony enacted before them. The Buddhist scholars and ministers sat with great sadness upon their faces. Some had tears in their eyes. Trisong's other two wives sat in silence, their grim faces hard as the turquoise and coral on the headdresses they wore. Standing attendants and courtiers clenched their hands together. Some covered their eyes, not wanting to watch. Trisong heard the soft weeping of a woman behind him, perhaps that of an attendant or lord's wife.

It was too much killing, too much suffering, placed before them. They all ate mutton and yak, yet the lowly butcher saw to the bloody gore, allowing their hands to remain clean. Their hearts need never feel the terror and sorrow of the life taken for their sustenance.

Beyond the heaped carcass of the horse, throughout the courtyard the slaughterers' voices called out as they ended the lives of hundreds of animals.

"Here is a Ewe," a slaughterer cried, as he cut the artery, draining the life from the beast.

"Here is a deer!" the call rose from the carnage.

"Here is a yak!"

"Here is a sheep!"

"Here is a she-goat!"

"Here is a hind!" The man called out, his voice could hardly be heard as the animal he bent over screamed in pain when he cut into its hind legs, severing them from its live body. After a few heartbeats of the screams of intense pain given up as sacrifice, only then did he cut the suffering animal's throat, quickening its death.

Nine Bon scholars seated on cushions placed upon the ground in the center of the courtyard watched, as around them animals were slaughtered. Then, more animals were brought in from the holding pens. Deep in trance, nine Bon magicians, Gyaltsen among them, seated to the right of the scholars, chanted their magical incantations. The stench of blood and gore filled the nostrils of the nine Bon priests seated to the left, their eyes closed deep in concentration as they silently prayed to their Gods, inviting them to attend this spectacle performed on their behalf.

The whining and high-pitched yelping of several dogs mingled with the chanting as the tied animals met the cruel blades of the ceremonial slaughterers. The stench of hair and flesh permeated Samye as the many fires accepted the dead. Blood-letters, their red hands welding sharp knives, filled copper bowls with blood from the sacrifices, then arranged them on the skins lain before the priests. The butcher Bon cut up heaps of selectively-chosen severed and flayed limbs that had been roasted in a fire. Piling the meat on platters they were placed behind the bowls. Then the Sorter Bon divided the meat and passed out pieces to the various functionaries to eat.

When the bowls were all arranged and the work done, the priests began chanting their invocations. The Diviner Bon sat on their rugs, casting divinations.

The invocations of the priests, the drums of the shaman and the incantations of the magicians all floated upward with the dark pungent smoke of the many fires fueled by the hundreds of carcasses. As the last of the victims lay dying and dead in pools of their blood, attendants went around lifting their limp bodies and tossing them into the flames.

Trisong looked up into the sky to see vultures circling high above. A gasp from Mune brought his attention back to the ceremony. Trisong's breath caught in his throat as he watched the bowls of blood placed before the priests begin to steam and boil. Trisong glanced at Queen Tse-pongza who looked back at him, a smile of triumph on her face.

From the steaming bowls rainbow-like wraiths sparkled. Those of the court gasped as shrill disembodied voices, first in whispers then growing in volume into raucous laughter, emanated from the ether around them. The sounds could be heard by all who sat in attendance. Trisong's young third wife held her hands to her ears to stop the voices, yet she could not deafen them.

Mune sat frozen in fear. "Father, this is evil!" he whispered.

"Be still, my son," Trisong whispered back, as he placed his hand on Mune's knee.

Trisong turned his attention to Santaraksita, who was seated with the Buddhist ministers. Santaraksita looked back at him with an expression of incredulity and fear on his face.

"These are the voices of the Swastika Gods!" Gyaltsen called out as he and the other magicians stood up and began dancing before the assembly. Each magician wore a real animal head or one made of wood in depiction of the beast. Spellbound, they danced their power animal before the court assembly.

His hands held high, his face in rapture, Gyaltsen had donned a bear-head. All dead fur and shriveled eyes, its lifeless fangs made red dents in his forehead bouncing as he danced. Stopping, he held his arms out wide, bellowing, "It is the voice of Cha, the God of Chance and the voice of Yang, the God of Fortune!"

Turning suddenly, his bear-cloak swirling, he motioned to several attendants who ran to him, holding bowls of boiled blood. Taking a hot bowl in his hands, he danced over to stand before Trisong and the assembly. Holding the bowl out toward the Emperor as offering, he shouted so all could hear him, "This is for you, great Emperor." Looking up at Trisong with great pride in their achievement, he said, "Drink this bounty."

Keeping his voice steady and calm, Trisong asked, "Of what virtue is this bloody rite?"

Gyalsen froze, uncomprehending. "It is for the good of Your

Majesty," Gyaltsen answered, holding the bowl up higher toward Trisong. The blood now warm and congealed, he pressed on, "This is not for us, this is all done for you, our Emperor."

Resisting the urge to lean back, sickened by the metallic stench of the bowl of warm blood held before him, Trisong controlled his expression, looking unimpressed.

"This is of no worth to me," he said coolly.

Confused at the response of the Emperor, Gyaltsen gestured around him, "Oh King, is not your heart full? Are you not amazed at the sights you have seen here? Does this not prove the power of Gyu Bon?"

Panicking, Gyaltsen gestured wildly with his hand to the attendants. Obeying, they rushed up to Trisong, dropping to one knee as they held out the platters of the cooked flesh of the sacrifice high, as offering to him.

"Take as food this flesh of the offerings to our Gods," Gyaltsen roared.

Disgusted, Trisong waved the servants away. They rose quickly and stepped back bowing. Abruptly, Trisong slid off his high-cushioned throne. Mune stood, as did Trisong's wives and all seated in the assembly. All bowed before their Emperor as Trisong stormed away heading for the Utse Pagota, his son and minsters in tow. His wives, sickened and distraught, followed.

Only Queen Tse-pongza remained, watching her husband Trisong and son Mune's departure in shock at their insult to her Gods. Angrily, she grabbed the bowl held in Gyalsen's limp hands. Glaring at the back of her departing husband and son, she drank defiantly of the thick cold blood.

62

"How can we live side by side with this religion that breaks every tenet of our practice, breaks every vow we make to find truth and realization?" Santaraksita implored Trisong, who sat on his high-cushioned throne upon the dais before the assembly of Buddhist and Bon scholars, translators, ministers and monks in the Utse Pagota.

"Not to mention the karma of these actions," Santaraksita concluded.

Bon Priest Drenpa Namkha stood, imploring Trisong, "Great Emperor, what you witnessed out there is not the same as the Inner Bon we have been practicing for generations here in Tibet, in peace, side by side with the Buddha's followers. The founder of Inner Bon and Lord Buddha are as mirror images." Pointing accusingly in the direction of the bloody courtyard, he exclaimed, "Those Gyu Bon are extremist fanatics, they do not represent the Inner Bon."

Santaraksita broke in. "It is true, your sect is the reformed Bon, yet it came from those roots," he challenged, gesturing toward the courtyard. "The Gyu Bon confuse the people. There is no clear distinction between the practice Master Namkha describes and the practices of men such as those out there." Looking up at Trisong, Santaraksita implored, "It is not possible to mix the doctrine of the Buddha dharma with that of these extremist fanatics. The wise man abhors evil companions." With a wave of his arm toward the Buddhist ministers in attendance, he declared, "We will not live side by side with those evil practitioners. We will not drink the same water from the valley those men live. If they stay here, then we will depart in peace to the border areas and it will be they who will remain, along with their demented practices, here in Tibet."

A roar of voices rose as all in the hall began to argue.

Trisong tapped his knee with restless fingers as he considered the matter before him.

"Silence!" Goe, the elder, exclaimed. With stiff painful joints, he struggled to rise from his cushion. Standing, he leaned on his walking stick, frowning that no one had responded to his words. Raising his walking stick, he pounded it on the floor, thump, thump, thump, as he called out as loud as he was able, "Silence, I say!"

The room fell silent. All looked at him

His robe, once a deep red, was now faded with the springs he had spent in the courts of two Emperors. A single thick braid of white hair fell down his back, reaching to the faded gold silk sash around his waist. Behind the long wisp of a white mustache, his wrinkled leathery face was stern. He glared around the room with milky brown eyes. Shaking his head slowly, Elder Goe began, puffing out a few words at a time as though each were his last breath, "My King... we have had this dispute... for a very long time. When Bon is on the rise... the Emperor is disconsolate... and full of doubt... and fear. When the teachings... of the Buddha... spread... the Bon ministers... loose their confidence... and their purpose... in government wavers. When Bon... and Buddhism... are given equal status... they become enemies... like fire and water."

Elder Goe fell silent, breathing hard as he looked around at the assembly. Then, looking up at Trisong, he declared, with a thump of his stick, "It is evident... this agony... must finally cease."

Trisong looked down at the old wise minister, giving him a nod of acknowledgment, considering his words. To Mune, who sat next to him, Trisong inquired, "What say you, my son? What is your council?"

Mune felt all eyes upon him. This was a chance for him to prove he was capable of being a leader, of taking his place as Emperor one day, when his father passed. He considered what to say. Clearing his throat, he began, hesitantly, "It is clear to me, that these two religions can not co-exist." Straightening his spine, he went on more confidently, "We must choose. Either we establish the teachings of Lord Buddha exclusively here in Tibet and banish all practice of the Bon. Or we allow Bon to continue to flourish and Buddha's teachings shall depart to the border."

Trsong nodded his agreement. "Very well, Prince, and how do we choose?"

Mune sat thinking. Then, his eyes widened as the spark of an idea came to him. "We need to prove to the people which is the better path. We cannot just simply decide our favor. We must weigh the qualities of each in a metaphysical debate." Looking at his father, the spark becoming a flame of certainty, he went on, "We shall require a competition between both sides. The winner will be declared the religion of Tibet. The loser shall be banished." Looking around the room at the upturned faces, intent on his words, he concluded, "All must agree to the terms."

Murmurs undulated through the room as everyone in attendance considered this proposal. Trisong looked at Elder Goe, who was nodding his approval.

"Elder Goe," Trisong called out, "will you devise for us the method of debate?"

Elder Goe leaned hard on his stick, his head bowed in thought. With his legs growing weary from the effort of holding himself upright, he sank down on his cushion with a sigh. Placing his hands on his walking stick in front of him, he fell deeply into contemplation. The silence in the room was thick with anticipation as all waited for the old man to speak. After a time he pulled himself up straighter on his cushion and cast his gaze around the room.

Then, he declared, "Emperor Trisong... shall preside. His courtiers... shall sit... in the front row. To his right... the Buddhist faction... shall sit. To his left... the Bonpo. A contest... of metaphysics... shall be initiated. The rivals... must demonstrate... miraculous powers... as evidence... of their righteousness. Their creative skill... fully potentiated... through psychic strength. If the Buddha's doctrine... is proven valid... it will be preserved... and strengthened... and Bon... will be eradicated. If Bon is validated... then Buddhism... will be destroyed... and Bon... will be established." Puffing with the exertion of his long speech, he concluded as he looked up at Emperor Trisong. "My King... this is...the method... that no one... can deny."

Trisong nodded his approval. Sliding off his cushion throne, he stood, looking out over the hall. "It shall be so," he declared. "I will promulgate a decree to this effect. All must abide by it, whether it be a King, a Queen, Minister or subjects. Whomever would disobey, shall be delivered up upon the law. All must vow to abide by it."

Addressing Santaraksita, Trisong asked, "Will you and all ministers, translators and monks leave in peace should your side lose?"

Santaraksita stood and bowed as he answered, "I may vow for all of the Buddhist faith. The answer is yes, we shall, my King."

Turning his attention to Minister Tsenpo, Trisong asked, "And will you vow for all Bon ministers?"

Minister Tsenpo stood and bowed. "I will vow for all Bon practitioners, my King." Straightening, he declared, "We shall not lose. Bon is greater than the Buddha's teachings, as you shall see. However, I will vow that if we should lose, we will leave Tibet for the border lands forever."

Looking to his court, King Trisong asked his Queens and courtiers, "The side that wins shall be that which you will abide by. Do you all vow?"

All stood and bowed as they murmured their vow.

Trisong stood addressing all in the hall. "Messengers shall be sent throughout the Kingdom of Tibet. All of the Royals and lords of the provinces will hear my decree and must attend. The outcome of this debate must be told to the people by their Kings and Princes, their Queens and Princesses. The people of Tibet must hear of it by their rulers, who must tell of it, having witnessed it with their own eyes."

Trisong cast his gaze over the assembly. All in the hall were still, listening with suppressed excitement at their Emperor's words.

"I shall consult the astrologers for an auspicious date, giving enough time for all to prepare and for all to assemble. This great debate shall take place in the middle of the great plain of Yobok, which is not far from Samye," Trisong sang out. "I, your Emperor, will consult with Master Santaraksita and Minister Tsenpo to decide on the details of the contest and will have all written and presented to both sides. The Bon may then choose the nine best among their covens, the Buddhist ministers will choose the nine best of their practitioners as contestants."

Trisong stood silently thinking. Then he concluded, as he looked at the throng of serious faces before him, "Thus the religion of Tibet will be decided. Once and for all."

The hall erupted in whispers and murmurs. Trisong motioned to Mune. Emperor and Prince made their way down the steps of the dais and departed the Utse Pagota among a circle of warrior guards. The room fell silent as all bowed low before them.

63

Tsogyal sat high upon the huge ledge that jutted out from the cliffside, enjoying the swirls and play of the clouds filling the empty space below her. She followed the paths of the birds as they swooped among the tops of the tall pine trees below her, their songs and chirps echoing off the rock face. In the background was the soft ever-present murmur of the waterfalls she had passed when, a moon ago, she had traveled up the steep and winding trail that led to this secret place.

"Tea?" Padma asked, coming out of the cave entrance, one of several caves that honeycombed the mountain.

Tsogyal turned and smiled, watching as he approached the firepit, then stooped to pick up the pot of hot tea nestled among the wood coals.

"That would be wonderful," she replied, as she scooted to the side of her small woven rug to make room for him.

Moments later, he handed her a cup, then made himself comfortable next to her. Their thighs pressed together, cushioned by their robes of woven wool as they sipped the sweet earthy hot liquid and gazed below at the thick undulating mist.

Breaking the silence, Padma said, "I think we will have a visitor today; friend not foe."

"Yes," Tsogyal said, "I have been feeling the same thing. Any sense of the nature of their visit?"

"It feels urgent," Padma replied.

The mist below rose up on a draft, surrounding them in white.

Tsogyal had left her meditation cave at Senge Dzong, as too many people were curious of her presence there. She had achieved what she had gone there for, so no longer needed to remain. Taking Atsara and Dewamo, they had gathered their horses and mule from the farmer and traveled south, then west, across Bhutan to the Paro Valley. Then, they proceeded to look for the place Padma had told her to come to when she had achieved her goal. Traveling from the Paro Valley northwest, they followed a path through forests and over streams, finally coming to a rise with a clearing. From there, the horses clearly could go no further. Tsogyal was surprised to see Abaka exit a yak-felt tent that stood on the clearing at the base of a steep mountain; its cliffside rising two leagues into the sky. Near the tent, in a corral made from small timbers, Garkan and Batur whinnied, making a chorus as the mule bayed at the arrival of their horses and pack mule. Their gaze was drawn up in awe at the near-vertical slopes of the mountain before them covered in a blue-green blanket of pine forest.

"Abaka!" Tsogyal greeted, surprised to see him. "How good to see you here."

"Noble Daughter, you have arrived, what a delight. I came from Chimpu with Master Padma," Abaka greeted as he walked up to Tsogyal and took a gentle hold of Dawa's bridle. "I have been waiting for your arrival. From here, you must go on foot and it is difficult to find the caves. The horses will remain here."

Abaka nodded to Atsara and Dewamo, who dismounted, as did Tsogyal.

"How was your journey?" Abaka inquired.

"It was beautiful. A lovely country, this Bhutan," Tsogyal answered as she looked up into Abaka's eyes. There she could see his true heart. A flash of his many previous lives passed before her mind's eye.

Abaka looked down at her, a feeling of wonderment filling him. "Noble Daughter," he said tentatively, "I can feel ... are you enlightened now?"

Tsogyal chuckled, "No, no, Abaka, I am just ordinary."

With a laugh, he said, "Yes, of course, it is so. Just ordinary."

Turning his attention to Atsara, Abaka instructed that he should remain at the tent to care for the horses while Abaka led the women to the caves. With their bags slung over their backs, they began up the steep trail. After a long climb, the trail coursed downward again. All struggled with the rocky terrain. Then the path turned up again and after climbing for a long time, they were greeted with a roaring waterfall. Stretched across the two rock ledges, one on either side of the tall falls, lay a bridge made of logs tied together. Cold clean water sprayed them as they traversed the bridge. When they had all crossed, Abaka stopped and filled the water-skins he had brought with him for the trip up to the caves. Tsogyal and Dewamo gazed down, mesmerized by the water crashing into the pool below.

Proceeding onward, they finally came onto a large ledge jutting out of the cliff-face, its size welcoming all to sit and wonder at the view of thickly-forested hills cascading down into the Paro Valley far beyond.

Tsogyal was stunned at the size of the flat area of rock that fronted the doorways into the mountain caves. She looked along the cliffside to see there was another smaller, yet still large ledge, higher up around the bend of the cliff-face.

As they explored this unusual secret place, Padma had come out of one of the caves to greet them.

Looking down into Tsogyal's clear eyes, he could see truth. "I see you have reached your goal," he said.

"Yes, Master, I have," she replied.

Gesturing to rugs placed near the edge of the large ledge, Padma invited, "Come let us sit out here and have tea."

There was a small cook-fire near the rugs with a pot of hot tea in the coals and four cups sitting upon flat rocks placed around the fire-pit.

"It is so spacious here," Dewamo said, as she made herself comfortable on one of the rugs. "These ledges are large enough to build a temple."

"Indeed," Padma answered as he poured tea into each cup. Handing one to Dewamo, he continued, "I think seven temples, all in one complex, will be built here."

Tsogyal looked at Padma with a knowing smile. As she took the cup he held out to her, she asked, "And in which life will you build them, Master?"

Padma chuckled, seating himself, then taking a sip from his cup. He gazed out, yet seemed to be looking inward. "It will come, far in the future, when the time is right; it will be done," he declared.

Now, having been here for a full cycle of the moon, Padma and Tsogyal sat enjoying their midday tea. Tsogyal looked directly at Padma seated next to her. Lifting a lock of his long hair between her fingers, she said, "Master, there are many more gray streaks."

Padma smiled. "Yes, it is true," he said, looking down at the suspect strand held in her small fingers. Looking into her eyes, he said, "I will not be here much longer."

Dropping the lock, she looked at him in surprise.

Shaking his head, he said, "We will not speak of this now." Then turning his attention outwardly, he pointed as he said, "There."

Tsogyal looked to see the clouds had parted, revealing a section of the trail below. There they could see Abaka making his way up the steep trail that was visible from the ledge. Seeing them sitting on the ledge, Abaka waved. A man struggled up the trail behind him.

"Our visitor," Tsogyal confirmed

Sometime later, Padma rose and turned when they heard the arrival of the men behind them. Padma was surprised to see his student Drenpa Namkha, a Bon priest, following behind Abaka.

"Master," Priest Namkha said, stopping to bow.

"Priest Namkha, come and sit," Padma greeted, with a gesture toward the rugs. Tsogyal rose and began pouring tea for everyone.

Seating himself, Priest Namkha took the proffered cup from Tsogyal, then realized who she was.

"Queen Tsogyal?" Priest Namkha inquired in wonder.

"No longer a Queen, only a simple practitioner," Tsogyal answered.

"What brings you here?" Padma asked.

Pulling his gaze from Tsogyal, Priest Namkha began, "Master,

382

our Emperor Trisong granted me leave to find you. Santaraksita has sent emissaries out as well, looking for you. I knew you would be here as you did tell me yourself you had intended to practice here. I came straight to this place as fast as I could travel. There is little time. Emperor Trisong wishes you and Lady Tsogyal to know of his decree and to come at once to Samye."

Priest Namkha pulled a rolled parchment from his robe. Unrolling it, he read, "Pay heed! Buddhists and Bonpos treat each other as enemies. Neither gives credit to the positive qualities of the other. The King, Queens and Ministers have no trust in either. Both Buddhists and Bonpos are awash in doubt and fear. Therefore, on the fifteenth day of the new season, on the great plain of Yobok, each religion shall choose nine of their most wise and capable practitioners to compete in a test of signs of truth and proof of superior power in magic and psychic strength. Whichever dharma inspires confidence in the Emperor and his ministers, in that dharma we shall place our trust and that dharma shall be the dharma of Tibet. The loser shall be proven untrustworthy and so shall be utterly rejected. They that lose the contest shall be banished to the barbarian tribal borderlands. This is the decree of your Emperor, Trisong Detsen."

All looked at each other in stunned silence. Priest Namkha held out the parchment to Padma. Taking it he read it silently, then passed it to Tsogyal,.

"He must mean the Gyu Bon," Padma said.

Nodding Priest Namkha said, "Yes, the Gyu Bon presented their spectacle of sacrifice to the Emperor. Needless to say it did not please the Emperor nor the Buddhist ministers."

Shaking his head, Padma laughed, "Indeed, I am sure it did not!"

Looking in wonder at this exchange, Tsogyal inquired, "Priest Namkha, you are a Bon priest. Yet you are a student of Master Padma?"

Nodding as he sipped his tea, Priest Namkha answered, "Yes, I am a practitioner of Inner Bon. Our founder, Shenrab Miwo, taught a path which is a mirror image of that of the Buddha Sakyamuni. Master Padma has shown me the depth of the Buddha's wisdom, it helps me understand my own practice more."

Nodding, Padma interjected, "Priest Namkha has shown me texts and teachings of Inner Bon; it is as he says."

"Shenrab Miwo? I have heard of this name in my lands," Abaka said.

"Yet there are the Gyu Bon, they follow a different path," Priest Namkha explained, "They call on Gods and spirits. They travel to underworlds and talk to beings there. They are only interested in mundane power; that of fortune, healing sickness, creating circumstances for favorable crops and hunting. Their power is formidable and the evil among them seek to control others to their own corporeal ends and desires."

Silence fell between them as these last words faded, taken away on the breeze blowing up the side of the cliff face. It swirled around them then away, around the bend.

"Will you and the Noble Daughter succeed in a contest with them?" Abaka asked, looking from Padma to Tsogyal.

Padma looked at Tsogyal. "Will we?" Padma asked, with a smile.

All sat in silent expectation of her answer.

Tsogyal stared into the steaming teacup held in her hands, considering the question. Looking up at each man seated around her, she answered, "We must."

64

Queen Getso bowed low to the Emperor who sat high on a gold brocade cushion that lay upon the wooden backs of the intricately-carved forms of snow lions making base of his throne. Incense smoke wafted up through the open mouths of the large bronze dragon incense burners placed on either side of the dais, filling the hall with the scent of sandalwood and pachouli.

His emerald silk robes glistening in the light of the many butter lamps that were set up around the throne, Emperor Trisong greeted each in the line of nobles filing before him.

"Greetings, Queen of Karchen," Emperor Trisong said to Getso after having greeted her husband, King Pelgyi, standing next to her.

Dressed in dark-blue silk robes trimmed with the white belly-fur of the fox, Getso answered, "Great Emperor, I am honored to be here," as she rose up to meet his eyes.

"Your daughter is here," he went on, looking down at the Queen of Karchen, whose beauty was undiminished by her advancing age. Looking from Getso to Pelgyi, he said, "She will be one of the great nine for the Buddha dharma."

Hiding her surprise, Queen Getso replied, "I will be glad to see her."

Trisong looked to the next Noble in line, thus dismissing Getso.

Bowing, she retreated, following King Pelgyi away from the throne. They struggled through the crowd of Kings and Queens, Princes and Princesses, Nobles and their attendants, representing all of Tibet gathered in the great hall.

Getso could not help herself looking into each woman's face to see if she would recognize Tsogyal, her daughter, who had been gone from her for so long.

Seeing Getso's searching eyes, Pelgyi took her hand. "She must be with the Buddhist ministers planning their strategy," he suggested. "We will send word to her, let her know we have arrived." Then he added, "She will most likely have to wait until after the debate to visit with us."

With a sigh, Getso nodded. "Of course, she is one of the great nine for the debate." Shaking her head slowly, Getso said, "I had no idea she had become one so advanced." Looking up into the eyes of her husband, her lips trembling, she asked, "Will we know our daughter when we see her?"

"Of course," Pelgyi assured. "We will know her."

Pelgyi turned to Chudak who stood near, watching the crowd. "Chudak, we will return to our tents for tea and tsampa," Pelgyi ordered.

Chudak bowed, then moved in front of them to clear a path through the crowd for the Royal couple of Karchen.

Morning dawned as the rays of the sun burst over the snowy mountain range in the distance under a crystal blue sky. Long shadows played over the ground as the throngs of people made their way to the area set aside for all to observe the great debate. Rab-ten stood alone at one corner of the dais where sat the high throne of Emperor Trisong. She was invited to sit in this honored place by Trisong, as she was the highest-ranking court healer and one of few whom he trusted in his court. Gazing over the multitude making their way across the plain from the many tents set up for the Noble families and their attendants, she marveled at how many had come to witness this event; that which would decide once and for all the spiritual path all in Tibet would follow. She cast her gaze beyond the tent city to the large herd of horses that belonged to the many that had traveled here. There on the plain they grazed peacefully, unconcerned for the toiling of men's minds.

Rab-ten watched as the Buddhist scholars and translators, that made up the panel of judges, file into their seats to the right of the throne. The judges made up of the Bon shamans, Gyaltsen among them, priests and ministers, Tsenpo and Lutsen among these, murmured to each other as they seated themselves to the left of the throne. As the visiting Kings and their families, ministers and courtiers filed below her to sit on the cushions set in front of the Emperor's throne, she saw King Pelgyi and Queen Getso making themselves comfortable. She noticed Queen Getso's hair was no longer silky black, many streaks of silver glistened in the morning sun. King Pelgyi's lined face expressed the seriousness that reflected the mood of the day. Seating themselves next to King Pelgyi were King Wangchuk and Queen Dechen and her sister Queen Nyima and King Zhonnu. Rab-ten felt herself cower at the sight of King Zhonnu, hoping he would not see her. Then she forced herself to rise up straight, she was the Emperor's healer after all, no need to cower before King Zhonnu.

A booming voice called out, "All bow before the Emperor Trisong!"

All fell silent as those seated rose to their feet then bowed low as Emperor Trisong, surrounded by his personal guard, rode up before the dais on his beautiful black steed. The gold decoration of his saddle glistened brightly in the morning sun. Attendants ran up to take the reins of the horses as the entourage dismounted. The Emperor's warriors made a wall around him, escorting him to the steps that rose to his high throne. Only the soft footfalls of his felt boots mounting each step could be heard in the silence. Then the screech of a falcon, circling high above, pierced the cold morning air as the Emperor reached the top of the dais. Trisong looked up at the silhouette of the bird in the clear blue sky. Nodding to himself at the good omen, he turned and looked down upon the throng below as they settled onto their cushions. Gesturing to the attendant below that he was ready to begin, he remained standing. Two attendants ran to the large incense burners placed on the ground below the dais and lit the mound of sage that filled each. White purifying smoke wafted out of the flues. In moments a thin sweet cloud settled on the gathering in the still cold morning air.

"Those of the debate shall enter now," the attendant called out.

From the Bonpo tents the contestants filed out. Four, who were the Bonpo scholars, Norbu, Kungha, Tsalpa and Trompa appeared first. Under their long black beards they wore woolen robes died a deep black, making them look as one with the long shadows cast from the sunlight that struck their forms. The next to appear out of the tent were four magicians. In striking contrast to the scholars, their robes of shimmering white silk sparkled, making them look more like apparitions than men. Red sashes tied at their waists held their ceremonial knives securely. Each wore a large polished bronze mirror that hung at their chests, the convex mirrored surface warding off any negative energy that might threaten them. The ninth contestant to exit the tent was a woman, the Bon adept and shaman, Bonmo Tso. She was dressed in a black tunic on which were embroidered red swastikas, the ancient left-turning primordial spiral of the universe. To the Bon this spiral represents the primordial mother. Embroidered from each end of the geometric form were red flames of fire. Black wolf-fur ringed the openings at the arms. Over this tunic hung a lattice of bone ornaments. The openings of the lattice made perfect bone frames around each swastika. The long sleeves of her red silk undergarment was a striking contrast to the black of her tunic. Her necklace of amber beads from which hung a large silver locket inlayed with lapis lazuli swayed as she walked. From beneath the heavy head-ring of gold inlaid with turquoise and coral, raven hair spilled down to the backs of her knees. Her felt boots, black with silver embroidered spirals, kicked up a puff of dust with each step. Backlit by the sunlight, this made her appear to be walking above the ground on a cloud.

The throng watched in silence as the Bon made their way to their station. Their scriptures and texts, pages made of long narrow parchment stacked between wooden boards then wrapped in silk, were stacked like bricks making a wall half the height and the full length of a man. Their cushions were set out in front of this wall of scriptures.

Then the Buddhist tent door flap opened and Padma stepped out into the sun. His gold silk robes glistened in the morning rays, the pattern of emerald dragons seemed to dance with a life of their own as a breeze came off the still plain and fluttered past him. His long silver-streaked hair flowed from under his crown hat made of stiff red felt with clouds embroidered in gold thread and a large jewel of lapis lazuli adoring the front piece.

Behind him filed out three more Tantric adepts, Lodro, Tsemang and Chokro. Intent on their practices in mountain caves, they had arrived when summoned to participate in the great contest looking as common as farmers and herdsmen in their simple tunics of linen covered by dusty sheepskin zhuba robes hanging over well-worn felt boots. Their hair was long and matted from the dust storms they had traveled through on their route.

Then came the translator and scholar Vairotsana followed by Santaraksita, both dressed in simple red woolen robes. Each wore their long hair tied up into a topknot. After them appeared two more Buddhist scholars. Pelyang, who was an adept, was also dressed in red woolen robes with his hair in a long braid down his back. Vimalimitra, scholar and adept as well, appeared in a thick red silk robe adorned with a pattern of clouds in silver thread.

The last to appear was Tsogyal. Her white silk robe shimmered as she stepped out of the tent and walked last in line of the nine. A jungle of embroidered multicolored flowers wound their way up the back of her robe. Her hair was pulled back into a long simple braid that swayed with each step. Her beautiful solemn face shone bronze in the sunlight. A necklace of turquoise and coral set in glistening silver hung around her neck falling to cover her heart.

Queen Getso strained to see her daughter. The sight of her brilliant form passing before her caused her to gasp. Tsogyal looked toward the sound, seeing her mother. Her heart lurched at the recognition. Then, she realized, there too sat her father and her sisters. With a smile, she nodded in recognition, never altering her steps and continued on taking her place with the others at the cushions placed before the stacked wall of Buddhist texts.

Trisong raised his hands. All eyes looked up at his regal form as he addressed the attendants. "My ancestor, Emperor Songtsen Gampo, established Bon and Buddhism as equals in Tibet. Then Bon gained ascendancy and Buddhists were persecuted. I have renewed Buddhism in Tibet and allowed both Bon and Buddhism to co-exist equally."

Trisong shook his head slightly, as he projected his voice to reach every ear. "Yet Buddhism and Bon are inimical. Mutual re-crimination never cease and cause doubt and suspicion in the minds of myself, your Emperor, and all the Nobles and ministers."

Looking over the throng, Trisong raised his voice, "Therefore, this day we will compare and appraise the metaphysics of the two. Whichever system gains our trust will be adopted as a whole."

Looking sternly at all assembled, Trisong warned, "This is now the law. Whomever refuses to embrace the doctrine of the winner of this contest shall be destroyed by the law. Adherents to the system that loses shall be banished to the borderlands so that their doctrine shall be forgotten and die out."

Gesturing toward where Padma was seated, Trisong concluded, as he seated himself on the gold brocade cushion, "Master Padma, explain the course and purpose of this debate for the full understanding by all present."

A murmur rose from the audience as their attention fell on Padma's figure seated in a lotus posture. A gasp rose from the assembly as he began to slowly levitate off his cushion. In moments he was at the height of a man. The throng watched in stunned dismay as he continued to rise higher. When he rose to the height of a palm tree he stopped his ascent.

With all eyes looking up at him in awe, he spoke, "We have all assembled here to distinguish the metaphysics and tenets of Buddhism from Bon. It is right to do so. The first stage of all debate is to sharpen your wits with the customary exchange of riddles. Then each side will explain their tradition and present arguments; making clear their premises and conclusions. They will thus divide truth from falsehood.

In this way the difference between these two doctrines will be made clear. Then each side must give evidence of their accomplishments. These displays of magical skill will show the strength of each doctrine. The winner will inspire the Emperor, ministers and all the Noble families with confidence."

As Padma finished his final words, his form transformed into the figure of Buddha Sakyamuni, sending a wave of gasps and ejaculations through the crowd. Then, as he slowly descended toward the ground his form changed again, this time into Dorje Drolo. A Noble woman stifled her scream of fear as the wrathful being, its hair a wild black tangle, lips curled back exposing sharp teeth and long fangs danced in flames of fire. In its hand, finger nails long as claws, it held a sharp blade high in the air.

Gyaltsen glanced in dismay at Tsenpo, who sat rigid as stone, an expression of cold anger etched on his face. Bon adept, Bonmo Tso looked at the apparition, her lips pressed together tightly as she struggled to keep her face expressionless. However Lutsen, the other Bon scholars, magicians and the Bon contestants could not help but admire the display and what it showed about the abilities of this great master. Returning to his own form, Padma settled down onto his cushion, gesturing to the first two contestants, "The Bon shall begin, giving the first riddle," he said.

Buddhist scholar Pelyang stood up facing Norbu, his Bon opponent.

"What has notches like wrinkles and a big gullet?" Norbu said, clapping his hands for the answer that Pelyang must provide instantly. Pelyang stood dumb, not knowing the answer.

Norbu answered his own question, the time for Pelyang to answer having elapsed, "A set of scales."

Continuing, Norbu asked, "What has a head that grows and gets fatter?" Clapping his hands, he smiled as Pelyang shifted, trying to decide the meaning.

"A potho!" Norbu answered.

Pelyang shook his head, he should have known the answer. Pothos are the small heaps of earth covered in grass one sees while traveling in the highlands to the north. They resemble human heads and every spring they grow larger and larger.

Pelyang was shaken out of his self recrimination as the next riddle flew at him with a clap of Norbu's hands. "What is a coral purse full of gold coins?"

Pelyang felt his blood rise as he stood helpless, he did not know the answer to this silly riddle.

"A chili pepper!" Norbu said triumphantly.

On and on, the Bon Norbu proffered riddle after riddle, leaving Pelyang mute. Finally, obvious that the Bon had won the contest of riddles, their standard was raised in victory. The Bon entourage received the customary cup of wine from the Emperor, handed out by the attendants. The Bon ministers nodded their approval and prayed thanks to their Gods. Rab-ten was surprised to see Nyima laughing in approval with her husband Zhonnu. *So, Nyima has become Bon, following her husband,* Rab-ten mused.

Emperor Trisong shifted uneasily on his cushion at the first win of the day by the Bon. Elder Goe leaned over to him, whispering, "Quick to win... quick to loose. Riddles... have nothing... to do...with the Buddha... dharma... my King."

Trisong nodded, the words settled him and he relaxed into his cushion.

Elder Goe struggled to his feet. The crowd quieted seeing him rise. Leaning on his stick, he announced, "Now... the Bon scholars... and... the Buddhist scholars... will debate... on the truths... of their religious... doctrine."

As Elder Goe fell back on his cushion, the Buddhist sage Vimalamitra rose. Holding his hands out in supplication toward the audience, he declared, "The Buddha Sakyamuni explained that everything arises from a cause." Looking from face to face, he asked, "Yet, what effects the cessation of the cause?" Holding his finger up, he answered, "The Buddha explained it in these very simple terms; do no evil whatsoever and cultivate virtue in full measure, in this way your mind will become fully disciplined."

"Where is he?" the voice from the crowd called. All gasped as

Vimalamitra disappeared right before their eyes.

"Up there!" a man yelled, rising. All eyes followed his out-stretched arm pointing above everyone. There Vimalamitra sat in a lotus posture floating in the sky. A bright aura of light surrounded him. He snapped his fingers three times. The snap, snap, snap cut through the air. At the third snap the Bon scholars fainted.

Trisong sat up straight in his seat at what was occurring. Then, one by one, Santaraksita, Vairotsana and Pelyang rose before the audience and expounded truths set down by Sakyamuni Buddha and realized as truth by those who had followed after in his footsteps. Meanwhile, as these scholars spoke to the audience, Bon minister Tsenpo and magician Gyaltsen ran over to the contestants, shaking each man to wake them up. Lutsen looked on anxiously as Buddhist scholar Vimalamitra, stood once again, addressing the crowd on scripture. His audience sat in rapt attention listening to him. Lutsen could see the people were being won over. There was no Bon scholar awake, able to take the stage.

Gyaltsen spoke urgently as he shook each man, "Wake up!"

Groggily, Kunga and Tsalpa started to awake, then Norbu followed. But try as they may they could not stand and present their doctrine. Their tongues were numb and their lips stiff, their legs were weak and trembling. They sat pathetically on their cushions unable to utter a word nor stand up. Tsenpo finally gave up. Throwing up his hands, he stormed off to his seat in disgust as the ceremonial cups of wine were given to the Buddhist winners of the debate.

Resigned to defeat, Gyaltsen encouraged the magicians who were feverishly casting spells to enable the contestants to speak again. "They may win this part of the debate, but you can redeem yourselves by displaying your magical powers!"

65

Bonmo Tso stood, her hand raised up "Wait!"

All fell silent.

Casting her gaze over the Buddhist contestants with contempt, she declared, "I am not struck dumb by these barbarians!" Turning toward the audience, her voice raised so all could hear, she said, "I challenge Tsogyal to debate. I, Bonmo Tso, will show you all the superiority of our doctrine."

A low murmur went up from the crowd as she turned and walked into the debate ring. A strong wind came from the open plain and swirled around her, softly rattling the bone ornaments that hung around her garment. Her long black hair was lifted by a great gust, creating a halo of black spikes as she waited for Tsogyal to enter. Tsogyal rose, all fell silent as she glided toward the debate ring. The wind retreated and all became still as she halted, standing five paces before the Bon adept and shaman.

Turning toward the audience, her arms held out wide, Bonmo Tso began. "Our tradition spans many generations past. We, the shamans, are the liaisons to the spirits of the mountains and the forests, the rocks and the waters."

Raising her hand, finger pointed to the sky, Bonmo twirled her finger. The wind returned, softly caressing the flowing robes of the two women. "We, the shaman, speak to the Gods that control the weather. We keep the crops safe and make travel over the passes possible," she continued, as the wind grew stronger, whipping around the two women in the circle.

Tsogyal stepped forward, her hands held apart, then she make a loud clap. The wind instantly stopped. Raising her palm open up to the sky, she closed her eyes. Clouds began to form in the sky above. The crowd murmured, as the clouds became thick and dark, then a rumble of thunder rolled. Then, with a wiggle of her fingers, rain came showering down upon the groggy Bonpo contestants sitting on the side lines. They all jumped up, running to get out of the showering tumult. The crowd laughed as the rain poured down upon only them as they tried to get out of the path of the clouds, which seemed to followed them. With a snap of Tsogyal's fingers, the rain suddenly ceased. Bonmo Tso, looking skyward, stepped back in disbelief as the clouds disappeared. Then Tsogyal held her right hand up, from each of her five fingers appeared whirling wheels of five-colored fire. The crowd sat transfixed by the sight. Closing her hand, the fires disappeared.

Her voice loud and clear, Tsogyal spoke, "The path set forth by the great Buddha Sakyamuni, is the path to enlightenment. Shamanism is a path to mundane ends. It is a path seeking the power of the spirits of the outer world and the underworld to gain fortune, be freed from disease, and to remove obstacles placed in one's mundane life." Shaking her head slowly, her hands held out in supplication, she said, "This is merely trying to travel within samsara, making the best of it." Folding her hands, she continued, "The practices of Tantric Buddhism train the mind to see through the deception of the mind. To see the true nature of the mind, then use the mind to see itself; its sky-like nature."

Pointing at Bonmo, Tsogyal accused, "Shamanism is caught chasing the clouds of the mind. Whereas the practices of the Buddha allows the practitioner to realize the sky-like nature of the mind."

Tsogyal looked at the crowd, searching each face, as she asked, "Do you understand what I mean?"

The faces before her looked back blankly. Tsogyal bowed her head, considering what words to use for understanding, as she took a step, then two. She raised her head and looked from one to the next of each person sitting before her as she continued, "Day by day there will be clouds in the sky above, or it will be free of clouds and clear. Some days there will be storms bringing rain, hail and sleet. These forms and events occur within the sky." Holding her finger up, she declared, "Yet, these are not the sky itself. This is the same as thoughts, beliefs and emotions. These are but the energy of the mind, yet they do not affect the nature of the mind. It is the realization of this pristine true nature of the mind that frees you, that is the path to realizing your Buddha nature."

Pointing skyward, Tsogyal said, "You see I can control the weather." Gesturing toward Padma who was sitting with the Buddhist adepts, his eyes filled with admiration for her, she continued, "You have all heard the legends of Master Padma subjugating the spirits. We, those whom have practiced the Buddha dharma, can do all that. Those are simply siddhis, powers, picked up along the way, they are not the end and they are not the fruit."

Bending down, Tsogyal picked up a stone the size of her hand. Breaking it easily, she began to mold it, the hard rock becoming like clay. She continued, as she molded the now soft substance, "You see? This is child's play. These shaman can only manipulate the delusion of the universe."

Throwing the molded shape away, Tsogyal looked over the crowd, who sat mesmerized by her actions and words. "We practitioners can also can do much more. Through these superior teachings and practices of the great Sakyamuni, and others that have come after him, you will find wisdom and the truth of being. This, in turn, will awaken you to your true nature, your Buddha nature, the awakened state of being. Being freed from samsara is the path that frees one from the unending cycle of birth, suffering and death, then rebirth again."

Looking at Bonmo Tso, Tsogyal asked, "What say you to this, Shamaness?"

Bonmo Tso turned to the crowd, her face grim. With determination she collected her thoughts. Raising her head high, she declared, "What will you all do without your shamans? Who will divine the auspicious dates for your marriages? Who will assist your dead to a propitious rebirth? Who will divine your future? Remove bad spirits to heal your sick?" Gesturing to the Bonpo contestants now sitting upright, their chests filling with pride at Bonmo Tso's words, she asked, "Who will make sacrifices to the Swastika Gods to gain their pleasure and power. Who will speak to the many spirits of the world around you without us?"

A murmur passed over the crowd as they considered. Then Bonmo Tso pointed her finger at a row of Buddhist monks observing the debate. A flash came from her fingers and all nine monks collapsed, face down in the dirt. Tsogyal ran over to them and turned each monk over, opening their mouth she spit into it. Each monk instantly awoke, feeling many times more aware then before. After reviving all the fallen monks, Tsogyal strode into the circle of debate, glaring at Bonmo Tso. Bonmo Tso glared back at her with contempt.

Raising her voice, Tsogyal addressed Bonmo Tso so all could hear her retort, "Even the spirits you overpower to assist you in your shamanic world are themselves trapped in a spirit world of delusion. What makes you think these ghosts and spirits have any more wisdom than the wisdom that will awaken within your own being when you are freed from delusion?"

Looking to the crowd, their faces all intent on her words, Tsogyal laughed. "These spirits you seek out are themselves deluded. You all muck about, the deluded seeking the deluded. And in this way you think you will become free? How is that possible?"

Becoming serious, Tsogyal addressed the crowd. As she did so emanations looking just like her began to arise from her crown chakra. They rose above her into the sky and fanned out. Twenty-five in all hovered above her.

"The way is finding your true Buddha nature." Pointing to each person before her, she said, "That wisdom that is within each one of you. Seek to be freed from delusion and samsara; this is the road to Nirvana, to true release. Then you can do all any shaman can yourselves. Or, until you are free you have us, the lamas and adepts, to deal with the Gods and spirits. As well you have much more, you have a path to

Nirvana, something these shaman cannot give you."

With a snap of her fingers her emanations dissolved into light making a rainbow above her. Tsogyal said, "Watch us now in the remainder of this day's contest. You will be shown the abilities we possess that proves the superiority of the Buddha dharma."

Bowing to the audience, Tsogyal gestured to the Bonpo and Buddhists contestants to continue the contest. Anger and fear filled Bonmo Tso as she watched Tsogyal walk to her seat and settle onto her cushion. Then Bonmo Tso removed herself from the circle, feeling as in a fog.

As the sun passed over the mountains ending the long day, Tsenpo sat looking on as Trisong passed out gifts of gold to the Buddhist winners. The flag of the dharma was unfurled and raised high by an attendant as all the Buddhists in the crowd of onlookers cheered. The crowd cheered all day as one after one Buddhist contestant taught the Buddha dharma while displaying siddhis.

Adept Lodro brought the crowd to the edge of a near pond and astonished all as he walked on the surface of the water. Adept Tsemang recited the scripture of Kangyur, the vowels and consonants appearing in the sky for all to read. Adept Chokro invoked boddhisatvas, Buddhist saints, who appeared in the sky. Padma brought down thunderbolts and directed them like arrows. Adept and scholar Pelyang expounded on logic and caused objects to change form, to appear and disappear in people's perceptions. Adept Lodro changed fire into water and water into fire. Adept and scholar Pelyang passed through a boulder.

Emperor Trisong sat high on his throne transfixed by the marvels unfolding before him. An unshakable faith in the teachings solidified in him. For a moment the sounds of gasps and cheers faded away and he found himself alone, the plain was empty, just himself sitting on his throne. A mist of soft rainbow colors surrounded him. He began to hear a musical chanting, it grew louder and louder, "Om A

Ra Pa Ca Na Dhih." From the sky, a form floated toward him, growing larger and larger. Reaching him, it hovered in the space before him. It was a young man sitting on a lotus. His hand was raised high, holding a brilliant sword, flames of fire burned along its sharp double edges. Trisong knew who this was, it was the boddhisatva Manjushri. Suddenly, Manjushri swung his sword down, cutting off Trisong's head. He sliced again cutting off both arms and severing his torso. He swung and sliced, cutting Trisong's body to pieces. It lay in a bloody heap. Then, out of this heap, like a phoenix, rose a new form of Trisong, it was Manjushri himself, now the Emperor of Tibet. Trisong shook his head, he was back, the crowd was cheering. He looked down at Padma, who was looking up at him, tears in his eyes as he nodded to Trisong. He saw it, Trisong realized. A peace and surge of power he had never known filled Trisong. He knew what he must do; as soon as he was able, he declared silently to himself.

The crowd was standing, shouting and declaring the superiority and their faith in the dharma.

Tsenpo muttered to himself, feeling pummeled with doubt and anger. "These Indian barbarians have contaminated our Swastika Gods. We will slay these Indian panditas." Looking around him, he saw all the Bonpos had grim looks upon their faces. The crowd was cheering the Buddhists with smiles of pleasure. Many had tears of rapture flowing down their faces.

It was no use, the four Bon magicians could not even draw attention to themselves, the crowd was so enthralled by the display of siddhis by the Buddhist adepts. At the declaration that the Buddhists had clearly won, the Bon contestants rose and left the assembly. With the cheers of the crowd fading away as they made their way to their camp, the contestants and ministers gathered in one of the large tents to have a conference.

"We will destroy them," Bonmo Tso declared, her voice shaking with rage.

"We will destroy Samye with magic," Gyaltsen chimed in.

"We shall all go to Ombu and create a spell that will rain huge hail upon Samye, turning it to rubble," Tsenpo growled.

Gyaltsen said, "We will send thunder and hail to destroy all of Tibet! Then we will return and take control of the minds of people. They will soon forget this day, when Samye no longer exists and their crops are ruined, their villages destroyed. They will beg for us to return to them. They will blame the Buddhists for the destruction rained down upon them."

Lutsen, asked, "And the Emperor?"

Tsenpo glared at Lutsen as he replied, "It is time his son Mune took the throne. We can control Mune after Tibet is in ruin."

Lutsen stared at Tsenpo, uncomprehending. "The Prince takes the throne at the death of the Emperor."

Tsenpo nodded. "Let me make my meaning clear. A bolt from thunder will strike him dead!"

66

"You were marvelous!" Queen Getso said to Tsogyal as they sat facing each other in the chambers granted for their stay in Samye.

Getso fell silent when the servant arrived with a tray. With a bow, he proceeded to place tea on the small table that separated them. When the man was gone, Tsogyal took up the cup and gratefully sipped the hot fragrant liquid.

"You must still be very tired, my daughter," Getso observed. "Have you had enough rest?"

"Yes, these days of rest have done me good." Lowering the tea to her lap, Tsogyal considered her mother. "Mother, your hair is no longer like that of a raven's wing, it is now the color of a snow-dusted mountain." With a frown, she said, "I am sorry I have been gone so long. I meant to visit you sooner."

A tear began to form in Getso's eye. Brushing it away, she picked up her cup, sipping the warm tea as she composed herself. Placing the cup on the table, she said, "Well, my daughter, I can see by the events of that grand debate your absence has been due to a greater cause."

Tsogyal looked into the steaming cup, shaking her head. "I am sorry, I have caused you and Father pain."

"My daughter," Getso said, "all parents are caused pain by their children. It is life. You were born to a purpose. You had to follow that purpose. I am glad for it. I observed great miracles I had never known possible. Many performed by you."

Tsogyal looked into her mother's kind wise eyes. Then a smile brightened her face. "You know, we care not for those displays. They were used to attract the attention of the people. To cause interest in the path. Tis the path that is important."

Both women turned as Chudak entered the room. Bowing to Getso, he said, "My apologies for disturbing you, my Queen." Rising, he addressed Tsogyal, "Noble Daughter, the Emperor has requested your presence, immediately. I will escort you."

Tsogyal looked to Getso, who had a look of alarm on her face.

"I think we are not done with the Bonpos," Tsogyal said wryly, as she placed her cup on the table and rose.

The two women walked to the doorway, then both turned, facing each other. Placing her hands on Tsogyal's shoulders, feeling their strength under the silk robes, Getso said, "I am truly astonished at your greatness. I am proud beyond my dreams. Be safe, my daughter."

Tsogyal placed her hand over Getso's and squeezed. Releasing her daughter, Getso watched as Tsogyal disappeared with Chudak. Turning, she faced the empty room. Sinking onto the cushion, a mixture of happiness and great sadness churned like a wind devil in her heart.

"Be safe, my daughter," she whispered.

Moving at a quickened pace, Tsogyal almost collided with Chudak when he suddenly stopped. Turning toward her, he hissed, "Noble Daughter, I must give you something. I fear to wait, as I may not have this chance again."

Tsogyal looked up at the warrior, a questioning look on her face. "We can take a moment, Chudak. What is it?" she asked.

From his pouch, in the front of his zhuba, Chudak pulled a long lock of black hair. Holding it out to Tsogyal, he said, "It is Lungta. She has passed. "

Tsogyal reached out, taking the lock of mane. Inspecting the care with which it was wrapped tightly around one end, to hold it together, with thread made of gold, she inquired, "When?"

"It has been almost a moon now, Noble Daughter," Chudak answered.

Stroking the silky black lock of Lungta's mane brought a torrent of memories. The feeling of her hands coiled into Lungta's lush mane for a secure hold. The power of the little mare under her, her pounding hooves on the earth as they raced across the land, changing direction and speed at Tsogyal's mere thought. Lungta's intelligence, warning of danger when Tsogyal was unaware. Her bravery, pressing onward at Tsogyal's need. Her loyalty; head raised and ears forward when Tsogyal came to her. And most of all, her grace and beauty. And now she was gone. A tightness clutched at Tsogyal's heart as a tear welled in her eye. Wiping it away, Tsogyal looked up at Chudak. His eyes were now filling with tears as he looked down at her.

Placing her hand on his thick strong arm, she squeezed it as she said, "Thank you, Chudak, for the care you gave to my love; my splendid horse."

Chudak nodded, wiping at his eyes trying to dispel his tears, he choked, "We must go now, to the Emperor."

Placing the lock of Lungta's mane securely into the fold of her robe, Tsogyal hurried after him.

Entering the assembly hall, Tsogyal hurried to where Emperor Trisong sat upon his high cushioned throne. At his feet stood Padma and Bon Priest Namkha. Tsogyal could see all had grim looks upon their faces as they watched her approach.

Arriving in front of Trisong's throne, Tsogyal bowed. "My Emperor," she said, through heaving breaths.

"Yogini Tsogyal," Trisong greeted, "we are glad for your presence." Gesturing to Priest Namkha, Trisong urged, "Priest, tell our

Lady what you have just reported to us."

Tsogyal turned her attention to the Bon priest as he bowed low before her. Rising, Namkha began, "Noble Lady, I have heard from my informant of a secret meeting of Minister Tsenpo, Magician Gyaltsen, Bonmo Tso, and many other old Bonpos in a coven in Ombu. There they are making mischievous plans to rain spells on Tibet. They will bring hail and thunder. They are gathering together in one place to perform a very powerful legion of spells. Their aim is to destroy Samye and Tibet, to make the people afraid so they will cast out the Buddhists. They hope the people's fear will usher them back into power."

Tsogyal addressed Trisong, "So, they renege on their promise."

"Yes, they have," Trisong said, resigned. "I am sending Prince Mune with troops to dispatch them. Yet my men may not arrive in Ombu in time. The Bonpo have their own warriors in Ombu who are loyal to their cause. There will be a fight. Therefore, I request you and Master Padma to do what you can to avert their spells."

To Padma, Tsogyal inquired, "We can stop their spells?"

"Oh, yes, we certainly can," Padma confirmed. "You and I must go to the Utse Pagota, I will explain what must be done there."

With hurried steps, Padma and Tsogyal rushed to the Utse Pagota. Climbing the steps, they entered the large empty room. The quiet and peace of the place seemed otherworldly in contrast to the emergency of their task.

Padma gestured Tsogyal to sit on the cushion as he found a small table alongside the wall of the Pagota. Placing it before her, he knelt, then lay two bundles that he had been carrying with him on the table. Tsogyal peered down at the brocade-wrapped items, wondering what lay inside, as she settled herself to follow Padma's directions.

She looked at him expectantly. Padma gazed back at her, a smile curling the edges of his lips.

"My yogini, it will be you who dispel the Bonpo's evil, not I," Padma said.

Tsogyal looked at him in disbelief. "Me? Why me alone? You are the most powerful practitioner in all of Tibet!"

Padma settled himself on a cushion facing Tsogyal, the small table with the bundles between them, as he explained, "My yogini, my days in this life are almost finished. I am leaving this existence very soon."

Tsogyal stared back at him in shock. "Over? Leaving? When?"

"Soon," he said, as he began to untie the silk cord that tied one of the brocade bundles closed. Unrolling the cloth, his purbha knife was revealed. He placed it on the table before her, its gold blade shimmered as a ray of the day's last sunlight entered the room through an open window at that moment, striking it, filling the space with a golden glow.

Looking around the Pagota, now filled with the golden light, Padma smiled. "You see? You are the light now. I am done with my work in Tibet, with this life." Gesturing to his ceremonial purbha, he said, "I pass this instrument on to you, my yogini, as you have shown your achievements as my principle disciple."

Tsogyal stared at the instrument that lay glistening on the carved lacquered table.

"Take it into your hands," Padma instructed.

Tsogyal sat motionless, not comprehending Padma's words, not wanting to believe their meaning. My guru is leaving?

"Take it into your hands," Padma said again.

Tsogyal reached forward, feeling the cool dry ivory of the handle as she lifted it. It was heavy, yet the balance was perfect. She felt a surge of energy fill her. Looking at Padma, she summoned the courage to place her feelings aside and face her destiny.

"We... I mean, I must perform the blade rite, the cutting rite?" she asked.

Padma nodded. "The indestructible blade that cuts through all obstacles and obscurations, you must perform the Vajrakilaya the method of the indestructible blade, practice." Then, Padma unwrapped the other bundle he had lain on the table. It glistened when the sunlight hit its surface. Holding the large polished silver disc aloft, Tsogyal could see the sanskrit letters that were etched along the outer edge. At the center of the silver mirror was an etching of a celestial dragon, its body seemed to coil as the light shimmered off the etched lines. She felt the power of this beast, serpent and lion combined. Tsogyal lay down the purbha and took the mirror offered to her by Padma.

"This too I pass onto you. It is very powerful and must only be used for extreme purposes, such as we have facing us now," he said. "You will turn their spells back onto them."

Reading the mantra etched on the edge as Padma spoke, Tsogyal looked at Padma in surprise, "Their spells mean death for many Tibetans. My turning those spells back will kill the Bonpos who sent them. You mean with this practice, I must kill them?" she asked.

Laying a hand on Tsogyal's knee, Padma explained, "We do not wish them harm, we wish them do no harm to others. Wrathful beings must be subjugated by wrathful means. That is the only way. Peaceful efforts will not dispel evil intent on doing harm. These men and woman wish to destroy the lives of Tibetans; innocent farmers and merchants who only wish to live in peace. They wish to destroy people's lives to satisfy their lust for power. They wish to destroy Samye, the place where the Buddha dharma will grow and where many generations will learn of the Buddha's teachings. We won the contest. They are breaking their oath and the law. They sit in their coven now working their spells, intent on killing us and many others. You will turn their spells back on them, thus they will die by their own hand. This is skillful means."

Tsogyal stared down at the mirror in her hands as she listened.

Padma sat quietly for a moment, then he rose to his feet. "You can do it," he assured.

Tsogyal looked up at him, their eyes met, she held his gaze. Thoughts of his days being few now flooded her, causing tears to press hard behind her eyes. Taking a deep breath, Tsogyal composed herself, willfully transforming the energy of her grief into determination to the practice she must perform until she succeeds. She knew not how long it would take to do so.

"I will succeed, Master," Tsogyal declared.

Padma nodded. "I will instruct the servants to leave your tea and meals outside the door. At sunup and sundown."

Tsogyal watched as he disappeared out the door. The silence of the space felt heavy upon her. The sunlight was gone now, the sky she could see outside the open window was turning purple. She rose, looking to where there were butter lamps sitting cold around the room. A sound came from the doorway as a servant entered, holding a lit butter lamp. Going around the room, he lit each butter lamp, illuminating the space. Silently he left, leaving Tsogyal in the flickering light. Tsogyal settled herself back on the cushion, focused her mind and began.

67

Chudak pulled his zhuba tighter around him against the biting cold of the wind. His horse began to step sideways in agitation. Chudak tightened his legs and the rein to hold the animal still. Placing his hand on the restless horse's neck, he stroked it, settling it. He looked over at Senge, who sat astride Skamar, standing as still as stone on the hillside overlooking Ombu in the distance. Under the full moon, they could see the small figures of warriors below, placidly walking as sentries along the parameter of the village. White smoke drifted up, into the cold moonlit night, from the smoke hole of a large house at the edge of the village. Prince Mune leaned over to whisper to the General. Senge turned his head to Chudak, making a slight gesture. Silently they slid away, back into the shadows of the hillside.

"They are unaware that we know of their plan," Mune whispered to Senge, when they joined their force of one hundred warriors who were silently waiting for them behind the hilltop.

This was a force hand-picked by Trisong and Mune to attack the Bonpo village in stealth and to kill quickly. Senge and Chudak volunteered to accompany them. Their offer was granted by the Emperor, and their King, Pelgyi, gave them leave. Mune was grateful to have the experienced General Senge with them as the Emperor's own general, Klupal, was fighting to take Hami, on the northern part of the silk trade route. Trisong's armies were in a continual effort to control the entire trade route, bringing wealth and prosperity to Tibet.

Senge nodded. "Their sentries are practically asleep," he grunted. "The large house at the edge of the village must be the coven. They must be performing their wickedness even as we stand here."

Looking to the horizon, Mune could see it would not be long until the glow of dawn arrived. "At first light then," he declared. To his attendant, Mune whispered, "Tell the men. At first light we will advance directly to the coven, all who stand before us will fall. We will kill all inside, let none escape."

Smoke wafted in an undulating mass at the ceiling of the large room as the men sat before the fire chanting. Bon Ministers Tsenpo and Lutsen sat with scholars and shamans Tsalpa and Kunga along with seventeen more shamans all in deep trance, journeying to the underworld, as they chanted. Bonmo Tso and the magician Gyaltsen, along with seven other magicians, were casting curses into fire, into water, into earth and into air. With each curse uttered by the assembly, one of the magicians would toss herbs onto the fire. The herbs crackled and flared, then smoke rose into the rafters eventually finding its way out the smoke hole. A goat and a chicken were tethered to rings in the wall, awaiting their slaughter at just the moment the curses were at their peak, able to wreak havoc.

Tsenpo unconsciously shifted in his seat to alleviate the nagging cramp in his leg. They had been there for days building power into the curses with their chants, invocations, herbs and intentions. Lutsen's eyes opened, awakened from his journey in trance. Looking around the room, his eyes fell on Gyaltsen, who, along with the other magicians, was deep in his journey to the underworld, assembling an army of demons to carry out their wrath upon Tibet.

In Lutsen's mind's eye, he saw warriors on a hill. He felt a wave of intention, of attack, upon the very house they all sat within. His body shuddered in fear. Uncoiling from his cushion, he slid to the door and silently stepped out. The cold night air, in contrast to the heat of the smoky room, shook him awake as he gazed up at the hills overlooking the village. The sky to the east had a slight glow of gray.

The ceremony is almost complete, he thought as he turned to go back inside. Then he heard words in his mind, but not his own thoughts, *We shall attack at dawn.* A shiver ran up Lutsen's spine, he knew there was an army intending to attack them somewhere close, though he could not see it. Seeing a Bon warrior slowly walking his sentry position in the distance, Lutsen hurried, to warn of the coming attack. As he hurried to the sentry, he formed a plan of defense to set the man upon. Then, he would return to the coven and they would cast the curse upon Tibet this dawn, to insure they would not be thwarted.

In the gray light of dawn, they flew over the rise, a wave of pounding hooves thundering over the ground. Mune could see sentries, surprised at the approach of his army, running to take cover. *Good,* he thought, *total surprise.* In the lead with General Senge, they took the army to the edge of the village where Mune split off, taking half the warriors around the edge outside the village toward the coven and Senge taking the remainder through the village houses so they would arrive at the coven covering each side of the house, thus surrounding it, able to catch any who might flee. Chudak urged his mount, staying close to the General. Nothing moved in the village.

Strange, Chudak thought, *it is too quiet. We are as thunder upon the ground. People should be coming out of their houses in wonder at our approach.*

They filed along the small road that wound between several houses, each abode enclosed by a short stone wall. Then it dawned on Chudak, *This is a trap, they know.* Just as his mouth opened to call his warning to the General, he saw them. Like a dark cloud, many warriors rose up in unison from behind the walls and on the roofs of the houses; their bows fully drawn. At once they loosed their arrows. The wall of spikes flew into Senge's ranks. Chudak spurred his mount forward to flee the first volley. He felt the surge of his men behind him as all the warriors saw the trap they had fallen into. Their horses leapt and bolted to get free of the danger. Though all the warriors in Senge's division rode into the village with bows and swords in hand, the opposing force was too overwhelming, their only choice was to spring free of the narrow teeth of the village houses and get to the coven to take up position.

Gyaltsen heard the chants around him as he arose from the depths of the underworld. He became aware that Lutsen was whispering words into his ear. Startled by their meaning, Gyaltsen stared at Lutsen, at first not comprehending, then Lutsen's words took hold. With determination, Gyaltsen prepared to throw his last handful of magical herbs onto the fire with the invocation to all the demons and Gods of the elements to become a torrential wind, sending hail and fire to destroy all who are not Bonpo, to destroy Tibet.

Tsogyal barely noticed the gray light of dawn filter into the Utse Pagota, as she was deep in concentration on the rite she performed. She had cut all obstacles to building a shield for Tibet. As now as dawn arose, she had completed the mirror. Their curses would fall not on Tibet, but would be reflected back upon themselves.

"Phat! Phat! Phat!" Gyaltsen chanted as he threw his last handful of herbs onto the fire. This would begin the fury that would take down all those of Tibet that were not Bon. And to slay at once the warriors set upon them now.

Suddenly, a great rumbling could be felt beneath the seated figures in the coven. The men and Bonmo Tso looked around as the house began to shiver. They all realized they were hearing the thunder of horses' hooves surrounding the coven. Gyaltsen looked at Lutsen who stood transfixed, waiting for the spell to slay these warriors, who where now just outside the door, to work its magic. Why was it taking so long? All in the coven stood up in fear at the sounds of rumbling of the warriors taking up position around the coven. The fire spat and flames rose high. Bonmo Tso's eyes grew wide as the flames in the fire grew higher and higher. She gasped as a wind inside the fire began to swirl the flames.

Pointing to the fire, she shouted, "Look what is happening!"

Gyaltsen stepped back as a wind swirled the flames around and around, causing the fire to grow larger and larger, filling the chamber. Tsenpo ran for the door but was grabbed by Lutsen, who shouted to him, "Stay with us, you will be struck down if you go out there. Wait for the spells to work."

Both men turned to the cries of Kunga, watching as the swirling growing flames had Kunga and ten shamans pinned into a corner of the stone house. Screaming, they cowered on the floor, trying to escape the raging heat. All in the room gasped as the flames swallowed their bodies. Their dying shrieks caused the wind to circle the room, stronger and stronger, carrying upon it hot flames. Lutsen was struck by a ball of fire and burned to ash in an instant, along with seven remaining shamans and six magicians. Gyaltsen and the last magician ran for the door. As his hand pulled at the cord, he and the last magician were hit from the side by a ball of flames, hurled by the wind, throwing them both down. Gyaltsen gasped at the incomprehensible pain of his searing body. His mouth opened to scream, yet no sound came as in moments, Gyaltsen and the last magician were turned to a heap of ash.

Horrified at the sight of Gyaltsen's body burned to ash, Bonmo Tso flew over Gyaltsen's remains. Pulling hard on the cord, she opened the door and ran out, behind her Tsenpo and Tsalpa followed.

Mune led his warriors around the edge of the village to the

coven where heavy pungent smoke was pouring from the smoke hole. He waved his arm, signaling his men to surround the coven as he shouted, "Take no prisoners, they all must perish!"

As the warriors rode to surround the coven, Mune heard rumbling and whistling coming from inside the house. He looked to his lieutenant, a question on his face. A chill went up his spine as screams came from within. Mune's warriors looked to each other in shock at the chilling sounds. They all raised their bows in anticipation of some evil readying itself to flow out of that house. Then, the door swung open, a figure inside a black cloud of smoke bolted out toward them, sparks flying from her robes.

Seven arrows pierced Bonmo Tso's chest. She was dead before she hit the ground. Behind her, two more figures poured through the doorway, carried on an evil wind of blackness. Each figure fell to the ground pierced by the many shafts of retribution wrought by Mune's warriors.

Tsogyal's mirror had done its work. All in the coven were killed by their own intentions, Tibet was safe, the Bonpo leaders were destroyed.

Just then two of Senge's warriors reached the coven. Mune was shocked to see they had been wounded and arrows were lodged in their saddles. Senge was not among them.

"Where is the General? Where are the men?" Mune demanded.

One warrior pointed back toward the village. "Sire, we were attacked," he said, breathlessly. "They knew we were coming. We turned to counter their attack. We are fighting to dispatch them."

Mune turned his mare as he gestured with a wave of his arm. "Follow me!"

They charged to the ambush site. Senge's men were dismounted, having taken cover behind walls and houses. The Bonpo warriors held fast to their positions secure on rooftops, behind the short walls and inside the houses shooting through windows.

Mune dismounted before his horse came to a stop. He ran to the side of the first warrior he saw crouched behind a short wall, his bow held fast in his hand. Mune's mare trotted away to join the other horses all gathered in an open area away from the village.

"What is the status?" he demanded of the warrior.

"Prince. They hold strong, we cannot dislodge them," came the man's clipped irritated reply.

"Mmm," Mune replied, "they think their magicians can help them."

The warrior looked at his Prince. "Can they?" he inquired, a tremble of fear seeping into his voice.

Mune kept his gaze to the Bonpo positions as he answered, "I think not, as they are all dead."

"Hah!" exclaimed the warrior. "If you would tell them, Prince, they will surely surrender."

Without looking at the man, Mune shouted out. "Hear me, warriors of Ombu!"

His voice carried clear and strong. A stillness befell all as he continued, "Those of the coven are dead, slain by our arrows. Their magic has no power any longer. Your leaders are all dead."

The echo of his last words reverberated through the houses and walls. A murmur arose as the Ombu warriors called to each other in loud whispers.

Mune called out, "Surrender to me, your true Prince. Give your allegiance and oath of fidelity to the Buddha dharma and to me! Do so, and I will grant amnesty for your treachery to the Emperor! Do so, and Ombu will live in peace and prosperity."

Mune waited for a moment so his words could sink in, then he warned, "If you do not, I will send for more troops and we will turn this village of Ombu to dust."

Muni's warriors waited. A bonpo warrior rose up from atop a roof-top throwing his bow down. Man after man rose from the rooftops, holding their bows high in a gesture of surrender then throwing them down onto the ground. Bows were thrown out of windows with shouts of surrender.

Mune stood up, ordering his men to gather the prisoners and their weapons.

"Where is General Senge?" Mune called out.

No answer came. A lieutenant ran up to Mune and with a bow, answered, "I know not, Prince. When we were besieged I saw the General turned in his saddle shouting orders for us all to find cover. I know not where he took up position."

"Come with me, we will find him," Mune said.

68

Senge stood on the wide plain. Looking around, he saw Skamar, grazing in the distance. *What is he doing there?* he wondered. Confused, he tried to remember why he was standing there. He noticed Chudak, a slumped heap on the ground in the distance. Then he remembered; the attack, the arrows, their fleeing. *Chudak? Is he injured?* he wondered.

At once, he found himself looking down at Chudak, yet he could not remember walking toward him. Hearing the pounding of hooves behind him, he spun to see a warrior charging toward him. Senge reached for his sword, Dragon's Claw, at his side, only to feel the empty scabbard. Keeping his eye on the approaching warrior, he cast quick glances at the ground around him, searching for the sword. Then he noticed the flicker of the hilt, beckoning him. Lunging for it, his hand grasped at the cool solidness. Yet try as he may he could not grasp it. His fingers passed through the bronze hilt. Frustration filled him as he struggled to grasp the sword. Then, at last, he was able to raise the shimmering blade up, just as the figure drew near.

Senge stood with his feet wide apart, ready for a fight, as he took in the large figure. The warrior held his hand up, in a sign of peace. Senge stood his ground, staring in awe at the man and horse standing before him. The horse was the tallest horse he had ever seen, its silky coat was as black as coal. The warrior was, as well, a very large man. His chain-mail glistened silvery-blue, like many stars in the night sky, with the movement of his horse. Strapped to his muscular thighs shimmered black-lacquered leather leggings that seemed more like deep pools of water at midnight than armor. His black felt boots were embroidered with red spirals. Senge stepped back at the sight of the spirals spinning, not comprehending how this was possible. Below the silver helmet that shined with a soft glow, like moonlight, a long mustache draped over a deep frown. His piecing eyes, like white lights, looked down at Senge.

Senge stepped back, raising Dragon's Claw.

The warrior drew his sword from a jeweled scabbard. Senge stared in astonishment at the sword that was made not of bronze or steel but of a ray of moonlight. Pointing the glowing blue-white blade of light toward Chudak's form on the ground, the warrior said, with a voice like distant rolling thunder, "Look more closely at Chudak."

Senge leaned over Chudak, then stepped back with shock at the horrifying sight.

Chudak felt numb as he sat upon the cold hard ground. The weight of Senge's body, laying limp across his legs, grew heavy. Chudak's hands were sticky with the now-cold blood that covered them. Holding Senge's head on his lap, Chudak's tears struck Senge's face which was serene around the arrow shaft that protruded from his right eye socket. A clean shot that had killed him instantly.

Chudak had seen the General slump over his saddle at a full gallop after giving the order to run for cover among the barrage of arrows attacking his warriors. He had followed behind Senge until they reached the plain beyond the village. There, Senge, whose hand had held fast to his sword, finally released it, and his body fell out of the saddle to the hard ground. His horse careened away. Galloping up to the General's limp body, Chudak leapt from his saddle, dropping to his knees beside Senge. Turning the limp body gently over, Chudak gasped in shock and disbelief at the sight of the shaft that had found a path through the eye socket. Chudak lifted Senge's head up as blood dripped from the wound onto his hands. Then he sat slumped over, as the truth of what his eyes told him, sank in.

Senge looked up at the spirit warrior in disbelief, then back down at his own lifeless body.

"You are dead, General Senge," the tall warrior said simply.

Senge strode away from Chudak, pacing back and forth, his sword hanging limply in his hand. *Dead? I am dead?* he questioned. Shaking his head, he thought, *No, no, no!*

Looking up at the warrior, Senge asked, "Who are you?"

"I am the Lord of Death, I have come for you," the warrior said, his gaze intent on Senge.

Senge shook his head, *No, this cannot be. I must be in a dream.*

Knowing Senge's thoughts, the Lord of Death answered, "You are not in a dream of a man alive. You are only your mind now, your body lies there." The Lord of Death pointed the shaft of light again at Chudak.

Senge looked down at his body again, limp and bloodied across Chudak's outstretched legs, looked into his own unmoving face. *It is true, I am dead,* Senge had to admit to himself.

Senge looked up at the Lord of Death. "What am I to do now?"

"We must go now," the Lord of Death said. "Here is your mount for our journey."

Senge turned away from Chudak, and stepped back as a most beautiful and familiar horse suddenly appeared before him. *Ketu?* he thought in astonishment. He ran his hand over the soft silver-gray neck, now whole and uninjured. Then he noticed his fine saddle on Ketu's back. With delight, he took the recurve bow from the quiver hanging at the side of the saddle. *My old bow,* he marveled, as he felt the smooth horn and strong wood that made its strong limbs. Images of phantom warriors on phantom horses filled the field before him now as he remembered the day it was broken in battle. Then the image faded. Sliding the bow back into its quiver, Senge mounted Ketu and looked at the Lord Of Death.

"Were are we going?" he asked.

No longer in the field with Chudak, they now rode up to a large house. Its high battered stone walls were white-washed. Shutters covering the windows were open, letting in light and fresh air. Over each window was a little wooden awning covered with tile. Senge realized it was his own house. Just then the wooden door opened and his wife Michewa stepped out with a basket held in her hand. Her colorful *chuba* apron sparkled in the sunlight.

Turning back to the open doorway, she called, "Sengemo!" She waited for a moment then, with irritation in her voice, she called again, "What is taking you? Come now!"

Senge could see a glimpse of the small courtyard through the open door. Then he gasped when his daughter Sengemo, now seven springs old, stepped out. *She has grown so much,* he thought, *have I been away so long?*

"I am here, Mother, " Sengemo said. "I had to say goodbye to Tashi."

"You are too attached to that little dog, we will not be gone long," Michewa said. Then looking Sengemo over, she gasped, "You look like a farmer's daughter." Setting her basket down and stooping before her daughter, she said, "Here, straighten up your robe." As she pulled at the wool robe that hung half off Sengemo's shoulder, she continued, "You want to look like the daughter of a General; like a Noble girl."

Sengemo hiked up her shoulders in a effort to help her mother straighten the robe. As her mother tucked the strands of hair that had escaped her braid behind her ear, Sengemo said, "I miss Father. When will he come back?"

Michewa, looked into her little girl's eyes. "As do I, Daughter. I know not when he will return. He is General to our King, so he is often away in service." Standing, Michewa took up her basket, saying, "Bearing his being away, this is our duty. As he does his duty for the people."

Senge dismounted Ketu and walked toward them. Tears in his eyes, he reached his hand to touch Michewa. Pain seared his heart as he realized he would never be by her side again. Looking at Sengemo, he could not bear that he would never see his daughter grow up and marry. He would never see them again.

"Stop! Do not touch them," the Lord of Death ordered.

Startled, Senge turned and looked at him, a question on his face.

"It will disturb their minds," he explained.

"Come now, Daughter," Michewa said. "We have much to do this day."

As they turned and walked toward the market, Sengemo said, "I hope Father will come back soon."

Tears filling his eyes, Senge watched them walking away from him, down the path to market. Holding out his hands out to them, he called out, *my precious wife, my precious daughter, I love you.* Yet it was a thought, not spoken words to be heard in their corporeal world.

Suddenly, Sengemo stopped in her tracks. Turning she looked back. Her mother continued on, not noticing. Taking a step toward Senge, she looked directly at the place his spirit stood.

With a perplexed look on her face, she whispered, "Father?"

"Daughter, come now. What are you looking at?" Michewa called.

Sengemo gazed to where the spirit of her father stood, answering, "I just felt... I thought I heard... nothing, I am coming." She turned away and hurried to her mother's side and they were gone.

Senge looked up at the Lord of Death, not able to bear his grief. Gasping, he bent over, his hands on his knees, letting his tears fall to the earth.

"You had your duty, you were a good servant to the King. You did what you thought was correct. You had honor. You provided your wife and daughter with a fine house and a good life. This is good karma," the Lord of Death explained.

Suddenly Senge found himself on Ketu's back and they were

traversing lands he had never seen before. There were large sharp rock formations with fires burning everywhere, the smoke made him cough. He looked around him, men were fighting, many men. As far as Senge could see, men were stabbing each other with swords and knives, hacking limbs and heads off. Men holding in their own entrails, large gashes cut across their bellies. Senge watched in shock as the men around him were screaming in pain. The stench of blood and feces was overwhelming. Then, after suffering terribly, the wounds healed immediately. Then they were fighting again, only to suffer, all over again, the pain and terror of being injured, the fear of being killed; yet with no final release.

The Lord of Death stopped his horse. "When you were young, General, you killed out of a desire for killing. You enjoyed taking other's lives from them," the Lord of Death said. "Yes, I realize it was war. But you were blood-thirsty, General. This is very bad karma and there is a consequence for this."

Gesturing around him, the Lord of Death said, "This is the Hell Realm, those with evil karma end up here for eons of time."

Senge swallowed hard as terror gripped him. Had his actions led him to spend eons in this horrid Hell Realm? Must he dismount Ketu and remain here?

Suddenly they were no longer in the Hell Realm. Now they rode their horses among orchards of fragrant trees laden with large apricots. There was a huge market of thousands of stalls that disappeared to the horizon. Each stall filled with grain or meat, tea or honey. Senge suddenly felt very hungry. Then he noticed the people here looked very strange.

The Lord of Death said, "Then you killed not for pleasure any longer, but out of the desire for power and wealth. This then consumed you."

Gesturing toward the people around them, the Lord of Death asked, "You see their small necks and big bellies?"

Senge nodded as he looked at them.

"They are surrounded with all this food yet their necks are so small nothing can pass through to their big bellies. They are always hungry, though they are surrounded by delicious food. They suffer greatly here in the Hungry Ghost Realm where they can never be satisfied. They will remain here for eons of time," the Lord of Death, said looking intently at Senge.

Senge looked at him as his fear grew, *by the Gods let me not have to remain here*, he prayed.

The market faded away and they stood on a mountaintop overlooking a small village. Senge did not recognize the place.

"Yet, later in your life you changed," the Lord of Death stated. "In your heart, you saw the error of your thinking. You truly did regret killing. You saw the folly of seeking only power and wealth. You valued life over death. When confronted with the duty to kill, you did so only when absolutely necessary. You righteously killed evil men who would harm others. And you killed in battle in the service of your Emperor. You offered prayers for those you had to kill in battle. And many times you showed mercy to those you could have easily killed. You began to refrain from killing whenever it was possible."

The Lord of Death looked intently at Senge. "Then you volunteered to fight a battle for the benefit of others. In the end you sacrificed your life so that others would have the dharma, the path toward their enlightenment, in their lives. This is not just one religious belief over another," the Lord of Death explained. "This is truth over folly. If a religion is folly and hurts others or creates bad karma in any way, those that practice the actions of malevolence will suffer the results. Karma is the law of the universe, none can escape it, no matter their religion. None can escape my judgment when their corporeal lives are over."

Nodding his head in approval, the Lord of Death continued, "This change in your thinking, in your actions, your truly selfless acts of love and right action and this final act of sacrifice for the benefit of others, have been the deciding factors that keep you out of the Lower Realms and allow you a rebirth as a human."

Looking down at the village below, the Lord of Death explained, "You will be reborn a human again in that village. This is fortunate. You will have a chance to improve yourself. Yet this village is very poor. It will be a hard life for you. Your previous bad karma must be cleansed."

Pointing toward the village below, the Lord of Death instructed, "There you will have the choice to use your abilities learned in your last life to help the people here. If you fall into bad habits or selfish habits, your abilities will end up abusing the people. You must use your abilities to good purpose or you will surely fall into the Lower Realms in your next rebirth. This does not mean you do not seek wealth or stature, there is no wrong in this. Indeed, in this way, it is most possible to help the entire village. What it means, is that you help others whenever you can and do not directly abuse others." With a hand on Senge's shoulder, the Lord of Death asked, "Do you understand, General?"

Senge looked down at the small village nodding slowly, relieved he was not going to be left suffering in the Lower Realms.

Then they were back on the wide field again, with Chudak slumped on the ground. Senge looked in the distance as a cloud of dust revealed Prince Mune and a warrior with him, riding up to Chudak.

Chudak disregarded the clatter of hooves that approached. Prince Mune and the lieutenant dismounted and slowly approached Chudak. Looking down at the sight of the slain General, Mune shook his head in disbelief. "By the Gods," he uttered.

Chudak looked up at the Prince, his face wet with tears. "He was my brother, he was my General. Now he is gone," he cried.

Mune knelt next to Chudak, placing his hand on the large strong shoulder, he said, "General Senge was a good man. He died for his Emperor and his King. He died to protect all of Tibet." Squeezing Chudak's shoulder hard, he encouraged, "He will be given a Royal funeral, full honors."

Standing, Prince Mune declared, "He died a warrior, this would have been his wish. He will have a fortunate rebirth due to his good deeds. Chudak, hold that in your heart and celebrate your brother's many triumphs."

Turning to the lieutenant, Mune instructed, "Get a wagon and catch his horse. We will bring him home in honor."

Senge watched as they placed his lifeless body into the wagon. Chudak noticed Dragon's Claw laying on the ground. He picked up the sword that had been passed down for generations to Senge and dusted the dirt from the fine blade and gold inlayed bronze hilt. Placing the sword next to Senge's body, he considered that it would be passed to Senge's daughter, as he had no son. She would pass it to her son.

Dismounting Ketu, Senge stood next to Chudak as Chudak tied Skamar's lead rope to the back of the wagon. He held his hand just inches from Skamar's neck, then remembering not to touch, withdrew it. Pain seared his heart as he stood with Chudak, watching the wagon rumble away.

Chudak stood watching until the wagon disappeared from sight. He looked to his horse, grazing on what grass it could find. Placing his hand on the gelding, he stroked the muscled neck, trying to draw from it the strength to step up into the saddle. Finally, with resolve, he drew in a breath and lifted himself into the saddle. Turning his mount, he followed the wagon tracks.

Senge watched as Chudak rode away. *Good bye, my brother*, Senge thought, with tears anew.

Looking up at the Lord of Death, Senge straightened. He went to Ketu and mounted, alighting on the horse's strong back.

Turning to the Lord of Death, he said, "I am ready for my next life."

The Lord of Death looked deeply into Senge's eyes, the piercing light of them boring deep into Senge's consciousness, as he said, "In future lives, you will become tired of this cycle of birth, suffering, death and rebirth. When that happens, you will be consumed with the desire to realize ultimate truth. You will seek the path to awakening from the dream of life into the realization of ultimate truth. Due to your good deeds in the life you have just left behind, you will be reborn a human. This results in keeping that path to release from this endless cycle open for yourself. For only in the human realm can one attain enlightenment and release from this constant cycle."

Turning his black steed, the Lord of Death beckoned Senge to follow.

With one last look back to the life he was leaving behind, General Senge and the Lord of Death rode into the west.

69

Rab-ten slipped silently into the shrine room. The cups clattered softly against the teapot as she set the tray down on the small table next to Tsogyal. Tsogyal's soft chanting filled the room. Abaka's mala clicked as he moved each bead through his fingers counting each mantra, his deep voice adding to the resonance. Rab-ten seated herself on a cushion and began pouring tea, the spiced smoke of the incense tickled her nose.

"Om, Ah, Hung" Tsogyal chanted, completing their session. Abaka stilled his beads and lay his hands in his lap, his legs crossed in a lotus. Rab-ten studied his face, his eyes were closed, his mustache hung limp around his solemn mouth.

Looking to the object of Rab-ten's gaze, Tsogyal placed a reassuring hand on Abaka's arm. "He is on his way," she encouraged.

Abaka opened his eyes and noticing Rab-ten, he nodded.

Rab-ten held the tea cup out to Tsogyal, inquiring, "He will have a good rebirth then? He will not end up in the Lower Realms."

Taking the cup, Tsogyal said, "Yes, absolutely. He will be reborn as a human again and that is good."

Then Rab-ten stood, taking a few steps to hand a cup to Abaka, who took it gratefully as he released his legs and stretched them out over the cushion.

Sipping the hot thick salty butter tea, Tsogyal shifted on her cushion, stretching her legs out straight in front of her. As she wiggled her toes, she considered, "You know, when I was a girl, General Senge, at that time in my knowing him, was a man who loved war. He was a man who reveled in battle and killing. That is what my father always said about him."

Abaka smiled, nodding his head. "He was formidable, I have heard."

Looking up at the large statue of the Buddha, Tsogyal continued, "But later, as he matured, his Noble qualities, his ethos, his principles, his honor, all came together to make him a most valuable man." Looking into her tea, she thought for a moment then said, "Not a beast as many men who have skills to kill become."

"He was a very complex man," Abaka said, "Noble at heart, even if not by birth."

"I think the journey with us to the south, to Sikkim and Nepal, to the sacred retreat and caves, opened his mind and heart," Rab-ten said.

"This is true," Abaka confirmed. "He was moved by what he saw and experienced, even if he would not embrace it for himself. It changed him." Abaka chuckled. "He became light, even jovial at times. I saw compassion for others arise in him. In a way, I think he found a sense of his true nature on that journey. It settled him and gave him a higher purpose in life. Well, in the end it was for that reason he fought to save the Buddha dharma; for others." Looking from Tsogyal to Rab-ten, he chortled. "It was not for himself. He hated the whole idea of meditating in caves!"

Tsogyal and Rab-ten laughed. "He did say it so many times!" Rab-ten confirmed.

"He confided in you?" Tsogyal inquired.

"That trip was when we became brothers," Abaka said softly. "That journey was when I saw the heart of that man. I shall miss him greatly."

Falling silent, they all sipped their tea as the butter lamps sputtered. Images paraded through Abaka's mind of the sky burial of

General Senge's body that had come after the Royal funeral. The large flat area made of rock, on the mountainside. The body wrapped in thin cotton. Dark shadows of the large vultures circling above, passing over all in attendance as the butcher cut through the shoulder, severing the arm. With might, he hurled it away. The large birds swooped down, landing on the meat. Then the other arm was flung aside, then one leg, then the other. Many vultures had arrived, devouring the meat, tearing at the cloth. Then the entrails and organs were scattered before the birds. They lunged and fought, each grabbing a piece in their large beaks, swallowing piece by piece the corporeal form that was once a man. A man with a consciousness, with desires, with capabilities. A man that had strode upon the earth, had fought in many battles, had loved his wife, had sired a daughter, had served his King. Had spoken, laughed and sang. And now in the end, the birds having devoured all, flew away on the wind high into the sky and disappeared.

"Jigme is a good man," Tsogyal said to Rab-ten, bringing Abaka back into the temple, "He has always been kind and good?"

Swallowing her tea, Rab-ten nodded emphatically. "Yes, Jigme in truth hates war and killing. He does his duty." Then with a giggle, Rab-ten added, "He fools everyone because he is tough and stern with his men. If they saw the man I know behind closed doors, they would all be surprised."

Abaka looked up, a smile growing on his face. "Your husband is a great strategist and is very clever. His place in the General's tent planning wars, not on the battlefield."

Then, looking into the past once again, Abaka added, "The field of battle, that was Senge's arena. He was as a gladiator there."

"Mmm," Tsogyal intoned, "well, General Senge has earned a fortunate rebirth, as his last moments were fighting for the dharma, for the safety of the people of Tibet and for his men. All good karma."

"How much longer will you both sit doing this ceremony for him?" Rab-ten inquired.

"We will be guiding his consciousness through the Bardo for five more days. We want to make sure he does not become confused there. This ceremony will help him into his next life," Tsogyal answered.

428

"I will tell the Emperor then," Rab-ten said.

"And the Bonpo prisoners?" Abaka asked.

"They can wait. The Emperor wants you both and Master Padma to be in attendance when determining their fate. They just arrested six more old Bon yesterday, that did not obey the law and go to the borderlands, and have added them to the many now filling the dungeons," Rab-ten informed.

"Fools," Abaka muttered. "They should have just gone north and kept to their promise, now look at their fate. They may all be executed." Shaking his head, he repeated, "Fools."

"Yes," Rab-ten agreed, as she took the empty cups and placed them on the tray, "they have made it much worse for themselves."

Standing, tray in hand, she said, "I will return at dawn with your meal and tea."

Then she left the room as silently as she arrived. Abaka and Tsogyal both pulled their legs into a lotus position, and straightened their backs. Taking up his mala, Abaka concentrated on the mantra. The hum of their recitations filled the room.

70

Seated upon the royal high-cushioned throne, Prince Mune absently tapped his knee with his fingers as he looked at the assembly of Bonpo prisoners before him. His expression was stern. He was angry that these Bonpos had broken the very clear law and now action must be taken. He did not want to see a mass execution. *What a bloody mess*, he thought. Seated next to him, Emperor Trisong was serene.

"Prince Mune," Trisong began, "take my place in this affair. What would you do with these lawbreakers?"

Surprised at his father's request, Mune answered, "Father, you wish me to decide their fate?"

Trisong turned his attention to his son. "Prince Mune, I trust you will find the correct manner of deciding their fate."

Mune took in a breath, this was very unexpected, gripping his knees, as he thought for a moment. Then, addressing Padma, he asked, "Master Padma, as the foremost master of the Buddha dharma, now the official religion of Tibet, what would your advice to me be? Shall they be put to death?" Mune asked.

Padma looked at the group of chained Bonpo men and women kneeling before the high throne of the Emperor, their heads bowed. The stench of their unwashed bodies and their fear wafted over him. He paced before them, considering. His silk robes, red with garudas embroidered in gold thread, made a soft swish, swish, swish, with each sliding step.

"Mmm," he considered. Turning to look up at Prince Mune and Emperor Trisong, he said, "My Prince, these Bonpo have broken their oath to abide by the results of the great debate. Thus they have broken your law. As well, their leaders had conspired to murder innocent Tibetans. In their wretched plan, their leaders had also conspired to remove our Emperor, Trisong, from the throne by murder."

Turning to look over the prisoners before him, he could hear sobs of grief from within the huddle. With a wave of his arm in gesture toward the prisoners, he declared, "However, I see no benefit in the death of these men and women here. Their covens have been laid waste. Their most powerful teachers have brought death upon themselves by their own black magic."

Gazing from face to face now turned up to him in awe and with hope in their eyes, Padma continued, "These Old Bonpo are heathens. My advice is to allow them to abide by their oath now. They must go to the lands of the north. To the lands of Treulachan in Mongolia. If any shall return to Tibet, they shall then be put to death."

Murmurs of relief issued from the throng. Padma held up his hands, silencing them. "As for the reformed Bon, their teachings and texts are in harmony with the Buddha dharma. They shall go to the lands of Zhang Zhung and any border lands they choose and remain there to live and practice in peace."

The room fell silent as Mune considered Padma's advise. Trisong sat in stillness, a slight nod of approval.

"And their texts and teachings?" Muni inquired, "What would you advise be done with these?"

Padma held a finger up as he answered, "All texts and writings shall be sorted out separating the old Bon from the reformed Bon. All texts of the old Bon shall be burned! In this way their evil magic and sorcery shall be erased from knowledge, never to arise again. Those texts of the reformed Bon have no harmful practices. Therefore, they should be allowed to take their texts with them and do what they may with them; so as to be retained for future generations."

Looking up to Mune and Trisong, Padma concluded, "This is my advice, my Prince."

Mune looked at his father's serene face. It struck him, that, in fact, Trisong seemed somewhere else. Having hoped to receive his father's word on the decision before him, Mune realized his father truly had left this matter in his hands. Mune was to decide.

"I agree with you, Master Padma," Mune said, "thus, it shall be done."

Tsogyal, Abaka and Rab-ten watched as the prisoners were taken from the room by the guards. All filed out to the clink and rattle of the many chains. The Buddhist ministers in attendance filed out after the prisoners, to attend to their duties. At last, all fell quiet in the hall, Padma, Tsogyal, Rab-ten and Abaka remained in audience.

Then Trisong stood. Standing, they all bowed before him. Trisong gestured as he said, "Seat yourselves. I have made a decision I wish you to hear," Trisong began. Turning toward Mune, he said, "Son, you have shown me you are intelligent and strong in matters of state."

Turning toward Master Padma, he continued, "Master, I have had a vision of Manjushri. He came to me as a youth of sixteen springs, his skin was clear and white. He held a sword raised in his right hand. Swinging it down upon me, he has severed all delusion."

Padma's eyes widened a bit, then he nodded in approval. "It occurred at the contest," Padma said, more as a statement than a question.

Trisong nodded. "Yes, Master, it was very powerful. And I have had other visions since that day, when in practice. Therefore," Trisong said to all in the room, "I am handing my throne to Prince Mune. He shall be Emperor now. I will declare this formally on the morrow before all the ministers and it is to be sent by messenger to all the Kingdoms."

Tsogyal and Rab-ten looked at each other in surprise. Abaka caught Padma's eye, a smile growing on his face.

With alarm, Mune slid down from his cushion. "Father, no!" he said. "You are Emperor, you are still young and strong. What will you do, if not be our Emperor?"

Trisong took his son by the shoulders, he felt their strength under his hands. "My son, I wish to achieve enlightenment in this life. I have now had very good signs that it is possible for me. I must go away, far into the mountains, into solitary retreat. This is the only way for me to deepen my practice and realization. I have no doubt, I leave Tibet in strong and capable hands in you, Mune."

Mune sank, his knees feeling weak. He looked down at the small assembly. Realizing he could not change his father's mind, he raised himself up. Squaring his shoulders, he turned to his father, declaring, "If this is your wish, Father, then I shall obey. You can be assured, I will take the throne and rule as you would."

Trisong chuckled. "My son, you have a good mind and a noble heart. Therefore, it is my wish that you rule as you will; I trust in that more."

Trisong turned, speaking to Padma, "Master, will you join me in my chambers?"

All rose and bowed, watching Trisong disappear through the doorway, Padma right behind him.

Mune turned to his audience, a torrent of thoughts spinning in his mind. His heart was pounding in his chest at what responsibility had been lain in his hands. Then, his eyes met Tsogyal's. Suddenly, his thoughts stilled. His mind became clear. His heart slowed to a steady beat. He felt a calm bliss come over him. His course of action became very simple, his confidence in himself was strong. Amazed at the experience that just washed over him, a questioning look formed on his face.

"This is what my father follows?" he asked Tsogyal.

"Emperor Mune," she began, "it is what inspired him to seek a deeper path. In the beginning, just being able to still the mind is very helpful in all matters."

Mune considered. The clarity he was experiencing was full and rich. He noticed thoughts were trickling back, then they began to flood his mind again. Try as he may to grasp for the clarity now receding from him, it eluded him, like grasping at a ray of sunlight.

To Tsogyal, Mune asked, "Will you teach me, Noble Yogini?"

With a nod, Tsogyal answered, "Yes, Emperor, I will teach you."

71

MANY SPRINGS LATER

Mist hung low over the sharp craggy outcropping as Tsogyal clung to the hard cold rock under her wool-wrapped fingers, making her way around the ledge. This was a very narrow section of the route that wound up and around the rock formations of this very secret place. The strap of the bag she carried dug into the muscle between her neck and shoulder, yet she took no heed of the discomfort, it had been there all day. Looking to her destination, now not far, she saw the tall figure standing there, his zhuba waving in the wind. A smile parted his long white mustache and beard as he called out, "We have arrived! Only a few more steps."

Dropping her bag at Padma's feet when she reached his side, Tsogyal gazed out at the whiteness. Every now and then the clouds separated to reveal a breathtaking view below them of the empty pristine land they had traveled to get here. Looking out, they could see the mountains in the distance all covered in snow and sometimes obscured by the mist around them.

"We will hide many termas, texts to be saved for future generations, here," Padma said, with a nod toward the dark cave entrance below them in a ravine.

"These are the last ones. We have completed our task," Tsogyal confirmed.

Looking into Tsogyal's eyes, Padma nodded solemnly. "We will remain here for twenty-one days. I will give you your last instructions and practices. After that, it will be from this place I will take leave of this life and leave the teachings in your hands. You will continue the lineage. When your time comes to leave, you must pass the lineage on to a disciple of superior accomplishment. You may leave this life only when you have found such a vessel to pour the teachings into. One who can continue the lineage when you are gone." Looking down to the dark doorway of the cave below them, Padma continued, "This is why we leave these treasures, these teachings. When there are breaks in the lineage, these texts will be found to continue the teachings, so the dharma will never die out."

Tsogyal swallowed the lump that formed in her throat. "Yes, Master. I am fortunate to be witness. To be here to be with you these last days," she said softly.

"Very well, let us complete our task. But first, let us rest," Padma said as he turned and began climbing down the rocks to the cave. Looking up at Tsogyal, he enthused, "We shall make tea."

Tsogyal picked up her cup of tea and sipped, then she looked at all the faces of the group of nuns seated before her. All sat transfixed, intent on her words as she told them the story of her last days with Padma, the hiding of the terma teachings, his last instructions to her and his manner of leaving this world.

This was an often told story here in the nunnery Tsogyal had built at Zhoto Tidro. Though many springs had passed since the event of Padma's leaving, she felt it was just a short time ago as she now told of it for perhaps the hundredth time. She loved remembering that day and telling of it, to inspire faith in her many devotees and disciples, those that flocked to her after Trisong went into retreat, Mune took the throne, and Padma left the world, leaving the lineage to her.

"We had been traveling for many moons to many places hiding

termas," Tsogyal continued, setting her cup down. "Padma subjugated evil forces and blessed many places too, so they would be power spots for practitioners to advance in their practice. Finally, we arrived at our last destination, the cave of Tsasho. There we hid the last terma texts, thus completing the hiding of all the terma. Padma gave me final instruction on Dzogchen. He gave me the highest teachings, of which I was then capable of understanding and practicing. We practiced together. Then, on the final morning of our stay," Tsogyal recounted, growing solemn as the memory filled her, "the time for his leaving had come. Bidding me farewell, he stepped up upon a boulder that jutted out from the cliffside. Below it, the mountainside fell away into space. I stood watching him. Sadness overwhelmed me. I simply could not believe he was really leaving this world. That I would never be with him again." Tsogyal looked from one face to the next. "I threw myself onto the boulder, grabbing his feet. Crying out, I pleaded, 'Master, please stay. I cannot bear for you to go.' Stooping down, he raised me to my knees. I was sobbing. 'Tsogyal,' he said softly, 'you must release me now.' I was kneeling before him, my legs too weak to hold me up," Tsogyal said, looking from the faces of the nuns seated before her to her disciples seated at the side of her audience. "Gently, he urged me back away from the rock. I stepped backward off the rock, away from him. I stood before him, looking up at him, sobbing. Then, to my amazement, his body began to glow, the light coming from within. It grew stronger and stronger. The shock of what was happening dried my tears. I shielded my eyes, trying to gaze upon his form for as long as I was able. His light radiated out into the sky above. He looked at me, smiling, and said, 'You have done well this life, My Lady. You will achieve your goal.' Mantras and music came from the ether above. Then to my amazement, dakinis appeared, and Buddhas. Many dakinis and Buddhas. Padma's body was completely light now. It shrunk from the form of a man into a glowing ball of light, only the size of my fist. It floated to the center of the retinue of dakinis and Buddhas. Then, it rose up, with them as escort, high into the sky. In an instant it all disappeared. I was alone. Shocked by the sudden disappearance, I began sobbing again, I called out Padma's name, over and over again. Feeling so alone, I prayed, 'Oh, venerable Padma, father and protector of Tibet. Now you have gone. Tibet is empty without you. What will become of Tibet?' A ball of light appeared in the sky and illuminated the northwest. I knew, somehow, that all of Tibet was engulfed in that light. Then the light that had engulfed Tibet became concentrated into a small ball of light and shot into the southwest, where Padma had gone. His voice came out of the ether all around me, saying, 'Queen of Wisdom, you now will achieve the happiness of all beings of Tibet. You will travel and teach the dharma. Many will follow you. After many springs, you will find a disciple who will carry the teachings forward. Then you will join me here on the Copper Colored Mountain. Forever your emanations will be reborn in Tibet to keep the dharma fresh and alive. Tsogyal, you and I will never be parted. But on the relative plane I say farewell, until we are joined forever. My compassion will never be taken from Tibet. All who call upon me will be answered.' Looking into the faces of each woman seated before her, Tsogyal ended with, "I felt full then, the pain of his departure ceased. I feel the Guru within me always," looking over the small assembly of nuns. Then to the side where her eleven disciples and Atsara were sitting, Tsogyal asked, "Have you any questions?"

A young nun seated before her glanced from side to side, then, seeing no one was speaking, said, "I have a question, Mistress Tsogyal."

Tsogyal nodded for her to proceed.

Clearing her throat, the young woman asked, "I have heard it said that you wrote down all of Master Padma's teachings. That it was you who wrote the terma. Is this true?"

Tsogyal smiled at the young nun, saying, "This is true. I began recording Master Padma's teachings, as his scribe, since the time I was Queen of Tibet. Almost from the first day that I met my Guru. Emperor Trisong made sure my writings were kept safely hidden away."

"And now?" the young nun asked. "Precious One, who scribes your teachings?"

"I do," Tsogyal answered. "As well, I have a scribe in each of my nunneries and my learning centers to copy my writings. I have hidden many terma that I have written, to be found by terma-finders in future generations."

The nearby stream, tumbling over rocks and boulders, hummed as all sat silently contemplating Tsogyal's words under a blue sky. White clouds gathered at the tops of the tallest peaks that surrounded Zhoto Tidro.

Tsogyal gazed over all in attendance. Raising her voice, she began, breaking the silence, "As you all know, I have been traveling and teaching since the day Padma left this life. Many springs have passed. I have created several nunneries and centers of learning. I have many nuns, scholars and eleven disciples to carry the teachings forth into the future." Tsogyal looked at all the faces rapt in attention on her. "I wish word to be sent out by messenger to all of my nunneries, to Chimpu and to Samye, that all practitioners who are able are to assemble at the Heart Cave on Zapu Mountain on the eighth day of the bird moon. There, they will be witness to a profound spectacle."

72

The soft grinding of stone on stone was the only sound in the room. Golden rays of sunlight shone through the window. The strong scent of herbs rose from the grinding stone as Rab-ten toiled at her work.

"Mother?"

Rab-ten turned from her mortar and pestle to the voice at the doorway.

"Oh!" Rab-ten said in awe as she gazed upon Nam-kha who stepped into the room. She walked up to him, reaching out to touch the metal armor covering his strong form. "Oh, my son, you look magnificent," she enthused. She ran her fingers over the many overlapping thin metal plates. "This armor is like the scales of a dragon," she said.

"Indeed, it is." Jigme's voice came from behind Nam-kha. "And it is as strong," he said, entering the room. His gaze fell upon Rab-ten. He marveled at how the sight of her always stirred him. Even now, with her hair streaked with white, her face lined, she was beautiful. His heart felt tight at the thought that he must leave her for so long. For he and Nam-kha must go with the Emperor's army, west to the Sogdian capital of Samarkland, a city on the great silk road. There the army would join with the Qarluq Turks to assist the rebels in Samarkland against the

Arab Caliphate, who sought control of the city. If the Muhammadans succeeded in taking the city, they would seek more cities on the route.

Turning his attention to Nam-kha, Jigme placed a hand on his shoulder and took stock of his son's armor. Releasing his hold on his son, Jigme asked, "Can you move easily, son?"

Nam-kha raised his arms and twisted at his waist. "Yes, father, it is a skin of iron."

"The Persian armorer does fine work," Jigme said nodding in approval. "It will do very well."

Nam-kha turned to Rab-ten. With a slight bow, he said, "Mother, I have come to say farewell."

Looking up into his eyes, Rab-ten took his head in both hands and gently pulled it toward her. Nam-kha bent his head to touch his forehead to his mother's forehead. Closing her eyes, Rab-ten said, "My son, you make me very proud. You will be in my thoughts. Fight well and come back to me."

Raising his head, his throat tight, Nam-kha could only nod.

"Son, go check on the horses, I would like a moment to speak with your mother," Jigme said.

With a last gaze to his mother, Nam-kha turned and was gone. Looking up at her husband, Rab-ten choked back the tears pressing behind her eyes. "Husband?"

Jigme pulled Rab-ten close to him and held her tight. Releasing her, he placed his hands on her shoulders and looked down into her eyes. "Do not worry for your son, he is a trained warrior, a skilled fighter. I have trained him and he has learned his lessons well. He will not fail on the battlefield."

Rab-ten nodded, tears now falling.

Gently brushing the tears from her cheeks, Jigme assured, "And I will be overlooking the battle from the observation place. It is unlikely I will be called on to fight. Those Arabs are no match for our forces and our allies. As well, Emperor Ral-pa-can has supplied us well. Our new Emperor is young, yet he understands the need for strength," Jigme added.

Rab-ten nodded, unable to speak.

Jigme pulled her close, his passion rising. He assured, "Wife, we will return."

Rab-ten listened to his footfalls fade away from her. Heavy of heart, she returned to her herbs. The smells of the room once pleasant now sickened her as she tried to push away the fear of never seeing her husband or son again. Unable to work, she sank into a cushion. *Our new Emperor Ral-pa-can,* she mused. *There have been two now since Mune's murder.*

She sighed. "Poisoned by his own mother, Queen Tse-pongza," she whispered to herself. "He sat upon the throne for less than two springs. That Queen was such a spiteful jealous woman. To be sure, jealous that Trisong had Mune marry his beautiful youngest Queen. Jealous of her son's wife and so she murders him!" Rab-ten was still incredulous after all these springs. "How is it possible for a mother to murder her own son! Oh, it is so evil." She shook her head, dispelling the painful memories of the past. The trill of a bird filled the silence of the room. She raised her head, listening, feeling the joy of its song fill her.

"Mune was a good man," Rab-ten said to herself. With a chuckle, she thought, *I remember the uproar when he tried to take the wealth owned by the Nobles and distribute it to the farmers and poor people. It was an honorable idea...* Shaking her head slowly, she said softly to herself, "Perhaps there were others who also wanted him gone from power and so encouraged his mother in her evil deed."

Pondering the motes of herb dust swirling in the sunlit room; more memories returned to her. After Mune's murder, since he had no son, his younger brother, Sad-ne-legs, took the throne. Sad-ne-legs was a good Emperor, Rab-ten had thought during his reign. He had firm command of the government and he had a magnanimous heart in all matters. He was faithful to the dharma as he had received instruction by Master Padma when he was a young boy. Sad-ne-legs had given high government appointments to some of his Buddhist teachers. For Rab-ten, this mattered greatly as she knew there were Nobles who were still Bonpo. These men were waiting for an Emperor they could influence, to attain power in an effort to take down Buddhism and reassert Bonpo power. Now, Sad-ne-legs was dead and his son of twelve springs, Ral-pa-kan, is Emperor.

So much death, she thought, looking at the empty doorway her husband and son had passed through. She prayed softly, "Please let them live to return. I know life is impermanent, but I want to see them again." Holding back tears, Rab-ten rose from her cushion to go back to her grinding stone.

"Noble healer?" A voice from the doorway startled her. There a messenger stood.

Rab-ten turned to the man. "Yes?" she inquired.

"Noble healer, I have a message from the great yogini Tsogyal," he said. "All are to meet at Zapu Mountain. She sent me to tell you that you must come."

73

Rab-ten marveled as she walked along the path at the base of Zapu Mountain. There were so many people. Tantric Buddhist practitioners were reciting mantras all around her as she looked on. Standing at the edge of the throng, she strained to see over the heads to find the cause of a wave of movement inside. Then the crowd parted before her and there was Tsogyal. The crowd was gathered around her. Stopping before each, she offered them the cup she held in her hand. As they sipped from it, she broke off a morsel of a brown substance she held in her other hand. As the person returned the cup, she gave them the broken-off morsel to eat.

"It is beyond explanation!" the man standing next to Rab-ten said, as he shook his head.

Rab-ten looked at him. His hair was long and braided, his mustache framed a mouth open in wonder.

"What is?" Rab-ten asked.

Gesturing toward Tsogyal in the large crowd, he answered, "Our Lady, Yeshe Tsogyal, has a morsel of molasses in her hand and a cup of chang beer. All those people have drunk from same cup, yet she does not refill it. And all receive a piece from that chunk of molasses she holds, yet it never shrinks."

Rab-ten stared at him, incredulous. "That is not possible," she said.

"Sister!"

Rab-ten stepped back, surprised that Tsogyal was standing before her.

"Oh, Sister, you startled me," Rab-ten gasped, holding her hand to still her leaping heart.

Tsogyal giggled. "Oh, my dear, I am sorry."

"No... no, my Sister, it is well, I am fine," Rab-ten said with a gasp.

She took in Tsogyal's form. Her long hair, streaked white and gray, draped over her shoulders. Rab-ten noticed a small turquoise stone woven in a single narrow long braid on the left side of her head. Looking down at Tsogyal's hands, she saw the cup full of chang and the morsel of molasses.

Tsogyal lifted the cup to Rab-ten. "Here take a drink from this, Sister."

Drinking the tart liquid Rab-ten felt a wave of calm come over her. As she held the cup, she watched Tsogyal break off a piece of molasses which she offered to Rab-ten. Taking the morsel, Rab-ten returned the cup, whose contents she saw had not diminished. She looked at the morsel in Tsogyal's hand. It had not shrunk in size, though the piece in Rab-ten's hand was easily half its size. Placing it in her mouth, she let it melt, tasting the earthy sweetness. Filling her, like a wave of warm liquid, was a sensation that she could only characterize as the greatest feeling of satisfaction she had never known.

Looking into Tsogyal's eyes, Rab-ten's expression asked the question for her.

Tsogyal smiled. "Sister, I will explain later," she assured her. "I will see you at the gathering when the sun is setting." Then she moved on. Rab-ten watched as Tsogyal gave each person a drink from the cup and a morsel of molasses. Her eleven principal disciples followed solemnly behind her.

The many fires flickered in the waning light as Rab-ten looked at the last of the day's glow dim behind the distant mountains.

"Lady Rab-ten?" came a voice from behind her.

Turning, she looked up at the tall man, his beard long and streaked with grey. A smile formed on his face.

"Abaka?" Rab-ten asked, as she took in his once very familiar form. Yet now older. "Abaka," she said now with confidence. Stepping toward him, she took his hand in hers. Looking up into his leathery and lined face, she said, "Abaka, it has been so long. Where have you been these many springs?"

Gesturing for them to walk, Abaka began. "I have been in retreat for the past three springs." Walking alongside him, Rab-ten listened in rapt attention as he told her of his many springs with Tsogyal receiving her teachings. His extended stays in solitary retreat. His many springs traveling and teaching others, and, as well, what he had learned by his experience on the meditation cushion.

When he finished his story, Rab-ten looked at him in awe. "You have been very busy, my friend."

Abaka chuckled. "Yes, indeed. And how are your husband and son? Is your practice progressing?"

Arriving at the place she had set out her rugs to sit on, she sat down on one, inviting Abaka to sit with her.

"They are well," she said, gazing into the distance. "Yet, I pray they will remain so."

Abaka nodded knowingly. "Ah, so they are off to another battle for Tibet."

Rab-ten looked into Abaka's eyes, the kindness there made her feel safe. "I practice everyday, though in truth I know not what progress I make."

"You can never know really, until you arrive at the higher places, then you begin to be a watcher with understanding," Abaka assured her. "Yet I can see, you have progressed. Keep your practice alive, my sister. That is most important, do not look for achievement, just practice with diligence."

Wanting to change the subject, Rab-ten asked. "Why has Tsogyal asked all to come here?"

Abaka's face lighted with surprise. "You do not know?"

Rab-ten shook her head. "I was summoned by Tsogyal, yet I have only seen her for a moment. She has not told me."

Abaka glanced around and Rab-ten followed his gaze.

Noticing that all had fallen silent, they turned their attention up to the base of Zapu Mountain as Tsogyal walked out and stood on a flat-topped boulder. On either side of her, a short distance away, stood two of her disciples. Tashi Chidren who had been with Tsogyal for many springs after meeting her in Bhutan when she was a young girl. And Kalasiddhi, a woman from Nepal. The remaining disciples sat cross-legged below the boulder, looking up at her form.

Two large fires illuminated her as she spoke. Her voice carried clearly over the throng, all could easily hear her words.

"Practitioners of the Buddha dharma, the Tantra, yogis and yoginis, nuns, monks and friends," Tsogyal began with her hands held out. "I have spent many days now giving each of you individual instruction and your last teachings. I have answered all of your questions and I have given prophesies of the future. I have given you each all you need. Now, my time has come to leave this life and join Master Padma. You need not beg me to stay, as I will not heed your requests."

Rab-ten shot a look at at Abaka in shock. He looked back at her, nodding solemnly.

"Knowing Buddha's teachings to be the way to positive, personal evolution, you must strive to apply to your lives the instruction on the Ten Virtues," Tsogyal's words rang out. "Understand that your many forms of behavior, these negative karmas, are leading you eventually to hell. To keep from drifting toward this end, fasten your body and speech to virtue, to purify the Lower Realms."

Tsogyal stopped, looking at the faces turned up to her. "Integrating the body, speech and mind, you must travel the path of virtue. If you desire to attain Buddha-hood, you must purify your mind, composing yourself in Mahamudra. When Emptiness and Awareness are set free, you are a Buddha," she declared.

Gesturing with her hand from her head to her feet, she said,

"This body is the seat of all good and bad. If you wish to obtain rainbow body, dissolve corporeality, absorb yourself in the continuous peak experience of Dzokchen Ati. When you arrive at the extinction of reality, there is nothing but the spontaneity of pure potential. There is no other way to dance in the sky. With conviction, practice Dzokchen and enter the place where Ati ends."

Tsogyal's gaze traveled over the crowd until she met Rab-ten's eyes, now filled with tears. Looking at Rab-ten, yet speaking to all in the crowd, Tsogyal continued. "Practice diligently. When your split minds are whole, then you and I will be reunited as one," she assured.

Raising her hands high, gesturing toward the mountaintop, Tsogyal called out, "I will now go up to my cave at the top of this peak. When I have left this world, the sign will be clear. At that time, you may go to retrieve what remains of my corporeal form. Even when my body is gone, know that I am never separate from you. All who call upon me shall be answered. May good fortune and happiness be everywhere!"

Rab-ten felt a pang of longing watching as Tsogyal leaned over to whisper into Tashi Chidren's ear. The intimacy of their many springs together was clear in the easy way they interacted. A wave of sorrow washed over Rab-ten at the feeling of loss. She had been Tsogyal's closest friend since so long ago. Yet she chose to have a husband and son, she could not follow Tsogyal these many seasons past. Surrounded by a crowd of people, Rab-ten felt separate and alone. The pain of the loss of her friend seared her heart.

The crowd was calling out to Tsogyal, begging her to stay and not leave this life. Many sat sobbing, some chanted.

Rab-ten suddenly realized, *Tsogyal is leaving! Yet she has not spoken to me as she promised. Has she forgotten me?* Tears welled in her eyes, she wiped at them with her sleeve, not wanting Abaka to see her pain.

"Noble Lady?" Rab-ten looked up with surprise to see Tashi Chidren standing before her. With a bow, she continued, "The Buddha Yeshe Tsogyal wishes you to come with me." Looking at Abaka, she added, "Abaka, you may accompany us."

Moments later, Rab-ten's hands were being held in Tsogyal's.

The love in Tsogyal's eyes melted away the pain in Rab-ten's heart.

"My spiritual sister," Tsogyal began. "Many springs ago you helped me. You took a great risk, you risked your very life defying Prince Zhonnu, setting me free from his grasp." Firming her grip on Rab-ten's hands, Tsogyal said, "Now I am going to that place I told you of in those days, so long ago."

Tears streaming down her face, Rab-ten choked, "Sister, I shall miss you greatly."

Tsogyal smiled. "This has been a great life." Looking up at Abaka, she said, "We have had a great adventure, haven't we?"

Abaka smiled through the tears now wet on his face. "Yes indeed, we have had a fortunate life. A wonderful adventure."

"I am going to Nirvana now," Tsogyal said, releasing Rab-ten's hands. "In two lives hence, you will join me, sister," she declared to Rab-ten.

Then she turned and was swallowed in the embrace of her disciples who escorted her up the steep winding path to the cave at the top of Zapu Mountain.

74

"Om, ah, hung," Rab-ten chanted the end of the long mantra she had been given by Tsogyal. The visualization she held in her mind, of herself as the Deity, faded as she opened her eyes. She laid the string of sandalwood mala beads in her lap, then raised her arms up, stretching her back. She felt a soft crack release in her spine. Staring at the butter lamp before her, Rab-ten listened to the sounds of people outside her large felt tent who were walking by in a soft conversation.

Rising from her cushion, she threw the tent flap open and stepped out into the cold morning air. The scents of dung smoke, horses and people filled her nostrils. Looking to the mountains beyond, the light of the sun's imminent rise glowed behind them. Stooping, she stirred the coals in her small fire pit, gratified to see the soft orange glow still alive beneath the ashes. Placing small tuffs of grass and broken sticks she had brought with her onto the hot coals, the fire rose anew. Then, she carefully set pieces of dried dung on the tiny flames. She sat back on her small carpet and poured water from the water-skin into a pot. As she broke a piece off the brick of tea, she mused, *How much longer?*

"Good morn, Lady Rab-ten."

Rab-ten looked up up to see Abaka standing a short distance away, calling a greeting to her.

Smiling, Rab-ten waved. "Abaka, come sit and have tea."

Moments later, they sat companionably, sipping tea and eating balls of tsampa.

"How much longer do you think? Until we will see a sign," Rab-ten asked.

"I am not sure," Abaka said. "Yet, Master Richen Chok told me he feels it will be soon now. It has been almost seven days since she entered her hermitage."

Rab-ten nodded, considering. "Two days ago I saw one of Emperor Trisong's former Queens here, Li-za Dronma," she said. "I had heard she became one of Tsogyal's disciples when Emperor Trisong went into retreat, so many springss ago."

Abaka set down his cup and folded his hands in his lap. "Chudak is in retreat now," he reported.

Rab-ten swallowed a sip of tea. "Really? He is a practitioner?" she asked in surprise. "I had wondered what became of him. I had not seen him for many seasons now."

"Yes," Abaka said, "he is a lay practitioner. He left the service of the King, when King Pelgyi died. The death of Senge, then Pelgyi, moved him to consider what is important in life, to consider that all is impermanent. He went to Tsogyal and received teachings that allow him to be with his family most of the season, then take retreats for deepening his practice."

"Why is he not here?" Rab-ten inquired.

"I can only guess that Tsogyal gave him teachings and suggested he not break his retreat to be here," Abaka answered.

Suddenly, Abaka felt a chill up his spine. He looked up at Zapu Peak. "Lady, I think we should go now to the base of the peak, I have a feeling something is about to happen."

All the gathered people sat or stood looking up at the rainbows forming in the clear cloudless sky above the tip of the peak. Murmurs of this impossibility rose from those, perhaps one hundred in number, in attendance.

"Look!" a shout came from someone watching the peak.

Gasps of shock and wonder rose from the crowd as the sight of a ball of bright light shot from the top of the peak, where Tsogyal's hermitage was, straight up into the sky, like a shooting star yet from earth into the heavens.

"She has gone," a cry rang out from within the gathering. "The Buddha Yeshe Tsogyal has left us. The world is doomed to darkness."

Just then the sun's rays broke over the mountains, sharp rays of light bathing all. Out of the bright light of the sun's rays, a form appeared. She wore flowing robes of light, her hair was silver and long, flowing over her shoulders and down her back. Her eyes were piecing, the rays penetrating into the hearts of everyone there. Her voice, soft and soothing, from the ether, could be heard by all. "Practice the Buddha dharma. Call on me, Yeshe Tsogyal and I will answer. We are, in truth, never parted. Remember my teachings. Practice and realize your true Buddha nature. We will be rejoined. My love for you will never cease. I will send emanations of my true self to be reborn in future lives. Remember, that for all time, my love of the people of Tibet will never cease. And any, in all the world, who call my name in sincere desire for enlightenment, will be answered."

Then the form dissolved into the light of the sun's rays and was gone.

People shouted and cried out. Some were staggering in disbelief and awe at the sight they had just witnessed. Some fell to their knees in prayer and meditation. Some threw themselves onto the ground and wept.

Rab-ten found herself on her knees, not remembering sinking to them. She felt unbearable love in her heart. Looking to where Tsogyal's apparition had been, she could not believe it had really happened, yet it had. Looking to where Abaka had been standing, she saw him sitting on the hard rocky ground, cross-legged in deep meditation.

"Come, we must go to the hermitage," a voice called out.

Rab-ten tried to rise to her feet, feeling disorientated. Just then a strong hand grasped her arm. She looked up into Abaka's serene face.

"Come, Lady, I will help you. We must go to the peak," he said.

Rab-ten approached the opening of Tsogyal's cave, now guarded by Tsogyal's disciples. One of the guards held out his hand to stop her. "Only two may enter at one time, you must wait," he declared.

He looked familiar to Rab-ten. "What is your name, sir?" she inquired.

He looked down at her, then at Abaka, recognition glowing on his face, he said, "Lady Rab-ten! It is I, Atsara Sale."

Recognizing him, Rab-ten clasped his hand. "Oh, Atsara, you are here. This is very good."

Just then two men exited the cave. Atsara gestured for Rab-ten and Abaka to follow him. Giving orders to make way, he lead Rab-ten and Abaka inside.

Ducking their heads, they entered the small cave. The light of butter lamps flickered on the canted rock walls. The scents of sandalwood incense and damp stone was thick in the air. Atsara stepped back against the wall and gestured to the cushion. There Rab-ten saw a mass of gray streaked hair flowing over a heap of robe. The twinkle of turquoise stone winked up at her in the braid that lay intwined. The robe was stiff with a red dried paste that was also dusted around the cushion. Scattered in front of the cushion on the floor were ten fingernails. Rab-ten stepped back in shock, noticing a set of teeth laying at the hem of the robe. She looked at Atsara, a mixture of question and disbelief.

"She attained rainbow body," he said simply. "This is all that remains."

With a quizzical look on his face, he bent to his knees and pointed to an object partially seen from under a fold of robe. "We do not know what this is, though."

Abaka knelt, spying the object, and asked, "May I retrieve it?"

Atsara nodded. "Yes, you may inspect it."

Abaka carefully edged the object from between the folds. Holding it carefully in his hand, he stood, gently smoothing the black lock of hair. The gold thread binding at the one end glistened in the lamp light. A tear began at his eye as he looked up at Rab-ten.

Rab-ten bent, looking down at the object. Shaking her head slowly, she whispered, "It is Lungta's mane." Looking at Atsara, she added, "Chudak gave it to her many springs past."

Abaka nodded. "Yes, it is."

In wonder, Atsara murmured, "She kept it in her robe, always."

Kneeling before the remains of the Buddha Tsogyal, Abaka gently placed Lungta's mane on top of a fold of robe.

"What will become of these?" Rab-ten asked, gesturing to the heap of robe, hair, fingernails, toenails and teeth.

"All these remains will be taken to Emperor Ral-pa-can. He will want an account of what happened here. These sacred relics will be distributed to the holy monasteries," Atsara said.

Rab-ten looked at Abaka, feeling his gaze on her. She looked down, shaking her head slowly, choking back her tears. "She was a Buddha. Now, only her teachings, her memory and these remain."

"Let us meditate now," Atsara said. "We are very fortunate to have shared this life with her. That is something to remember."

Rab-ten wiped at her eyes, nodding. They all sank down on the cold rock floor. Crossing their legs, they felt peace and love fill their hearts. Then all three fell deeply into bliss.

75

MANY SPRINGS LATER

Sengemo stumbled, her foot stepping on a loose stone on the rocky path. Reaching out, she grabbed the hard cold stone of the rockface to stop her from falling.

Jampo turned to look down at her from the path above, concern on his face. Sengemo smiled, waving that she was not hurt.

"It is perhaps a half a day more to reach the cave," Nam-kha said, coming up behind her, adjusting his heavy bag on his shoulder as his eyes searched the mountain above them.

Following his gaze, she craned her neck, looking up.

"Do you see it?" she asked.

Nam-kha shook his head. "No, not from here."

Sengemo pulled on the strap of the bag that hung across her back, taking the weight off the soft muscle on her shoulder. She sighed at the moment of relief, then letting it settle back into its place, she resumed her climbing up the steep path. Nam-kha followed behind her.

"You are sure you know how to find the old Master's cave?" she asked, gasping with the heavy breathing of the climb.

"Jampo knows, his father told him many springs ago, how to find it," Nam-kha assured her.

She pulled herself up over boulders that blocked this part of the path. Reaching the top, she stood on the narrow flat path looking down at Nam-kha as he made his way up, following her.

When he reached her, she asked him, "How does he get food up here?"

Gasping to catch his breath and pointing in the direction of the village they had passed through two days before, he answered, "A disciple brings him food every moon. He does not need to eat much." Gesturing up toward the mountain, he added, "I suspect there is a stream nearby the cave, that will be one way of finding it."

Shaking her head as she continued up the path, Sengemo said, "Up here all these seasons, alone? He must be enlightened."

Nam-kha said, solemnly, "He is said to be, yet not many know of him as he has been in seclusion for so long. Jampo's father claimed he is. My mother knew him, many springs past, before he went into seclusion."

They looked up to see Jampo waiting for them at a level place. Sitting on the ground, he was drinking water from a water-skin. Reaching him, they let their bags thump to the ground and sat, pulling water and tsampa from them.

"We will rest for awhile here," Jampo said. "I think we can make it before nightfall."

Hours later, Sengemo looked out at the reds and oranges of the sun's last rays playing on the clouds, becoming lost in the display, as Jampo called out to the opening in the rocks above them.

"Greetings, Master, we have come to ask for your teachings," his voice rang out.

Jampo and Nam-kha stood staring at the black opening in the rocky cliffside, waiting for a reply. Only the whistling of the wind swirling around them answered their call.

Nam-kha looked at Jampo. "Do you think he is in there?" he asked.

Jampo pressed his lips, thinking. "Wait here," he ordered.

Climbing up to the cave entrance, Jampo crouched just outside.

"Master?" he called into the cavern. "We have come to ask for your teachings. You knew my father, he told me of you."

Suddenly, a figure appeared at the doorway. Jampo scurried back, startled at the sudden appearance of the man. Looking up in awe at the man standing before him, Jampo had a moment of dread, wondering if he really wanted to meet this old warrior he had heard so much about. The old warrior's long white hair draped over his shoulders and down his back. His white beard flowed to the belt tied around his worn sheepskin zhuba. His bare feet were planted solidly on the ground as his stern gaze seared Jampo, who was clinging to the rocks looking up at him in terror. Then the old warrior noticed Nam-kha and Sengemo below.

His stern face relaxed. "I recognize you," he said, his voice resonant and strong. "Enter," he commanded, turning back into the cave.

Jampo remained frozen, as the meaning of the old warrior's words sunk in. Wildly, he waved his arm for Nam-kha and Sengemo to come. They scurried up the rocks, excitement coursing through them.

Gathering together at the doorway, Jampo whispered, "Are you ready?"

Sengemo and Nam-kha nodded, wonder and dread swirling through them, like the wind gusting up the mountainside, as they entered the cavern behind Jampo.

The dank damp smell of rock and earth mingled with the soft scents of butter lamps, wood smoke and tea on the fire in the small pit at one side of the cave. A natural draft, coming from deep inside the mountain, blew the smoke out the cave entrance, so the air inside the small irregularly-shaped room was not smokey.

Seated on a worn cushion, the old hermit's eyes twinkled from his wizened face as he watched the threesome seat themselves before him. He took a deep breath at the recognition of their youth, the contrast to his age was stark.

The old warrior Abaka smiled to himself as he gazed at these young people. He could clearly recognize his old friend Senge in

Sengemo's features. The determination in her expression reminded him of the General. He could see the essence of the healer in Rab-ten's son, Nam-kha. Abaka chuckled at the spitting image of Chudak, in his son Jampo, seated before him now.

"You wish teachings?" Abaka asked. "Who is your teacher now?"

"Nam-kha and I have studied with the principal disciple of Master Richen Chok and with the old yogini Kalasiddhi in Chimpu. My father, Chudak, trained us all in meditation" Jampo answered. "He died three seasons ago," he added.

Nam-kha leaned forward anxiously, saying, "My mother's last words to me, when she was on her deathbed, just days after my father died, was her plea that I save the dharma. She pleaded that I find you and receive teachings from you and keep the teachings safe, because the Buddha dharma is once again under persecution. All is in disorder in Tibet."

"Is not the Emperor supportive of the Buddha dharma?" Abaka queried.

Nam-kha shook his head. "Emperor Ral-pa-can has been assassinated."

Abaka's eyes grew wide. "By Bonpos?"

"They say he slipped on the steps of the temple, yet all know it was murder," Nam-kha explained. "Some of the Nobles, of the clans rebellious of the Buddha dharma, and reformed Bon have always been uneasy with the influence the Buddha dharma has had on all of Tibet. They feel our cultural heritage is being inexorably altered. These Nobles and those in their service turned a blind eye when some of the old Bonpo religion, defying the law, began to return to Tibet and mix with the reformed Bon."

Sengemo chimed in, "They set out to discredit Ral-pa-can by spreading rumors that his Queen, Nang-shul, and a monk named Yon-tan, were... well you know," she said, blushing, "Yong-tan was assassinated and the Queen committed suicide!" Sengemo looked down shaking her head. "It is such evil."

"So now," Jampo said, "These Bonpos and Nobles have backed

Ral-pa-can's brother Lang-dharma. He is now Emperor of Tibet and they have influence over him."

"They have already begun their persecution. One by one Buddhist monasteries and translation centers are being closed. Monks have been required to return to lay life. Some of these monks are being forced to become butchers and hunters. causing them to go against their code of never taking a life," Nam-kha growled. "Already two Buddhist Masters I have heard of have been killed."

"And the statue of Sakyyamuni Buddha, brought to Tibet over two hundred springs ago by Sonsten Gampo's Chinese wife, has been hauled out the great temple and buried," Sengemo said.

Abaka frowned, declaring, "Padma prophesied this. That the dharma would once again be under attack. That is why he and Tsogyal hid many teachings."

Jampo nodded, imploring, "So you see, Master, that is why we have come to you. You are one of the last living who knew the Buddha Yeshe Tsogyal and you received the teachings directly from Padma and Tsogyal."

Looking at Sengemo, Abaka asked, "My Lady, how much teaching have you received and practice have you done?"

"My uncle, Chudak, told me many stories about my father, Senge." Looking up at Abaka, her eyes brightened. "He said you and my father were like brothers."

Abaka nodded. "Yes, we were," he said simply.

Sengemo went on. "Chudak was so kind, he taught me meditation and through him I met and received teachings from the old hermit Atsara Sale and also I received instruction from the old yogini, Tashi Chidren. I went into retreat for three springs with her guidance." Looking down at her hands, Sengemo said softly, "But now they are all gone. There are still some teachers remaining, yet most of the old ones have passed and those disciples that are masters are in hiding; gone to the east and to the north."

Looking at Abaka, her fist clenched on her knee, she pleaded, "We must keep the teachings alive. So we come to you, Master, please give us teachings so we can help the dharma remain in this world. As well, we wish to realize our Buddha nature and be freed from the ocean of suffering."

All grew silent in the cave as Abaka considered the threesome. Then he said, "Very well, you three are ready enough. You will remain here for many moons. Do you have food?"

Nam-kha nodded, "Yes we have enough to remain for a moon. After that, we will go to the village and get more. We have barter, we can remain here for as long as you will teach us."

"Very well, " Abaka nodded. "We will begin now."

76

SIXTEEN MOONS LATER

Tampo turned to watch as Sengemo and Nam-kha made their way down the path behind him. He was not the same man who had traversed this way for the first time, many moons past. He was quite different since that day. Looking at the light steps of Sengemo, he could see how much different she was as well, and Nam-kha too. After sixteen moons of extensive teachings and practice they had each achieved a higher level of realization of their true nature. Within them, they held knowledge of the essentials of the path, as taught by Padma and Tsogyal to Abaka and added to by his own realization. Now they could continue to practice on their own, reaching higher levels and teach secretly to others. They could find other adepts and share their knowledge.

Meeting up, they stayed together as they negotiated the steep rocks making their way down into the world beyond them. After a full day, they set up camp to stay the night. The next morning they continued down the mountainside. Before turning into the canyons, leaving behind the last view of the mountain hermitage, they turned to look up at the mountain that held Abaka's cave. The sky was a clear deep blue. The threesome stood, gazing at the mountain, silently saying their last goodbyes to the old warrior, thankful for his teachings.

With a gasp, Sengemo said, "Do you see that?"

"Yes, but that is not possible," Jampo and Nam-kha said in unison, as they watched rainbows appearing in the pristine blue sky above the mountain peak.

"It is so beautiful," Sengemo whispered.

Then a ball of light, like a shooting star, flew from the mountain peak into the sky and disappeared. They all gasped at the sight.

Suddenly, Jampo sat down hard on the ground, putting his head in his hands. Nam-kha stood frozen, an expression of dread on his face.

Sengemo looked from Nam-kha to Jampo, pleading, "What was that?"

"He has gone. The last of them is gone," Nam-kha said, swallowing the lump forming in his throat.

Jampo slowly stood up. "Now I understand why he said his farewell to us days before we left and told us not to disturb him," he said, looking up at the mountain, the weight of his sadness bearing down hard on his heart.

Finally understanding, Sengemo felt the life drain out of her. She sagged on weak knees. Placing her hand at her heart, the tightness grew at the realization of the loss of one more Master of the dharma. One of the last few remaining in this world that had direct teachings from Padma and Tsogyal.

Looking up at the sky, the rainbows now fading, Nam-kha turned to Jampo and Sengemo. "It is now up to us. We must carry the teachings and protect them."

Jampo nodded, declaring, "We must find the others who also hold the teachings and help to keep the dharma from fading and disappearing from the world altogether."

Sengemo pulled herself up straight, resolve replacing sorrow, her hands tightened into fists. Looking up at the empty blue sky above the empty hermitage, she called out, "We will not fail, Master!"

Nam-kha and Jampo joined her, shouting as loud as they could, "We will not fail!"

A deep silence fell upon them as the last echo of their words faded into the vastness of the remote mountains. With determination planted firmly in their hearts, they stepped onto the path and strode onward.

Tᴂ ᴇɴᴅ

"If you know me, Yeshe Tsogyal
Mistress of samsara and nirvana,
You will find me dwelling in the heart of every being.
The elements and senses are my emanations,
And emanated thence,
I am the twelve-fold chain of co-production
Thus primordially we never separate.
I seem a separate entity
Because you do not know me."

Mayra Sonam Paldon

AUTHOR'S NOTE

Yeshe Tsogyal is a true historical figure. Her life story can be found in Tibetan Buddhist texts. Translations in English of these Tibetan texts are available in book form. This novel is a work of fiction based on her life story.

After Emperor Ral-pa-can's death, Emperor Lang-dharma took the throne and began the persecution of Buddhists in Tibet. Buddhist practitioners and teachers went into hiding. Historians vary in accounts but it is clear that for seventy-five to one hundred and thirty-seven years Buddhists struggled to keep the teachings from completely dying out in Tibet. Slowly Buddhism began to resurge. In 1038, the great adept Atisa came to Tibet and later came the great teacher Marpa. Buddhism began to flower once again, growing to become the religion of Tibet. In the mid-fifteenth century, the First Dalai Lama took his seat as head of the Buddhist religion in Tibet under Mongol Khan rule in Tibet. Eventually Reformed Bon was recognized as the sixth principle spiritual school of Tibet, the five other schools each being of a Buddhist lineage.

Tibet embraced Buddhism and turned away from its warrior past, becoming a peaceful and pacifist nation sequestered behind the high Himalayan Mountain Range.

In 1949, Chinese Communist Leader Mao Tse-tung invaded Tibet. Communist forces destroyed thousands on monestaries and killed hundreds of thousands of innocent Tibetans. The facts of this invasion are easily obtainable. Buddhism was outlawed in Tibet as well as in China.

Avoiding capture by the Chinese, the Fourteenth Dalai Lama fled Tibet to India where he now heads the Tibetan Government-in-exile, headquartered in Dharamsala, India. From Dharamsala, the teachings and practices of Tibetan Buddhism have spread to the West. Thanks be to Yeshe Tsogyal and Padmasambhava, who hid the teachings, thus keeping them safe for future generations, they remain in the world today.

In this novel General Senge was given a sky burial. It is true that sky burials did not become a common practice in Tibet until the 13th century. However, sky burials had been pracriced for 11,000 years in Asia, as evidenced by excavation in Soutern Turkey at Gobekali Tepe. Some religions practiced sky burials in Persia for 3000 years. Both the ancient Jaina and Buddhist monks in India subjected themselves to the sky burial. Though sky burial was not common in Tibet in the 8th and 9th centuries it would have been known about. Since Tsogyal and Abaka wanted General Senge to have the best chance at a fortunate rebirth, the act of giving his body to feed the vultures would have been a gesture resulting in merit for him. It would therefore not be unheard of.

The subject of rainbow body is too extensive to discuss here. Advanced practitioners attain rainbow body to this day. It is a subject I suggest the reader google to read about this phenomena

PRONUNCIATION OF NAMES

Most character names can be sounded out, like they are spelled. Like Rab-Ten and Klu-pal. Below are examples of how to pronounce Tibetan names.

Tsogyal - So-gee-al
Pelgyi - Pel-g-yee
Getso - Get-so
Dechen - De-shen
Nyima - Nee-ma
Chudak - Choo-dak
Senge - Sen-gay
Trisong - Tree-song Detsen - Det-sen
Santaraksita - Santa-rak-sita

Made in the USA
San Bernardino, CA
03 October 2015